# An Unsuitable Man

. . .

*Elisabeth Leigh*

ARROW

Published by Arrow Books in 2001

1 3 5 7 9 10 8 6 4 2

First published in the United Kingdom in 2001 by Arrow.

Arrow Books Limited
20 Vauxhall Bridge Road, London, SW1V 2SA

Random House Australia (Pty) Limited
20 Alfred Street, Milsons Point, Sydney,
New South Wales 2061, Australia

Random House New Zealand Limited
18 Poland Road, Glenfield
Auckland 10, New Zealand

Random House (Pty) Limited
Endulini, 5a Jubilee Road, Parktown 2193, South Africa

Random House Group Limited Reg. No. 954009

www.randomhouse.co.uk

A CIP catalogue record for this book is available from the British Library

Papers used by Random House
are natural, recyclable products made from wood grown in sustainable forests.
The manufacturing processes conform to the environmental regulations of the
country of origin

ISBN 0 09 928064 7

Typeset by SX Composing DTP, Rayleigh, Essex

Printed and bound in Denmark by
Nørhaven A/S, Viborg

For Vivian

# One

• • •

Nicola said she was coming to stay but I half expected her to cancel. She was always changing her mind at the last minute, but I was probably like that at her age. I could scarcely remember what it felt like to be nineteen, only that I was engaged to marry Henry.

I was just getting into bed when the phone rang. Only my daughter would ring so late.

'I'm not sure if I can make it this weekend,' she began.

'But I thought you'd arranged to go with Paul to the new club. I hear it's a fantastic place.'

'Maybe. But it won't be as good as the ones in London.'

'You haven't been home since you started college.'

I couldn't hide my disappointment.

'I've called you loads of times.'

'It isn't the same.' There was a glum silence. 'Has something happened? What's upset you?'

Nicola sighed. Sometimes she would confide in me, at other times I'd be left in the dark. I never knew what to expect.

'I don't really want to go to the club with Paul. He should have realized by now.'

'What do you mean?'

'I'm not that keen any more. It isn't like it was. When

he comes to London, he never wants to do anything interesting. We're always having rows. And then he's so jealous all the time. He thinks now I'm at college, I must spend all my time chatting up boys. It's crazy! Why shouldn't I want to meet new people?'

I could understand how Nicola felt. She was in the middle of her first term, carried away with the excitement of it all, living in London, sharing a flat for the first time, starting to discover herself. We were all very fond of Paul, but she wasn't nearly ready to settle down and I knew they hadn't been getting on for some weeks.

'Why don't you tell Paul how you feel? It's only fair,' I said.

'I suppose I should.'

'It doesn't mean you have to stop being friends.'

'I don't believe in all that. You can't be friends with an ex-lover.'

'Is that what Aunt Ginnie says?'

'No. I do, actually.'

I smiled to myself. This was Nicola trying to be worldly and sophisticated. I knew she felt at a disadvantage having grown up out of London. Still, I was sure she was making up for it now.

'So you'll be coming on your own, then?'

'I hope you don't mind, but I'd rather stay here this weekend. One of my flatmates invited me to a party. Should be a good one. How about the weekend after?'

I didn't give her an immediate answer. Even if we did arrange another time, it was likely to be postponed. I sometimes felt as though I hardly had a family any more. Joel was away at boarding school and Henry spent the week working in London. When he was home, he was either playing golf or working in his study. I missed Nicola most of all. We had an intuitive understanding of one another, although we both resented it sometimes. I thought quickly, trying to find a way of inducing her to come.

'How about this? Why don't you meet Paul on Saturday as arranged – and ask him back here for lunch? After that, I'll leave you alone so you can talk to him. Say there's been a change of plan, that you're going out with Daddy and me later on. Then you can make up your mind what you want to do.'

'Could do, I suppose.'

When Saturday came, I was still uncertain whether she'd arrive or not but I was prepared. The fridge was stocked up with everything she liked and there were fresh flowers in her room. When I heard Paul's old van bumping up the drive, I smiled with relief, threw a jacket over my shoulders and rushed outside. After he'd stopped in front of the house, Nicola immediately jumped out and came towards me without waiting for him.

'Hi, Mum,' she said, giving me a hurried kiss. 'What do you think? Auntie Ginnie's present.' She turned round in front of me, showing off her long black velvet coat with a bright pink fake fur collar. Although we shared the same kind of looks – fresh complexion, hazel eyes and fine straight brown hair – Nicola tried to disguise herself by experimenting with every fashion gimmick possible. Today her hair was pulled back tightly from her face, which was heavily made up with an overdose of rouge. I'd never had the courage to look so theatrical.

'Really glam,' I said, with a smile. Underneath the coat, she was wearing a thin black cotton T-shirt and tight shiny trousers. 'But aren't you cold?'

'No. Why should I be?'

'You're lucky, not feeling the cold.'

'It's warm in London.' She glanced back at Paul, who was standing on the lawn a little way away, gazing at the few red and gold leaves that still clung to the trees.

'Come on in,' she called out. 'Let's eat, I'm starving.'

I wondered if Nicola had worn her London outfit to make a point. They didn't look as though they belonged together. Paul was wearing a thick navy fisherman's sweater and old jeans. Or was it he who was setting out the distance between them?

'Good to see you, Sally.' He shook my hand, then added, 'Sorry I'm a bit of a mess. I've been working this morning.'

'You look absolutely fine,' I said.

A faint blond line of stubble shadowed his chin, but it suited his masculine, strong-boned face. There was something of the Viking about him. He looked far more confident than when I'd last seen him in the summer. Within a few months he'd made the subtle change into manhood and I could no longer ask his age. Twenty-five or twenty-six, he must have been. Everyone loved having him around and even though his background was very different from ours, he seemed to fit in naturally. Paul had been a visitor to the house off and on for two years. I felt sad that Nicola was turning her back on him.

We sat down round the kitchen table. If Henry had been home, we would have been in the dining room.

'I forgot to tell you. I've gone veggie,' Nicola announced, as she helped herself to a mammoth portion of baked potatoes and salad.

'When was that? Yesterday?' said Paul.

She frowned and continued directing her remarks to me.

'Auntie Ginnie eats Japanese. She says it cleanses the system.'

'I hope it's not one of those diets. You're thin enough already, darling.'

'Size ten isn't thin,' she replied.

Paul was already attacking his steak.

'Girls always want to be thinner. They wouldn't if they worked outdoors.'

'What's so great about outdoors?' said Nicola, looking straight at him for the first time. 'All that fresh air is bad for the brain. And it's all polluted anyway.'

'My brain seems OK. At least, nobody's said anything. What do you think, Sally?'

'In good working order, I'd say.'

I'd always appreciated Paul's dry sense of humour but Nicola wasn't responding.

'We've got a professor at college who's written twenty books.'

'What's his name?' I asked.

'She. Why did you automatically . . .?'

'Sorry. I wasn't thinking.'

'Brain-rot, Sally. You must have been spending too much time outdoors in the garden,' said Paul.

'If you don't mind, I was telling you about this professor,' Nicola interrupted. 'She's famous and been on TV lots of times. And her books are published in France. She's giving a special seminar on Racine. In France they say he's better than Shakespeare.'

'They would,' said Paul.

'You haven't a clue about the French. You haven't even been on the ferry to Boulogne.'

'How do you know I haven't been to France?'

'You would've told me,' said Nicola.

'Would I? Not necessarily.'

'Oh. So what are you hiding? Come on, tell us Paul. Who did you go with?'

'Mum and Dad.'

'Expect me to believe that?'

'All right. I had a date with Juliette Binoche.'

Nicola looked at him disdainfully and then turned to me. I hadn't realized she felt such hostility towards him. Inviting him to lunch was a bad idea, I decided.

'I saw a film of hers in French. Really good. It hasn't been released over here yet. Not that you'd ever get to see it in Wengrave.'

'Heard of video?' said Paul, with a smile. 'You put in this cassette and press a button . . .'

I sensed that he was trying his best to hide his irritation.

'I don't know if you'd like a pudding. But I've bought a fruit flan, just in case,' I said, quickly.

'Great,' said Paul.

'No thanks, Mummy.'

'And coffee?'

'No caffeine either. It's bad for you.'

'Brain-rot again?' asked Paul.

'No,' said Nicola, crossly. 'If you must know, it's bad for the cardiovascular system.'

'I can't keep up. I didn't know you were studying medicine as well.'

Nicola stretched out her arm, took an apple from the fruit bowl and bit savagely into the russet skin. I was becoming more and more uncomfortable. Was she brewing up for a row? I recognized the signs, the increasing impatience that could suddenly erupt into a shouting match. Or perhaps they'd been having a go at one another on the way from the station. I wanted them both to be happy together as they once were, but Nicola was growing up so quickly and I couldn't blame her for wanting to move on. You don't often stay with your first boyfriend, although I did. I was lucky to have found the right man so young, to have avoided the storms of broken relationships. I hoped it wouldn't be too long before Nicola found someone who suited her.

'I'll make us some coffee,' I said to Paul.

'I'll do it.' He went over to the dresser and took down two mugs. 'Is it still in the same place?'

'Second cupboard from the left,' I replied. He took down a jar of instant coffee, found a spoon, doled a heap into two mugs and put on the kettle.

'Mummy doesn't like instant,' remarked Nicola.

'Where did you get that idea? I often have it,' I said.

Suddenly, she leaped up from the table.

'I've got to be off. Julie asked me over for a game of tennis at the club.'

'You'll freeze to death. What's wrong with a game of football?' asked Paul.

Nicola gave a cocky smile.

'Nothing. I know a girl who's in a football team – as a matter of fact. Mum, did you put my tennis gear in the wash?'

'It's all in your drawer.'

'You're the best.' She gave me an affectionate hug. 'When's Dad coming?'

'He'll be here around six.'

'I'll be back before then.'

As she ran out of the kitchen, Paul looked at me with a resigned smile.

'I'd better go, too.'

'There's no need,' I said. 'Let's have another coffee.'

Paul stood against the window, staring out as though he was longing to be elsewhere. I wanted to comfort him, to say that my daughter had always been headstrong, that she might change her mind. But he spoke first.

'I don't think Nicola was too keen to see me.'

'She's been swept off her feet – moving to London, first term at college. It's all new and exciting for her. I'm sure she'll settle down in a few months.'

'People grow apart, don't they?'

'Some do. Not all.'

He came and sat opposite me, leaning his elbows on the table.

'We want different things, anyhow.'

'Does Nicola know what she wants?'

'In the morning she does. By evening she's changed her mind.'

We smiled at one another. He understood her, too, but in a way that I never could. However hard I tried, I never managed to imagine how men saw women. If Henry and I were both asked to describe my women friends, we'd have come up with completely different pictures.

'Anyway, I'm glad I came. I've always liked coming here. How's Joel doing at boarding school? When I last saw him in the holidays, he told me he was the best at athletics and the best swimmer. Is there anything he isn't good at?'

'Talking. He never says much – to me, anyway. Now it's only physics that counts. He wants to do research somewhere. All rather beyond me, I'm afraid. But he's fascinated.'

'And Henry?'

'In London. He's coming later today but he'll be sorry he missed you.'

Before Paul left, we strolled round the garden, even though there was little to see in November other than leaves. Earlier in the year, Paul had helped me to dig out a couple of beds and plant the shrubs that were now establishing themselves in the rich earth. I was just pointing out where I had put the spring bulbs, when Nicola appeared, cycling furiously down the drive as though she was leading the tour de France, her tennis racket balanced precariously on the back. She waved at us without slowing down.

'So it's goodbye, Nicola,' said Paul, quietly. Then he walked towards his van.

'You can come by whenever you like. You're always welcome,' I told him.

'I will,' he replied.

I'm sure he was only being polite. Why should a young man spend time visiting the parents of his former girlfriend? He would have had better things to do.

*

Nicola was in high spirits when she returned. She had won at tennis and was determined to enjoy herself. Julie would be joining her later at the new club, which was called, for some obscure reason, the Red Hot Chicken Shack. Everyone was going there, Nicola told me. As usual, she'd taken over my dressing table and had covered the bed in skirts, trousers and tops that she intended to select and put together for her night out.

'When did Paul go?' she asked, covering her face in some muddy substance that Ginnie had given her.

'Not long after you.'

'He always manages to annoy me. I can't help it. We had a row before we got here. I didn't mean it to come out, but I told him it was finished between us. I don't want him to see me in London again.'

Her eyes suddenly looked sad through the muddy mask.

'It's always painful, however you say it. But you were right to tell him,' I said, gently. In spite of her bravado, I knew it was hard for her.

'He doesn't stimulate my mind. I couldn't say that, could I?'

'Not really. But you might find out later that his other qualities are more important.'

'Important than what?'

'Discussing Racine.'

Nicola smiled and the mud cracked round her lips. 'I only talked about that to gee him up. I'm wicked, aren't I?'

'Sometimes.'

'I bet you've never been wicked.'

'I never had the chance. Being married at twenty doesn't give you much time, does it?'

'If I get married, I'll wait till I'm thirty,' Nicola said, firmly. 'When I'm that old, I might get sensible. But I can't imagine staying married for years and years and years. Like you and Dad. I can't imagine it, being with

9

the same person all that time. How do you stop getting bored?'

'Perhaps it's because I don't expect life to be wildly exciting. You don't, not when you're my age.'

'I wish you wouldn't say that.'

'All right.'

'If life wasn't exciting, I'd take off round the world. You could if you wanted. Dad wouldn't mind. Then he could work even harder.' She went over to the bed and lifted up a leopard-print top. 'Is this sexy? I want to look sexy tonight. Or should it be black? I can't make up my mind.'

'How about this?' I suggested, holding up a velvet shirt.

'Boring,' she retorted.

'Or this, perhaps?' I pulled out a red cutaway satin top and black trousers.

'Mm.' She pondered, then placed the satin top against me. 'That'd look good on you. Why not wear it to your dinner party tonight?'

'Daddy would have a fit!'

'So what? Whose dinner party is it?'

'Maggie and Jeff's.'

'And I bet I know who else there'll be.' She counted off on her fingers. 'Angela . . . Douggie . . . Patsy . . . and Mustafa. Am I right?'

'Yes. And a few others I'm bound to know.' We grinned at one another. If my life was safe and predictable, I often thought Nicola preferred it that way. 'But you've missed out Martin.'

'So I have. Martin. I like him. He's all right.'

There now followed Nicola's long immersion in the bath. An hour later, her skin shiny and blooming, she tried on a succession of ensembles and finally opted for a short dark red, clingy dress. It took at least half an hour for her evening make-up to be applied and for her

10

to reach a conclusion about the right shade of lipstick. Now it was my turn. She stayed long enough to turn up her nose at the black grosgrain suit and white blouse with a lace collar that I'd chosen for later.

'You haven't bought any new stuff for ages.'

'I don't need anything.'

Nicola sighed impatiently.

'It's not about needing things.'

She was always trying to push me into something I'd never dream of wearing. Young people could get away with cheap, fun clothes but I certainly couldn't.

'Am I all right?' she said, coming to stand in front of me.

'Sexy and gorgeous.'

'Really? You mean it?'

She'd rearranged her hair so that it hung all round her face and I pushed it back a little. I knew she'd pull it down almost over her eyes when she was out of the house.

'Have a lovely time and don't drink too much,' I said, beginning to step into the black skirt of my suit.

'I never drink too much,' she said, with a cheeky smile. Then she looked me up and down. 'Meet me in London and then I'll choose you some proper clothes.'

'I'll think about it,' I answered.

Even before Nicola had moved away from home, she and Ginnie had been trying to persuade me that I should uproot to London. I couldn't face the thought of leaving our comfortable house and beautiful garden. It had been too long since I'd lived in the city and in any case, what would I do there? Even though Joel would have loved to spend his holidays in London, I knew Henry would never consider living there full-time. For the past two years, he'd been forced to spend all week at his London office and when he wasn't working, there were usually important clients to entertain. He couldn't wait for Fridays, when he could leave his small flat in Dolphin Square and come speeding home. It kept him sane, he said.

I was occasionally tempted by the idea of taking off in another direction but I couldn't really see myself making any radical change. Sometimes I wondered what life would be like in ten years' time. I hoped I'd be a grandmother by then, giving to the new generation. Now the children were almost grown-up, I ought to have been considering new horizons. But where were they? I couldn't imagine where to start. What do women do after forty? Sometimes I thought I might try and find some kind of work. My friends came up with different suggestions, none of which appealed to me. I filled my days and tried not to dwell on what might have been.

I was just about to order a taxi to take us to Maggie's, when a call came from Henry. I was getting worried, as we only had an hour or so before we were due to leave. Henry sounded weary.

'The car's broken down. I was just setting off when there was a horrible grinding noise. I didn't want to risk it. I'm really sorry, darling. You'll have to give my apologies to Maggie.'

My heart sank. I couldn't go to Maggie's on my own.

'Can't you get the car rescue?'

'They're bound to take hours.'

I made another attempt.

'I'll come and get you and then we can turn up later for coffee. I'm sure Maggie won't mind. And I can drive you back to London on Monday morning.'

'That's kind of you. But I've had a grisly day. I'd probably fall asleep over the coffee cups. If you don't mind, I'll get an early night and come home tomorrow. I'm sorry to let you down, I really am.'

'It's not your fault, Henry. Lousy car. I thought it was

12

meant to be reliable.'

'So did I. Anyway, you'll go, won't you?'

If it hadn't been a formal dinner party, I might have considered it. But there'd be around twenty people there, all husbands and wives. I couldn't bear the thought of everyone asking me where Henry was, feeling sorry that he wasn't at my side.

'Maggie spends hours working out her seating plans. She mightn't like having a spare woman.'

Henry sniffed.

'That's ridiculous. Go and have a good time, Sally. You might meet some interesting people. Tell me about it tomorrow.'

'Will you be playing golf as usual?'

'Oh yes. Back for lunch. Will Nicola still be there?'

'She should be.'

I held onto the phone, wondering what I would say to Maggie. Even though it wasn't his fault, I couldn't help resenting Henry's absence. Cars went wrong when you least expected it but I suspected that Maggie's dinner party wouldn't be high on his list of priorities. He was probably making an excuse. I really ought to have had more sympathy for him. Poor Henry! Why should he want to drive to Wengrave and go out to dinner when he was tired and his mind was elsewhere? He'd be expected to tell amusing stories, to charm the other guests and be the centre of attention. And there was always someone who'd buttonhole him for advice on some tedious legal problem. If he had come, it would only have been for my sake. He knew I hated letting down my friends and until fairly recently, he would make an effort to turn up for special social engagements. I knew he was working too hard but you couldn't put the brakes on Henry. I hoped Maggie would understand.

\*

'You are coming tonight, aren't you?' Maggie sounded fraught, as she always did before her guests had arrived.

'I'm really sorry but Henry's stuck in London.' I was about to say that his car had broken down, but that might sound like a lame excuse. 'He sends lots of apologies but he's got tons of work to do this weekend. You know what Henry's like.'

'Come on your own, Sal. It won't matter a bit. As it happens, Elaine has the flu so there'll be a spare man anyway. It's hopeless having dinner parties at this time of year. You never know when someone will go down with something. I don't know why I do it. But you will join us, won't you? You won't change your mind?'

'Of course I'll come,' I replied.

Nothing surprising happened at Maggie's – not that I expected it would. I knew everybody there. The men talked mostly about the fall of the pound and the women discussed the merits of a London hairdresser who'd opened up in Wengrave. Maggie told a funny joke that I couldn't remember and I drank too much wine. I was rather relieved that Henry hadn't come with me.

The next morning, I'd just finished breakfast when I thought I heard Henry's car coming up the drive. I opened the front door and could see him getting out of his BMW, briefcase in one hand and an enormous bunch of golden yellow roses in the other.

'Hello, darling.'

'So you risked the car? I thought you'd be coming by train.'

'A neighbour had a look at it for me. He started it up and it behaved perfectly. Typical isn't it?' He kissed me on the cheek and put the roses into my arms. 'With love from a hopeless husband.'

'Oh! What a wonderful colour.'

I was slightly taken aback. Henry wasn't in the habit of buying flowers – if he did bring me something, it was usually a bottle of special champagne for a birthday or wedding anniversary.

'Any chance of some coffee?' he said, throwing off his coat in the hall.

'There's some still hot. I didn't get up till late.'

He came into the kitchen, sat down in his favourite old Windsor chair and began to open his mail.

'Nicola still in bed?'

'Naturally. It's the morning after party night.'

'I don't know how she does it. Always going to parties.'

He looked up with a relaxed smile.

'How was dinner? What did I miss?'

'Not a lot.' Then I grinned. 'Maggie was deeply shocked that you couldn't come.'

'I don't imagine Maggie's ever been shocked by anything.' Henry took a few sips of coffee and glanced at his watch. 'I must phone Joel. I expect he'll have come out of chapel by now.'

'I phoned him yesterday. He wants to talk to you, he's worried about his choice of A levels.'

I knew what Henry's movements would be, as Sundays usually followed the same pattern. He'd spend half an hour talking to Joel, lying with his feet up on the sofa, and then he'd head off to Wengrave Golf Club. Two hours of golf, then back for lunch. If Nicola was home, there'd usually be an argument but, this Sunday, she spent most of the time yawning. She probably had drunk too much the night before. Soon afterwards she caught a train to London, saying she had an essay to write. I suspected that she was more depressed about finishing with Paul than she cared to admit.

The moment we'd finished having tea and crumpets, Henry disappeared to his study. After he'd been gone a couple of hours, I came in to find him bent over a pile of papers. He'd probably lost track of time, as usual.

'Can you take a break?' I asked.

'Of course.' He raised his head and turned round to face me.

'I never like interrupting you, but we don't seem to have much time to talk things over.'

'Just give me half an hour. This shouldn't take too long.'

My head was teeming with things I wanted to say, yet it had become more difficult to allow them to emerge naturally. I was aware that every moment of Henry's time was so valuable. Even though I was his wife I sometimes felt like an insistent client who was over-running her time. I felt it was my duty to give way to the pressure of his work, guilty that what I had to deal with was so trivial in comparison. I suppose I might have asserted myself more. Perhaps I admired him too much, but I always had. Ginnie used to say I had married my father. Lots of girls do, I suspect.

Henry poured us both a gin and tonic and then he settled into a corner of the sofa, stretched out and put his feet up. I sat on the edge of an armchair opposite him.

'You know Paul came over for lunch yesterday?'

'Oh? Nicola didn't mention it.'

'It was all rather sad. She seemed to resent him being here and they certainly didn't seem happy together. Apparently they've decided to part. Or, rather, Nicola's decided.'

'Probably for the best, don't you think?' Henry said.

'What do you mean?'

Since Henry knew so little about the stages of their relationship – Nicola never discussed intimate matters with him – I was surprised at his comment.

16

'Well, she's a bright girl. Nicola has a lot going for her. If only she'd learn to apply herself, she'd do well. Though I'm sorry she isn't studying law.'

'But you know she's always been against the idea.'

'Because I suggested it, no doubt.' He gave a slight smile.

'Still, I'll be sorry not to see Paul any more.'

'He's a nice enough lad but I'm sure she'll find somebody else.'

Henry was turning the ice round and round in his glass, as though he didn't want to pursue the subject. I couldn't understand why he was so indifferent.

'I thought you liked him.'

'I didn't say I didn't.'

'But he's been almost part of our family for months. You can't just suddenly pretend he doesn't exist.'

'I'm not. Only I was getting concerned. I sometimes wondered if Nicola might end up marrying him. Which wouldn't have been a good idea, would it?'

I was silent. If they'd been happy together, why ever not? But Henry's attitude to Nicola was different from mine and nothing she did seemed to meet with his approval. I thought he was often rather hard on her. Even if she ended up marrying a barrister – which I'm sure he wanted – he would have found something to criticize. It was the only thing about Henry that pained me, his relationship with Nicola. I rapidly changed the subject.

'Listen, darling. I thought it was time we started planning out the summer holidays. Apart from anything else, it would give Nicola and Joel something to look forward to.'

Henry shrugged.

'I'm afraid I haven't had time to give it much thought.'

'Last night Angela mentioned that she and Douggie

17

were renting a villa in Portugal for July and August. She asked if we'd like to share it with them. How about it?'

'It's an idea,' Henry said, without enthusiasm.

'Don't you like Portugal?'

'Quite.'

'Apparently the villa is high up on a hill and there's a pool and a beautiful garden. It's wonderfully wild around there . . .' I made another attempt to arouse his interest. 'And there's a golf course you can get to in an hour.'

Henry looked at me doubtfully.

'I'm not sure if I'll be able to get away this summer. I hate to disappoint you. Obviously, I'll do all I can . . . But there's nothing to stop you going with the children. I can always join you for a weekend, anyway.'

'A weekend?' I stared at him in amazement. 'But you've always said your summer holiday is sacred. You've never worked through the summer. And it's the one time of the year when you can get away, when things go quiet. Why is it different now?'

'I'll . . . do my very best. I'll have to see . . . what's possible.'

He appeared hesitant and I presumed he was running through a diary of events in his mind. Then he got up, went over to the drinks cabinet and refilled our glasses. Having placed a heavy log on the fire, he stood leaning against the chimney breast.

'Sally, I really didn't want to bring it up now, but the partnership has been under rather a strain.'

I instantly jumped to my feet.

'Henry! Why on earth didn't you tell me? Why did you keep it to yourself? If things have been going badly, shouldn't I be the first to know?'

'It's not . . . not what you think. I don't quite know how to say this.'

He was bending forward, looking into the fire. I came up to him and put my arm round his shoulder.

'You don't have to hide things from me,' I said. I assumed that he had had a terrible disagreement with his partner, that everything was falling apart. I suddenly felt icy cold. Then Henry gently moved my arm away and took a deep breath.

'There's another woman in my life.'

At first I thought I hadn't heard properly.

'What? What did you say?'

'There's someone else.'

'Someone what?' I stammered.

'I've been seeing someone else.'

'You've been seeing . . .?'

'Another woman.'

'Henry! For Christ's sake, what are you saying? Are you being serious?' I could hear my voice sliding out of control, as though I might break into hysterical laughter at any moment.

'I'm afraid I am being serious.'

I left his side and collapsed onto the sofa. My head was swimming.

'Are you telling me you've been sleeping with someone else?'

'Yes,' he said, with a sigh.

'How long?'

He didn't reply. He didn't need to. Was it days, months, years? It made no difference. I stared at Henry as though he was some distant relative I'd never seen before. This man standing in front of me with his head bowed, clenching his fingers tightly round his glass, was a total stranger. He wasn't my husband. I was having a hallucination. He seemed to be receding further and further into the distance, his voice sounding almost disembodied.

'She works in my chambers. She's called Sheila. Around thirty-two, divorced, eight-year-old son.

Enormously helpful, kind . . . and we're . . . we're both in love.'

'I don't need to hear this,' I whispered.

'Sally. I can't change what's happened. I never expected to fall in love. I wasn't looking for it, I really wasn't. I thought we had a happy marriage but now we'll both have to come to terms with . . .'

'With what? Come to terms with what exactly?' Suddenly Henry Farringford came into focus and I was filled with rage. How dare he? I stood up abruptly and glared at him. 'What are we talking about? A cheap little office affair? A quick grope when nobody's looking? Hope no-one will find out. For God's sake, don't tell my wife. How can you? You? I hope you'll have the sense to put an end to it.'

Henry put down his glass and began to pace slowly round the room.

'I know it's difficult. But do let's try and be calm about this.'

'Why have you only just decided to tell me?'

'I don't know. I didn't want to hurt you. I couldn't bear the thought of it.'

'You're a coward!' I shouted.

'I know I am. I should have told you earlier.'

Henry turned and went to sit down on the window seat, as though he couldn't bear to be anywhere near me. I remained standing in the centre of the room, my hands tightly clasped.

'What difference would that have made? How can you have been so stupid? Aren't you ashamed? Why couldn't you control yourself?'

'Please, Sally. Let me try and . . .'

I cut across him. 'And even worse, why did you lie to me all this time? I thought you of all people believed in some kind of standards? Or am I just being old-fashioned?' I could hear my voice beginning to crack up, my mouth was quivering. 'You know I love you and you've been deceiving me. Is that what the roses were for? A little token of guilt?' Now I began to gather momentum. I didn't care any longer what I came out with. 'Were you with her when your car broke down last night? Or did it break down? Was this just another lie? No wonder you've been spending so much time in London. How convenient! While you're there you can forget that you have a wife.'

'That didn't cross my mind,' Henry said.

'Are you sure?'

'You're not giving me a chance, Sally.'

'All these years we've been together. They mean nothing. Nothing at all. You've ruined everything. I thought we were happy. I wish I'd never met you.'

I walked towards the door, as the first tears started to run down my cheeks. 'I'm going to make some coffee. I'll be in the kitchen.'

I went to the downstairs cloakroom and stared into the mirror. I looked as though I'd just witnessed a terrible road accident. My face was streaked, grey and awful, my eyes pink and watery. My hands were shaking as I turned on the tap and threw water over my face. I wanted to be ugly, to remind Henry of what he had done.

I made a pot of coffee and tried to pull myself together. Henry came in quietly and stood by the kitchen window. It was almost pitch dark but neither of us switched on the light. We couldn't bear to look at one another.

'I'm sorry I burst out at you like that,' I said softly.

I was telling myself that the adult thing to do was to be as calm as possible. I was trying my utmost to be rational even though I felt I could break out into hysteria at any moment. There was no reaction from Henry, so I forced myself to continue. I felt a sudden need to reassure him.

'We still have a good marriage. Just because you . . .

went elsewhere, it doesn't mean I'm about to throw you out. But I'll need time to get over it. As long as you promise you won't see her again. I couldn't bear it if . . .'

I couldn't continue and covered my face with my hands. Henry came up to me and rested his hand on my shoulder.

'Do you mind if I put on a light?' he asked.

I shook my head and he turned on the spotlight over the cooker. There was silence except for the sound of trailing branches tapping against the window in the wind.

Then he sat at the table, his arms tightly folded, avoiding my gaze.

'When I started seeing Sheila – eighteen months ago – I thought it would pass. I kept thinking how banal it was and that I couldn't be so foolish. Which is why I said nothing to you. I assumed it would all be over in a couple of weeks. Then, when it went on . . .' He paused, perhaps waiting for my response.

'I'm listening,' I said.

'. . . there came a point when we tried to put things on an even keel, to see one another as little as possible.'

I raised my head and looked straight at Henry.

'You tried to stop having sex, you mean?'

I would have to hear him out even though I wanted to let out a stream of abuse. I dug my nails into my palms as though waiting for the dentist's needle.

'It didn't work. We had to be together. I can't change my mind or reason myself out of it. I'm in love with Sheila.'

Henry looked so terrible that for a moment I felt his pain as though it was mine. His broad, jowly handsome face looked as though it had been beaten into submission.

'You call that love?' I said, trying to keep the bitterness from my voice.

'It's not a word I use lightly. And I've never stopped loving you.'

'Oh? Who would have guessed?'

'Only I love Sheila in a different way.'

I didn't want to go into why Sheila was different, namely better, than I was. I felt as though something inside me had been forcibly removed without anaesthetic. Henry had reached a conclusion. It had nothing to do with me.

'I want to live with her,' he said.

'So you intend to move out of the house?' I said, blankly.

'Yes.'

'And forget about me and the children?'

'I'd never do that. You know I wouldn't.'

The sentence had been passed. Uncontrollable tears began to stream down my face. He'd turned his back on me, taken away my self-respect and left me in pieces. I could only sob.

'Who's going to tell the children? What'll happen to them? What is my role to be? What am I meant to do? What will I say to everyone?'

'I'll do everything I can for you and the children. I want you to have a good life,' Henry said, gently.

'A good life? How is that possible? How can I look forward to the future? There isn't one, not for me. There's nothing more to say. Please go. Go, Henry. I want you to go.'

'How can I leave you like this? Please don't make it worse. I've been very happy with you and I owe you a lot. You've been a wonderful wife, a caring mother. I couldn't have asked for more.'

I grabbed hold of a tea towel to wipe away my tears. Then I stood up. Everything inside me froze.

'Henry. Please get out. Get out now. I've heard enough and I don't want to hear any more. If you want to live with your tart, that's your business.'

*

I rushed from the kitchen, ran downstairs to the children's playroom and banged the door shut. I don't know when Henry left but when the dawn came and I was exhausted with tears, his car had gone.

# TWO

• • •

It was barely light when I left the house. I don't remember what I packed but when I arrived at Ginnie's flat I was carrying a small holdall. I don't remember driving to London. I do remember Ginnie holding me tightly and saying everything was going to be all right. I heard her making an official-sounding phone call – it must have been to her office – saying her sister was sick and she'd be off work. I cried a lot and drank a lot and at some point I must have gone to sleep.

The next day my head was leaden. I couldn't take in what had happened and kept thinking of Nicola and Joel. How would they take it? What could I say to them? I couldn't let them see me in this state. Somehow I would have to keep sane for them. Might they think it had been my fault? Although it was Henry who had walked out, it was as though I had been partly responsible. I had failed in a way I couldn't understand.

I lay curled up tightly in bed, wishing that I could lose consciousness and blank out for weeks. Around ten o'clock, Ginnie came into the room with some herbal tea.

'You can stay there as long as you like,' she said.

With an effort, I sat up straight and sipped the unsustaining liquid while she sat cross-legged on the end of the bed. I tried to put on a brave face.

'Henry will be back. He's bound to realize what an idiot he's been,' I said. It might have been a false hope, wanting everything to remain the same, but I had to find a way of carrying on.

'You must eat something,' Ginnie urged.

'Some toast, perhaps. And a little black coffee . . .?'

'It'll be decaff. OK?' I nodded. 'Good. You're recovering.'

She pulled her kimono above her knees, jumped off the bed and opened up the wooden venetian blinds over the bay window. The weak sun brought out the rich colour of the apricot walls, the oak cupboards and the dancing figures painted by one of her boyfriends. Ginnie was always better at bringing a room to life than I was. Then she tripped out of the room. The inviting smell of heating-up bread wafted out from the kitchen, across the corridor and into her bedroom, which she had given over to me.

'Let's face it, Sal. It's unlikely that Henry will come back,' Ginnie said, as she set down the breakfast tray.

'I have to believe that he will. How else can I pick myself up?'

'You're going to, sooner than you think. Believe me.'

I wished I could have shared Ginnie's confidence. She had such definite views on everything that I was often won round by her certainty. This time I doubted her. I doubted everything, unable to believe in myself, my marriage, my life. And I feared for my children.

'What makes you think he's gone for good?'

Ginnie looked at me for a moment, as though deciding whether this was the time to embark on the analysis of Henry.

'You said it's been going on for some time. How can it have been an impulsive decision? Men aren't like that. They ponder.'

'I know what Henry's like.'

26

'Are you sure?' Ginnie gave me a questioning look as she divided a sliver of toast in two.

'First, Henry will spend hours pondering. Then he'll see that he's made a mistake and come home. He'll have to, if only because of the children. Joel hasn't even left school and Nicola's still very dependent on us. You can't walk out, just like that. If Henry thinks I'm so hopeless, he can wait a few years and then shack up with that . . . with that bitch if he really wants to.'

I began to hear Henry's words again and struggled to fight back the tears.

'It's not your fault,' said Ginnie. 'And she's not necessarily a bitch. I bet she's rather ordinary, not terribly bright and wants to get her hands on a man with a reputation.'

I gulped down some coffee.

'How do you know? She might be blonde and gorgeous.'

'I doubt it,' said Ginnie, loftily. 'Otherwise she'd have found someone available. And younger.'

'She might like older men.'

'Then there's plenty of choice,' retorted Ginnie.

I knew that she was trying to comfort me. I didn't want to think about Sheila.

'I still feel as though I've done something wrong,' I continued. 'I can't think what – so it can't be anything obvious. Perhaps I should have worn sexy underwear or got a pilot's licence.'

'Why not both at the same time?' suggested Ginnie, with a grin. 'You could always go for a job with Virgin Airlines.'

I managed a watery smile.

'Maybe I should have been more daring, had interesting opinions, been more exciting company . . .'

'What a thing to say! You didn't stand a chance. Henry always wanted to be the centre of attention. Remember when we were kids? You were pretty wild then, always ready to say what you thought. But afterwards it became "Henry this", "Henry that". He was always number one. No wonder Nicola had tantrums.'

I glared at Ginnie, feeling my face flushing with anger.

'What do you know about my marriage? I don't expect you to understand. But when you've been married and had children, you have to adapt.'

'Adapt to what? Being a wife and mother? An appendage?'

'That's not how I see it. Anyway, you seem to forget I've been in love with Henry ever since I met him.'

'I know you have,' said Ginnie, in a resigned tone. Then she sighed. 'I've said too much, as usual.'

Ginnie had mixed feelings about my husband, which she usually tried to hide for my sake. Not being married herself, she must have resented him for taking up so much of my life.

'Oh, never mind, Sal. We should stop talking about Henry. It's you that matters.'

I assured Ginnie that I'd look after myself while she went off to her magazine in Covent Garden. I envied her. Whenever her life became intolerable – boyfriends letting her down, for example – she could dress up in outrageous clothes, daub on the make-up and swan off to a glamorous office. There'd be plenty of people to distract her, as well as deadline panics, crises and tempers to deal with. But she'd take it all in her stride and always see the funny side. She was bound to come back home and give me a blow-by-blow account. At least it might stop me thinking about Henry and the children for a while.

It seemed to take hours for me to bath, to dress and even longer to disguise my face, as though the world had suddenly slowed down. I would try and act as though Sunday had never happened. I wandered round Ginnie's flat trying to blank out the pain, staring at her piles of books spread over the floor, the stacks of CDs about to fall from the shelf, the flowers beginning to wilt in the overcrowded vase. There was some mouldy yoghurt in the fridge and empty bottles to be taken down.

After washing up, I went back to the bedroom and arranged the shoes littering the floor in neat pairs on the rail. Automatically, I folded up the pile of clothes waiting to be sent to the cleaners. What would I say to Joel that evening? I'd have to phone him, otherwise he wouldn't know where I was. He might need something. There was always something. The school concert. I hoped Henry hadn't forgotten. I'd have to remind him. We'd make an appearance together and pretend life was normal. I'd do it for Joel's sake. He was going to do well and I wasn't going to let Henry hamper his progress. Lots of couples had to go through this. There were plenty of rocky marriages, even in Wengrave.

I hunted for a duster and found one, screwed up underneath the kitchen sink. The Hoover needed emptying. There was one bin bag left and I stuffed it full of rubbish and took it downstairs. Mail was spilling over on the shelf by the front door, as though the postman had tipped out his bag and walked away. I looked warily outside. There was nobody in the street, not a child or even a stray dog, as though each occupant had fled towards something far more important. Work. Career. Business. I wondered where the children were or if it was an adults-only zone. Bulging bin bags took up most of the small paved space in front of the house. I placed mine beside them. Would the dustmen ever come? Or would the bags mount up day by day into some impenetrable barricade?

I needed to calm down before I could bring myself to talk to Nicola. How long should I be evasive? She'd worm it out of me. Nicola usually did. I could tell her it was a temporary separation, a few weeks to gather our thoughts. I wouldn't mention Sheila. What reason would I give her? Daddy and I haven't been communicating very much. She'd laugh. Like you and Paul, we seemed to get on each other's nerves. I hoped she'd understand that. I wasn't ready to tell her the truth.

I ran back up the stairs and my legs started to crumple halfway up. Was I past it already? Once it was two steps at a time, not so long ago. Breathless, I sat down in the kitchen, cleaned out a mug and boiled up the fur-lined kettle. I'd do the kettle next. Ginnie didn't believe in cleaning ladies and couldn't get one anyhow. I'd be a cleaning lady. If Henry asked me how I spent my time, that's what I'd say. I'm doing houses. Hadn't you noticed? I'm quite good at it. And a bit of domestic cooking, nothing fancy, as a special favour. My husband left so I'm doing some cleaning.

I thought of packing up his clothes and sending them to London. It was one way of forcing myself to realize that he'd gone. But if I opened his wardrobe and saw all the familiar suits, I knew I'd expect him back at any moment. If I wished hard enough he might come home. Was Henry destined to go right from the beginning? Was I being tested by some superior power? Was some fairy-tale prince testing my capacity to love? Why had it happened? And how would I react if Henry did come back? Would we carry on as before? Fill in the cracks? Pretend to the children that nothing had happened? Daddy's been away on a case. It had happened before, six weeks in the States.

After I'd cleared out a couple of Ginnie's kitchen cupboards and washed down the shelves, I suddenly stopped dead in my tracks. What on earth was I doing? What would Ginnie have thought? She'd have sent me straight off to some counsellor. My sister needs therapy, she can't stop cleaning. I was sure my complaint would be given a name. Lady Macbeth syndrome, something like that. Was I losing my mind?

I wasn't used to allowing panic to take over. I was terrified of everything now. I'd never been like this, not even when Joel fell off his bike and was almost hit by a car or when Nicola set her dress on fire. Then I was overtaken by an unexpected calm and automatically knew what to do. Now I didn't. If I opened my mouth, I was sure the words would have stuck in my throat.

I gradually became a little calmer. I tidied away the cleaners and sponges under the sink and hoped Ginnie wouldn't notice the work I'd put into the transformation. A low wintry sun crept through the kitchen window and brightened up the pink begonias on the sill. I would force myself to go out.

I could see a bus slowly approaching the stop at the end of the road. It felt like a triumph when I was aboard and settled into a seat but I had no idea where I was going. When I found myself in Oxford Street, I jumped off. The conductor was shaking his fist at me as the bus drove away. It took me a few moments before I realized I hadn't paid. He thought I'd done it on purpose. I wanted to run after him, catch up with the bus and cry out. Here it is, here it is, here's the money, my fault, my fault. But my legs still felt weak. I was scared.

I was bumped and jostled down Oxford Street and I went on walking past blurred shops and sizzling streetfood, round Oxford Circus until I was swept into Regent Street. A group of tourists were pointing their cameras into the sky. I looked up, curious to see what had attracted them. Bulbous reindeers were crudely etched in lights and a Santa leered and winked from a sleigh. I suddenly came out of my daze. Christmas? We were still in November. Weren't we? Had December arrived without my noticing? I hadn't thought beyond tomorrow. What on earth would happen at Christmas? Where would I be? Where would the children be? Would Henry be there, pretending to be a father? I just

31

stood stock still, mesmerized, staring at the lights. Then I felt a sudden jolt to my elbow.

'Fancy bumping into you with all these crowds. Still, it's best to shop early for Christmas, isn't it?' I was aware of Maggie's beaming face, framed by a fake fur hood. 'Isn't London dreadful? Come for a coffee. I was just going to pop into Fortnum's.'

I looked down at Maggie's clutch of carrier bags.

'I'm afraid I have to . . . I've got to . . . I'm late for . . . it really isn't . . .' I stammered, feeling utterly confused, as though I'd just been mugged and forced to identify my attacker.

'That's fine by me, Sal. You meeting Henry? If you are, tell him we all missed him at dinner.'

'I'm really sorry . . .'

Maggie stared at me for a moment.

'Is everything all right?'

'Oh, fine.'

She looked at me doubtfully.

'You look a little pale. Everyone's going down with something. Take lots of vitamin C and echinacea and give me a call when you get back. I'll be home tonight. Promise?'

'Echinacea?'

'Marvellous Red Indian remedy. Native American, I mean. Get it from Boots. You'll feel on top of the world again. Just you see.'

I watched her weaving her way across Regent Street and disappearing down Swallow Street. I felt a pain cramping my stomach and my head began to throb. I would have to tell them all, eventually. How long could I wait? I couldn't bear the thought of seeing my friends and putting on an act, pretending that nothing had happened. I was never good at disguise. I'd have to make excuses to keep away from everyone until . . . until I'd come to terms with Henry not being there. If he stayed away, that is.

I jumped into a cab, relieved that I would be invisible behind the darkened windows.

'Where to?' the taxi driver shouted, pushing back his glass partition.

'Royal Academy. No, not Royal Academy. Too many people. But I do want to see some pictures. I used to know quite a bit about art, a long time ago.'

'Tate, then. Tourists go there.'

'No, no. Cork Street. Somewhere around there.'

'Make up your bloody mind.'

'Sorry,' I said, but he didn't hear.

With a jerk the taxi lurched forward and we set off down Piccadilly towards Bond Street.

I hadn't been inside the Themis Gallery for over twenty years. The exterior was almost the same, except that the gold lettering above the entrance was more modern. A huge canvas filled the window. It was covered in oily, jagged swirls of paint that were interspersed by what appeared to be scraps of hair and fragments of bone. When I looked closer, I could just make out a child's face, half stripped to reveal the skull beneath. The word of the title was written below. *Aftermath*. Had the artist used paint or blood? It looked like blood. I recoiled in horror. Then I pushed open the glass door. At the end of the gallery an old man with grizzled curly hair, dressed in a dark pinstriped suit, was sitting in an elegant office chair. His back was turned, but he appeared to be reading a catalogue. I walked slowly past the few large canvases placed round the spotlit walls and stopped a short distance behind him. After a few moments, he swivelled round to face me.

'May I help?' he said, without smiling. 'We have further works in the back room, should you care to see more.'

'I was just passing. I used to work here.'

'Ah.' He scrutinized me as though I was an

unattributed painting that a stranger had brought in. 'You look familiar. I'm dreadful with names.'

'Sally Farringford.'

'Farringford? Farringford?' He looked up at the ceiling, as though my name would be written there.

'I mean, you must have known me as Sally Linton.'

'Good gracious!' The old man rose slowly to his feet. I could only recall his first name – Theodore. He had seemed old even then.

'Sally. Of course. Why haven't I seen you before? Now I remember, of course I do. Are you living abroad?'

'No. Out of London, though. I don't come up that often.'

'A pleasure. A real pleasure. Are you still in the art world?' I shook my head. 'A shame. You had real perception. I used to value your judgement, even when you had little experience.'

'Did you? I don't know why. I was terribly young.'

'You still are,' he quickly replied.

'You were always gallant,' I said, smiling.

'Gallant? I haven't heard that word in years. Just one moment.'

He punched out a code on a back-door lock and disappeared. When he returned, he was carrying a decanter and two glasses.

'For special customers and Sally Linton. My particular favourite.'

He poured out some dark red port and beckoned me to sit down on a chair beside him. It suddenly came back to me. I was offered a glass of port then, all those years ago. All my feelings of excitement and fear suddenly returned. Fresh out of school, I had no idea what you were meant to say at interviews but Theodore appeared satisfied with my halting answers. My first – and, as it turned out – only job. I suddenly remembered what I wore, a pale green

Arabella Pollen dress with a dark green velvet bow.

'Just a moment,' said Theodore, peering at me through tinted, silver-rimmed glasses. 'Didn't you get married to a barrister?'

'That's right.'

'And you left immediately afterwards. You should have stayed on a while.'

'I wanted to, but Henry wasn't keen. We had a family early on.'

'Ah. Very wise.'

'My son is sixteen, my daughter three years older.'

'Quite extraordinary.'

'Not really.'

I never quite knew what Theodore thought about anything other than art. He lived on his own, or he did then. I couldn't imagine him changing his way of life.

'Sally, I'd like your opinion on the new artist we've taken on. Have we acquired the works of a future master or a sensationalist poseur?'

'I'm rather out of date,' I said, apologetically.

'Come and have a proper look.'

He led me round the small gallery, ill at ease with the paintings. But he had been in the business for so many years that his shrewdness must have prevailed. Twenty of the canvases had been sold for a hefty price. I wondered who would want to be reminded of suffering and outrage every day.

'Banks. Mostly banks. A collector or two. And the odd American gallery,' Theodore said dryly, when I asked.

I had something to tell him. Insulated from the street, away from anybody I knew, I felt safe. I wanted to hear myself say it, in order to banish the wild hopes that kept returning.

'I think my marriage is over,' I said quickly.

Theodore gave me a penetrating look, a mannerism

35

which had frightened me at one time. I used to imagine he could read my thoughts, that my head was transparent as a jellyfish.

'Do you want it to be over?' he asked.

'No. It's come as a shock. And I haven't thought about what I want for a long time. I'm not used to it.'

He smiled, but said nothing. I appreciated the way he reacted. I didn't want an outpouring of sympathy, or feigned shock or curious questions about how it happened. I just wanted to see if I'd be able to say it. And I had. We were both silent and I got up and began to walk towards the glass door. Theodore followed me.

'Have you thought of going back into the art world? I might be able to help.'

'I have my children to think of and anyway I couldn't see myself moving to London,' I said. 'But thank you all the same.'

'Come in again. Any time you wish.'

While I sat in the bus returning to Fulham, I wondered what I'd been like before I met Henry. I tried to feel my way back into being Sally Linton. If I could manage that, I thought, I might be able to go forward. Everyone was talking about going forward. Did forward mean better or worse? I had no idea. People had plans and aims and used their energy pursuing them. What had I pursued? I had to feel I was doing something, however insignificant. I would start by making a list. I needed lists. My children had to feel that everything was under control. First, I would phone Joel at six thirty when he was allowed to take calls.

'Why are you phoning, Mum? I'm OK. Is anything up?'

I lay on Ginnie's bed, exhausted. I longed for her energy.

'I just wanted to say that I'm with Auntie Ginnie, in case you'd tried me at home.'

I could hear a rustling of paper. He must have been in the middle of his homework.

'Have you done anything special in London?' he asked.

'Not really.' I made an effort to disguise the tiredness in my voice and hoped I sounded as I normally did. 'I've been round the shops, wondering what you'd like for Christmas.'

'How about a Ferrari?' He giggled. 'Only joking. I'll let you and Dad know when you come to the school concert.'

'Thank goodness you reminded me.'

'You wouldn't have forgotten. Dad might have, though. Will you check that he's put the date in his diary? Then if he's coming straight from the office he won't forget.'

'Of course I will. Anyway, I'll be back home at the end of the week.'

I was relieved that Joel hadn't asked more questions. When I'd finished the call, I sat by the phone wondering whether I should ring Henry. The school concert. Would he turn up? Christmas. Did I want him to come? When he would be going straight back to her?

'I tried you at home,' Henry said, when his secretary had put him on the line. 'Thank God you're with Ginnie. I was worried about you. I felt terrible about leaving so suddenly, rushing off like that. Only I couldn't face . . .'

For a second, I had the wild hope that he might have changed his mind.

'Yes?' I said, my heart thumping.

'I know I should have said something earlier.'

'Like what?'

'I don't quite know. One never knows the right way.'

'So you will definitely be staying in London . . .?'

'Yes.'

Now I was certain. There was no going back.

'I haven't said anything to the children yet. Would you rather tell them or should I?' I said, in a strained voice.

'I will, if you think it's better . . . Or perhaps we should do it together.'

'Nicola's coming home at the weekend. I'll try and find a good moment to talk about . . . about what you've decided. Though there won't be a good moment.'

'No. Of course not. There never is.'

I could sense Henry's awkwardness. He must have been longing for our conversation to be over. But I knew there was more to say and I took a scribbled list from my pocket. It helped if I pretended to be his secretary.

'Don't forget, we'll be seeing Joel at his school concert.'

'Ah, yes. Glad you reminded me.'

'So we might find a moment.'

'I'm sure we could.'

'And you'll have to decide what you're going to do about Christmas.'

'I've been thinking about it. Would you like me to come down?'

At first, the thought horrified me. How could you pretend to be a couple when you weren't any longer? Then I wondered what would be best for the children. Should we both behave as though it was a friendly reunion? Or was it better to start setting out the distance between us? Both alternatives appalled me.

'I honestly don't know.' I was feeling torn in two.

'We can decide later,' Henry said. 'I'll do whatever you wish.'

Towards the end of the week, I was longing to be back at home. I couldn't expect Ginnie to give more than she had. I wasn't used to leaning on people and she had her own life – which couldn't have been more different from mine. However generous and good-natured Ginnie was, I couldn't help being sucked into her chaos. Her work and private life constantly jostled for space and attention. Phones rang endlessly. The right people weren't available, the wrong people talked for hours and every day there was a frantic last-minute decision to make. Friends dropped round, rushing from one place to another. There was hardly a moment's calm. I wasn't quite sure what I needed except a little silence.

Finally acknowledging that Henry had left, I drove home and began to make a host of plans I would never carry out. For the first time, I was consumed with anger. Now I understood why women longed to burn things, trample on things, throw things against the wall, and destroy everything within their reach. In my fantasies, I would spew out a stream of invective and watch Henry cringe. But I knew it would change nothing. I imagined myself constructing a vast Guy Fawkes bonfire in the garden, throwing everything that reminded me of Henry onto a flaming pyre. Then I would walk away with my back turned. I wanted to blot out his existence. When reason returned, I merely set about rearranging the rooms and packing Henry's clothes into boxes. I did make a fire in the garden, but I only burned dead branches and shrivelled leaves. When the flames leaped up and the smell of smoke invaded the house, I felt elated. By the time Nicola arrived for the weekend, my rage had subsided.

We were both wrapped up in scarves seated on a wooden bench by our favourite part of the river, with a view through ancient weeping willows of the high water moving swiftly round a bend. It used to be a stopping point during the Sunday walk that we took as a family. I vowed I would never create rituals again. The same swans floated past, followed by large grey cygnets laced with white. I had to tell Nicola now but I dreaded sounding angry or bitter, making her dislike her father more than she already did. In the end, she forced it out of me.

'Dad's never home much any more, is he?' she said, swinging her muddy booted legs over the arm of the seat. 'What does he do all the time in London?'

'I'm not quite sure. With his kind of work . . .'

I couldn't finish the sentence.

'He should take you out more. You never go any-where, not even the cinema. I don't think that's fair. If you're married, you do things together. I would, anyway.'

I could see that Nicola was scrutinizing me, waiting for a comment. This was the moment I had been dreading. Once I'd told her, she'd remember this cold, sunny November day for ever.

'It's possible that . . . I mean . . .'

'What is it? What's been happening?'

'Isn't it better to talk at home?'

'No.' Nicola swivelled round and clasped her knees tightly.

'Daddy might . . . be in London for quite some time.'

She looked around her to check that there was nobody approaching.

'Say what you mean, Mum. Are you saying Dad's left? What are you hiding? I'm not a child any more.'

No wonder she was irritated. She had every right to be.

'He's . . . we haven't been getting on too well for a while. It's just . . . Henry prefers life in London.'

Nicola grabbed hold of my hands.

'Listen. I know he's left home. He has, hasn't he? And he's been sleeping in one of the spare rooms, hasn't he? Do you think I hadn't noticed? I'm not blind.'

I waited a few moments until I could look her in the face.

'Daddy's got another woman. It's been going on for some time.'

'What?'

I swallowed and tried to continue as calmly as I could.

'He told me last Sunday. And then he went back to London. He's going to stay there.'

'You mean Dad's screwing someone else?' she shouted, pulling away her hands. We neither of us noticed the families and dogs walking past. 'Fucking bastard!'

'Please don't.' I tried to gather myself together. 'I know he wants to tell you himself. There are always two sides to everything. Try not to blame him.'

Nicola stared angrily at me as a tear began to trickle down her cheek.

'Why didn't you stop him? How could you let Dad cheat on you like that? You must have known, surely? You must have suspected something. I can't believe it.'

I took a deep breath. I couldn't begin to answer her questions.

'It takes a while . . . to realize that there is something wrong. Perhaps I didn't want to face up to it. I thought our marriage was solid.'

Nicola put her hands round her ears and turned away, as though refusing to hear more.

'Why did you wait to tell me?'

'It was only a few days ago,' I said, gently. 'And I wanted to get over the shock.'

I wiped away Nicola's tears and we started to walk slowly back home, arm in arm.

'It's happened to lots of my friends' parents. I don't see the point of marriage. Or having one guy around all the time. I'd rather be on my own. Who needs it?'

'I know this has come at a bad time. It would have helped if things had gone better with Paul. But you won't feel like this for long, I promise you.'

Nicola suddenly stopped and looked at me wide-eyed.

'What's going to happen? Will we see Dad again?'

'Of course. He'll want to see you both, anyway.'

'Does Joel know?'

'Daddy's going to tell him.'

Nicola said little until we returned for tea. She refused the cakes I had bought and sat hunched at the kitchen table.

'How will you manage? Will you be all right? What are you going to do?'

'I've no idea. Something will turn up. I'll get over it. Something always does turn up. You mustn't worry about me. I'm tougher than you think. Watch this space.'

I was relieved to see her smile.

'Honestly?'

'I might get a job, take in students . . .'

'Good idea. And who knows? You might meet someone else.'

We both laughed.

'At my age? That's highly unlikely. Anyway, I might enjoy being on my own. You'd approve of that, wouldn't you?'

Nicola grinned.

'You can still have a wild affair. Serve Dad right if you did.'

'Don't, darling. It doesn't make things any better.'

'OK. OK.'

Slowly we were returning to normal. By the time Nicola left for London, she was chattering away as usual. I admired her resilience and optimism, even though I didn't think I could live up to the reassurance I had given her. For the few remaining weeks before Christmas, I could only concentrate on repeating the pattern I had made for myself even though my heart wasn't in it. I tried to enjoy my usual activities with friends, but it only seemed the most convenient way of passing time and obtaining a little comfort and sympathy. Life had been too easy and I sometimes wondered if I was being punished for it. When had I made an overwhelming effort? What had I risked? What had I achieved? I couldn't feel justified in blaming Henry for everything. I began to question myself.

I went quite mad over Christmas, as though it was the last one on earth. Was I trying to prove that I would make up for failure in an excessive celebration? Or was I determined to show Henry that I was happily standing alone? Or giving the children the best time they'd ever had? Whatever the reason, I didn't care. I raided the joint account for every extravagance I could find. I went up to the limit on my credit cards. I wanted to spend and spend so that Sheila couldn't do the same. I refused to feel guilty and asked everyone I could think of to share in my excess. I proudly counted my list of guests for Christmas lunch: Nicola, Joel and friend, Martin, Angela, Douggie and family, Maggie, Jeff and family, Patsy and Mustafa. There'd be at least twenty people. And Henry would come in the morning bearing gifts for the children and see the dining-room table laid to capacity. I'm having quite a crowd, I'd say. You can stay if you like. But I knew he wouldn't. He'd have another engagement. Everyone knew why he'd be absent. I think above all I felt relief at not having to hide what had happened. I was celebrating the promise of a new life. Well, that's the idea of Christmas, isn't it?

My only clear memory was of the morning when Henry came – the rest of Christmas passed in a warm blur. He complimented me on the huge tree reaching up to the ceiling in the drawing room covered in starry lights, the trailing pennants of silver silk and Eastern baubles, the glittering stars fixed to all the windows. Joel and Nicola were lying on the floor, tearing open the presents I had gathered from all my friends. Henry hesitated as he entered the room, then put down his case and knelt down beside them. Joel gave him a hug but Nicola merely looked up.

'Hi Dad. Are you staying for lunch? Mum's done fantastic things,' she said.

'You know Daddy can't stay,' I said, quickly.

'Shame,' she replied.

Henry opened his case and placed some profession-ally wrapped presents under the tree.

'Will you have a gin and tonic? Your usual big one?' I asked.

'I'd love one.'

He surveyed the presents he had brought with him, checked the labels and then extracted the largest, which he handed to me.

'If you don't like it, I can always change it.'

I smiled uneasily and took it from him, as though he was some actor dressed as Santa Claus. Then I pulled off the paper, aware that Joel and Nicola were watching me intently, and placed a large wooden box on the carpet.

'Let me open it,' said Joel. 'I bet it's tools. Mum'll need some of those.'

'Why should she?' retorted Nicola.

'In case anything goes wrong when Dad's away.' Joel glanced at Henry.

'I'll never be far,' said Henry.

'That's not the point.' Nicola held up a large embroidered sweater and shrieked. 'It's from Maggie and Jeff. Wouldn't you guess?'

By this time Joel had pulled back the lid of the box.

'Oh. Oil paints. Why did you buy her that? Mum's never painted a picture in her life.'

'But she did work in an art gallery once. And I think she might be rather good.'

44

I looked up with a start. I wasn't used to receiving compliments from Henry.

'We'll see about that!' I answered, hastily. Then I looked at Henry. 'I'd never have thought of it. Lovely. Angela can start me off.'

There was an awkward silence while I poured out his usual measure of gin into a glass. I wished he would go. I wished I hadn't agreed when he asked to come. He'd said it would be better for the children.

'Dad, we've put your presents from us under the tree,' Joel said.

Henry crawled on his hands and knees and started reading the labels. I wanted it to be over. I longed to see his car disappearing down the drive.

'Silly. I left my glasses in the car. I can't read this,' said Henry.

'Oh, never mind.' Joel took a few parcels and held them in front of him. 'Here's mine. I'm afraid I've bought you the same as usual. I couldn't think what to get. Mum said it wouldn't matter so I hope it doesn't.'

Nicola rose to her feet and looked fixedly at Henry as he began carefully tearing the paper. She waited until he had opened everything, her hands on her hips. I tried to distract her.

'Why don't you get the walnuts? Daddy likes those.'

'I'll go,' said Joel, walking away towards the kitchen before I could stop him.

Nicola went over to the sofa and pretended to examine a pair of earrings I'd bought her. Suddenly she leaped to her feet.

'I'm off,' she announced.

'Where?' I said, in alarm.

'Anywhere. See my friends. There's no point. We're all being dishonest. I can't stand it. You've made a beautiful Christmas and Dad wants to be with . . . with her.'

'I like being with you. I want to be here. That's why I

45

came,' said Henry. He went over to sit next to Nicola but she shied away.

'No, you don't. You're thinking, I'd rather be . . . wherever she is. Not with us, anyhow. We're not a family any more. Why pretend?'

Joel had returned and was standing by the door.

'I'm glad Dad's here,' he said. 'Anyway, it's not pretending. He's still Dad.'

'Not to me he isn't. Not after what he's done to Mum. He's spoiled our Christmas.'

Henry turned to look at her. There was pain in his face and I could see him struggling for words, his mouth half-open. I felt an overwhelming compassion for him and wanted to protect him.

'It's hard for all of us. Not least for Daddy. But it was important for us to be together today. We're not pretending and we're not going to stop loving one another.'

'He's spoiled Christmas,' repeated Nicola, angrily.

'He has not,' shouted Joel. Then he turned round abruptly and we could hear him stamping heavily up the stairs. Nicola started to follow him.

'It's best to leave him,' I said, going towards her.

'I'm going upstairs, too. Until Dad goes,' she retorted.

Henry and I looked at one another. Then he came over to me and put his arm round my shoulder.

'I've made a mess of everything. I'm sorry. I tried . . .'

'I know.'

I gently released myself and went over to pour some more gin into his glass.

'We'll find a way of dealing with . . . I mean, the children will. Perhaps it would be better if you left. It was all too . . .'

I was unable to finish. Henry remained on his feet, with the debris of torn-off wrapping scattered around him.

'I should never have come. Would you mind if next time I saw the children in London? Wouldn't it be easier for all of us?'

I watched helplessly as he walked into the hall and put on his overcoat. Then I heard him go up the stairs and call out to the children.

'I'm going now. Will you come and say goodbye?'

A door slammed shut upstairs. Then Joel appeared on the landing.

'Bye, Dad. Thanks for the present. You'll come and see me at school, won't you?'

'Of course I will.'

'Wait a moment, Henry.' He was hovering by the front door, a tormented expression on his face. I ran into the drawing room and returned with three unopened parcels from under the tree. 'You missed these. They're for you.'

He gathered them in his arms and I opened the door for him. Without saying anything, he walked over to his car, put the parcels in the boot and slammed it shut. Then he quickly got into the front and started up the engine. I stood watching him, in utter despair. I couldn't understand how this woman had been able to wrench Henry away from all that he loved. It was as though he was under some horrendous spell. I still couldn't believe what had happened, even though he had been away for over a month.

The moment he had disappeared down the drive, Nicola came running downstairs. I was still gazing through the window in the hall, wondering if I'd just seen Henry for the last time.

'Come on, Mum. We've got to get a move on. Lunch to do. Joel's in his room. He said he'd come and help finish the tables in a minute.'

Then the front door bell rang. A smiling Angela carrying a large basket decorated with red and green ribbons stood next to a slightly pink-faced Douggie.

'We came early to give you a hand. Douggie's already had one or two . . .'

'Getting into the mood . . .'

'. . . but he'll be fine. And I made you a Christmas cake for later.'

'That's wonderful. I'll open some fizzy,' I said, forcing myself to smile.

Then I ushered them in.

# THREE
• • •

'Work? That sounds dreadfully serious.'

Maggie pulled down her short skirt a fraction and settled into her chair. We were sitting round a circular table in the Café Rouge – Maggie, Angela and me – surrounded by shopping bags. Every Saturday we met here and it was one of the few rituals I still enjoyed, no doubt because it had nothing to do with Henry.

'I know I ought to do something,' I said.

Angela gazed in front of her. She was enveloped in a Peruvian sweater and scarf, as though setting off for the mountains.

'I spend hours wondering what I'll paint next. Why do people have to rush around doing things all the time?'

Maggie chuckled. 'Because they don't want to end up knitting bedsocks. Sally must find something to take her mind off things. An adventure. What about that gorgeous young man over there?' She turned round to smile invitingly at the new young waiter whose name she was itching to find out.

'He's not my type,' I said, to discourage her.

'Pity,' she sighed. 'He's mine all right. Lovely profile.'

As soon as her husband was out of sight, Maggie felt a compulsion to flirt with every desirable – or undesirable – male within reach. In one way I rather admired her for it, not allowing herself to be deterred just because she was over forty. But I still felt a little uncomfortable.

'Where does one find work around here, I wonder? What do women do? Nobody seems to have secretaries any more.'

I couldn't think how I was going to begin. If only I was Nicola's age, when nobody cast a critical eye wondering how old you were.

'Who wants to be a secretary, anyhow?' said Maggie, dismissively. 'You want a challenge. Monica is doing very well with her gift shop. How about something like that? I'm sure we could find the right premises.'

Maggie and Angela looked expectantly for my reaction. Ever since they heard about Henry's departure, they had been trying to find something to arouse my interest. Maggie always sounded so enthusiastic about everything.

'I'm hopeless at selling things,' I remarked.

'So am I,' Angela said, with feeling.

'Well, we know that.' Maggie gave Angela a slightly reproachful look, being unable to understand how she could spend hours perfecting a painting and then leave it in the attic. 'Listen, Sal. How about a course at Patsy's college? Business studies? That would be fun. I'd love to learn to cook the books.'

'It's an idea,' I said, trying to be positive.

'And there'd be lots of interesting men to meet there. Think of all that brainpower. Not that one would be looking for that! How about it?'

'It's not quite me.'

'What is you, I wonder?' asked Angela, leaning back and gazing into my face. 'If you could do anything you liked, what would you choose?'

I thought for a moment. I had never even considered having total freedom. Nobody I had ever met seemed to have achieved it.

'I could try being an explorer,' I said, remembering a

book I had read about intrepid women roaming through deserts and jungles. Then I rejected the idea. 'No, I'm not fit enough. I'd quite like to be a botanist, travelling around hunting for rare plants.'

'You wouldn't meet any normal men doing that,' said Maggie, even though I was sure she'd never come across a botanist – male or female – in her life.

'That's not the first thing on my mind,' I said, with a smile.

Maggie looked so astounded that we all burst out laughing. She half-finished her third cup of coffee and immediately ordered another so that the waiter could come up to our table yet again. She was starting to scoop off the thick layer of froth and chocolate when she suddenly put down her spoon and reached into her bag.

'What is it?' asked Angela, in alarm.

'An idea for Sal,' she answered, pulling out a glittery pink mobile phone.

'Can I know first?'

'I should have thought of it before. Major Carter said he wants to stand down as fund-raiser for Last Retreat. Sally would be the ideal person. I'll ring him now.'

'Stop, Maggie,' I cried. 'I don't know anything about raising money.'

Maggie waved aside my objection.

'It's really rewarding work, having lunch dates with people who are loaded and appealing to their better nature. All you have to do is ask for some money and use a bit of persuasion.'

Angela looked impressed.

'Sally would be perfect. She'd do it in such a convincing way.' She turned towards me. 'Didn't you raise some money for Joel's school?'

'That was different. I only ran a stall.'

'All the same,' said Maggie, who was now searching in a tiny phone book. 'I'll give him a call.'

Before I could rustle up any more objections, Maggie jumped up and walked over to the coat rack where she couldn't be overheard.

'If it doesn't work out, we'll think of something else,' said Angela. 'I bet Patsy would come up with a practical idea. With her contacts . . .'

It was far too long before Maggie returned to our table. What could she have been saying? She looked triumphant.

'I persuaded Major Carter that you'd be ideal. Now all you have to do is to go along for a chat and he'll fill you in.'

'An interview, you mean?' I said, starting to panic.

'A chat,' Maggie confirmed. 'And I've fixed a time.'

I knew my friends were doing everything they could to help, but I was hopeless at pretending to be confident and putting on a bold front. Unlike Maggie or Patsy, I'd never been good at projecting myself with people I didn't know. And when Henry walked out, I was left with the feeling that I was useless and incapable of doing anything. Still, it was a first step. Even if I failed the test (I was sure there was going to be a test) I'd make an effort to find something.

Maggie told me as much as she knew about Last Retreat. Apparently it was a charity that enabled those without means to have twenty-four-hour nursing and die with dignity in their own home. I was attracted by the idea for personal reasons. When my father was dying and the hospital surgeon wanted to cut out bits of his insides to see if he could save him – a twenty per cent chance – he opposed all the staff and insisted on discharging himself. How terrible it would be, to die in some impersonal ward with the curtains drawn and the television on at full volume. With much trepidation, I phoned back Major Carter then and there and said I would meet him. He sounded rather brusque and forbidding but Maggie said that was just his manner.

When I left the Café Rouge, it was gusty and pouring with rain. On the way to collect my car, I caught sight of myself reflected in the gilt mirror placed in the window of Wengrave Antiques. What a sight I looked, how tired and worn! Nicola often said her face had good days and bad days. This was definitely a bad day for my face. I had forgotten to bring a scarf and my hair was tangling up and straying in all directions. I hurried off to the car park, praying that the Range Rover would behave. It was due for a major service and had been spluttering badly. Henry was responsible for things like that. It was his car and I didn't care if it rusted into the ground. If it packed up, I'd use Nicola's bike.

I was feeling triumphant as I'd managed to get the engine to turn over. When you're feeling a little fragile, as I still was, you tend to think that if something breaks down, it's your fault through being stupid or careless. And if everything works, life seems more bearable. My elation was short-lived. I'd reached the traffic lights in the middle of the High Street and when they changed to green, the Range Rover cut out completely. However much I tried the ignition, there wasn't a spark of life. Serve me right, I thought, for tempting fate. I switched on the hazard lights, got out and began ferreting in my bag for the number of the RAC. Everyone was getting extremely shirty and angrily swinging out to avoid me. The lights changed from green to red. Then I noticed a young man cycling towards me. He stopped on the pavement, straddling his bike.

'Hi Sally. What's up? Can I help?'

It was Paul. I hadn't seen him since that Saturday in November, the day before Henry left. Neither of us would forget that weekend. Suddenly every detail came flooding back to me. He wouldn't have known about Henry, as it was hardly likely Nicola would have told him. I couldn't decide whether I should let him know or not. We were no longer part of his life, after all. I felt so awkward that my words came out in a rush.

'The engine suddenly went dead and I was just about to ring the RAC and I can't think where I put their number. Isn't it ridiculous? I know I've got it somewhere.'

He leaned his bike against a lamp post and walked over to me.

'It happened to my old van. Suddenly one morning it gave up the ghost and died. But I bet yours is OK. Why don't I have a quick look?'

'Can you spare the time?' I asked.

'Of course.' He flashed me a warm smile and rolled up the sleeves of his thick woollen sweater. Then I opened the bonnet for him and flicked the ignition a few times while he peered inside.

'It's flooded,' he remarked, raising his head. 'There's probably something wrong with the choke. Leave it for five minutes and then you can try again. I'm sure it's nothing serious. How about a quick drink?'

'I really . . . I really ought to stay here . . .' I said, hesitantly.

'No-one's going to drive it away. Have you got some lipstick?'

I gave him my Chanel pink, assuming that it had hidden chemical qualities that could start an engine, rather like making a drawer slide freely with candle wax. He had always found unexpected ways of solving problems, I remembered. I was taken back when he used it to scrawl over the windscreen: Broken Down Awaiting Tow. He handed the lipstick back to me, covered in grime.

'It's not much good now, I'm afraid.'

'I never liked that colour,' I said, with a laugh.

I followed Paul into the Raven pub, feeling uneasy. I knew it was the pub where he and Nicola used to meet

54

and it seemed tactless to see him there alone. But, unlike me, he didn't appear to betray any embarrassment as he strolled over to the bar and ordered our drinks. Standing beside him, I found myself staring at his strong, well-formed wrists and the layer of straw-coloured downy hairs on his forearms. His hands were blackened from fishing around under the bonnet. I wasn't used to seeing working hands. He suddenly noticed that they'd attracted my attention and grinned.

'Filthy aren't they? I need a scrub. Sorry about that.'

'It doesn't worry me at all,' I said. 'You should see mine when I've been digging around in the garden.'

'I have, many times.'

He pulled up a high stool for me and stood by my side. I hadn't realized before how tall he was. As I slowly sipped a lager, I was suddenly tongue-tied.

'I've got a job in another yard since I last saw you,' Paul began. 'Edgeworth Marine has taken me on. They're a strange bunch but they're very friendly.'

'Are you happy there?' I asked.

'Much better than the last place. Nicola couldn't understand why I stuck it out. Why don't you get out of there? she was always saying. But I had to look around till I found somewhere good. Jobs like this one don't drop from trees. Though she thought they did.'

'I'm sure it'll be different when she's left college and has to find work herself,' I said. It must have sounded as though I was apologizing on her behalf. In a way I was. 'Did you hear from her over Christmas? I would have asked you over but . . . well it was rather difficult this year.'

'I sent her a card, then she sent me one. But that was it. I didn't expect to hear really. She was off to other things,' said Paul, with a wry smile.

'You must have been very upset, though. She didn't have to cut you off so abruptly.'

'Better that way. We'd been having arguments for

ages, anyhow. In the end I was glad it was over. First love and all that. It peters out, doesn't it? And then you wonder why you got so steamed up in the first place. Though I don't believe she was ever that mad on me.'

'I'm not so sure about that.' Paul finished his beer and although I still had half a glass of lager left, I started to edge off my stool. 'That was lovely. But I really ought to be going back to the car.'

'Don't I get another then? I'm not a one-pint man, you know!' he said, with a grin. His grey-blue eyes were looking straight into mine. I was confused, wondering whether he was teasing me and why he wanted to stay in my company. I leaned across to the barman.

'Another pint, please.'

'And a half of lager,' Paul added quickly. 'You can stay ten minutes longer, can't you?'

A table had become free and we both sat down facing one another.

'You seem a bit nervous. Don't worry about the car. I guarantee it'll start and if it doesn't, I'll lend you my bike.'

I don't know exactly how he managed it, but I felt able to trust Paul. I believe I always had but it didn't seem so important in the Henry days. He communicated a certain fearlessness, as though nothing would faze him or drive him to anger.

'Do you ever have some days when something easy appears amazingly difficult?' I asked. He laughed.

'Only after I've had a heavy night at the pub. I bet you don't have many of those.'

'To be honest, I don't.'

We both smiled. I was trying to decide whether to tell him. Why not? We knew one another well enough.

'It sounds ridiculous, but I've let myself in for a job interview. I didn't want to but my friends insisted . . .' I hesitated, trying to gauge Paul's reaction.

'What's it for?'

'Well, it's not really a job. Charity work. Now the children aren't at home, I decided I had to do something.'

Paul looked puzzled.

'I never know exactly what that is. That's only because I don't know anyone who's a charity worker.'

'I'm meant to raise money for a good cause. I have to see someone called Major Carter.'

'Sounds OK. Why the interview, though?'

'To see if I'm trustworthy, I suppose. I might run off with the money.'

'And pigs might fly. Can't Henry put in a word for you?'

I said nothing for a few moments. Should I mention what had happened? What would Nicola have thought? I was sure she would never have wanted him to know. However 'cool' she and her friends might be about the break-up of marriages, it was always different with your own parents.

'Oh, I suppose he might,' I said. Then I added, 'If he's around.' Paul must have detected that my tone had changed.

'And is he?'

I looked down and instinctively covered my ring finger with my other hand.

'No. He's left home. I didn't mean to tell you.'

'Is that why Nicola was in such a bad mood when I came for lunch?'

'He left the day after. She was terribly upset and angry.'

'I'm sorry, Sally. It's the last thing I would have guessed. But we won't talk about it if you'd rather not.' Paul reached out and softly touched my hand.

'I'd rather not,' I said, moving my hand away. For a moment he appeared hurt, as though aware that he'd touched a nerve. We both finished our drinks quickly in silence and then Paul got up.

'I'll walk you back and get you started.'

I waited in the car with the window wound down, watching Paul as he checked the engine. There was a sureness and deftness about his movements that I liked, as though he was familiar with each part.

'You could do with some more oil. Now turn her over.'

I did as he suggested and the engine came to life.

'I can't thank you enough,' I said, reluctant to drive away.

'Glad to help.' He was waiting to say more and then we both spoke at the same time.

'If you like . . .'

'You could always . . .'

I got in first.

'I could always what?' I leaned out of the window.

'Come and see me at Edgeworth Marine. There are some lovely boats there. I could show you round. Do you know where to find it?'

'I've a vague idea.' I was so delighted at his invitation that I didn't for a moment think what his offer might imply. 'I'd love to come.'

'Then take this.' He pulled out a flimsy card from his pocket. 'I'm official now. They printed this up for me. I've never had one of these before.' I read the heavy black letters. Paul Burridge, Technical Assistant. Edgeworth Marine. 'Maybe when you get your job you'll have one, too.'

I grinned and put the car in gear.

'We'll see about that. I will come and see you, though.'

'Great. Give me a call first, to make sure I'm in. Bye Sally.'

As I drove off, I could see him standing with his bike as though he was making sure that I was safely on my way.

*

The moment I reached the house, I abandoned everything I had planned to do. I even forgot to fret about my interview with Major Carter. I tried to work out why my spirits had suddenly lifted. Was it just that I was unused to having the undivided attention of a very good-looking man for an hour or so? Why had my reaction to him changed? My elation quickly gave way to confusion and embarrassment. Had I made a fool of myself? Did he feel sorry for me? Why had I told him about Henry? Hadn't I accepted his invitation a little too quickly? He was so young! What if he thought that I was manoeuvring him into a rendezvous, like some dreadful middle-aged woman on the loose hunting down a toy boy? But I wasn't a stranger. He knew me as Nicola's mother. How humiliating to even think . . . I would have to accept that I found him attractive and leave it at that. Nicola would never talk to me again if she even suspected. What if I did turn up at the boatyard? There would be no harm in that . . . but no. I knew I shouldn't. He would assume I had other things in mind. I tried to follow everything through, logically. It was going to be quite a challenge, learning to operate as a single person again.

I tried to reassure myself. After all, many women on their own would have had the same reaction. My behaviour wasn't so difficult to explain. During my visits to the hairdresser, I would devour any article I could find on the psychology of the abandoned wife. (There seemed to be quite a few, though admittedly I was looking out for them.) If you've been dumped by your husband, you're liable to react quite unreasonably when someone comes along who shows an interest in you. That rang true. I was at the vulnerable stage, when I could make the most awful mistakes. And this would be the most serious mistake of all, showing an interest in my daughter's ex-boyfriend. It was completely mad. The temporary loss of reason and judgement – I'd been informed – is an affliction to be treated as seriously as post-natal depression. Just as well that in the evening I would be having dinner with Angela and Douggie and others of around my own age. Seeing them would bring me to my senses.

I was about to throw Paul's card in the rubbish bag, when I hesitated. He had given it to me, after all. I put it carefully inside the box of fuse wire that I kept in a kitchen drawer. Then I laughed at myself. Sally Farringford, what has come over you? Go and put the food away and clean up the kitchen. There's nothing like putting on an apron and a pair of rubber gloves to banish foolish thoughts. And there was Major Carter to think of.

You know how it is when you sense instantly that a decision is wrong, but you seem impelled into making it? Major Carter was very persuasive, if not bullying, and was convinced that my particular qualities as a wife and mother would be ideal for this sensitive work. I didn't have the opportunity to make my prepared speech about raising funds for Joel's school, which was probably just as well. I couldn't face the idea of selling myself, even though Patsy had coached me in 'presentation'. After a fifteen-minute lecture delivered from behind the large desk in his tiny office, Major Carter announced that I was now the official (whatever that meant) fund-raiser for Last Retreat and demanded that I start immediately. I didn't have a clue how to begin, so once again I consulted Patsy and Maggie.

Their idea that I would have endless opportunities for meeting desirable men went straight out of the window. I was told that it would be more convenient to work from my home as there was no room for a second person in Major Carter's office. All the same, Maggie insisted on dragging me round Wengrave boutiques to hunt down the 'get-up-and-go' managerial look. This turned out to be a bright magenta tailored jacket with lightly padded shoulders and a short black skirt to be worn with high-heeled court shoes. When I looked in the mirror, I gazed back at somebody I hardly recognized. I felt a complete fraud.

By the end of my second day, I already knew that I wasn't cut out for fund-raising. Few wealthy people I rang actually had the time to come to the phone. Nobody seemed interested. Unlike Maggie or Patsy, I knew I lacked the ability to persuade. How did they learn, I wondered? I realized that I had made a serious error of judgement that wasn't listed in the wife-on-her-own articles – and I should have trusted my first instinct. This job was not for me. (They were always advising you to trust your initial instinct but mine was hardly in working order. The incident with Paul was an obvious example.) However, I couldn't possibly let Major Carter down, or Maggie for that matter, so I tried to soldier on in the hope that I would soon be replaced by someone more suitable.

That evening I spoke to Joel, who was puzzled when I related my experience with Major Carter, as he couldn't understand why on earth I'd volunteered to do such a thing. He said I should leave if I wasn't enjoying it. And what's more, why wasn't I being paid? I wish things were that simple, I told him. When you're that age, life is so much more straightforward. Sometimes I envied him.

I was just about to settle into an evening watching television in bed (Henry used to hate me doing this) when the phone rang beside me.

'Hi, Sally. It's Paul. Just ringing to see how it went. The interview, I mean. Are you in the middle of something?'

'No, no . . . Just a moment.'

I leaped up and turned down the television. Remember. You're Nicola's mother, I told myself. Be friendly and natural, as you would normally be.

'Are you still there?'

'I was watching TV.'

'Shall I ring back later? Or would you rather I didn't?'

'No, no, it's quite all right. How nice of you to phone.'

I wasn't being natural. How could I be? Paul instantly picked it up.

'Is anyone else there? You can always ring me back.'

It would have been so easy to lie or make some excuse to put Paul off, but I'd been caught unawares. I've always been hopeless at avoiding the truth. Henry used to say – half seriously – that I'd never have been any good in court. No doubt his ability came in useful with me. Avoiding the truth is not quite the same as lying, he insisted. Yes, Henry.

'I'm on my own – tonight,' I said.

I was quite proud of having said 'tonight' as though it was a rare occasion. That was a slight lie, as I spent several evenings a week on my own. I didn't want to dwell on those.

'How did it go with the major?'

'He forced me into the job. And now I'm making a complete bosh of it. How do you make it sound attractive to sign a fat cheque for Last Retreat? I can't imagine how people do it. How can you ring up someone you've never met and say please give us some money?'

'I'd feel the same. I suppose you have to give them an incentive. Meeting a film star, something like that. Or getting a free ticket for a Cup Final.'

'I'm sure you know far more than I do.'

'I doubt it.' I could almost see the expression on his face. His eyes would be slightly crinkled, his mouth hinting at a smile. 'I was only guessing.'

'Actually, I have been invited to lunch by one of the people I phoned. Or rather his secretary arranged it. He's called William Murphy.'

'I've heard of him, haven't I? I'm sure he was one of our school governors.'

'Very likely. He's often in the *Wengrave Gazette*, chairman of this that and the other. That's why I thought of him.'

'Brilliant idea.'

'Do you think so? But I can't think where to go from here. At what point do you say, "By the way. Thank you for lunch. Now could you please sign a cheque?"'

'Try it. You could hit lucky. He might like the direct approach.'

'Yes, perhaps he might.'

I suddenly realized I had been talking far too long. It's one of the symptoms of being on your own — you prattle on and forget about time. Was I sounding too friendly, too familiar? I had to set a distance between us. Nicola's mother. I needed to remind myself once more.

'Anyway, I'm glad you called.'

'Mind if I do it again?'

He sounded uncertain. A young man unsure of himself.

'Of course not,' said Nicola's mother, reassuringly.

Most of the time while I was sitting opposite William Murphy across a vast bird's-eye maple table, I was thinking of Paul. I imagined him sitting next to me. What would he have thought of this short square man whose nose reminded me of a small Jerusalem artichoke? We would have exchanged impressions afterwards. He would have prevented me from feeling so tense. I tried hard to appear poised and relaxed as a succession of silver dishes passed in front of us.

'What a lovely room,' I remarked, glancing at the shiny oil paintings strung in even lines around the walls, showing different species of game being dismembered.

'My wife designed it. She's busy looking after the estate in Kerry. So, you see, I'm left on my own.'

I wasn't sure how I was meant to take this remark. He stopped tearing a king prawn to pieces and gave me a disconcerting smile. How was I going to bring up the subject of Last Retreat? It was a little too soon, I decided. Feeling increasingly uncomfortable, I attempted a neutral subject.

'What kind of work are you involved in, Mr Murphy?'

'Call me Bill. People I like call me Bill.' I could feel his eyes fixed on me and stared down at my plate. 'Since you ask, I'll tell you. Do you know anything about the road-haulage business?'

'Very little, I'm afraid.'

He ignored my reply and continued.

'I bet your husband does. He seems to know about everything. Clever fellow, Henry Farringford. He'll be taking on a case for my company later this year.'

'Oh? I didn't know that,' I said.

'Why should you?' he said, with a slight leer.

It was the last thing I expected, that he would know my husband, but in a small town like Wengrave most people did. I prayed that he wouldn't mention my visit.

'There's a lot of ignorance about road haulage, around here anyway,' Bill continued. 'Do you know how many lorries there are on British roads in one day?'

'I couldn't imagine,' I said, forcing myself to eat a thick rubbery mussel.

If I'd paid more attention instead of becoming panic-stricken as I tried to find the right moment to introduce my subject, I might have learned something. I could have become an expert on the challenges of transport, the gear ratio and pulling power of different lorry manufacturers, European vehicle legislation and how to beat the striking French at their own game. Once the pudding had been removed, I plucked up courage and took the plunge.

'Could I tell you about Last Retreat?' I began.

'Fire away,' said Bill, taking out a cigar from his pocket. He rocked back on his chair and fixed his gaze on my lower neck. I wished that I'd worn a blouse under the magenta power jacket but Maggie had said it was more stylish this way. Was he getting the wrong message? I tried to look straight at him and was met by a half-smile. Oh dear. I was sure he'd heard it all before.

'. . . and former Prime Minister John Major is particularly sympathetic to our case,' I concluded.

'Never liked the man,' he said. 'No good for transport, I'll tell you.'

'That's interesting. I'd never considered his transport policy.'

I thought he was about to give me another lecture on this subject and was longing to escape from his baronial house. Then he appeared to take pity on me.

'You can talk to my secretary about your charity. She'll fit you into our allocation budget.'

I smiled with relief. Perhaps I'd managed to achieve a result, after all. Now was the time to put Patsy's brief tuition into practice. I would 'close the deal'.

'Could you possibly give an idea of what you might give? Just so that I can tell Major Carter.'

Bill sucked at his cigar and then blew out a cloud of thick smoke towards the ceiling.

'The company usual. Well, no. I'll give a little more. You're very persuasive, Sally.' He must have noticed my startled reaction. Hearing him pronounce my first name had come as a shock. 'Sally's right, isn't it? That's what my secretary told me.'

'Yes,' I said.

Maggie had told me to smile as often as possible. My mouth was beginning to hurt.

'Lovely name, Sally. And a welcoming smile to go with it.'

'That's very kind of you, Mr Murphy.'

He started to rise from his heavy gothic chair, went over to the wall and pressed a gold button.

'Now we'll have coffee in the blue room.'

My heart sank as I followed him into a small room leading off from the dining room. As I sat down on the edge of a gilded armchair, Bill sprawled across a chaise longue opposite me. A young girl dressed in a tight black dress and a frilly apron brought in a tray and left it on a table in front of us. She shut the door behind her.

'I'll do the honours,' he said, stretching across and pouring the coffee from a silver pot. 'Why don't you sit beside me? It's easier to talk that way.'

He said it in such a commanding tone that I instantly obeyed. If it would make him favourably disposed to Last Retreat, it was the least I could do. I sat myself as far away as I could, but he slid towards me.

'Relax, Sally,' he urged. 'There's nothing to be nervous about. I'll give you what you want.'

The coffee cups lay untouched on the table. As I started to reach forward to collect my cup, he suddenly seized me fiercely round the waist.

'You're a lovely woman and very desirable,' he said. I was frozen, unable to move. Suddenly his hand slithered down the open neck of my jacket and he grasped hold of my breast.

'What do you think you're doing?'

With a frantic movement, I freed myself and stood up. My legs were quaking and I was struggling to keep my dignity and self-control.

'I have to get back to the office,' I said, coldly.

When I began to walk towards the door, he followed me and suddenly gripped my hand. By now I was so incensed that I hit out and slapped him on the face as hard as I could. He appeared not to react, almost as though he was expecting it, and then he slowly opened the door.

'You'll get your money,' I heard him shout as I ran through the dining room.

I kept running, unsure of the way out, passing through long corridors, straining to hear if footsteps were following me until at last I saw some French windows opening onto the garden. I stumbled onto the acres of lawn and followed the hedge round until I found where I had parked the car. As I turned the ignition key, my whole body was shaking and my teeth were chattering. Thank God it started first time. I put my foot down and roared down a narrow country lane, praying that nothing was coming towards me. When I neared my house, I was still shaking and shuddering as I gripped the steering wheel.

The moment I was through the front door, I went round the house securing every lock I could find. I felt as though I was under siege. Every room I entered, I imagined that Bill Murphy would be standing in front of me, leering. I quickly downed a brandy. I couldn't help feeling that I had brought it all on myself. What was I thinking of, going into a strange man's house and asking for money? How could I have been so stupid? Was I any different from a prostitute plying her trade? Thank God Ginnie was at home.

'Of course you didn't bring it on yourself!' she exclaimed, when I had attempted to give her all the details. 'And we're not going to let the bastard get away with it. Have you got a bruise? You can get him for assault.'

'I can't, Ginnie.'

'Why ever not? I'll help you out.'

'Anyway, I gave him a hefty slap on the face. He could get me for assault.'

'Self-defence,' Ginnie snorted. 'Quite legitimate. It's not as though you used a weapon. He should go inside for this. That'd cool him down.'

'I really couldn't cope with going to the police. It was

only a grope,' I said, trying to minimize the whole episode.

'Only a grope? Don't be ridiculous. You must take this seriously, Sal.'

'I'm all right now.'

'Sure? Why don't you come up to London and stay with me for the night?'

'I think I should stay here.'

'Don't be silly. There's no need to brave it out on your own.'

We argued a little longer, but Ginnie was unable to persuade me to take action. If it had been Nicola or Joel who'd been attacked, I knew I would have done something immediately. I vowed not to tell any of my friends. Couldn't I have seen the way things were going? How could I have been so naive? It was the first time I had seen myself as others must now see me – a woman of a certain age on her own. Fair game. Is that what they thought? I had listened many times to Nicola's brave assertions about being equal to any man and I admired her for believing it. But I felt I was fixed in another era. When I was her age, I was only vaguely aware of the new ideas of women's liberation that Nicola took for granted – but I never related them to my own life. Hard to believe, but I still expected men to behave like gentlemen. Of course they didn't, not even Henry, but my instinctive reaction was to believe they would.

This might explain why I behaved as I did when I had a drink with Paul. Now I was surer than ever that I'd made a complete fool of myself. What if one of my friends had seen me? I could imagine their sniggers. Chasing after anything she can get, young enough to be her son. Poor Sal. And how was I to know that Paul wasn't thinking the same thing? Get her into bed, have a bit of fun. I promised myself that I would keep a formal distance between us if we ever met again, which was quite likely to happen.

There was one man I'd always trusted and felt safe with – and that was Martin. He was one of Henry's oldest friends and godfather to Joel and over the years we'd become very close. When his wife Helen was alive, we would all go on holiday together. When Henry walked out he was outraged but he refused to write him off. Even if Henry's been a bad boy, he told me, he's still my friend. It didn't stop him from offering support and advice whenever I needed it. He had firm opinions about how one should act if confronted with a dilemma. No wonder he was so good at business. I couldn't decide whether I should brave out my job a few more weeks or hand in my resignation as soon as possible. Martin advised me to fix up a meeting with Major Carter. After talking it over, we decided it would be best if I gave up the job immediately.

The meeting was briefer than I expected and far more unpleasant. I'd abandoned the magenta jacket for a navy wool blazer and blue tweed skirt, hoping to feel more comfortable. But I was sweating with anticipation.

'How's this week's progress?' he asked brusquely, sitting bolt upright and arranging some papers in front of him.

'It hasn't been very rewarding, I'm afraid. Most of the people I phoned didn't show much interest. I really don't think I'm the right person for the job,' I said.

'Did the Murphy man cough up?' he asked.

'He said he would, but whether he will or not . . .'

'Good, good. I'll give him a nudge.'

'I'd rather you didn't.'

'Oh?' He looked at me sharply. 'And why not?'

'It didn't go very well. I probably bungled it.' I thought it was best to be honest but the major merely grunted. I hoped by now he was getting the message. 'In fact, I've found out that I'm not very effective at this kind of work. I'm sure it would be better for Last Retreat if you found somebody else.'

'That's for me to decide,' he said. As this so-called job was unpaid, surely it was my decision to leave? But I didn't dare interrupt. 'Perhaps you're unable to summon the dedication required, Mrs Farringford?'

'That's hardly the reason!' I exclaimed. He grunted again and placed his hands next to one another on his desk.

'Your attitude is somewhat negative, I might add. I'll have no other option but to ask you to relinquish your services. In which case, you will please return all the items of stationery that were loaned to you.'

'And my phone bill?' I said, rising to my feet.

'This time, it will be paid.'

'I should hope so, Major Carter.'

By now I had lost my fear of him. I felt I had been used.

'The person who takes over from me should be told about your conditions,' I said, indignantly.

'No-one will take over,' he said emphatically. Then his face seemed to collapse like a crumpled balloon. He looked old and defeated and I felt I had been too hard on him. 'Despite ailing health and dwindling resources, I will continue to carry on the good work myself.'

'I'm very sorry. I didn't realize you weren't well . . .'

I hesitated while he cleared his throat and stared gloomily at the unopened leather signature folder in front of him. Only then did I guess the whole sad story. Major Carter was destined to be one of the beneficiaries of Last Retreat. He slowly rose from his chair and came round to formally shake my hand.

'Thank you for your help, Mrs Farringford. I regret that you were unable to stay.'

I fancied others had heard the same words as they stood in front of him in his tiny office. As I left, I promised myself three things.

I wouldn't rely on friends to find me work.

I would put aside my fears about answering job advertisements.

I wouldn't use Henry's surname when applying.

# FOUR

### • • •

After my experience with Major Carter, my confidence
was shaken. If I started looking for another job, I feared
that I would merely repeat my mistake. How would I
know if I was letting myself in for a disaster? I didn't
trust my judgement any more. Every time I phoned
Ginnie or Nicola, they nagged me to make an effort and
came up with one suggestion after another, pulling me
in different directions. Ginnie favoured a short course
in counselling whilst Nicola suggested something in
interior design. Her friend's mum was doing all right at
it and unlike me, she had terrible taste so I was bound
to be successful. I was touched by their faith in me, but
it all sounded too daunting.

In the end, it was Martin who drew my attention to a
small advertisement in the local paper. Hedgehog
Graphics were looking for an office assistant. I thought
I should be able to manage that and I liked the name.
Yes, I could see myself typing the odd letter and
answering the telephone. Heartened, I dialled their
number and was answered by Matt. I had no idea what
his position in the company was, but he sounded
incredibly young. After a short friendly conversation,
he asked if I could start the following Monday as they
were desperate for some help. He hadn't brought up the
subject of previous experience – or even asked my
typing speeds – and I was so taken aback I dropped the

phone. When Martin heard that I'd landed the job, he was delighted and immediately booked a table at his favourite restaurant in order to celebrate my achievement. It was hardly an achievement and didn't merit a grand evening out but Martin refused to be put off.

I knew he'd arrive with a gift-wrapped package in his hand. And he'd be early.

Twenty minutes before our arranged time, I could see his old Mercedes – the one the chauffeur used to drive – coming through the gate. Then he accelerated. How could he park like that? He'd missed the rhododendron bush by inches.

'Sally, my dear. What a pleasure to see you!' He gave me a slightly damp kiss on my cheek. 'And I've brought you something.'

As soon as he'd taken off his traditional Savile Row coat, a relic from the days when he owned a highly successful furniture business, I had to open his surprise. He was so full of pleasure at his present that I had to do my little act.

'Oh, Martin. How absolutely gorgeous.'

It was a shiny belt with medallions, thick links and an ornate buckle, the kind of thing that Maggie would love.

'Different, isn't it? I knew you'd like it.'

I placed it over my navy pleated skirt and it hung awkwardly over my hips. Totally incongruous. I smiled. Henry would have had a fit.

He took me off to the Beetle and Wedge, the romantic place on the river that was one of Henry's favourites.

'You don't mind coming here, do you?' he asked, as we were led to our table. 'But the lobster is unbeatable. And I like that dark-eyed waitress over there. Not as pretty as you, of course.'

He always liked to flatter me and he was a wonderfully good-hearted man. It was impossible to be depressed in his company. However, when I looked round the restaurant at the shiny-eyed young couples, I couldn't help wishing that I was sitting opposite someone who was just a little younger, a little more handsome. Then I realized he might have been thinking the same of me. If only Sally was more like that pretty young waitress. If only she was in her twenties.

'She's far too young for me,' Martin commented, when she had taken our order. 'They like young chaps at that age. And if they don't, believe me, they're after something else. Like Henry's bird.' Realizing what he had said, he raised the wine list in front of his face. 'Sorry, shouldn't have mentioned it.'

'It doesn't matter, Martin. Let's face it, I have to stop pretending that she doesn't exist. After all, they've been living together for almost three months.'

'Then it's time she was getting on his nerves. Though if she was, I wouldn't be having dinner alone with you, would I?' I heard the rattle of ice and Martin whipped round in his chair. 'Good. They've remembered the champers. I told them to have it ready. Now you're a career lady . . .'

'Hardly,' I said with a grin.

By the time I had picked my way through half a lobster, my curiosity got the better of me.

'Have you met Sheila yet?'

Martin shifted the lobster shell to the side of his plate, then glanced up at me with a slightly guilty expression. He didn't like telling tales about Henry and I respected him for it.

'You needn't tell me if you don't want to,' I added.

'Er. Well, as a matter of fact I saw Henry at the Reform Club a couple of weeks ago. He asked if I'd seen you and wanted to know how you were. Full of plans, twenty years younger and beautiful as ever. That's what I said.'

'That's sweet of you. I didn't know you were so good at telling whoppers,' I said, attempting to gouge out the remains of the lobster.

'I'm not. I meant it.'

'Was he with her?'

'She turned up,' he answered, evasively.

'And? What did you think of her?'

'Well, she came for him in a taxi. I only got a brief impression. You know, average height, messy curly hair, and hardly any make-up. And badly dressed.'

'Really?'

'Square shoes, square shoulders.'

Since he was obviously reluctant to say more, I didn't feel I could press him. It was hard to work out whether I was relieved that she wasn't supermodel material, or upset that my replacement was so unimpressive.

'How did Henry seem?' I asked.

'Much the same. He's still very fond of you, Sal. But not as fond as I am.' Martin gave my hand a reassuring squeeze.

'He has a strange way of showing it,' I remarked, a little acidly.

'I know, I know. Rotten behaviour. I told him I didn't have a clue what he was up to. Or why. Funny chap, Henry.' He beckoned the waitress and the lobster debris was removed. 'How've the children been since Christmas? Amazing how they've coped, although you can never tell. One doesn't quite know what to say, whether to pretend nothing has happened or whether to let it out into the open. Don't let me do the wrong thing, will you?'

Not having any children of his own, Martin had always enjoyed being with Joel and Nicola. I sometimes thought they took him for granted, but I knew they were fond of him.

'I'm confused myself, about when to interfere and when not to. And it's often hard to keep out the bitterness. Nicola still refuses to speak to Henry. Joel is trying to carry on regardless. He keeps saying I mustn't worry about him. But I do, of course.'

'You're a really good mother. Do you know that? You've never put any pressure on your children and you've given them masses of love and affection. Isn't that what it's about? They're lucky, those two.'

'I've tried but I don't think I've been too successful.'

'The best I know. Though I sometimes thought you did too much. Never any time to yourself.'

'Watch out! That's going to change.'

'I can't wait.' He poured out the last of the champagne, picked up the wine list and pointed to an expensive bottle of burgundy.

'How about this one?'

'You're spoiling me,' I said, as he summoned the wine waiter.

'Only the best!' He edged his chair closer to the table. 'I must say, you really are looking good. You're a very attractive woman and I appreciate you enormously. Do you mind me saying so?'

'Not at all. We all like compliments.'

'And I find you extremely sexy.'

'That's one thing I'm not,' I said, with an incredulous laugh.

'And I'm not the only who thinks so.'

I suddenly thought of Bill Murphy. Had word got around? Suppose he'd been spreading rumours? I could just imagine him saying that I'd thrust myself at him. Luckily, Martin failed to notice my moment of panic.

'I often meant to say it but . . . I really am hopeless at making compliments. Would you allow me to take you away somewhere? I was wondering about a little trip to Rome . . . Paris . . .?'

'It's possible,' I said, vaguely.

Martin was obviously encouraged and gave me a beaming smile, even though I hadn't meant it to sound possible at all. He was the kind of man whom everyone liked immediately, with his round rosy smiling face, but I could never imagine it going further. After Henry had left, Maggie often hinted that Martin would be ideal for me. He was one of the rare eligible men around – a widower, rich, good company, loved the children and fancied me – so what more could I want? It was too soon. How did I know what I wanted? I couldn't even think of committing myself to someone else, least of all Martin.

'And then, in the summer . . .' He seemed unsure whether to continue. 'Oh, well. It was meant to be a surprise but what the hell . . . I'm going to tell you. I've decided to get a boat.'

'Oh?'

'I'm having a traditional slipper launch specially built. They're the smartest boats on the river. Everyone says it's the same as pouring money down a black hole, but everyone's got a black hole somewhere, haven't they? I don't go in for fast cars or fast ladies. And what's the point of my having a private mooring just for the ducks? What do you think?'

'I'll have to get used to the idea,' I said. 'I've never seen you as a river man.'

'Hidden depths.' Martin chuckled. 'I'm designing it with old Gabriel Edgeworth from Edgeworth Marine. Fascinating this boat business.'

On hearing the name, I immediately ran hot and cold. He'd be seeing Paul. The link would be renewed. There would be the perfect excuse to see him. How's Martin's boat coming along? I was ashamed I could even think like this.

'How exciting,' I said, as Martin filled up my glass.

'Marvellous place old Edgeworth's got. Have you ever seen it?'

'Joel has, I think. A friend of his kept a rowing boat there.'

'And you know Paul Burridge, that nice young man who used to knock around with Nicola . . .'

I quickly corrected him. 'Who was her boyfriend, you mean . . .'

'. . . old Edgeworth is putting him on it. He's done well, has Paul. Remember when I got him that grant from the Education Committee budget?' I nodded. Martin was proud of his activities as a local councillor. 'They think highly of him in the boatyard. Fast and reliable. You don't get much of that nowadays. And he's a good-looking young chap. I bet the girls fancy him like mad. But if he's going to do a good job on my boat, that's all that matters, isn't it?'

He looked at me expectantly. By now, my cheeks were burning. If I found myself in front of Paul, I'd have given myself away. I wished I'd been able to disguise my emotions but it was one of my failings. Martin appeared not to notice my awkward silence.

'You can come along with me to have a look while it's being built. Amazing what you can do with wood.'

'I'd love to see it when it's finished,' I said, quickly.

'I can see it now. Sally lying back on the velvet cushions in a lovely straw hat, picnic hamper, chilled champagne, sparkling river . . . We'll have wonderful times together.'

He took hold of my hand and kissed it. In half an hour, he would be happily tipsy. Martin's only fault was a fondness for downing the drink – Henry could never keep up with him.

'Wouldn't you rather find some gorgeous young girl to lie back on the cushions?' I suggested.

'There is one. Sitting in front of me,' he replied. 'You have beautiful eyes, a seductive smile and I can't talk about your body because unfortunately I'm not acquainted but it looks pretty perfect from here.'

I let out a giggle.

'You don't expect me to believe all that, Martin?'

'No, but it's the truth,' he said, his eyes crinkling with good humour.

A spectacular soufflé diverted us both. I found it hard

to take Martin's compliments seriously. To be honest, I'm sure I would have reacted differently if his words had been uttered by someone else. There must have been around twenty years difference between us. I know when you've reached your forties this is regarded as quite acceptable (according to Patsy and Maggie, anyhow) but I was feeling rather uneasy. I couldn't get used to the idea of Joel's godfather and Henry's golfing pal flirting with me. He had never behaved like this when Henry was around. Did he assume that because Henry had chosen to leave, I was now in the market for older men? Was Maggie right when she said, 'Let's face it, Sal. When you're our age, you have to be realistic'? Was I giving out the wrong signals? Did I seem as though I was on the lookout for another man?

I suddenly felt extremely depressed and struggled to be cheerful and appreciative as I slowly spooned up the soufflé. Martin finished well before me.

'Don't you like it?' he said. 'You can always order something else. Anything you like.'

'No, it's absolutely wonderful.' I looked up and attempted a smile.

'Good. Because tonight everything has to be perfect. And now we'll have some of that liqueur with the coffee beans on top. I know you love it.'

'We've both had quite a bit. And you must be over the limit . . .'

'Don't you worry, Sal. We'll take a taxi home.'

Once we'd driven up to the front of my house, we remained inside the taxi for several minutes while I attempted to persuade Martin to go back home, which was only a ten-minute drive away.

'I'm really sorry but I'm feeling absolutely exhausted. No stamina, that's my problem.'

He put his arm round me and whispered, 'Can't I come in? Just a cup of coffee?'

'Another time.'

'Good. Another time,' he said, showing no inclination to move. He couldn't hide his disappointment but then he suddenly rallied. 'Let me know how you get on with that job of yours. Anything I can do to help . . .'

'I'll call you, of course I will.'

I began to slide towards the door of the taxi but Martin took my hand and pulled me back.

'Just a moment, Sal. I know I've drunk a little, but . . . don't take it the wrong way. There's something I meant to say to you tonight. Do you know when I first met you, I was incredibly jealous of Henry? Because you were just the girl I'd always dreamed of.'

Martin had suddenly become serious. He rarely revealed his feelings and I couldn't bear the idea of hurting him.

'And when you got to know me better, you thought thank God Henry got there first.'

'Quite the reverse. I've always resented him for having you. Never said a word, of course. Do you think he ever guessed?'

'I'm absolutely sure he didn't.'

Martin leaned across and placed his hand on the door handle.

'You should have married me. Never mind. There's still time.'

He kissed me lightly on the lips, waited until I'd got out of the taxi and then settled back inside, waving as it pulled away.

All this was quite unexpected and bewildering. I sat down at the kitchen table thinking over what Martin had said. At first, I even wondered if I had heard him correctly. Did he really say I should have married him? When I wasn't even divorced? But for once Martin had been unsmiling and I knew he meant every word. This was practically a marriage proposal, yet I hadn't suspected for one moment that he would seriously consider me as a wife. Even though he was slightly drunk, it must have been on his mind. Although I was touched by his confession, on reflection I was quite horrified at his suggestion. Me marry Martin? Did he think I could switch so easily from living with Henry to living with one of his oldest friends? What had made him even refer to marriage? 'There's still time.' Had he even wondered if I could fall in love with him? Or was this just another of my delusions? Was falling in love merely a romantic state, which happened when you were young? Would I have to reconcile myself to being past the age of passion and dreams? Would I have to settle for affection and respect as a way out of loneliness? Was this the necessary compromise of maturity? If that was so, I had hardly outgrown childhood.

Standing in front of the bedroom mirror, I wondered if any of what Martin had said was true. Was I still attractive? How did you know if you were sexy or not? It hadn't occurred to me before. How would a young man view me? Someone like Paul, for example? No, not Paul. Someone else around his age. What would they think? Quite pretty and fresh-looking but nothing out of the ordinary. Conventional fine brown hair, cut short and lightly permed. Not exactly a teenage figure, but still slim enough. Wide hazel eyes. Breasts a little too large, out of proportion with the slight frame. Good legs, only revealed in tennis shorts or a swimming costume.

Henry used to say in the early days that I was a very good-looking girl. Nicola said I'd be fantastic if only I'd change my hairstyle, wear more interesting make-up and more modern clothes. I laughed at the time, but she was right. I hadn't thought about my appearance for years. As long as I fitted in, I had no desire to stand out in a crowd and I'd always regretted the magenta jacket. But now I would have to adapt to a completely different environment. Hedgehog Graphics. I don't believe I ever questioned why I had such a strong desire to merge into my surroundings. Perhaps I was afraid of being different. Unlike Maggie or Ginnie, I dreaded drawing attention to myself.

Next day I searched through my wardrobe to find something I could wear for my first day at work. There were rows of discreet, rather expensively tailored clothes in cream, navy and brown. What would they think? I couldn't see myself in any of them. Nicola had suggested jeans and a sweater, but I couldn't quite go that far. Maggie said everyone judged on appearances now and I really should give it some serious thought. That was the last thing on my mind. I was far more worried about getting my office skills up to scratch, spending every spare moment practising on the old computer in Henry's study, wondering how on earth I'd manage.

Maggie, as usual, took matters into her own hands. Instead of our Saturday session in the Café Rouge, she summoned Patsy – who was the expert on image – to give weight to our shopping expedition. As we traipsed round various boutiques I'd never been into except with Nicola, Maggie and Patsy selected various options and judged them on a scale of one to ten. Naturally, they couldn't agree. The get-up-and-go executive wardrobe was clearly out but I'd no idea what was in. Eventually a compromise was reached and I was persuaded into buying two different ensembles. I stopped saying 'I can't possibly wear that' and came away with a bag full of unsuitable clothes. Patsy informed me that there was no such thing as unsuitable. Even Coca-Cola executives were now going casual and City banks had dress-as-you-like days when investment managers would wear trainers and Diesel jackets. Young kids fresh from art school – with a name like Hedgehog Graphics, what else could they be? – wouldn't have a clue as to what was suitable and what wasn't. They'd be wearing rings all over their faces and tattoos up their arms. Patsy tended to assume that anyone who went to art school was either a raving lunatic or a wild anarchist, so I took her comments with a pinch of salt.

When I phoned Nicola to tell her about the result of our morning's trawl through Wengrave, she was over the moon.

'You will wear it all? Promise?' she said, when I'd described to her satisfaction the padded leather jacket, shiny shirt, wool waistcoat and matching short (by my standards) slightly flared skirt and ankle boots.

'I don't know what came over me. Still, I can blame Patsy and Maggie.'

'I wish Dad could see you,' she said, with a giggle. 'Why don't you come up to London and march into his office in your new gear? That'd give Sheila a shock for a start.'

'I'm about to be a working lady. No jaunts to London from now on.'

'Whatever you say. But when I'm next home, I'm going to check up on you.'

'No, you're not! Anyway, I might not last that long.'

'Yes, you will.'

She sounded in such high spirits that I was glad I hadn't conveyed my fears about my new job. Once the euphoria had worn off, I quickly came down to earth. How could I possibly lie about my abilities? I was about to be found out. Several times I was on the point of writing to say I'd given the wrong impression and that the job with Hedgehog Graphics should go to someone more qualified. Then I decided to come clean and let Matt make the decision. I phoned him up again, much to his surprise.

'You are coming on Monday?' was the first thing he said. He sounded quite anxious.

'Of course I am. But you might change your mind

after that. I'm really not terribly efficient. The only time I've worked in an office was a few weeks temping and that was years ago.'

'You'll soon pick it up. Go at your own pace. We won't hassle you, really.'

'I'll be rather slow on the computer. To start with, anyway.'

He gave a good-natured laugh.

'See you on Monday, then. Don't worry, I'm sure it'll work out.'

Golden rule, never apologize. I knew it in theory, but found it impossible in practice. Patsy, who believed all women were by nature apologetic, was very keen on assertiveness training to root out this weakness. She'd have had a fit if she'd heard my conversation with Matt, but for the time being I'd have to do things my own way. Even if it was the wrong way. At least I could work a computer. I'd rashly promised to type out Joel's essays during the summer holidays and he'd spent hours teaching me the basics.

I was fairly confident about that side of things, until Angela mentioned that they might use a complicated kind of software. Panic set in once again.

I put an urgent call through to Joel's school and eventually got him on the phone. I wasn't at death's door but it felt like it. When I asked him about the kind of software a graphics company might use, he became so technical and suggested so many options that my mind went totally blank.

'Just use Help, Mum. It's dead easy,' he concluded, after I'd asked a series of irrelevant questions. 'And don't forget to save.'

'Don't forget to save,' I repeated.

'Even Dad can just about manage and he's hopeless, so you'll do it easy. No problem.' This was one of the few occasions when I'd ever heard Joel criticize Henry or doubt his abilities. 'But if you're stuck, leave a

'I'm really sorry. I'm trying my best but I don't see how I can get all this finished today. Is it all right if I do some tomorrow?'

To my astonishment, Pickle swung round on her swivel chair and roared with laughter.

'What? You must be joking! If it's done by Friday, that'd be brilliant. We haven't had anyone for a month. The last girl was clueless, not like you. She got all the addresses muddled up and even with the checker, her spelling was crap.'

Instead of being relieved at the extra time I'd been allowed, I started going over what I'd done yet again. I couldn't bear to have made any mistakes. An hour later I had a small pile of completed work and felt wiped out.

'It's not always like this,' commented Pickle, ripping up a large sheet of paper covered in felt-tip scrawls. 'Well, mostly. What's the time?'

I glanced at my watch. Although I was meant to leave at five thirty, I had been going so slowly I didn't think I'd done a proper day's work. 'About six fifteen.'

'I'm fed up with this.' She slipped off her chair and ran onto the landing, yelling down the stairs. 'Jed! Matt! Take a break?'

They were all bound for the pub but all I wanted to do was to recover at home. And I was sure they'd only asked me to come with them out of politeness. I couldn't help feeling self-conscious about our difference in age. After all, they'd hardly want to have a boisterous evening in the pub with the mother of two teenage children.

'I've been rather useless on my first day,' I said.

'You've been great,' Pickle replied, as she chucked her pens into a jam jar.

And then she said something that made me want to come in the following day.

'And I like your jacket. Wicked. Can I try it on?'

*

87

After I'd been part of Hedgehog Graphics for a week, I was beginning to enjoy it. They worked irregular hours but I didn't mind. They seemed chuffed that I wasn't a nine-to-five person. I was surprised by them and I think they were equally surprised by me. Although they were all well under thirty, once I'd admitted that I still possessed an original copy of the Sergeant Pepper album and I could just about remember what Biba's looked like, I was regarded as one of the gang.

I began to look forward to my day, but the worst part was coming back to an empty house in the evening. It was particularly painful when Matt, Jed and Pickle started talking about what they'd been up to the night before. It wasn't quite the same, chatting over the phone to Nicola and Ginnie. I still missed Henry. If he had been home, I would have described everything around me at Hedgehog Graphics, what amused me, what projects were being developed and he would have advised me how to cope with any problems I had. My conversation used to be limited to telling him about local gossip, people I'd bumped into in the shops or at the sports club. Now I did have something to talk about, he wasn't around. I never went into the drawing room any more, where we used to sit in the evenings. Once, when I was feeling low, I started to pour out gin and tonic into two glasses and burst into tears. The next morning I gave myself a talking-to. Even if Henry had been there, would he really have been interested in hearing about the progress of an offbeat graphics company? I doubted it. His passion was discussing legal cases with the judges and barristers he knew. How could he possibly have understood 'the creative rumble' as Matt called it?

My second week at Hedgehog ended with a Friday night 'brainstorming'. They were putting together a package to write and illustrate a children's book on bears. I was there to make notes and keep everyone in order, but I didn't fancy being the Betty Boothroyd of the office and kept quiet when the shouting began. After I'd listened for a couple of hours, I came up with a silly suggestion for the front cover. There was an unnerving silence while Matt, Pickle and Jed seriously considered the idea of bears coming out of honeypots.

'Like it,' said Pickle.

'Not bad,' from Jed.

'Work on it,' from Matt. 'Now we'll buy Sal a drink. She works harder than any of us.'

This time, I couldn't refuse.

Walking to the pub with the gang, I barely noticed where we were going. It was only when Matt pushed open the door that I realized we were about to spend the evening in the Raven.

'I can't stay too long,' I said, once we had gathered round the bar. I was looking anxiously towards the entrance and trying to see who was passing in front of the windows.

'What's up? You trying not to be recognized?' asked Pickle. Then she giggled. 'You been barred or something?'

Jed grinned and pushed a packet of crisps into my hand. 'Or is it your husband's drinking hole and you're meant to be making the dinner?'

'I told you. Hubby's left. Sal got rid of the bastard.'

'Right.'

Pickle had already discovered a little about my life. As she was constantly telling me about hers, it seemed natural to tell her about Henry's departure. He had now become a character in the proposal for the Big Bear Book. Pickle's version was a particularly gross, bad-tempered animal called Henry the Barrister Bear who was always falling over and saying, 'Bear with me a moment.' (I sent a copy to Nicola, who loved it, but I made her swear not to show it around.)

'We don't mind going somewhere else, honest.'

'No, no. This'll be fine.'

The Raven was the liveliest pub in the area with a couple of outrageous barmen who seemed to be able to serve a dozen people at once and talk to them at the same time. I'd drunk half a glass of wine when a crowd of people pushed past and appeared to be greeting everyone in sight. It took half a second for me to pick out Paul. He stood at the bar and I couldn't take my eyes from him. He had a brown leather jacket over his shoulders and I could see him in profile, his firm chin and assertive nose. Beside him was a girl with blonde hair in a ponytail, almost the same colour as his, looking up at him, smiling. They both looked happy and easy with one another.

I started to rise to my feet.

'Same again? said Jed.

'No thanks. I'll just finish this and then I really ought . . .' Before I could finish my sentence, he made his way to the bar. Matt quickly followed him.

'There's Paul's mates,' said Pickle, pointing at the crowd who'd just come in. 'I wondered when he'd appear. He's a great guy but he doesn't fancy me. More's the pity.'

I longed to escape unobtrusively through the crowd but I couldn't back out now.

'How do you know he doesn't?' I asked, nervously.

'I just do. Can't you tell when a guy fancies you?'

'I'd probably guess wrong. You'll have to teach me.'

She reached for her glass and held it up, looking through the clear glass at the top.

'He's seen you. Looks like he knows you.'

Paul pushed his way through and came up to our table.

'Sally! Good to see you. What are you doing with Pickle? Learning bad habits?'

Pickle leaned back and giggled.

'Sal's working with us. Another Hedgehog. Creative input, that's what.'

'May I?' said Paul, grabbing hold of Jed's chair.

'Go ahead. The guys have deserted us. Bet they forget our drinks.' Pickle edged her chair away so that Paul could fit round our table. I glanced quickly past him at the blonde girl. She appeared to be flirting with some- one else. Was she the new girlfriend?

'What happened to Major Carter? I thought you were working for him,' said Paul, turning to face me so that our knees almost touched.

'It didn't work out. Or rather, I didn't work out.'

'That's a shame. I wanted to phone but . . . well, you know how it is. How did you land up with this lot, then?'

'I applied for the job and Matt was so desperate, he took me on. But no doubt he'll regret it.'

Pickle couldn't be silent any longer.

'Come on, Sal. How do you know Paul? What's between you two?'

'Nothing. Nothing at all. Except Paul used to go out with my daughter.'

'Cor! She's never that old, surely?'

Paul grinned at Pickle and then focused on me.

'Me and Sal are old buddies. Don't we look like it?'

Seeing him in a public place was unsettling. Seeing him anywhere was unsettling.

'Don't you want to join your friends?' I suggested.

'No. I like sitting here. You look fantastic. Quite different. It suits you.'

'Does it?' I glanced towards the bar and tried to remain calm. 'Is that your new girlfriend over there? She looks a real charmer.'

'That's Sam. From the boatyard.'

He hadn't exactly answered my question. Was it deliberate or not? It didn't matter, one way or the other. Was he trying to flirt with me? If he was, I wouldn't rise to it. If only he hadn't been so attractive. I kept trying to look past him, to focus on somebody else. Abruptly, Pickle stood up and pushed back her chair.

'Save my seat. I'm off to the bar.'

I think this was Pickle's way of being tactful. I would have preferred her to stay. Now Paul could demand my full attention.

'I like seeing you away from your house,' Paul continued. 'When you're there, you're different. Nicola's mum, I suppose. And I don't think of you like that.'

'How do you think of me, then?'

'You're a puzzle. I like puzzles. Sometimes I understand you, even when you don't say anything. And sometimes I don't have a clue.'

'Does it matter? Understanding me? I'd rather be a mystery. Far more interesting.'

I turned round. Matt, Jed and Pickle were having an animated argument at the bar.

'They're a nice bunch. Are you designing for them?' asked Paul.

'Heavens no. I'm just doing some office work.'

'I bet it's fun. Can I get you something else?'

'Thank you, but it's time I got going. We've had a long day.'

'Then it's time to wind down, isn't it?'

I sipped the little that remained of my glass of wine.

'Have you heard from Nicola?' I asked, deliberately changing the subject.

Paul looked at me intently and didn't answer. It was as though he guessed that I was using her as a defence but I wasn't going to be deterred. 'Joel's coming down this weekend. I know he'd like to see you. Why don't you drop round for Sunday lunch?'

'I'd much rather see you on your own.'

'I . . . well . . .' I couldn't think of an instant reply. 'Is it a good idea?' I asked, rather lamely.

'Yes, it is a good idea,' Paul said, with a smile. 'I'll

phone you. Then we can meet. Miles away if you like. And not in the Raven, I promise you.'

'You'd better get back to your friends,' I suggested. Pickle and Jed were making their way back to the table. 'And it's time I was going, too.'

The noise in the pub was growing so loud that I could scarcely hear what was being said. I wasn't used to it. My head was spinning, even though I had drunk little. I could see Matt talking to Paul but couldn't guess what was being said. When he came back to sit with us, Matt had to shout to make himself heard above the clamour.

'I've asked Paul to our party.'

'Who's he coming with?' Pickle shouted back.

'I said to bring someone but he said he'd come on his own.'

'That's cool,' she said.

'And he asked if Sally was going.'

'Did he now?' Pickle winked at me.

'Course Sally's going,' said Jed. He turned to me as I was putting on my coat. 'We haven't finished the design for the invite but you'll get one.'

Pickle leaned over and whispered in my ear.

'I could be wrong, but I think Paul fancies you, Sal.'

'How could he? He's far too young for me. You must find me a nice old man.'

'Rubbish,' replied Pickle. 'Get in there. I would.'

Once I was home, I imagined all the objections I would put to Paul. How could I possibly meet him alone? Even if he hadn't been Nicola's boyfriend, there was a yawning chasm between us. We could have a friendship, but no more. I couldn't take a repeat of Henry. He had stripped away my defences and the slightest, most trivial remark could cut me to the quick. I couldn't be like Ginnie, taking rejection with a smile, merely saying it didn't work out and going on to another unsatisfactory affair. In any case, I didn't see myself as the kind of woman who had affairs. How could I explain that to Paul without sounding prissy or defensive? And why should he even be interested in having an affair with me?

I was scared stiff of getting involved with anybody – let alone Paul. If only I was able to be bold and carefree. How do you stop worrying about consequences? How did someone of Pickle's age deal with the doubts and fears of having a relationship with a man? I would like to have known the secret. What happened if she got hurt? Wouldn't she have bled, like everyone else? Or, if things didn't work out, did she gaily go on to somebody else, still hopeful, keeping a distance, dancing in step for a while and then going her own way?

It was halfway through Monday morning and Pickle had just settled down at her drawing board. I was trying to make sense of a long letter of Jed's and put it into paragraphs. The scraping of her felt-tip pen suddenly stopped.

'He was tickled pink you're sorting us out.'

Pickle occasionally assumed that I could read her thoughts. Or maybe she'd said something earlier that had gone over my head. As she was constantly chatting, there were times when I shut off.

'Who was?'

'Paul was. He stayed on a bit at the Raven and then came with us for an Indian. You should've come.' I carried on typing. 'When I said "why don't you drop in and see us?" he said he might. I bet he does, too.'

'Oh?'

'Anyway, he's coming to our party so you'll see him then.' When I didn't comment, Pickle turned away from her drawing board. 'Do you like him?'

'Yes, of course.'

I still wasn't used to being distracted.

'He likes you, obvious. But he's a shy one, Paul. If it

was me, I'd ask him for a drink. Just casual. Why don't you, Sal?'

'I can't. Lots of reasons.'

Pickle came over and sat on the edge of my desk.

'You're only worried cos Nicola went out with him. That's no reason.'

'I'm afraid it is. Well, it's one reason. In any case, he's far too young for me.'

'And not enough of a toff?' Pickle said, with a giggle.

'That doesn't come into it.'

She leaned over and looked over my shoulder.

'Why does it matter? If you fancy someone.'

'I didn't say that.'

'Oh no?' she said. 'Time you enjoyed yourself. You keep saying no all the time. I bet you used to say yes once. Give it a whirl. Do you good. And Paul's a nice guy, not like some good-looking blokes I know.'

'How can you be sure?' I asked.

'Obvious,' she replied, going back to her desk.

That night, all I could think about was when I might bump into him again. It was like dreaming about an exotic place you would never visit. The temptation to see him alone began to be stronger than all my doubts. Would I have to wait until we came across one another again? I even considered going alone one evening to the Raven just to catch a glimpse of him and then coming home on my own. Or dropping into the yard to ask him about Martin's boat. Even if I had heard his voice, I would have been satisfied. He had rung me before. He might ring me again.

I had never harboured thoughts like this before. It began to seem as though I'd been invaded by a strange fever and sometimes I longed to return to my normal state. I was disturbed but I couldn't begin to understand why or how it had happened. Why Paul? Why had I fixed on the one person I ought never to have considered? I devoured books on psychology from the library, hoping to find an answer to my strange behaviour. Was I trying to regain my lost youth by supplanting my daughter and stealing her boyfriend? Was I releasing the hidden waves of sexuality that had always been repressed? Was it just a way of getting my own back on Henry? None of these explanations satisfied me.

Then I received a card from Matt, Pickle and Jed, headed Sally Linton and Partner.

*Hedgehog Graphics do It Again! Now we are Three! Come to our birthday party at the Red Hot Chicken Shack.*
*March 10th. 9p.m. Salsa till you drop. Dress: cool gear.*

I made up my mind to go, even though I knew that Paul would be there.

# FIVE
• • •

I knew that Paul would be coming, as I'd had to type out the list of acceptances for the Hedgehog party. There was no other name next to his. My heart almost missed a beat when I realized that he really was coming on his own. How could I hide my excitement? I'd be laying myself wide open.

I considered various alternatives. Could I find an excuse not to come? I could stay with Ginnie in London. No, that was the coward's way out. Sooner or later, I would have to come to terms with my infatuation. I couldn't carry on avoiding him. What if I came with somebody else?

That seemed a sensible solution. Then Paul would get the message that I wasn't available. It would also prevent me making a fool of myself. But who would I go with? The only unattached man I knew was Martin. Could I really see Martin turning up at somewhere called the Red Hot Chicken Shack? I would have to rely on my friends to find somebody suitable. Maggie could usually rustle up an escort when she put her mind to it.

Patsy, Maggie, Angela and I sat round a table in the Café Rouge as though we were company directors planning a giant takeover. They were a little mystified that I was going to a party at a club that their children frequented, but Patsy decided it was a good networking ploy for my future advancement in Hedgehog Graphics. (She was already planning my Route to Management.)

'The most important question is . . .' Patsy began, but Maggie didn't allow her to finish.

'. . . what is Sally going to wear. Black or something bright? All the young things insist on weird colours. Mind you, I'd go for pink myself.'

'You always go for pink.'

Patsy usually had a mild go at Maggie, as she rather disapproved of her style of dressing.

'That's because it's safe and feminine.'

'I thought I might borrow something from Nicola. We're about the same size.'

As soon as I'd said that, I recoiled in horror. I couldn't possibly raid Nicola's wardrobe. Was that a Freudian mistake? Mother wearing her daughter's clothes?

'On second thoughts, it's not a good idea,' I hastily added. 'I'll probably go for the green taffeta skirt with a black lace top.'

'Lovely, that,' said Angela with a smile. We were pretty familiar with one another's wardrobes. Maggie didn't seem convinced by my choice.

'You could be a bit more daring, Sal. Now you're a girl on the loose. I could lend you my gorgeous emerald green halter top, the one with the sequins . . .'

'She can't wear that,' retorted Patsy. 'How about your classic silk two-piece? The lovely pale grey one you wore for Mustafa's birthday party? Perfect for the girl who's heading for the top.'

'Oh yes?' I said, with a laugh.

I could see from her serious expression that Angela was contemplating wider issues. 'How can you decide if you don't know who you're going with? If the man is casual, the grey silk might be too formal. Have you made up your mind who it's going to be?'

Three faces were turned towards me.

'It's a difficult one. I can't really ask Martin. And I don't really want to go on my own.'

'Out of the question!' Patsy said in horror.

'Let's have a think,' said Maggie. 'I know a very nice man who's a good dancer. Ballroom anyway. So he could pick up on the Latin stuff.'

I had barely time to object, when Patsy jumped in.

'You're not thinking of Vic Fairstone? The one who has that sports shop in Reading?'

'He's quite nice, Patsy. There's no need to make a face.'

'I don't think so.'

Angela gave a start.

'Oh, him! I bought Douggie some trainers from his shop. They fell apart after a month. That isn't much help, is it? I know, there's Douggie's friend Sebastian who's just split up from his wife. He's very amusing and creative.'

Maggie pursed her lips.

'Mm. Isn't he the one who's a little . . .?'

Patsy instantly came up with another suggestion.

'And we mustn't forget Alistair, of course.'

Alistair was part of the golfing circle. He was a local architect who had lived alone for years and was often asked for Sunday lunches. We all felt sorry for him, but it was hard to see him throwing himself with abandon into salsa. Not that I could see myself doing so either, but I'd give it a try if it was dark enough.

'A bit old for Sally,' commented Angela.

'And he's always going on and on about the environment,' Maggie added.

Angela reached across for the sugar bowl and piled brown crystals into her cup. 'I don't see what's wrong with going on your own, Sally,' she said. 'Who knows? You might meet somebody wonderful.'

'At the Red Hot Chicken Shack? You must be joking!' Patsy usually brought us down to earth with a bang. We looked at one another blankly. Eventually she said, 'I could ask my cousin Peter, the one who lives in Shiplake, if you're really pushed.'

A few more suggestions were put forward and I was getting increasingly gloomy. I was very near deciding not to go. The party was assuming an importance that was quite out of proportion. Nicola would sometimes go to two or three in an evening without giving it a thought.

'This isn't getting us anywhere,' Maggie announced. 'Maybe Angela's right. Why not go on your own? There's no need to stay long. You can show your face, be there for half an hour and then say you're going on somewhere else. Come and have supper with us afterwards. You're always welcome.'

I immediately felt more cheerful and imagined what I would say when I came face to face with Paul. We'd have a brief chat for ten or fifteen minutes. Then I'd say something like: 'I really have to leave. Unfortunately I'm due at a friend's house for supper. It was so nice seeing you.' That way I would be in control.

'I think I will go on my own,' I concluded, relieved that a decision had been made.

On the day of the party, Matt, Pickle and Jed were out of the office decorating the Chicken Shack. I was left on my own, staring at the computer, feeling a nervous wreck and imagining the worst. Paul and I would be unable to talk. He would be dancing with a pretty young girl all evening. I would drink too much too quickly and abandon my plan. The Hedgehog crowd would try and persuade me to do the salsa and I'd make a complete idiot of myself. Paul would notice. Someone who knew Henry would be there – very unlikely but you never knew. I felt sure I was heading for disaster, even though it was far more likely to end up as nothing more than an unsatisfactory, uncomfortable evening.

Wengrave Cars were due to pick me up at nine thirty and I began preparing at least two hours earlier. I changed my mind about what I would wear several times and got to the point where everything looked dated and dull. In the end I reached for the ankle-length taffeta skirt and put on a shiny black clinging top with long sleeves and a cut-out neckline. I'd only worn it once as Henry said it made me look as though I was serving in a bar. A smart cocktail bar, he conceded when I pulled a face. It gave me unexpected pleasure to be wearing something he disliked. There was a very pretty jet necklace I had never worn as Henry's grandmother had a similar one and he disliked Victorian jewellery. I put that on, too. I'm sure I slapped on far too much make-up and the wrong colour lipstick and probably looked nearer fifty than forty. But after a while, I no longer hovered near the mirror. In the drawing room I knocked back a hefty gin and tonic, put on one of Nicola's CDs and tried to persuade myself into party mood.

Bill, the driver from Wengrave Cars, looked at me curiously when I gave him the address of the Red Hot Chicken Shack. As we drove down a track in the middle of a field off the main Reading road, he explained that it used to be a chicken farm in the old days. I was far too young to remember that, he assured me. As I certainly did remember it, I was flattered. I began to feel brighter as I heard the sound of loud Latin music blasting into the night. Bill escorted me as far as the outer door and then left me as I was approached by a hefty security guard in a T-shirt.

I wished that there had been someone to take my arm. I nervously pushed open the heavy black swing doors and was relieved to find that Matt was just inside, with his arm round a striking girl with long reddish hair and a full-length tight-fitting silver dress split up to her thighs. Matt gave me a kiss and introduced me by saying, 'This is Sally. My wondrous assistant,' before leading me through the crush to find a tumbler of sangria. I was glad that the lights were all smothered in dark red fabrics that gave everyone a warm glow. Gazing quickly round the dim hall, I saw only a mass of dark figures. Had Paul already arrived? Would he come? If so, would I be able to pick him out from the throng?

I found the darkest corner possible, hoping that nobody would notice that I'd overdone my face and was wearing a taffeta skirt that was more suitable for a tea dance than a Latin rave. I wished I could have responded to the fiesta atmosphere. Everywhere was full of colour and movement, with bright young people swinging their hair, throwing out their arms, swaying their hips, stamping their feet and shouting to make themselves heard above the music banging out from great speakers. I pulled down my top to show a touch more cleavage and wished I could have dressed with a little more style and abandon. I must have stuck out like a sore thumb. I saw young men in a glorious mix of fashion – trainers, boots, cowboy fringes, satin shirts, gaudy scarves, baggy combat trousers and hip-hugging jeans. The girls wore tiny narrow dresses suspended from sparkling straps, thigh-length skirts and mini shorts, boots and stilettos and platform shoes. I felt completely out of place, like a middle-aged tourist who'd been dropped off by coach in the middle of Rio de Janeiro at carnival time. And I almost hoped that Paul had decided to stay away. How awkward it would be if he caught me lurking in a corner, trying to keep a smile on my face.

I was beginning to wonder if I could bear it much longer. My glass was empty and I couldn't face pushing through the crowd to get a refill. Not far from me, Jed was gyrating on his own and Pickle was jumping around like a little firecracker, while her boyfriend

Miguel encircled her with expert steps. I was just plucking up courage to make my way towards her when someone came up to me.

'Hello. Having a good time?'

I gave a start and found myself confronted by a silver-haired man with a roguish face – a drinker's face.

'Oh. Yes, thank you.'

I tried to put him off by saying I was waiting for someone, but he insisted on talking to me. He turned out to be a property developer from Wengrave who had commissioned a brochure from Matt. Then he began to tell me about Hedgehog Graphics and how they had started.

'I know all about them. I work there,' I said, a little huffily. I peered round. If Paul was going to come, surely he would have arrived by now?

'You don't look the working type,' the property man continued, in a familiar tone that made me cringe. My spirits took a further nosedive. Had he approached me because I was the only woman over forty he could find? Did he think he might have a chance? Was this the kind of man I was going to attract? The fiftyish Jack the Lad with the roving eye? Or roaming hands like Bill Murphy?

'Fancy a dance?' he asked.

'No, thank you. I'm going soon,' I replied.

'Boyfriend stood you up, then?'

Luckily I was prevented from saying something angry and stupid, because Pickle was worming her way towards me. I was relieved when she ignored the property man and took my hand, pulling me towards the dance area.

'Miguel and me will teach you salsa,' she shouted over her shoulder. 'It's great. You'll love it.'

'I haven't got a partner,' I shouted back.

'No need.'

I was dying to ask her if she'd seen Paul, but I was

propelled into the whirling centre of the dancing mass. Girls were dancing with girls, some were with boys and some were making patterns on their own. I was reluctant to attempt the complicated movements but I wanted to show willing. Keeping my eyes on Miguel's feet, I tried to copy what he was doing as he followed every beat of the music with tiny precise steps and quick turns. Even though he kept yelling encourage- ment, I knew I was making a mess of it. Over my shoulder I could see Pickle as the light caught her short blood-red satin tunic. I was mesmerized, watching her swaying hips as she moved forwards and back, then twisted and turned in a deft circle, showing unre- strained pleasure in every inch of her body. How I envied her suppleness. (I promised myself I would go more often to the gym.)

I was slowly edging myself out of the centre when somebody touched my arm.

'Sally. I've been looking for you.'

I almost dropped to the floor. Paul was beside me, smiling, and I could hardly believe how handsome he looked. The red light made him seem tanned and glowing, or perhaps he had caught the sun and wind working outside. His long blond hair was gleaming. It was as though I'd seen him for the first time.

'Do you like the gear? It's the beach-boy look.'

I took a step back to admire his jazzy Californian shirt and tight white jeans.

'Only you could get away with that. Amazing! Now all you need is the yacht.'

'It's with the crew in Monte Carlo.'

Paul saw my look of astonishment and laughed.

'You look pretty good, too. I thought you'd be dancing with a gorgeous bloke. There are plenty around.'

'I was, just before you came.'

'Well now you can do it with me.'

'Pickle's boyfriend was trying to teach me salsa but he gave up.'

Paul glanced over his shoulder. Pickle and Miguel were now dominating the dance floor, sweeping across in a flamboyant tango.

'Too energetic for me,' he said, taking my hand and leading me towards them. 'We'll do something quieter. Though I'll have a go at salsa if you're game.'

I suddenly lost all my self-consciousness. I had forgotten my plan, forgotten to tell him that I couldn't stay long and was expected somewhere else. It seemed so natural to be in his company, as though we'd met only the day before. I unclasped the jet necklace, slipped it into my bag and stopped worrying about my unsuitable clothes or my face, which must have resembled a shiny apple by now. He clasped his hands behind my back and we swayed gently to the rhythm of another tango. Pickle gave me an enthusiastic wave. Then suddenly the tango mixed into a fast number and everyone began clapping to the rhythm. The whole room started to heave. Without thinking, I began to sway my hips and I could feel my body loosening up.

'Let's give it a go,' shouted Paul, taking a couple of steps backward. Then he put his hands on my hips and I followed his moves. 'You're good,' he said, speeding up the steps.

'Not so fast, though!' I gasped. But he didn't slow down. I could just about keep up but I was praying for the number to end. Suddenly the music stopped.

'That's finished me,' I said, laughing and heaving for breath.

'Me, too.' He took me in his arms, pressed my head against his chest and lightly kissed my neck. 'We need a drink.'

It was only when we reached the bar that I came to my senses. I stood watching him as he waited behind the queue of people. That was enough, I told myself. I have been in his arms, breathed in the sweet smell of his body and now it was time to leave. At parties, you did things you later regretted. I didn't want to regret anything. I could still go without guilt, even though I had felt his warm lips on my neck.

'Why don't you have a dance with Pickle? She's an amazing dancer,' I said, sipping from an ice-cold glass.

'I can't compete with Miguel. Anyway, why should I?'

I looked away and took a deep breath.

'I have to go soon. I'm expected at a friend's place.'

The smile faded rapidly from Paul's face.

'Which friend is that? Must you go?'

'I said I would. The taxi will be here by now.' He looked so disappointed that I almost relented.

'Who is it? Some anxious boyfriend wondering where you are?' he asked.

I suddenly realized that Paul had given me the opportunity of stopping everything now. If he thought there was someone else, I knew he would back away. One small lie and I would be saved from a fatal involvement. I stared at him for a moment. It was impossible.

'Maggie asked me over. I didn't think I'd be staying long. Well, it's not quite my scene, is it?'

'I don't understand why you said that. You seemed to be enjoying yourself. You looked so happy.'

'Did I?'

'I spent ages hunting for you. Matt said you'd be here. That's why I came. I wanted to see you. Will you stay?'

'I'm afraid I . . . it isn't really possible.' I could almost hear the gossip in the office next day. Did you see Sally at the party? Spent the whole evening with Paul. What'll happen next? I knew I couldn't face it. 'I can't. I really can't. Though I'd love to have stayed,' I continued, as firmly as I could. A moment later, I hated myself for refusing him. If only I'd been able to say that I was longing to see him, too. But my natural caution had taken over. I was terrified of the consequences.

'Then let's go and find your coat.'

We stood awkwardly by the entrance of the Chicken Shack while the taxi ticked over a short distance away.

'Don't keep running away, Sally. Not unless you want to,' Paul said.

'I don't. And I don't mean it to seem as though I'm running away.'

He took my hand.

'Then you could ask me over, couldn't you? Or if you'd rather, we could go out for a meal.'

'I'll call you.'

'You know where I am. Promise you'll phone? Otherwise, I will.'

'I promise,' I said. Then I jumped into the taxi.

Instead of going to Maggie's I went straight home, in complete turmoil. My head was throbbing, my body hot and feverish. I felt I was out of control, as though I was skiing downhill, bound on a fatal, inevitable course. However much I repeated to myself that it was possible to have a good time with someone and enjoy a light-hearted affair, I didn't believe it was possible with Paul. I didn't even know if I was capable of a summer holiday affair. How did you know if you'd never had one? And I had no idea how Paul regarded me. As a pleasant diversion from the young girls he frequented? A new experience? Was he attracted to older women, perhaps? Or, worst of all, did I remind him of Nicola? Did he see in me the older shadow of the first girl he had loved?

I couldn't wait to call Nicola. I hoped she might have given me the excuse I was looking for and I almost wished that she still had a relationship with Paul. Just when I was about to reach for the phone, I realized it was too late. She might be worried if I rang past my usual time. I would have to wait until the next evening.

When I eventually got through to Nicola, I was trembling. All I wanted to ask was whether she'd seen

Paul – or even spoken to him – since Christmas. If she had, I'd never meet him alone again. How would I bring up the subject? Would she guess by my voice that I was betraying more than mere interest?

'How was your party then? Was it wild?' she asked.

I was touched that she'd remembered.

'You wouldn't have thought so, I'm sure. I did enjoy it though. I managed a bit of salsa.'

I could hear her chuckling.

'Good for you! Who d'you dance with? Not Martin?'

'No, not Martin.'

'I was going to say! Who was it then?'

I could feel my cheeks flushing.

'Oh, it was Pickle's boyfriend. Miguel. He was very sweet and took pity on me.'

'He might have fancied dancing with you.'

I hoped she was unable to detect my invention.

'I doubt it. He couldn't be much older than twenty-four.'

'So? Why should that matter? I bet you were good, anyhow.'

'Well, I didn't fall over,' I said, with a laugh.

'Did you borrow anything of mine to wear? I said I wouldn't have minded.'

'That was a nice offer. But in the end I wore a little black top – and the green taffeta skirt.'

'That old thing.'

We both laughed and I promised it wouldn't be in the wardrobe next time she came home.

'Mum, mind if I tell you something?' I was on the edge of saying, 'Have you seen Paul again?' Then I stopped myself. 'Are you listening?'

'Yes, darling.'

'I've met this super guy. He's really fantastic. Not the kind I thought I'd go for.'

'That's fabulous.'

'I haven't told Aunt Ginnie, so – not a word. It's too

soon. But he is . . . amazing and different.'

I had learned to be tactful. One question too many and Nicola would have accused me of prying into her life.

'Can I ask where you met him?'

'It's bad luck if I tell you too much. But he's really nice. We've been out three times in the last ten days and we get on fantastically well. I think we do anyhow.'

She didn't sound entirely convinced, as though about to face my disapproval.

'You sound a little doubtful. Is something bothering you?'

'Not really.' She paused. I knew she was deciding how much to say. 'He's . . . well, he's much older than I am.'

'Is that important?' I asked.

'I thought that was the first question you'd ask. Since it always seems to matter so much to you.'

Nicola always hit out when she thought I would disapprove of something. I tried not to rise to her comment. She had an instinctive way of making me feel at fault.

'I'm sorry. I never realized it did.' Was she right? Or, looking back, wasn't it she who brought up the subject, after one of her rows with Paul? Saying he was far too old for her? There was no point in reminding her. 'As long as he's not a dodgy old man. And I'm sure he isn't.'

'Well, he's nothing like Dad, if that's what you mean.'

'Enough of that!' I said. I took a deep breath. I would try my best to make it sound like a casual enquiry. 'So does that mean Paul is out of your life now?'

'Paul? Why do you ask? I haven't seen him since before Christmas.'

'I thought you might have talked to him, now and again. I wasn't sure if you'd made a final decision or not.'

'Past history, Mum. I'm growing up now. Girls do, you know. Boys take longer, don't you think?'

'Some do, I suppose. Anyway, Paul seems to be doing quite well. Martin's having a boat built and he's going to work on it.'

'Good. Hope I get to go in it. What kind of a boat?'

'A slipper launch.'

'Oh yes. Whatever that is.' I could hear the sound of feet clattering in the background. 'Zoe's getting supper. I'd better help. Talk to you soon.'

My mind began to race. I was sure that Nicola meant what she had said. She was no longer interested in Paul. If anything did happen between us, I wouldn't be causing her pain. The most serious obstacle appeared to have melted away. I tried not to dwell on the other obstacles. If I met him again alone, could I trust myself not to get too involved? Other women managed. I suspected that Maggie, for example, had indulged in one or two affairs during her marriage and kept them hidden from her family. She once told me that you needed a light-hearted holiday from marriage once in a while, that married women deserved a little fun to keep them sane. I couldn't begin to imagine how she managed it.

For the next few days I veered wildly between deciding that I'd follow my impulses – which in any case was a contradiction as you can't decide to be impulsive – and being rational and sensible. In spite of my agonizing deliberations, I felt an overwhelming need to see Paul again, which grew stronger and stronger. One quiet afternoon in the office, I reached for the phone and automatically dialled the number of Edgeworth Marine, which I now knew by heart. I didn't have a clue as to what I would say. The moment I heard his voice, it came rushing out.

'I wondered if you might like to come to lunch one Sunday.'

He answered immediately.

'I was hoping you'd call. I was going to give you till

the end of the week. How about this Sunday? Or are you doing something?'

'No, no. This Sunday would be fine.'

'What time?'

'Whenever you like. Around one?'

'Great. See you then.'

After I'd put down the phone, I went into a cold sweat and sat motionless wondering what had come over me. Now I'd have to carry it through.

I spent the whole of Saturday afternoon cleaning and rearranging the furniture. I phoned Joel and felt immensely guilty. When he asked what I was up to this weekend, I said – oh, nothing special. Having a quiet one. I immediately promised to come down to his school and take him to see a film the following weekend. Then I rushed out to buy some flowers, rushed back and wished I hadn't bought roses. Tulips would have been better. I started polishing the dining-room table and then hesitated. Should we eat there or in the kitchen? The kitchen, with a simple tablecloth? The dining room, without a cloth but with informal mats? Flowers on the table or not on the table?

I knew perfectly well that it would have been much easier if we'd arranged to have Sunday lunch at a pub, but I couldn't possibly have suggested it. I was terrified that somebody might catch sight of us, that rumours would start. I found it hard enough dealing with Pickle in the office, as after the party she asked several times if I was going on a date with Paul. It was cowardly, I admit, but in Wengrave gossip went around like wildfire. How much easier it would have been in London. I wondered if Henry would have run off with someone else if his offices had been in Wengrave High Street. Somehow I doubted it. If you're part of a community – which we were – you have to abide by certain rules, whether you approve of them or not. I didn't believe I was strong enough to break them openly.

There was ironing to do. What on earth was I going to wear? I ran my hand down the long row of clothes hanging in the wardrobe. How had I managed to collect so many identical beige and navy tailored suits, so many silk and cotton shirts all interchangeable, tailored trousers, tailored jackets, tailored everything? There was absolutely nothing I wanted to put on, and just half an hour before the boutiques closed for the weekend. Once again I drove into town and came back with a burnt orange, long-sleeved Agnès b cashmere sweater with a dipping scoop neckline. I bought it in a hurry, which I'd never done before. Yes, it's perfect. I'll take it. Henry would have had a fit. I could just see him scanning down the credit card bill. What? You spent all that? I could buy a suit for that price!

Sunday took an eternity to arrive. I soaked in a long bath, washed my hair by mistake in moisturizing lotion, washed it again, ironed my black jeans and spent an hour in front of the mirror deciding if I could get away with wearing no make-up. I put some on, then removed it. My summer tan had faded to white, so I applied a touch of bronzer. Did it make me look younger? Or not? A little powder? And the sweater. Did it make my breasts seem a little too prominent? Had I fallen once again for the barmaid look? Oh well. I'd never had a knack with clothes. I closed the mirrored wardrobe door. I didn't look too bad, I decided.

I thought I heard the sound of tyres on gravel and ran down to the drawing room. Through the window I could see a figure on a bicycle, hurtling down the drive with stones spattering out to either side. Paul's mane of fair hair was streaming out behind him in the wind. I watched as he came nearer. What a splendid sight! I came out just as he was flinging his bike against a tree.

'Am I too early?' he said.

I shook my head and smiled. We both stood for a

moment, uncertain how to greet one another. Then I turned and walked briskly into the house. Paul followed me into the kitchen. He was here. How many countless times had he wandered into my house? And yet all week I'd been dreaming of the moment he would arrive.

'That's a good colour on you. Lovely. And so is everything else,' he remarked, giving an approving smile as he looked me up and down. I glanced away and could feel myself blushing. I was aware of his eyes following me as I moved around the kitchen. 'Do you need any help?'

'No, thanks. Not at the moment. I don't know if I've got the right thing. Just hamburgers and salad. Is that all right? I'll make something else if you like.' I must have sounded like a nervous, twittering hostess.

'Sit down for a moment. There's no rush, is there?'

'Not unless you're starving,' I said, with a smile. 'But we could have a beer, couldn't we?'

'That'd be great.' Paul took off his coat and flung it over a chair. 'You know, I kept thinking about the party. I wish you'd stayed. We should have gone on dancing and then walked by the river and watched the dawn come up.'

'That would have been a long wait,' I said, lightly.

'But worth it.'

'And I'd probably have been fast asleep by then.'

'I doubt it,' Paul said, with a lazy smile.

I wish I hadn't found him so compelling. When he looked at me, I felt I'd go with him anywhere. This frightened me. I was making every effort to resist him.

The hamburgers were overcooked and the potatoes floury, but as I'd prepared the salad earlier, I couldn't spoil that. We were sitting opposite one another and I was doing my best to persuade myself that this was an ordinary occasion, inviting a friend to lunch. Yet I was paralysed into silence by the weight of what I wanted to say, and couldn't. Paul seemed relaxed, even though he said little while we ate. The moment we'd finished, I began to clear away.

'I told Joel that you were going to work on a boat for Martin. He said he'd like to come to the yard at half-term. Would you mind?'

'He's welcome any time.'

'And he's bound to ask lots of technical questions.'

'I'll have to swot up, then. I bet he's doing well at school. I presume he'll be off to university.'

'It looks like it. He's set his heart on Manchester.'

I found it easier when I had something to do. It was as though I was about to have an interview, terrified of saying either too much or too little. I piled up the dishes by the sink and spent far too long making the coffee, cutting up a baguette and arranging the cheese on a board. When I eventually came to the table, Paul moved his chair round so that he was at my side.

'Did you go to university?' he asked.

'Yes. I read English at Bristol. But I never worked as hard as I should have, even though I scraped through my exams. My father thought English was a soft option.'

'What did he mean by that?'

'He said anyone can read literature. It's not a preparation for life and work.'

'You've never talked about it.'

I smiled.

'You don't, not if you haven't done very well. Or at least, I didn't.'

'And you cared desperately what your dad thought?'

'Yes. I'm afraid I did. I knew he considered Ginnie to be the one with brains. I would cruise along until I found a husband.'

'So that's just what you did.'

'Henry came along at the right time and . . .'

114

I couldn't finish the sentence. I'd never been in the habit of contemplating my past life, of drawing conclusions about myself from what had happened to me. Paul was looking at me intently as I brought a tray to the table.

'But you had a degree and letters after your name. What was it, before you married?'

'Sally Linton.'

'Better than Farringford,' he said, with a grin. 'I wish I'd known you then.' Paul seemed to sense that he'd touched a nerve. I must have looked down or given myself away somehow. 'I didn't mean that it would be better than knowing you now.'

'There's not a lot to know,' I said, taking up the coffee pot. My hand was unsteady as I splashed the coffee into the cups.

'You don't talk about yourself very much, do you?' he said.

'There's never been much time. With a husband and two children . . .'

'We've got time, though. Or have you got to rush off somewhere this afternoon?'

'No,' I said, uneasily.

'And you haven't invited the vicar for tea and cakes?'

'I don't think I did,' I said, with a slight laugh. 'Anyway, this is a very heathen household.'

'That suits me.'

When I began to collect up the cups, Paul stopped me.

'Leave that. I've brought you something.' He leaned over and took a small package from his coat pocket. 'I was going to get you a bottle of wine or some flowers and then I thought you'd like this better. Hope you do.'

I opened the package and pulled out a CD.

'What a wonderful present! I wasn't expecting . . .'

'I thought you'd like to have some salsa music in your collection. Let's go to the downstairs room and listen to it. I heard the first two tracks. It should be OK.'

The children's room in the basement was the most comfortable in the house, filled with bright modern furniture, posters, cushions, a large television set and a powerful sound system. I didn't want to be reminded that Paul used to spend hours here with Nicola.

'There's a portable stereo in the drawing room,' I suggested. 'It's rather old but it works.'

'Fine. If you'd rather.'

I usually avoided this room now, except on occasions when I raided Henry's drinks cabinet. It was full of heavy antique furniture that he'd selected from various auctions, a vast chintz-covered sofa with matching armchairs, dark landscapes and seascapes round the walls. I pulled back the moss green velvet curtains hanging from elaborately draped pelmets.

'I've only been in here once or twice,' remarked Paul.

'I don't come in much either. Henry and I used it for entertaining mostly.'

'Do you miss all that?' Paul said, as he went from one picture to another, examining closely the ones that showed sailing ships in rough seas.

'It was a lot of work. But I liked the house when it was full of people. It's not the kind of place for one, really. Even with the children, it's far too large.'

'So why don't you sell it?'

'I couldn't possibly. I've been here for years and years.'

'You could go somewhere else. You could go anywhere you liked.'

'I've never thought of moving,' I said.

I went over to a large inlaid cupboard and took out my old portable stereo, which I placed on a table positioned near the sofa. Paul was standing by a large oil painting of a ship keeling over in tempestuous seas.

'This painter knew about boats.' Then he pointed to

another one, over the other side of the room. 'That one didn't.'

'How do you know?'

'He's got the rigging wrong. I always notice. Or it could be a bad copy.'

'I can't wait to tell Henry. He was so proud of buying that for a silly price.'

Paul came over and slipped the disc into the stereo. He turned up the volume to the maximum, which wasn't very loud, making the Brazilian drumbeats sound rather restrained. Then he made himself comfortable in a corner of the sofa. I placed myself opposite him in an armchair.

'I love the music,' I remarked, after listening for a few minutes. 'I'd never heard it before properly till that night.' I almost said, Nicola never liked anything Latin American. She preferred house and techno but most of all reggae. But Paul would have known that. How could I avoid talking about his affair with my daughter? Would it mean we would never refer to the past? How long could you go on pretending that only the present existed? Would I have to ignore all the years I had spent with my husband?

'Are you in touch with Henry?' Paul suddenly asked. There had been several times when he seemed to guess the direction of my thoughts. Or it might have been pure coincidence.

'Occasionally,' I replied. 'Mostly to discuss practical matters. The children, school, what needs doing in the house, that kind of thing.'

'And do you miss him?'

With anyone else, I would have refused to answer such a question. But Paul asked it in such an open, straightforward way that I didn't find it offensive.

'I miss the good times we used to have once. But not Henry as he is now. He's changed a lot.'

'Or maybe you have,' Paul said, with a smile. Then he

117

leaned forward towards me. 'You seem a long way away. I'm not used to wide open spaces. And I'd rather you were close to me.'

Reluctantly, I got up from the armchair and sat beside him. He rested his arm behind my shoulders and I gradually became a little less tense. We were silent, as the music continued to the end of the tracks.

'I wasn't sure if it was a good idea to come here today,' said Paul. 'It might have been easier if we'd gone out somewhere.'

'Then I would have been worried.'

'Why?'

'Because . . . because I haven't been out with anybody . . . since . . . for a long time. Well, I mean, only with Martin . . . and he's just an old friend really . . .'

'I don't believe that can be the reason.'

'Do you want me to tell you? I'm rather ashamed of admitting why.'

'You needn't be. Not with me.'

The tone of his voice was reassuring, straightforward and direct, as though he genuinely cared about what I thought. I tried to reply with the same directness but at first I was hesitant. When you've never expressed something before, especially to a man, it's hard to find the right words.

'I'm not very good at coping with . . . I don't know if you'd understand . . . People say things. Specially around here. I know you should ignore them but somehow I can't. It was dreadful when Henry walked out. I felt that everyone was blaming me.'

Paul looked at me in astonishment.

'What on earth made you feel that?'

'Many of the people we knew, if they saw me, they looked at me in a strange way. It wasn't pity. It was a kind of disapproval, as though I'd let them down in some way. I still feel that everyone's dying to point the finger. No wonder her husband walked out. Who's that

118

young man she's with? Sally Farringford! Who'd have guessed? I know it shouldn't matter but it does. I've always wanted people's good opinion. Or maybe I was just trying to protect Henry. In some way, I needed us to be the perfect couple so that nobody could criticize us.'

I wasn't used to making such a long speech. Paul looked thoughtful.

'I'll try to understand, though it's hard for me. I've never minded what people think, but then it wouldn't have made a difference to me one way or the other. I wasn't after being a politician or anything like that.'

'Thank goodness you weren't!'

Paul leaned back and smiled. For the first time, I began to feel at ease.

'Myself, I don't see why other people should dictate what you do,' he said, reflectively. 'Why can't you just be you?'

'It's easy to say that. Maybe one day. I've only been on my own since last November. Will you give me a few more weeks?'

'Days,' he said, with a grin.

I suddenly felt as though I was falling into a trap, that we were becoming too intimate. I'd said too much. Everything was happening too quickly.

'Perhaps the answer is to move to London. Ginnie's always trying to persuade me. Then I needn't worry about what people thought.'

'Don't do that, Sally.'

'Why not?'

'I'd hardly ever see you if you did.'

I got up from the sofa and started pacing round the room, trying to collect my thoughts.

'I can't get it out of my mind. You and Nicola . . . However much I . . . I wish I could,' I began, hesitantly. I stopped by the window and turned to look at Paul. He leaned forward, staring in front of him, his hands clasped tightly.

'If we hadn't gone out together, would that have made all the difference? What's stopping you, Sally? Are you really so worried about what people might say? Or is there another reason? Are you afraid I'll take advantage of you in some way? I don't know what's going through your mind. Are you saying you'd rather we didn't meet any more? If that's how you feel, I'll go away.'

I walked slowly back to the sofa, and crouched at the furthest end, my feet curled up under me.

'It frightens me that I might become too involved with you. That we might have an affair for a few weeks or a few months and then you'd . . . well, you'd want to move on.'

'I don't see it like that. All I see is a wonderfully attractive girl who's unlike anyone I've ever met. I want to make love to her and make her smile. Is that wrong of me? Am I completely out of order? Acting like a lunatic?' I shook my head. 'Then nothing else matters.'

'Yes, it does.' Now I looked him straight in the face. 'I have to trust you.'

Paul stretched out to take hold of my hand and gently caressed my fingers. Then he slowly pulled me towards him.

'Will you give me the chance?'

His hair fell round my face and he was holding my breasts. My head swam, my eyes were closed. I don't think anyone had ever kissed me like that. Then I came to.

'Paul . . . please . . .'

He gently released me and then he took my hand, pressing it to his lips.

'I kissed you because I meant it.'

I slowly rose to my feet, dazed, wanting and not wanting him to touch me again.

'You can tell me to go away if you like,' he said.

'No, no. I couldn't . . . I wouldn't do that,' I stammered.

'Have I upset you?'

'I don't think so.' I was frantically trying to compose myself. 'You've confused me.' I was unable to look into his face. A thousand thoughts were rushing through my mind. I felt as though I was being swept out to sea by a giant wave.

'It'll take me a while . . .'

I was unable to continue. I was thinking of Henry, his dishonesty and his deception. I feared I might allow myself to be deceived again. What I intended to say was – it'll take me a while to trust any man again.

Paul came up to me and put his arms round my waist.

'I need time. You mustn't rush me,' I said.

# SIX

. . .

I was determined to put Paul at a distance but I kept
running over every minute he had spent at the house
that Sunday. There were moments when I was with
him that I was able to forget my fears and stop looking
into the future with apprehension. And after he had
kissed me, I felt only tenderness and joy. He seemed so
open in his feelings and there was nothing he had said
or done that could be interpreted as a calculating act. I
could no longer imagine how I had come to regard him
with such suspicion. Then my doubts returned and I
almost wished he would disappear from my life. I
couldn't see how we could possibly have any future
together – the obstacles seemed impossible to overcome – and I couldn't face the idea of having a part-
time, secret lover. Better, I thought, to have none at all.

If I heard nothing from Paul, I planned to give
myself a week before speaking to him. Even if we had
been lovers for only a night, I couldn't bear the
thought of never referring to it again, pretending that
nothing had happened. Before going to work, I waited
as late as I dared. Paul might phone. Had he written
down my mobile number? Every time I heard the
ringing tone, I was certain it would be him. Every
moment of the day while I sat at my small desk in
Hedgehog Graphics, I willed Paul to phone me.
Wouldn't he want to say hello, thank you for lunch,

how are you? At the end of each morning and just before I left in the evening, I asked Matt, Jed and Pickle if there had been any calls for me. I refused to go out with them to the pub, in case Paul might show up. I couldn't face seeing him.

As the week passed, my anxiety grew worse. I hardly slept, racking my brains for all the reasons that had prevented Paul from calling. Why should he get involved with a woman with all my complications? Perhaps he thought he had gone too far and wanted to back away. I had hardly encouraged him. I might have put him off. What if he thought I really didn't want to see him again?

On Friday morning, I gave myself an ultimatum. It was impossible, going on like this. What on earth would Nicola say if she knew that her mother was acting like a lovesick teenager? I felt ashamed. At half past four, when Pickle was in Matt's office having tea, I took a huge breath, picked up the phone and dialled Paul's number.

'Is Paul Burridge there?'

'Mr Edgeworth's secretary speaking. Can I tell him what it's about?' Certainly not. My mind was a blank. The voice went on, 'Are you still there?' Quick. I had to think of something.

'A boat. He was going to look for a boat . . .'

'I'll get someone to see if he's around. Would you please hold?'

What was I going to say? Would it come to me? Should I refer to last weekend? Would he speak first or would I? Would he rather I hadn't called him at work? When he came to the phone his voice sound impersonal. I couldn't think how to begin and my words came out in a rush.

'Are you busy? I can always call back later'

'Sally? They didn't say who it was . . .'

The moment I heard my name on his lips, everything

flew out of my head. I made an effort to collect myself.

'We're having a tea break, so I thought I'd call. See how you were . . .'

'It's really good to hear you. I've been just outside Reading most of the week, doing some repairs on a boat. A messy job. How about you?'

I could hear a hammer banging away in the background. A girl's voice was shouting, 'Paul, Paul, give us a hand, can't you?'

'Just a moment, Sally. Don't go. I'll be back,' Paul said.

I waited with baited breath, praying that Pickle was taking a leisurely tea break. I heard her heavy footsteps coming down the stairs, then pausing outside the door. The door handle turned, then she swore loudly and went rushing up again. I heard the phone crackle.

'Sorry about that.'

I tried to sound casual. 'I wondered if you'd like to come round to my place one evening after work.'

'Tonight?'

'This week's difficult.'

'Sunday then?'

'I'm going to see Joel on Sunday.'

'Send him my best.'

'I will.' Did I give the impression of being lukewarm? I quickly added, 'How about Monday?'

'Sure.'

'We could have a drink and then maybe . . .'

'I'll take you out somewhere.'

'Couldn't be better.'

The door burst open and Pickle deposited a mug of tea on my desk.

'Around six thirty?'

'Fine.' I saw Pickle raise her eyebrows, curious about the caller. I merely grinned, then said to Paul, 'Must get back to it now.'

\*

I was completely impossible for the rest of the afternoon. Pickle asked if I'd won the lottery and Matt returned several letters that didn't make sense. I was just deliriously happy and quite irresponsible. We were going to meet again. And I'd taken the initiative. To anyone else, without my stilted upbringing, it would have been quite unremarkable to phone up a man and suggest a date. For me, it was a milestone and I never imagined I'd be able to do it. Something that Nicola – or my friends – would take for granted, I'd never dreamed of attempting.

All I knew was that everything had to be perfect and that there must be nothing to spoil our pleasure. Where would we go? What place could possibly live up to my expectations? I suddenly realized that I had a very narrow view of the area in which I lived. You could be somewhere for years and always go to the same places. A pub? A restaurant? I'd leave it to Paul but I hoped it wouldn't be anywhere in Wengrave and that we'd avoid the restaurants frequented by Henry or Martin. Of course we would. To have dinner for two would probably cost Paul a week's wages. Even if he wanted to, I couldn't bear him spending a lot on our meal. Or should I offer to go Dutch? Wasn't that what the young ones did, when they went out with their friends? I hoped we'd end up in a country pub. That way, we'd both feel at ease. I conjured up elaborate visions of what would happen at the next meeting. And the next. I would seek out hidden places where we would never be found. I hunted down an ancient school copy of Shakespeare's sonnets. I listened to Heart FM. I looked longingly at the seascapes hanging in Wengrave Gallery. Everything made me think of Paul. I would experience the madness of love and nobody would stop me. Then, on Sunday night, I almost rang him up to cancel.

There's nothing like visiting a school to make you feel older. On Sunday morning I put on the expected uniform for a Visiting Mum – tweed skirt, tailored jacket and sensible shoes. Then I drove down to Sussex, watched Joel playing football and met Mr Peters, his housemaster, to discuss his progress. Henry had informed him of our separation, without telling me. I did my best to be affable and not to show my resentment but it was difficult, especially when he insisted on calling me Mrs Farringford at every opportunity and using pointless jargon like 'separation anxiety'. I bet they didn't talk like that when Henry was there. Still, it was probably worse in his day. Many of the masters looked almost half my age. Far too young, anyhow.

The White Rose Tea Rooms in a nearby village was Joel's first choice for his Sunday outing, because they made cream teas and gave double helpings of cream if you asked. Later, we'd be off to the Lewes Multiplex for an action movie starring a twenty-two-year-old American actress whom Joel admired, though I couldn't understand what he saw in her. While we sat in the black-beamed, crowded tearoom, I noticed other parents on their own, smiling a little too much, being overattentive with their sons.

'Dad came last week,' Joel said, as he piled jam and cream onto a hefty scone.

'I know. Mr Peters told me. Did he come on his own?'

'Yes. I said I'd rather Sheila didn't come. She offered, though.'

'That's very sensible of you,' I said.

'I'll see her in the holidays anyway. Did you know? She's got a new car.'

I prickled immediately.

'How would I know something like that?'

'Dad bought it for her. It's second-hand, though. A Japanese job. Sheila's paying for me to have driving lessons in the summer. Then she'll let me have a go in it.'

I pursed my lips and hoped Joel wasn't expecting a comment. Sometimes it felt as though I was living in a horrible limbo. How much longer would I continue being Mrs Farringford, how much longer would I be wondering what Sheila was up to and whether she was running up huge bills that Henry would pay? Her plans were obvious. By getting herself in Joel's good books, she was already preparing herself for the role of stepmother. I wasn't ready for that.

'But don't you remember? I promised I'd give you driving lessons this year,' I said, unable to keep the emotion from my voice.

'It's much better if she pays. Then you'll be able to buy something for yourself. Like a new stereo.'

Dear Joel. He always took refuge in logic and I'm sure he hadn't for one moment questioned Sheila's motives. And maybe it was just as well that he wasn't aware of the subtle ways in which adults could wound one another.

'Maybe I will buy a stereo. And you can help me choose it. How did Daddy seem?'

'OK.'

'Is that all?'

'Just the same, really.'

'I suppose parents are,' I said, with a smile.

'You're not. You've changed a bit. Since you got that job.'

'Better or worse?' I asked.

Joel stared for a moment. 'Better, I'd say.'

'Thank God for that.'

Then we both laughed.

'Mr Peters made me see the school doctor. He's trained in psychology or something.'

'Oh? Didn't you have a say in it?'

'Not really. He asked me if I was sleeping properly. And he said I could talk to him about my parents any time I wanted to. I didn't see the point.'

'And did you tell him that?'

'Yes. Then he went on about not repressing things, better to talk and so on. That was about it, really. Anyway, I said I was more worried about coming second in the physics mock.'

'But that was a brilliant result!'

'I should have come top.'

'I don't think it matters. You've been doing fantastically well.'

'It does matter. There's no point in being second. I was silly and read one question wrong. My answer would have been spot on.'

How like Henry he was. He had the same driving ambition, even at sixteen. His pride wouldn't allow him to be less than the best. I should have been proud of him. In one way I was, but he sometimes disturbed me. There was a hint of ruthlessness about Joel that I feared.

'And is it still going to be Manchester?'

'Yep.' Joel ladled out another thick spoonful of cream onto his plate. I could see there was something else on his mind. After he'd half demolished the remaining scone, he suddenly stopped eating. 'Mum?'

'Yes?'

'Will you and Dad get divorced?'

'Why?' I said in alarm. 'Has he said something?'

'No, he hasn't. I just wondered.'

'We haven't discussed it. But if things go on as they are, I suppose . . . well, when the time comes . . . but you'll be away at college by then.'

Joel grunted and looked at his watch.

'Can we go, Mum? I don't want to miss the beginning of the film.'

It was late by the time I arrived back in Wengrave. All the way home, I'd been worrying about Joel. The children were always at the back of my mind. It was not

128

that I saw them as an extension of myself – some women did, I know – but I constantly wondered if I had done my best. I wished we'd offered Nicola a less academic and more creative education. I wished I'd stood out more firmly when Henry insisted that Joel went to his old boarding school. Henry believed that an education away from home was character-building for a boy and bred independence. I believed that other qualities were more important. Why didn't girls need their characters building? What did it mean anyway? Why had I never said anything? Why did I always assume that Henry was right?

When you start questioning one thing, it's so easy to question everything. As I lay in the bath, I wondered what on earth had come over me during the week. If I thought of what mattered most, it was my children. Paul could never share that part of me. For the greater part of my life, I had been a mother. In reality, I couldn't see myself as a lover. Could I somehow manage to keep Paul at arm's length, to destroy the ridiculous fantasies I had built up? At first I'd been overcome with a heady mixture of panic and excitement that I might end up in bed with him. I'd imagined being swept into his arms to be carried away in the graceful dance of sex, playing out the scene of some glossy Hollywood romance where the bodies are smooth and beautifully formed, the lights low and everything leads up to a perfect, satisfying, loving climax. How could I possibly fit that role? I was far too old for the part.

After my bath, I examined myself in the full-length mirror. The towel slipped to the floor and there I was, naked. I came nearer the glass, so that every imperfection was magnified. How could he possibly find me attractive? Wouldn't he long for the peachy skin of a young girl? He'd never have seen a body as old as mine. My breasts were no longer as round and firm as they once had been, my hips had filled out a little and there

129

were a few faint stretch marks to remind me of childbirth. Looking more closely, I could detect the smudgy hint of a varicose vein on one of my legs. Now was the time to confront the question. Could I really allow my body to be touched – or, even worse, scrutinized – by someone as young as Paul? Wouldn't he shy away in revulsion or leap from the bed and invent some excuse to rush off? How could I lay myself open to such a rejection?

I would do everything in my power to hold back, even though I knew that my desire for Paul was too strong. I picked up the phone to call Ginnie, praying that she would be at home and hadn't had too many vodkas.

'Ginnie, are you in the middle of something?' I asked, in case she was trying to finish a piece for her magazine.

'Only a bottle of wine. I've been watching a useless movie. You're up late. Is that good or bad?'

'I'm not sure. I've been to see Joel at school.'

'Is he all right?'

'Absolutely fine.'

'You sound anxious.'

'I've done something stupid. At least I think I have.'

'Henry isn't coming back, is he?' she said quickly.

'No. It isn't to do with him.'

'Who then?'

'Someone else.'

'Someone else? A man?'

'Mm.'

'Hang on a mo. This needs a fill-up.'

I was trying to think how I could give Ginnie just enough information without submitting to an in-depth investigation.

'All ears,' she said, having picked up the phone again.

'I've fallen for someone and . . .'

130

There was an explosion from Ginnie.

'Christ! Why didn't you tell me before? I've been waiting to hear this for weeks. Who? How? When?'

'Well, it probably won't come to anything.'

'And why not?' Ginnie said, indignantly. Then she changed her tone. 'Ah. So he's got a wife.'

'He hasn't. But the point is . . . he's years younger than I am. I should have put him out of my mind right at the beginning.'

Ginnie let out a groan.

'Oh dear. You're impossible sometimes, Sal. What every girl dreams of, and there you are complaining. Is he nice-looking?'

'Oh yes.'

'Bright? Interesting?'

'To me, he is.'

'And a fantastic lover?'

'I . . . I don't know yet.'

'Not gay? Or weird?'

'Not at all.'

'He sounds perfect. So what's stopping you?'

Unless I made an effort to be honest with Ginnie, this conversation would be pointless.

'I'm terrified that if we go to bed . . .'

Ginnie instantly cut in. 'When you go to bed . . .'

'He'll take one look at my body and say to himself – Christ! What am I doing with her? Do I look forty-two? I want your honest opinion, Ginnie. He doesn't know my age. Should I tell him? I can't make up my mind whether to or not. What do you think?'

'Hang on, hang on. If he asks, which I doubt if he will, lie about your age. That's what I'd do. Lose five or six years. Who'd know? Anyhow, you could easily be young thirties.'

'Hardly, Ginnie.'

'Nonsense. You're pretty and sexy, at least when you wear your sporty gear. And you still look smashing in a

131

swimsuit. Remember that picture I took of you last summer, by Martin's pool? Star material!'

I knew Ginnie meant it but I wasn't convinced.

'But supposing when it comes down to it, that I'm hopeless?'

'I don't get it. Hopeless at what?'

'I haven't done it for months and months.'

We were both silent for a moment. Eventually Ginnie spoke.

'I once went thirty-two weeks without a man,' she remarked, as though it was a notable achievement. 'Do you fancy him?'

'Like mad.'

'Then that's all that matters. It'll all come back, like riding a bicycle. You'll wobble a bit at first and then you'll start freewheeling down the hill. When's the next date?'

'Tomorrow.'

'I'll be rooting for you. Oh, you haven't told me his name? And do I know him?'

'Er, you haven't met him.'

'What's he called? Give me a clue.'

I thought for a moment.

'It's bad luck if I tell you now.'

'So it is,' Ginnie said. She respected superstition, unlike me. 'Anyway, have a great time and I'll call you on Tuesday. And here's a tip. Get some wildly expensive perfume and throw some in the bath. And make sure the bed's facing the right way. Have you still got that feng shui book I gave you?'

'Oh, yes.'

'Don't forget!'

'Thanks a lot, Ginnie,' I said, with a laugh.


Luckily, Monday was a quiet day at Hedgehog, as they were out at meetings the whole day. Feeling slightly guilty, I left early in the afternoon and rushed home to prepare myself. I swept round the house with the Hoover, polished the furniture in the dining room and filled every vase I could find with leaves and daffodils. When I'd finished the bath ritual and the hair ritual, which took twice as long as I'd allowed, I lit some logs in the drawing-room grate. Then, when I'd failed to think of anything more to do, I put on Paul's salsa CD and waited. My heart started beating fast as soon as the clock chimed six. Half an hour. I hoped he'd be on time, otherwise I'd be impossibly tense when he arrived. Promptly at six thirty, the phone rang.

'Hi, Sally,' came his soft, relaxed voice. My heart was beating overtime. Was he ringing to cancel? 'I went home to shower and change. We had a dirty day. I'm sorry. I wanted to be with you earlier so we'd have a long evening. Would you rather meet me in town? At the Raven?'

'Could you come here?' I asked.

I couldn't face bumping into the Hedgehog gang, who were bound to be propped up at the bar by now.

'Sure. Then we could go and eat somewhere. Anywhere you like. Just say.'

I couldn't think. All that mattered was that he'd called and I was about to see him.

My mind was a blank and I was unable to come up with anything.

'Why don't we go to an Indian place I know?' he suggested. 'I went there when Mum and Dad came up. It's really good, about ten miles away. Is that OK?'

'It sounds ideal.'

'I know I can't take you to the kind of places you're used to. It'll take me a while to earn that kind of money.'

'I don't mind where we go. I'd be just as happy eating in a country pub somewhere.'

'Honestly?'

'Of course,' I said, with feeling.

'Could we go in your car? Otherwise we'd be going for a long hike.'

I was only used to driving the children around. Henry always insisted on taking the wheel and said I made him feel nervous. I still felt I had to apologize.

'As long as you don't mind my driving.'

'Mind? Why ever should I?' he said, sounding astonished. 'Don't dress up too much, though. This place isn't fancy.'

'I won't be either,' I said.

The moment I'd put the phone down, I ran to my bedroom, exchanged the black low-cut sweater I was wearing for a velour T-shirt and removed my pearl earrings.

Paul directed me to the Light of India, set in an alley-way in the middle of a row of shops where the Thameside country abruptly changes into suburban commuterland and 'executive estates'. I was relieved to be somewhere I had never been before and I couldn't imagine that there'd be anyone I knew eating in a place like this. At the brightly lit entrance the owner greeted Paul and me with grave familiarity, as though we were important relatives. I had a sudden twinge of apprehension. What was going through his mind? That I was a mother taking her son out for a meal? Through a gap in the plastic leaves, I quickly surveyed the dining area. Everyone seemed to be in their twenties. I was expecting the manager to refer to me as 'Madam' and was pleasantly surprised when he asked 'the young lady' to follow him to a back table. The place was packed and there was a constant sound of clattering as waiters passed to and fro on the quarry-tiled floor, weaving round the room balancing trays of silver dishes and great platters of rice.

We were crammed into a corner, the chairs were hard and the table far too small but I hardly noticed. We sat opposite one another, lit by a guttering candle in an orange glass, enveloped in the warm spicy smell of an

Indian kitchen. Paul's eyes were shining. I could feel his foot against mine. I was determined to draw out every second, to imagine the seconds were days.

'I'm really pleased you phoned me,' Paul said, emptying a bottle of Indian beer into my glass.

'I wasn't sure whether I should have. I wondered whether you might have had second thoughts.'

'That's mad,' said Paul, with a laugh. 'There was me thinking I bet she doesn't really want to see me again.'

'Why? Did I give that impression?'

'I tried to imagine what was going through your mind. He's taken advantage of me, we've got nothing in common, that kind of thing. Mind you, it could have seemed like that.'

'It didn't, not at all,' I assured him.

'I'm glad, then. I thought a lot about you . . . since last time. And I wondered what you were doing, who you were seeing. I want to know about your life.'

'You used to see me around the house. There's nothing mysterious about me.'

'Oh yes, there is. There's something driving you but you're holding back. I don't know what it is. Not yet, anyway.' He stretched forward and took hold of my hand. 'Can I tell you a story? I once had a dog when I was a kid. He loved tearing across open spaces, rushing into the bushes, but only if he knew a place. When I took him for the first time to a great long sandy beach, he wouldn't move. Just stood there sniffing and quivering. Then I threw a stick and he hurtled off like a thunderbolt.'

'I'm not ready to hurtle off just yet,' I said. 'And I'm not sure if it's in my nature. I'm quite ordinary, Paul.'

'That you're not.'

'What have I done? Brought up two children, been an efficient housewife, supported my husband and done some gardening. Oh yes, and taught myself the basics of using a computer. There are hundreds of women in Wengrave who've managed that.'

'It doesn't matter what you've done,' he said, drawing my hand towards him and kissing my palm.

'Paul, please. It's not . . .' I couldn't think of a suitable word but I could feel myself blushing.

'Right?' he suggested.

'That will do,' I replied, with a smile.

'I'm not bothered with right. That means there's a wrong and there isn't. I just wanted to touch you.' He suddenly leaned forward again and kissed me lightly on the lips. 'Do you think they'll throw me out?'

'They might like you to order some food.' I giggled as I picked up the menu.

'We're not in a hurry, are we? And the waiters aren't bothered.'

I had been so used to making a drama out of the ordering of dishes, weighing one up against the other. Henry would specify exactly how he wanted each one cooked and Martin spent ages consulting the wine waiter. I'd never thought about it before. In fact, I was quite at ease in a place where people came to have their plates piled up and didn't admire them first.

'Why don't we have the set menu for two?' I ventured. 'Then we don't have to work out the difference between mughlai and biryani.'

'That's fine by me. It all tastes pretty much the same anyhow – some things with more chilli, some with less.'

We gave our order and Paul once more clasped my hand. I felt like a young girl on her first date.

'I love being with you, Sally. I want to see you again, see you often,' he said quickly, as though he'd been storing up the words for days. I was enjoying the moment and he was thinking about the future. I wasn't ready. I was thrown into total confusion.

'I'm not sure whether . . . that I'm the person for you.

Do you really think it would be a good idea if you . . .'

'If I what?'

'Became involved with me. Or me with you. Might it be better if we just stayed friends? Then neither of us will get hurt.'

'It's not what it's about, staying friends. I want you, Sally.'

I could feel myself colouring, a flush racing up my cheeks.

'I can't imagine why. I don't see how you can find me attractive. I mean, all the pretty girls who surround you . . .'

'Is that really how you think?'

'I suppose I'm trying to see things how they are.'

'I find you beautiful. And I'm seeing things how they are, too.'

'I wish I could believe it,' I said, looking down at my hand resting on his.

'Then I'll convince you. If you'll allow me to.'

We both leaned back as a waiter moving like a tornado deposited an array of bowls and platters on our table. My appetite had deserted me. I watched as Paul dished out the portions. It seemed such a comfortable familiar act. I barely noticed that we had been given dishes we hadn't ordered, that we must have been eating someone else's choice. When I pointed it out to Paul, he laughed.

'Another table will be getting a surprise. But we've done all right, haven't we?'

'Shouldn't we say something?' I said.

'No need, not unless they notice,' he answered, with a grin. I must have appeared a little disapproving. 'Are you shocked?'

'Course not.'

Did he sense that I was hiding my reaction? I felt that he did. Although it was hardly worth thinking about, I couldn't have kept silent and would have allowed

137

everything to be taken back to the kitchen. Secretly, I admired Paul for being so relaxed about it.

The bill came, with no questions asked. Paul pulled out some crumpled banknotes from his trouser pocket. I felt awkward and hoped that he hadn't just spent all his cash for the week. Should I offer to make a contribution? Is that what he'd expect? I quickly decided that I would do so – if we ate out again.

'Thank you for the meal. Really good.'

'You liked it?' said Paul, as he took my jacket from the back of the chair. 'Then we'll come here another time. You never know, they might make the same mistake.'

As I drove along the country route back, passing through long tunnels of thickly interlinked branches, my thoughts were running ahead. What would happen when we arrived back at the house? Should I suggest running him home? Or should I ask him in? 'Do come in for a coffee.' I couldn't bring myself to say something so banal. Whatever the etiquette was for a first date, I was going to ignore it. I hoped that as I opened my front door, he would follow me in. Further than that, I dared not imagine.

After I'd parked the car outside the house, Paul instantly got out and stood watching me as I unlocked the front door. Then he suddenly walked forward.

'Shall I come in? Or is it too late?' he suggested.

'I do stay up once in a while,' I replied with a smile.

We were barely inside the hall when Paul pulled me towards him in a fierce embrace and covered my face with kisses. All my fears about whether I should, whether I shouldn't, dissolved. I kissed him back, at first timidly and then I abandoned myself completely. I felt him lifting me up, carrying me into the drawing room as though I weighed little more than a bundle of grass. Then he set me down on the sofa, where I lay full length as he gently began to pull off my clothes. I was only aware of his warm hands stroking down my body. The curtains were drawn back but the room was dark except for a glimmer of moonlight making ghostly silhouettes of the furniture. I ran my hands over his long back, my face buried in his hair. I knew that he would come inside me, that I wouldn't resist and that I wanted to return his desire. As he caressed every part of me, I was oblivious of my fears about my body, my fears about the future. That night, our first date, we were lovers. I wanted it to go on for ever.

What luxury it was, to wake up at some unearthly hour in the morning with Paul's arms tightly round me. We were crushed up together, naked against the padded back of the sofa. The room had grown cold. I gave a slight shiver. Paul reached for his sweater and wrapped it round me. The drawing room seemed to have undergone a transformation. Even though I could just make out Henry's pictures, Henry's bureau and Henry's chest, the objects were remote, as though they'd been standing in the anonymity of an auction room. Paul suddenly rolled off the sofa and jumped to his feet.

'Aren't you stiff? I am. We should be in bed.'

I slowly sat up and swung my legs to the floor.

'How about a hot drink first? You'll laugh if I tell you what I feel like.'

'I'll guess. Ovaltine. I bet you used to drink that as a kid.'

'Wrong. Hot Bovril. We were allowed it at school in the winter.'

'Allowed? Why?'

'If you liked something, it had to be rationed.'

'As long as you're not.' Paul pressed himself against me and clasped my waist. 'Fancy you going for Bovril. Any chance of having it with bread and dripping?'

'Bread and dripping's off tonight. Kitchen can do buttered toast, though.'

We retrieved our clothes and hurriedly dressed. Then Paul followed me down the corridor to the kitchen. Everything was still and quiet, as though a spell had been cast over the house. I was back to the unselfconsciousness of childhood, as if the Henry years had never been.

'Now I could climb Everest,' said Paul, as he drained his mug. 'Have you ever been up a mountain?'

'On a ski lift.'

'That's cheating. I'd like to go to Kathmandu. Wouldn't you?'

'I doubt if I'd have enough stamina.'

'We could always find out. I bet you have.' He wandered over to the kitchen window and lifted up a corner of the blind. 'Why do you have the blind down?'

'I always do, at night.'

'Why?'

'Security, I suppose. Doesn't everyone?'

'I like to see out.'

He pulled up the blind and the light from the kitchen window illuminated a patch of the back garden. Two eyes glinted from deep in the darkness.

'Look! It's a fox. Have you seen one here before?'

'No, not in the garden. Are you sure it's a fox?'

'The eyes couldn't belong to anything else. Let's go outside.'

'It'll be freezing,' I said, hugging my arms tightly together.

'Come on. I'll get you a coat.'

We fished out some old boots from the hall cupboard, a Barbour jacket Henry used to wear and a padded jacket I wore for gardening. Then we crept out through the kitchen door into the back garden. I assumed the fox had taken off, but Paul suddenly gripped my hand and pointed to an apple tree.

'He's there. Not in a hurry. Can you see?'

'Yes,' I whispered, as I caught sight of a furling

140

brownish tail. We both crouched down and soon the fox emerged from some long grass. Two shiny button-like eyes were fixed on us for a moment, and then the animal quickly turned away and ran into the bushes.

'I hope he escapes the hunt,' Paul remarked.

We rose to our feet and he led me round the garden into the orchard. I was becoming used to the cold, leaning my head on Paul's shoulder and staring up at the clear night sky.

'Isn't it breathtaking? Can you see the Great Bear? Up there! You don't often see it like that, all those stars. Wouldn't it be wonderful to float round the stars for a while? In the old days, people would know every inch of the sky and now most of them don't have a clue.'

'I'm afraid I don't either.'

'I'll teach you, the main ones anyway. I'd love to navigate by the stars. I will, one day. Imagine setting off from Bergen and sailing into the midnight sun. Would you come with me?'

'Yes,' I said, breathing in the sharp night air.

'We could go next week.' Paul laughed and then placed his hands under my jacket. 'I think we should go back to bed. Or we could do it right here, leaning against a tree.'

'Inside would be better.'

'Are you sure?' he said, slipping his hands down my thighs. I laughed and gently forced myself free.

'Let's go into the warmth,' I said.

We ran inside and up the stairs to my bedroom. It overlooked the back garden and was cluttered with inlaid chairs, frilled furnishings and satin-shaded lights. The bed was wide and highly sprung, and for a long time I had been its only occupant as Henry had preferred to sleep in an adjoining room. Now it would belong to us both. Paul drew back the heavy curtains, then threw back the bed linen so it fell all over the floor.

'You're not too tired?' he whispered, planting kisses

141

down my face and onto my breasts. He couldn't have heard my murmured answer.

As the pale dawn light began to creep into the room, I woke up with a start. For a moment, I couldn't think where I was. I heard the sound of gentle, rhythmic breathing. A warm stranger was lying in the bed that I'd only ever shared with Henry. He was sprawled over it with one arm resting across my body, the other curled round his head. His straw blond hair streamed out over the pillow. In sleep, he looked so impossibly young and healthy, like an exhausted child who had been playing in the fields all day. I could feel his soft skin as he lay pressed up against my body. He had been inside me, yet I felt that I barely knew him. I had no idea what time he got up, what he liked for breakfast, whether he would talk or remain silent until he was fully awake.

Still drowsy, my eyes reluctant to remain open, I seemed to hear Paul bounding down the stairs. I drifted off again and then he awoke me with a mug of tea and handed me a newspaper that he'd retrieved from the letterbox.

'Room service. I know it's early but it's a fantastic morning. Can I open the window?'

'You may.' I felt awkward and buried my face in the pillow. I didn't want him to see my unmade-up face in the harsh morning light. We were lovers. It was hard to believe.

'Am I required to iron the paper? Isn't that what they do in posh hotels?'

I had to turn round and answer him. He'd wrapped a towel round his waist and was looking at me with such good humour that I giggled and sat up in bed.

'Not nowadays. They don't do things properly any more, you see. Can't get the staff.'

'Then I won't bother,' he said, smiling at me.

The morning sun began to stream into the bedroom. As Paul moved round the room looking for the clothes he'd thrown off the night before, I was aware of the beautiful shape of his body, his broad shoulders and long waist. His legs were dark brown from the thigh downwards so he must have worn shorts in the heat of the summer. His shirt was open and loose around him and he was dressing as though he was in a hurry to leave.

'Where are my shoes? I can't find them,' he said, impatiently.

I leaned over the bed and hunted under my pile of clothes.

'Here. You've plenty of time.'

Was he already regretting our night together? I caught my breath. All I had wanted to do was to luxuriate in bed for a while, revelling in thoughts of the night before.

Without a word, Paul slipped on his shoes and hurried out of the room. I got out of bed and immediately pulled up the sheets and threw over the cover, as though I was a guilty lover hiding my traces. Then I pulled on a robe and went down to the kitchen. Paul was staring out of the window, a mug of tea in his hand. I was unable to express how raw and vulnerable I felt. I longed for him to take me in his arms.

'What time do you have to be at work?' he asked.

I looked at him anxiously.

'Oh, about ten o'clock.'

'That's nearly lunchtime!' he exclaimed in mock horror. 'Cushy number, you've got. I wouldn't mind your job. Can we swop?'

He sounded so cheerful and calm that my mood suddenly changed. Now that I was in his presence again, my anxiety faded away.

'Time I was off. Or they'll think I've been up to no good,' he said, grabbing a biscuit.

I came to the front door as he was swinging himself onto his bike. He glanced up at me.

'I'll call you. And I might even come again. Would you let me through the door?'

I smiled nervously. I couldn't quite believe what he was saying.

'It's possible,' I said.

'What are you up to tonight? Anything special?'

'Nothing I couldn't put off.'

'Good!'

He blew a kiss and wheeled off towards the front gate. Halfway down the drive, he gave a jubilant wave.

# SEVEN
• • •

For the next couple of days my head was permanently in the clouds. I remember once travelling on a train and marvelling at a girl who kept an ecstatic, secretive smile on her face for the whole journey. Now I knew what she must have experienced. I relived again and again our voyage from awakening desire into passion. I no longer worried when we would see one another, neither did I hover near the phone. Paul called me to say he would be in the Raven for lunch in the middle of the week. I rashly promised to be there. This time I'd go with Jed, Matt and Pickle instead of eating sandwiches in the office. It made me happy to think that Paul wanted to see me in company, that he didn't regard me as someone to hide away.

I could only live from one day to another. I couldn't begin to imagine what would happen if our relationship continued, how I'd break it to Nicola and Joel, how I'd cope with the reaction of my friends. I kept telling myself that we'd only be together for a few weeks at most. Even though I was briefly carried away, my common sense usually got the upper hand. I didn't see how we could remain lovers for long. There would be a time when the passion would fade and we'd each go our different ways. By foreseeing the end of my romantic story, it would make it easier to bear when we eventually parted.

Pickle pushed open the door of the Raven, and I followed behind Matt. I could feel my pulse racing as I quickly surveyed the crowded bar. He was there, standing at a distance with a glass in his hand, talking with animation to an old man in overalls. It took a second for him to register my presence. He gave a wave and I could see him watching to see where I would sit. Pickle, Matt and I squeezed behind a table while Jed went over to the bar to make our order.

'Paul's in,' said Pickle, grinning in his direction. Then she turned to me. 'Why don't you buy him a drink, Sal?'

'Yes, I might.'

I probably sounded a little vague.

'Or why don't I? I bet he'd rather be sitting with us.'

'Do you think so?'

'After the Hedgehog bash, I said he fancied you – but you didn't believe me. I know these things. I bet you never got in touch.'

'Well . . .'

'Anyway, now's your chance. Look, he's coming over. I'll get another chair.'

Pickle leaped up and started wandering round the bar looking for a spare seat. I instantly stood up when I saw Paul coming towards me. I couldn't keep my eyes from him.

'Hi, Sally. How are you?'

His formal greeting made me smile. Then I realized that he meant it.

'Fine. Wonderful.'

'Me, too. I've never been better.'

By now Pickle had tracked down a chair and was dragging it towards us.

'Let me,' said Paul, placing the chair by my side.

'Will you come and sit with us? Then I'll go and buy you a drink,' said Pickle. She had clearly given up hope that I'd take the initiative.

'There's an offer!' said Paul.

'Pint of Brakspear's Special, as usual?' Paul nodded and Pickle gave him a toothy grin. 'Right. I'm off. Save my seat.'

Putting one hand on my shoulder, Paul gestured over to a corner of the bar. 'See that old man I was talking to? He's one of the best in the business. We're preparing the wood for Martin's boat. It'll be pretty pricey. I hope his bank account's in good shape.'

'I'm sure he'll pay,' I remarked.

'Yes, he seems a good sort. When it's done and we're trying it out, we'll go for a spin.'

'When will that be?' I asked.

'Early summer, I guess.'

I made a quick calculation. That would be weeks away. Would we still be together by then?

'Martin might not approve, if I'd been in his boat before him,' I commented, anxiously.

'He'd never know. No need to say anything,' said Paul, with a laugh.

Jed arrived at our table with a tray of beers and set it down.

'Food's coming.' Then he glanced at Paul. 'Pickle's ordered you a chicken sandwich. Lunch on us.'

'Can't I . . .' I began.

'Entertainment budget,' said Jed. 'It'll stretch to a sandwich. Just.'

Pickle soon joined us and put a huge platter of sandwiches on the table. Then Jed began to hand round the beer. There was an easy atmosphere between them, which helped to quell my nervousness. Pickle pulled out a large black portfolio from under her feet and balanced it on her lap.

'Want to see what Sal's been working on?' Opening the portfolio, she handed it to Paul. 'This is our latest. They're roughs for the Big Bear Book. Take a look.' While Paul scrutinized the pictures, I was staring at his

147

hands and strong fingers as he delicately turned the pages. They had caressed my body and stroked my hair. I thought of him naked. I knew I was blushing and looked away.

'Brilliant. Lovely colours. Kids'll go for it,' Paul said.

'They'd better. Otherwise we'll be skint. Anyway, Matt's promised we'll have a launch party when it's finished. Fancy coming?'

'Why not?' Paul glanced at me and smiled. 'Will it be salsa again?'

'Absolutely no dancing,' said Matt, lightly reprimanding him. 'This one'll be for grown-ups. Serious stuff.'

When Paul moved away to order another round of drinks, Pickle leaned over to me and quickly whispered in my ear.

'Listen, Sal. Have you been out with him?'

I couldn't think how to reply.

'Why?'

'Go on. You have, haven't you?' she exclaimed.

'We just went out for a meal. That's all,' I said, reluctantly.

'Knew it. Knew it. Knew it,' Pickle shrieked. Then she put her hand over her mouth.

'Sorry, Sal. Won't say a word. Honest.'

Jed was in the middle of describing a film we all had to see when Paul returned. He insisted on repeating the résumé of the plot for his benefit.

'We get the idea,' said Matt, good-humouredly. 'It's called *Play Easy* and it's about a high-tech cop who's a nut.'

'Fantastic direction. And great visuals. You should go. It's on at the cinema down the road. Have you seen it, Sally?'

'Not yet,' I said.

I suddenly felt very old hat but I was pleased when Jed assumed I might have seen it. On the few occasions when I did go to a local cinema, the film was chosen by

Joel or Nicola. Martin was a rare cinemagoer and preferred eating out. I couldn't remember the last time Henry and I had seen a film.

'I'm afraid I don't go very often. Though I'd like to,' I remarked.

'I fancy it. My kind of movie,' said Pickle.

'Come with us. We'll all go one evening after work,' suggested Matt.

Pickle glanced at Paul. Paul looked at me.

'I'd come with you, Sally,' he said quietly.

I knew an involuntary frown had crossed my face. I pretended I hadn't heard.

'I'm up for that. When's it to be?' I said, turning to Matt.

'We'll fix a day when we get back to the office.'

Paul couldn't possibly have guessed why I hadn't jumped at his suggestion. Seeing his downcast expression, I longed to explain why I couldn't go with him alone. It wasn't long before he rose from his chair.

'Sorry to leave you. Must get back.'

I instantly realized how a casual conversation could hide so much. The slightest thing could shake my confidence. Now I realized that Paul had felt the same. He must have felt I'd rejected him and my first impulse was to run after him. He barely looked at me before walking out of the bar.

It wasn't until later that evening that I was able to get hold of Paul. I desperately hoped that he hadn't taken offence. When I called the number of the house where he was lodging, I was answered by a foreign voice. It seemed ages before he came to the phone.

'Did you have a good lunch? I wanted to stay but I couldn't,' he said. He didn't ask the reason for my call. His voice sounded friendly but a little cool.

'About the cinema,' I began. 'I wanted to explain but . . .'

'What is there to explain?'

'Of course I wanted to go with you . . .'

'But you were embarrassed to say so in front of the others?'

'No, not at all,' I said, heatedly.

'I don't understand what's going on.'

'I know it sounds crazy, but if the film's on in Reading, would you mind if we went there?'

'What!' Paul laughed in disbelief.

'It's just the kind of thing Nicola's friends would go for. Just for the moment, I couldn't cope with going to the cinema and them seeing you and me . . .'

'Is that really the reason?'

'Yes. I know it must sound pretty feeble.'

'It does.' We were both silent. Then Paul continued, sounding both resigned and cheerful. 'If it makes you happy, we'll go to Reading. And we'll just have to pray that nobody sees us. I'll wear a disguise if you like. I'll put on my Ray Bans and borrow a baseball cap from one of the lads. How about you?'

He made me smile. It all seemed so trivial but I couldn't hide that it mattered to me.

'I'll think of something.'

'Make sure you wear that perfume you had on the other night. Otherwise I might not recognize you. Which evening? Or doesn't it matter?'

'Tomorrow?'

'Sounds good to me.'

When I answered the door to Paul, he was swathed in a large scarf, wearing mirrored glasses, a strange felt hat and a long raincoat. I couldn't match up to him, dressed as I was in jeans and a heavy woollen sweater. It had seemed too ridiculous, to disguise my appearance.

'Hi, kid. We're taking in a movie tonight.' I burst into laughter as he hugged me to him. 'Think I'll be noticed?'

'Are you really coming like that?'

'Sure. Now let's go,' he said, as he walked over to my car.

We sat in the front row, having taken the only seats available. Paul insisted on buying two enormous boxes of popcorn. I leaned back to take in the huge screen. The sound from the speakers echoed in my ears. Halfway through the film, Paul took my hand and rested it on his knee.

'Like it?' he whispered in my ear.

'Like everything,' I said, although I was hardly following what we were watching. I was a teenager again. The smell of popcorn mingled with my perfume and Paul's warm body was squeezed up against mine. Soon we would be in bed again. We left as soon as the credits began to roll. Paul took my hand and we ran into the car park. Then I handed him the keys and he drove us home. The moment we were inside the door, he began pulling off my sweater.

We were lying together in the darkness, exhausted and damp with sweat. I leaned my head on Paul's chest, trying to remain awake.

'You asleep?' Paul asked, softly.

'No.'

'Thinking?'

'Not really. Are you?'

Paul turned on his side, keeping his arm on my thigh, so that I was facing him.

'Thinking I couldn't be happier.'

'Me, too.'

'We should spend a whole weekend together. I hate getting up early and leaving you.'

'We will.'

'When?'

'Soon.'

We kissed and then I rolled over to my side of the bed. He preferred sleeping on the right side, while I had always slept on the left. With Paul, nothing seemed difficult. I couldn't understand how easily we fitted into one another's lives. I wanted to be with him more than anything. I wondered if I was falling in love.

I was dreading the weekend. If it hadn't been for Paul, I would have been looking forward to it all week. Martin had it planned for some time, as he liked everything to be settled well in advance. On Saturday afternoon Ginnie was coming down with Nicola and in the evening Martin would take us all out for a meal. The following day, there was Angela's art exhibition. We would all drop into the Wengrave Gallery and then go back to tea with Angela and Douggie. I didn't know whether Ginnie would decide to drive to London on Sunday evening or early on Monday. I would have to wait until at least Monday evening before seeing Paul again.

'I feel awful about this but I'm afraid this weekend is out. I won't be able to see you because Nicola's coming down with Ginnie,' I said to Paul over breakfast.

'It sounds as though you're getting anxious already.'

'I do find it easier when Nicola's in London. When she's here . . .'

'I know. Are they staying the whole weekend?' Paul said, sounding a little disgruntled.

'More or less.'

He grinned. 'What about the less? Couldn't you fit me in?'

'If only I could. But my family is . . .'

'Important. I know. I can't help wanting to have you all to myself.'

'Well, you can't,' I said, with a smile.

Paul persisted, demanding to know the whole schedule.

'If they're not coming till mid-afternoon, we can have till then.'

'But I've got to get the house ready, the shopping . . . there's so much to do.'

'Come on. You'll be out most of the time, there'll be hardly any cooking. And doesn't your lady come on Friday to clean?'

'Suppose so,' I said, grudgingly. I felt a twinge of resentment that Paul was so familiar with my pattern. 'What's the plan then?' I added.

'There isn't one. I just thought you might like to visit the boatyard because I'll be working there this Saturday. See what I'm up to. Then – well, whatever you like.'

'You'll get tired of seeing me all the time.'

'That's up to me.'

'No, it isn't.'

We were half joking but I didn't want him to feel that he had complete control over my life. In fact, it seemed that he had. I knew I'd relent. He was just about to leave for work when I stopped him.

'Paul? Why don't I come to the boatyard when I've done the shopping? Around eleven on Saturday?'

He beamed. 'It's muddy in there. Wear your wellies.'

The instant he'd gone, I reached anxiously for the phone. I'd become so immersed in thinking of Paul that I'd completely forgotten my previous conversations with Ginnie. It only needed one indiscreet comment . . . It was early, so she was bound to be at home.

'Ginnie?'

'Yes?' I could hear her yawning.

'Something I forgot to mention. My young man . . .'

'Ah, yes.' She was instantly awake. 'How's it going? Have you seen him again? Have you had another night of wild passion? And when will you tell me his name? I'm going crazy trying to think of everyone I've ever met in Wengrave who's under thirty.'

I paused and took a breath.

'You won't say a word to Nicola or Martin, will you?'

'What do you think I am? Completely brainless?' she said, indignantly. 'I'm hardly likely to tell Nicola that Mum's got a toy boy, am I?'

I stopped myself just in time from showing my irritation. Ginnie had a right to see it that way. From her perspective, that's what Paul would always be. A toy boy. How I hated the phrase.

'Sorry about that. Only I was a bit anxious, as you can imagine.'

'Shall I bring anything for the weekend? Sergei's brought me some Russian caviar. I couldn't remember if you liked it.'

'That was Henry,' I said.

'Huh. I'll just bring some vodka then. If we're late, it'll be Nicola's fault. She's seeing her boyfriend for lunch.'

'Do you know anything about him? She seems very keen but she still won't tell me his name.'

'Me neither. I expect she's embarrassed. Remember how sensitive we were at that age? He's probably called Maximilian or Valentine. Or Brad or Rocky or Leonardo. Anyone's guess.'

'I wonder when you'll meet him.'

'She's not ready, she says. I suppose she's afraid I'll take against him or disapprove. Why, I can't imagine. What a bloody family. I can't cope with all these secrets.'

I was happy that Nicola had found somebody she was wholehearted about. It was the first time I'd ever heard her going overboard about a boy she'd met.

'I could try asking her if she'd like to tell me a bit more about him. A casual enquiry?'

'Yes, do. You're better at that than me. Christ! I'm late. Must rush. Bye.'

I could only pray that Ginnie would go easy on the

154

vodka. When she was reasonably sober she was fine, but her over-exuberant moods sometimes led to disaster – like the time she phoned up her boss and said the March issue of the magazine headlined 'Spring Greens' reminded her of overcooked cabbage.

By ten o'clock on Saturday I had everything ready for Nicola and Ginnie – house done, shopping done, all the bags of salad, fruit and cheese arranged in the fridge. My usual coffee meeting with Maggie and Angela at the Café Rouge had been cancelled, my excuse being that Ginnie was bringing Nicola down in the morning. I hope I sounded convincing. I was veering between elation and guilt at having agreed to see Paul before they arrived. Couldn't I have waited just two more days?

As I followed Paul's directions out of Wengrave, I left behind all my misgivings. By inviting me to his place of work, I felt that Paul was letting me more and more into his life. If it was going to be merely a lightning affair, I thought, he would never have asked me. In spite of my attempts to keep a level head, I half believed that we might stay together more than a few weeks.

I drove far too fast along a cracked, muddy road that ran along the edge of a field, straining to see a sign for Edgeworth Marine. There was none, but as I rounded a bend I caught sight of the great iron gate that Paul had mentioned. As I stopped to open it, I gazed at the straggling bushes and trees almost blocking the entrance. Then, with twigs brushing past my window, I drove through into an area of cracked, mossy stones. There were two large sheds in front of me, with some of the windows crudely boarded over and, beyond that, several large boats were moored in a river inlet. Everywhere was rampantly overgrown, like a Douanier Rousseau painting, so that I almost expected to see the face of a wide-eyed lion staring at me from the bushes.

Skeletons of old wooden boats were half protruding from the ferns and clumps of nettles. Old heavy anchors and rusting chains were spread at random over the long unkempt grass. I drank it all in, for this was the backdrop to Paul's daily life. I wanted to learn everything about him, to find out what made him what he was.

I walked up to one of the sheds. Huge sliding doors had been pushed back so that I could peer inside. I instantly saw Paul in the distance, his sleeves rolled up, sanding down a long wooden strut. I stood still for a few moments, waiting for him to notice me. Then he looked up and waved at me to come over.

'Mind if I finish this? Won't be long,' he said, continuing his sanding. Then he stopped a moment, and pulled up an old paint-spattered stool. 'Here. Have a seat.' At the last moment, I'd swopped my cream tailored trousers and silk sweater for old jeans, a tight T-shirt and my Hedgehog jacket. It was taking a conscious effort to shake off the kind of image I'd always assumed was appropriate. In my circle, casual meant smart except for barbecues or gardening, when jeans were allowed.

'I'm glad you put the wellies on,' Paul added, looking me up and down with approval. 'You look good.'

I laughed. 'Only you could say that. I look a mess.'

'I must like mess then,' Paul replied, as he swept down the length of wood. When he was satisfied with the surface, he put it on a bench. 'Now I'll introduce you to the boss. Follow me.'

We walked across the yard to an even more dilapidated shed and stood at the entrance. A little light was coming through cracked dusty windows and I could make out an old man with long straggling grey hair who was vigorously hammering nails into the curved shape of a hull. It was as though we had entered some medieval workshop.

'Hi,' Paul shouted. As the man looked up, Paul took me by the hand. By the time we'd reached him, he was once more bent over his work. 'Mr Edgeworth, this is Sally. It's her friend Martin who's ordered the launch.'

'How do,' was all he said, while I stood rather awkwardly, wondering if I ought to continue the conversation.

'Sally's come to have a look,' Paul continued.

'Best when it's done. But please yourself.'

When we were outside again and out of earshot, Paul led me towards a blue sheeting tent erected on the grass by the moorings.

'Edgeworth seems crabby at first but he's OK. Not much social chat, unless it's a customer and he can sell a boat. I've told him all about you, of course.'

'What?' I said, startled. 'What have you said?'

'That I met this wonderful girl who's nutty about boats. And who's a real stunner as well.'

He was grinning. I didn't know quite whether to believe him. Often he said something to surprise me, to stop me in my tracks.

'Why should your boss be interested in knowing about me?' I asked.

'Everyone else is.'

'Like who?'

'Oh, the whole of Wengrave.'

Before I could reply, he pushed through a gap in the sheeting and pulled me after him. As soon as we were hidden from view, we came together in an embrace. Then he gently pushed me away.

'I'm happy you came. How long can you stay?'

'Only a little while.'

'Look behind you. We've started on Martin's slipper launch. There's not much to see, but you can get an idea of the shape.'

He stroked down the smoothly sanded wood. To me,

it just looked like a rather wide rowing boat with a tapering tail at the back and I couldn't imagine how it would turn into a glossy launch, like the ones I'd seen on the river.

'All I know is it seems beautifully made.'

'No point in doing it otherwise. I'll show you the boats and then we'll go over to the stores. We've got a kettle there in the back kitchen so I can make you coffee. Not as good as the Café Rouge, but the best I can do.'

We walked along the ancient jetties that divided off the boats. The season hadn't yet begun, so the mooring was crowded with launches and large wooden boats. There was one, though, that seemed ill at ease with the others.

'I wouldn't have thought your boss would approve of that,' I remarked, staring at the cumbersome white fibreglass cruiser with darkened windows.

'He doesn't. But he's persuaded the owner to sell it and get a proper boat. He's letting him moor up for free, so he can be in his good books. With any luck, we'll get the commission.'

'I'd never guess Edgeworth was that canny. I bet you're learning a lot.'

'Some people just have a natural instinct but I don't. I'd never be sharp about the business side.'

'You never know. If you had your own yard . . .'

'I don't think that far. I'm thinking about the next time we can get together.'

We wandered off down a small path running beside the river and stopped by a prefabricated shed, which looked newer than the others. There was a badly written sign over the door: 'Edgeworth Marine Stores'. Inside were rows of shelves with boat parts, varnish and paints neatly ranged along them. I sat down on a massive rope coiled up on the floor while Paul disappeared round the back.

'Paul? You there?' a voice called out. I heard the door creak open. A young girl burst in and bounded towards me. She looked astonished to see me sitting on the ground.

'You waiting for someone?' she asked. Her accent had a slight burr, like Paul's, so I imagined she must have grown up in Devon or Cornwall.

'I'm a friend of Paul's. He's making me some coffee.'

'I can get you a chair, if you like.'

'Thanks, but there's no need.'

We inspected one another and I suddenly realized I had seen her before. She had been with Paul once, standing at the bar of the Raven. Then her blonde hair had been tied up in a swaying ponytail but now it was falling around her face. Her skin was pale gold and her complexion had a glowing sheen, even without make-up. Her tight dungarees were covered in oil and there were smudges up her arms.

'Do you work here?' I asked.

'Yeh. Along with Paul. I'm Sam, short for Samantha. They thought I was a boy when I wrote in for the job. They think different now! I'll get that layabout to make me some coffee as well.'

She took off towards the kitchen. I heard giggles and laughter and the whistle of a kettle. It was as though I'd suddenly been doused in icy-cold water. Were they more than friends? How could he possibly resist such an appealing, pretty young girl?

I stood up, wondering what on earth I should do. My imagination was beginning to run riot. What chance did I have? Given the choice, what young man wouldn't prefer this elfin creature? Apart from being so much nearer his age, she worked beside Paul all day and drank with him at the pub. They must have known one another well. Had they been to bed? In the past? Would it happen again? They shared a familiarity that I hadn't earned. Could I bring myself to ask Paul about her?

What could I say? Have you ever . . .? What did she know about me?

I couldn't think clearly but I knew I couldn't bear seeing them together. If I stayed, I would only be intent on watching for the smallest sign that might betray them. Even the briefest intimate glance I would take as the proof that I feared to find. How did I know that Paul hadn't been lying to me? I was shocked at how quickly I could close up but I could do nothing to prevent it. Everything was so fragile. I had to prevent myself from falling into the trap. Older woman making a complete fool of herself. Poor Sally, taken in by a handsome young lad. Should have known better. Went off balance after Henry left.

I rose to my feet and ran through the stores, seeing nothing, intent only on reaching the door, the yard, my car. When I arrived home, the phone was ringing. I needn't have looked at the number display, but I did. I knew it would be Paul but I didn't answer. Somehow I had to calm myself before Nicola and Ginnie arrived. I never imagined that I could lose control so easily. My pulse was racing, my head throbbing. And I resented Paul for being the cause of my state. I regretted everything. And then something else occurred to me. Why had I never thought that Nicola might have had good reason to leave Paul? What had she left unsaid? What was the real cause of their disagreements and rows?

After I'd soaked in a bath, I put on the cream trousers and silk sweater that were still lying on the bed and carefully applied a layer of make-up. Now I was once more Nicola's mum. I wasn't sure I could endure my double existence any longer. It had taken so little to shake me to the core. I waited impatiently for Ginnie and Nicola to arrive. I heard the phone ringing several times but I refused to go near it.

*

160

They were late, of course.

'Martin's coming on the dot of seven,' I said, setting down a pot of herbal tea in front of Nicola.

'He won't mind waiting,' Nicola remarked, with a grin. 'How many men get to take out three girls?'

'We should have been here earlier, but . . .' Ginnie began.

'My fault. But I had a very important date.'

I could see that Nicola was having a hard time concealing her joy.

'With your boyfriend.'

'Who else?'

'Isn't it time we found out his name?' I said gently. 'I can't keep saying "how's your boyfriend" for much longer.'

Nicola bit her lip.

'OK then. He's called Mark.'

'That's a good old-fashioned name,' said Ginnie, brightly.

'He's really cool, not old-fashioned at all.'

'How am I meant to know? You haven't told me a thing about him. Anyone would think you'd signed the Official Secrets Act.'

Nicola got up and opened the fridge, turning her back to us. I knew she wouldn't find anything. Sure enough, she banged it shut.

'I'm longing to meet Mark,' I said.

'Soon,' said Nicola. She looked anxiously at Ginnie, then at me 'I don't want Dad to know.'

'Why? Is Mark working in a rival firm?' said Ginnie, rather flippantly I thought, which brought a stony reaction from Nicola.

'There's no reason for Daddy to know. It'll be strictly between us,' I said, soothingly.

'I'll think about it.' Nicola collected up the cups and took them to the sink. 'Now I'm going to get ready.'

*

When Martin made his appearance we were immediately rushed off to La Bella Italia, which he assured Ginnie had superb Italian wines and very presentable waiters. As I tucked into the risotto with truffle and the sea bream with a ginger sauce, I could only think of Paul. Had he had enough of me already? Was he planning to make Sam his next conquest? What should I do? Confront him or keep quiet? Was I expecting too much? I was holding my breath as though Nicola was able to read my thoughts but she was giggling away happily, as Martin reminisced about our family holidays.

She remained in high spirits and started bringing Mark into the conversation. She teased Martin, saying he'd be wildly jealous because he was a fantastic dancer and dressed in fabulous gear and knew about everything. Her enthusiasm was infectious but I still felt the urge to protect her. I was hardly the one to advise anybody but I wanted to make sure that she didn't repeat my mistakes. I didn't yet know what effect Henry's leaving had really had on Nicola. She might have fallen for the first boy who could give her some kind of security. I had no idea why she had chosen Mark. I was looking for an opportunity to enter into her confidence, but she kept resisting my attempts. It wasn't until breakfast on Sunday that I was able to have a talk. Fortunately Ginnie was still soundly asleep.

'I'm glad everything's going so well with Mark,' I commented. Nicola was spreading lashings of honey on her toast and flicking through the Sunday magazines.

'Mm. Like I said, he's a cool guy.'

'Are you in love with him?' I asked.

'Probably,' she answered, looking up with a grin.

'Is that yes or no?' I said, lightly.

'I don't fancy anyone else. So it's more yes than no.'

I went over to put more bread in the toaster.

'You can ask him down whenever you feel ready.'

'Not sure about that,' she said between mouthfuls. I

knew she was only pretending to read the paper placed to one side of her. She must have been reluctant to ask the obvious question.

'I can always put a double bed in your room. I'm not like Daddy. If you're having a serious relationship with a boy, I'd never pretend you weren't sleeping together.'

Nicola stopped reading her paper and looked straight at me.

'But you wouldn't be easy about it . . .'

'If I'd got used to seeing you together, if you got on really well . . .'

'Not like Paul, you mean.' She opened the magazine and became absorbed in the fashion pages. Without looking up, she said, 'Did you know I did it with him?'

'Oh. I rather assumed you had,' I said. I was glad I didn't have to look her in the face. That was the other Paul, I told myself. Paul in the past. 'But it's different now you've found someone who means a lot. I'm sure Daddy would be pleased and want to meet him.'

'Oh yes?'

I could see from her hostile frown that she had no intention of introducing Mark to Henry, but I continued nonetheless.

'It's easier in one way, with Daddy living in London. Why don't you and Mark get together with him in a pub somewhere?'

'Maybe.'

'Or would you rather I met him first?'

Nicola closed the magazine, got up from the table and stood at the window with her back to me. Her shoulders were hunched. Then she suddenly turned round.

'Mum. Mark's black.'

She was scrutinizing my face, her lips pursed, holding her breath to gauge my reaction. It took a few seconds for it to sink in.

'And you thought I'd be shocked . . .' I ventured.

'Well, I bet you are, really.'

163

'Why on earth should I be? If he's a decent boy, and I'm sure he is . . .'

'Your daughter with a black man. That's different, though.'

She continued looking at me intently. I did my best to be honest without offending her.

'All right. I hadn't thought of it. But we all come from a ragbag of different races. You either like someone or you don't. If you're happy with Mark, I'm sure I would like him. It wouldn't be anything to do with the colour of his skin.'

'Honestly?'

'Have I ever said anything to make you think I'm prejudiced?'

Nicola gave a half smile. 'Not really. I just thought you would be. Since you don't know any black people.'

'If Mark treated you badly, I'd speak my mind and it wouldn't matter where he came from.' She came back and sat beside me, twiddling the rings on her fingers. 'And I'm sure that Ginnie would do exactly the same,' I added.

'You sure? But not Dad,' she said vehemently.

'You might be surprised. If you're confident about him, it doesn't matter what anyone thinks, does it?'

'Maybe not,' she said, giving me a warm smile for the first time. 'Would you come up to London one weekend and see us?'

'I'd love to.'

'Mark's a great cook. You could come over to his place. Actually, he's already suggested it. As I've met some of his family, he says he should meet some of mine.'

'He's absolutely right.'

'So you're on?' Nicola threw her arms round me. 'Great. And then Joel could meet him in the holidays. I bet they get on.'

*

164

As so often in the past, my daughter had shocked me into thinking about her in a different light, which also meant I was changing my view of myself. Now that she was starting to become an adult, she was challenging me to think about who she was, who I was. I didn't yet know about Joel, but I was beginning to think my family was far less conventional than I – and everyone else, come to that – had assumed. We had all taken for granted that Ginnie was the only wild card until Henry had surprised everybody by moving in with Sheila. And now, Nicola was breaking away from what was expected of her.

In spite of my denials, I was taken aback when I heard about Mark. All I knew was that he'd be very different from anyone Nicola had met before. She made a show of acting the rebel but only as teenagers do, and until now she had seemed little different from the daughters of my friends. I'd never imagined that she would be attracted by somebody so far removed from her experience and background.

But what about Paul? If my secret was out, isn't that exactly what everyone would say about me? What a strange coincidence that I found myself in exactly the same situation. I dared to hope that if my fears about Paul proved to be groundless and we remained together a little longer, Nicola might come to accept us. Seeing her strike out for her happiness had encouraged me to value my own. I began to feel more optimistic about Paul. If I thought about the times we were together, I had nothing to fear. And I felt ashamed of my childish attack of jealousy in the boatyard. But I also had to accept that the journey ahead was going to be bumpy, that my confidence would wax and wane like a candle guttering in sudden draughts and coming to life again.

Early on Monday morning, as I watched Nicola and Ginnie leave with bundles of spring flowers from the garden and smiles on their faces, I still felt optimistic. The evening before, Nicola had volunteered a little more about Mark. He lived in Brixton and was a librarian, slightly older than her. She preferred me to meet him first, before she introduced him to Ginnie, so I suggested one Sunday. Even though Ginnie pressed me to stay with her for the weekend, I declined, unable to bear the thought of two whole days away from Paul.

I knew he would be at work early, so I was able to call before I drove to Hedgehog.

'Can I see you tonight?' I said breathlessly, before he could say anything.

'It's a bit difficult. I've got to check over a boat in Marlow and it's going to take a while. It would be very late by the time I got to your place.'

I could understand his reticence but I wasn't sure if he was making excuses or not. Perhaps he didn't want to see me for a while. I couldn't blame him after my sudden departure.

'I do need to see you. You must have wondered what on earth came over me on Saturday.'

He was silent for a moment.

'I assumed somebody had come through the door that you knew. And you didn't want to be seen in my company.'

'That's not how it was. Will you let me explain tonight?' I paused but he didn't reply. 'I'll come over to your place if it's easier.'

'You would? It's fairly basic. Do you really want to?'

'Yes, I do,' I said, firmly.

Late that evening I slipped out into the dark, following Paul's directions like a burglar who'd been given a tip-off. The Victorian house in which he lived was at the end of a cul-de-sac on the edge of Wengrave. It looked tall and daunting, with steep steps leading up to a peeling door. At the side was an array of bells. I pressed number seven and the door swung open. I attempted to walk steadily up the flights of stairs covered in a thin worn carpet. There was a musty smell, overlaid with stale aromas of cooking, and on each floor naked light bulbs swung overhead disturbed by the wind whipping round the house. I felt like an unwanted intruder. When I reached the top, Paul was standing outside an open door.

'Welcome to the Burridge mansion,' he said, with a faint smile. I followed him into a large room, barely furnished. Standing on a corner shelf was a lighted gas ring with a small saucepan balanced on top. 'This is my supper but there's enough for two. Could you manage some or have you eaten?'

'No. It smells inviting,' I replied, settling myself in the hollow of a worn sofa.

'Heinz best.'

'Here,' I said, bringing out a bottle from my bag. 'I brought some wine, in case you felt like some.'

'A good thought.'

He put the bottle to one side and then found two bowls that he set down on a small coffee table.

'I'm looking for somewhere else,' he remarked, as he poured out the soup. 'But it's not easy around here.'

'I know. I'll keep my eyes open. You look exhausted.'

'I am, a bit.'

We were uneasy with one another. Even though he was tired and his blond hair hung down lankly, his skin glowed. I was unable to show how much I wanted him, nor could I tell him that I didn't care where he lived. He appeared as though I'd discovered his secret and was about to reject him. We finished our soup in silence and I began to collect up the bowls.

'I'll do that,' Paul said, taking them from me and going over to a small sink next to the corner shelf. I watched as he rinsed them out and turned them upside down, then I looked around me. There was so little in the room, just the grubby Dralon-covered sofa I was sitting on, a melamine wardrobe, two wooden chairs and a coffee table. A narrow bed was pressed up against the window. The heat of an inadequate gas fire became lost in the dank space. The only thing that marked Paul's presence was a wooden plank balanced on some bricks, on which was a row of books, mostly about boats.

'I wanted to apologize. I felt dreadful all over the weekend.'

'Why?' He looked genuinely surprised.

'Running out like that. Not answering the phone. I'm not normally so . . .'

'You don't need to apologize,' he cut in. 'There'd have been a reason. I knew that.'

'There was. Or rather there wasn't. I couldn't face . . . Oh, never mind.'

He came over and sat on one of the wooden chairs.

'Come on, Sally. I'm not about to give you nought out of ten.'

'All right then. I was jealous.'

The words dried in my mouth. I couldn't spell out what an idiot I'd been.

Paul waited, then he said, 'Do you mean Sam?'

'Yes,' I mumbled.

'Are you going to be wildly jealous every time I'm within an arm's length of the opposite sex?' he said, teasingly.

'Of course I'm not,' I replied, with little conviction. 'But isn't it understandable? You spend every working day with an extraordinarily pretty girl, who knows she is, who shares your passion for boats, who . . .' I came to a halt.

'And who? What else?'

'Who's much nearer your age.'

'So you think that's enough to tempt me away from you? What's the magic number then? When do you start getting in a state? Do you spend your time working out the age of every girl who's anywhere near me?'

His bantering tone had suddenly changed to anger. Had he never considered that I might have felt threatened by Sam?

'Can't you understand?' I burst out. 'There she was, right under my nose. I heard her giggling, then you were laughing and it was taking a hell of a time to make a cup of coffee. I'd seen you with Sam in the Raven and you, well, I noticed you looking at her in a certain way. Or I thought you were. I'd rather know now if . . . whether . . .'

Paul leaned back and stretched his legs out in front of him, his eyes half closed.

'You'd rather know if we've been to bed. Is that it?' I nodded. 'The answer is no. I haven't. Do you believe me?'

'Sort of,' I admitted.

'Some of the lads can't keep their eyes off her, but she doesn't do anything for me. She's fun and a good worker and that's about it. And she's a flirt. She likes winding me up because she wants me to fancy her. As I don't, that makes me a challenge. Sam's the one who's jealous – of you.'

'Do you expect me to believe that?' I exclaimed.

'That's how it is.' He rose slowly to his feet. 'Now I'll open that bottle. Then I'll have to be getting some sleep. I've had a rough day today and I've an early start tomorrow.'

It was only after Paul had refilled our tumblers that he started to ask me questions about the weekend, so I gave him a brief account of our dinner with Martin, and Angela's art exhibition. He seemed polite, little more, and I decided it would be tactful to leave before long.

'How was Nicola? Is she doing all right?'

I was glad he'd asked.

'She's got a new boyfriend in London and seems to be having a good time with him.'

'So she's happy?'

'I think so.'

'Good.'

He sounded absorbed in his own thoughts or perhaps he was simply exhausted. I was longing for some reassuring physical gesture but I feared to make the first move.'So what did you get up to over the weekend?' I asked, with a nervous smile.

'Oh, I had quite a wild time. Went up to London. Took in a few clubs. Met up with the gang. Got drunk. Sobered up. Got drunk. Just the usual weekend.' Then he laughed. 'You almost believed me, didn't you?'

'Yes.'

'I could keep you guessing but I won't. Come over here and I'll whisper.'

I moved towards him and he suddenly seized me in his arms. As he kissed me, my eyes began to be moist with tears.

'I love you,' I said, with my eyes closed. I felt his fingers stroking down my face, then his lips were close to my ear.

'I love you, Sally. Do you trust me now?'

# EIGHT
• • •

After I'd got back home, having stayed the night with
Paul, I found that Nicola had left a message. I was
thrown into confusion and immediately dialled
Ginnie's number.

'Yes, Sal?'

I could hear her fingers punching away on the
keyboard.

'This won't take long,' I said, apologetically. 'But
Mark's asked me over for this Sunday. He's going to
cook lunch at his flat in Brixton. I wish Nicola had
given me more notice. I can't say no, can I?'

'Relax, Sal. Play it by ear. I'm sure it'll be fine,' said
Ginnie. The rattle of the keyboard stopped.

'I know you're busy but I have the awful feeling I'm
about to commit some dreadful gaffe. I don't want to let
Nicola down. And I'm worried about what she's got
herself into . . .'

'Well, that's nothing new.'

I let that pass and continued.

'I didn't realize he lived in Brixton. It sounds a pretty
dangerous place to me. Lots of people involved in
drugs . . .'

'So that means Mark must be a heroin addict. Is that
what you're saying?'

Ginnie was in the kind of mood where she'd be
irritated by anything I said, but I pressed on.

'Of course not. He's obviously decent, working in a library . . .'

'Even librarians do drugs nowadays.'

I sighed. Ginnie must have been suffering from the night before. The last thing she would have wanted was an anxious phone call from me.

'It's just that I don't want to put my foot in it,' I said.

'I know what's bothering you,' Ginnie went on, relenting a little. 'Let's be straight about this. If he wasn't black . . .'

'It's nothing to do with that!' I protested.

'Come on, Sal. You've lived for years in a white-ghetto land. Once a year in Regatta Week you see a black rowing team walking down Wengrave High Street. Big deal. And look at Henry. An appalling racist.'

'I don't know how you can say that.'

I was beginning to feel defensive. Compared to Ginnie's life in London, mine was sheltered and perhaps a little narrow-minded and provincial – as she often reminded me – but that didn't mean I was totally unaware of life outside or how other people lived. And I didn't see why she had to bring Henry into it.

'Do you remember what he said once over supper?' continued Ginnie. '"That stupid black bastard should never have got off."'

'I don't remember him saying anything of the kind. And even if he did, it didn't affect his judgement.'

I heard Ginnie let out a snort. So often in the past, I'd automatically come to Henry's defence whenever she attacked his views. I'd forgotten for a moment that I was no longer responsible for protecting him. 'All right, he could be a bigot sometimes. And he's sure to go up the wall if he finds out about Mark.'

'Stuff Henry,' said Ginnie, dismissively.

She expected me to tidy Henry away and pretend that he didn't exist. Although we rarely spoke, there was too much around which reminded me of him. You can't get someone out of your system in a few months. And I still heard his voice in my head, although the words were getting fainter.

'I feel rather out of my depth,' I said.

'Just go along and be yourself.'

'It's all very well but black culture is different. What will happen when I'm face to face with Mark? What can we talk about when I know so little about him?'

For once, Ginnie seemed hesitant.

'Well . . . I suppose you could ask him about his family. That's safe, isn't it?'

'Then it might seem as though I'm checking up on him, trying to find out if he was born here or not.'

'There's always music.'

'How can I possibly talk about music? The nearest I get to their kind of music is listening to Radio Two.'

'You're making assumptions. He might like Beethoven. Or Indian raga. Or Shirley Bassey, for all I know.'

'I can't talk about any of them. Can you?'

'How about Bob Marley? We used to listen to him, didn't we?'

'That was years ago, probably before he was born. Really, Ginnie! This is crazy.'

We were both silent. Eventually Ginnie said, 'You'll just have to let Nicola do the talking.'

I laughed. 'Yes. She's good at that.'

I always got in a state when I couldn't find my way somewhere, one reason why Henry always drove rather than me. There were no proper signs and I was getting horribly lost. It would have helped if I knew where Brixton began and where it ended. I thought I was going roughly in the right direction, up Brixton Hill, past a strange place with fridges stuck over the entrance that Nicola said was a famous club, then I turned right into Coldharbour Lane. The road was frighteningly narrow, especially for a Range Rover, and there were plenty of large vehicles jostling for space, with people leaning out and shouting to one another over their booming speakers. In spite of feeling uncomfortable, I recognized the electric energy here – London in the raw it seemed to me – and I began to see why it appealed to young people.

Glancing at the map Nicola had drawn that I'd stuck to the dashboard, I made a left turn and slowed down as I approached a massive tower block with other towers behind. I had never been to an estate like this. It doesn't matter where you live, I kept telling myself. There was scrubby grass in the front where children were playing and acres of wall punctuated by small windows, with balconies linking one to the other. An ambulance with flashing lights and open doors was waiting in the concrete area by the entrance. I didn't dare ask anyone the way because anything might have happened. I wished it had been cleaner and better kept. I parked the car behind an overflowing skip, locked it nervously and walked quickly towards the entrance, hoping nobody would approach me. Once I had gone in, would I ever come out again? It was totally confusing. Arrows pointed everywhere, even up in the air, and I couldn't work out where I was meant to go for number three hundred and seven east.

A mother clutching several plastic bags of shopping was struggling into a lift with three small children and another in a pushchair, so I hurried forward to give her a hand. Plucking up courage, I asked her for directions to Mark's flat. She was very friendly and insisted on taking me right to his door. I tried not to look at the rubbish strewn down the corridors, the old fridges and abandoned cookers and the graffiti on the walls.

Nicola opened the door, looking pleased and surprised.

'You found us, Mum! Brilliant!' She took the bouquet

of flowers I'd bought and gave me a hug. 'Lovely colours. Thanks a lot. Come inside. Mark won't be long, he's getting some wine.' We stood in the tiny hall facing one another, reflected in a pink glass mirror. 'Do you like my hair? I had it done yesterday.'

'Fabulous,' I said, even though I had my doubts.

Nicola's appearance had completely changed since the previous weekend, as though she was an actress trying out for a new part. Her long straight hair had been cut short and was scattered with a variety of glittery slides and clips. Even her figure looked different and her lanky teenage body seemed to have acquired new curves, emphasized by the stretchy black dress she was wearing. There were several silver studs stuck round her ears and bangles on her wrist. She pointed to a small brooch in the shape of a star clasped at her neckline.

'Mark bought me this. They're real little diamonds.'

'Beautiful, darling.'

She took hold of my hand and pulled me inside.

'Come and meet Millie. She lives in the flat with Mark.'

The flat was larger than I'd imagined from the out-side. The walls were plain white and clusters of leafy pot plants lined the edges of the room. A bulky three-piece suite took up much of the space, and crouched in one of the wide-armed chairs was an old black lady with grizzled hair.

'I can't get up with these legs,' she said.

I shook her hand and we introduced ourselves.

'I'm Mark's mum though to most others I'm Auntie.'

She gave a hearty laugh and I couldn't help feeling shocked at how old she looked, more like Mark's grandmother. I should have realized.

'Mark, he's been married before but this one is a good girl. Much better. Estelle, she runs off with a Turkish man and takes the children abroad. She's no good. No education to teach her sense. My husband, he died two years ago so Mark he say I should live here. He's a good boy. You got a husband?'

'Yes, but he doesn't live with her,' Nicola said, while I was wondering how to reply.

'Your man was no good, too?'

'Not exactly,' I said, rather awkwardly. 'It's just, well, he found someone else.'

'Then he's no good. You better free.'

Nicola was hovering.

'Come and look around, Mum.'

Led by Nicola, I dutifully inspected the small bathroom, the kitchen and Millie's room.

'Mark's room is next to Millie's. Shall I show you?' Nicola said, pausing by a closed door in the narrow corridor.

'I'd love to see it,' I said.

When we were inside, I caught Nicola glancing at me from time to time, as though she was testing my reactions. Against one wall was a low double bed covered in a glowing embroidered kelim, with a table next to it laden with books. The black painted wardrobe was ajar and I recognized Nicola's pink silk dressing gown hanging in the front, as though she wanted me to notice it.

'It seems a happy place,' I commented, smiling at her.

I was suddenly confronted with the evidence that Nicola was now a woman and sleeping with the man of her choice. A black man. There was no logical reason for my feeling of unease and I had to admit that Ginnie was right when she accused me of living in a 'white-ghetto land'. I hadn't been prepared for this and I distracted myself by examining the books neatly arranged along a shelf. Some seemed quite new and one or two were in French, but there were no authors I recognized. He must have had very modern taste.

'Mark gets loads of books to take home from the library,' Nicola said.

'I can see he does.' I went over to admire the brightly coloured abstract prints hanging round the walls. 'And he obviously likes pictures, too.'

'He got some of those when he was working in Paris. He speaks French much better than me.'

'How clever of him, darling.'

'No. He's just good at picking up languages.'

As we walked back down the corridor, Nicola heard the rattle of keys outside and hurried to the front door.

Mark was smaller than I expected – only a couple of inches taller than Nicola who was about five foot six – but that wasn't the first thing I noticed. It was his age. Now I really was at a loss. I guessed him to be around forty, or at least twenty years older than Nicola, which made Millie the right age to be his mother. He held himself proudly, a proper man, not a boy. Was he a father figure for Nicola? A father who took notice of her, the reverse of Henry in every respect?

He had a well-cut beard and a lively, kind face. He was someone you wouldn't mind approaching in the street, conventionally dressed in a light, well-tailored jacket, dark trousers and shiny brogues. I felt ashamed of my preconceptions and ingrained fears, for he was courteous and charming from the start.

'Did you find your way OK?'

'Oh, yes. Nicola's instructions were very clear.'

'Mum didn't think Brixton was in London.'

'Well I am just a country pumpkin.'

Nicola giggled. 'Bumpkin we say, Mum. Us what speaks English.'

We all smiled. Mark began checking through a straw basket.

'Nikki, did you get some tacos?'

'Yeah. A big bag.'

'Nikki helps out with the shopping but I do the cooking. Which is just as well, because what she calls cooking I call heating.' He gave a cordial laugh. 'Mammie could teach her a thing or two.'

He glanced at Millie, as though giving her some predetermined signal, and she nodded. Then he helped her out of the chair and handed her a stick.

'I'm going to watch TV. I've my very own TV in my room,' Millie said, as she slowly edged towards the door. 'I'll be back for one o'clock. That's when we'll be eating. One o'clock, mind.'

The conversation went in fits and starts. It seemed as though we were all being quite amiable but I couldn't tell what Mark was really thinking. How could he avoid seeing me as 'one of them'? Still, if either of us disapproved of one another, it wouldn't make Nicola change her mind about him.

'Nicola showed me round the flat. You've a lot of interesting books.'

'I have to read a lot but it's not a chore. When people come into the library, it's best if you can give them ideas. If you know what you're talking about, maybe they'll try something new.'

'How wonderful to have a job like that! I do envy you being surrounded by books.'

Mark laughed. 'It's people reading them that counts. And you can't say I'm in it for the money. Nikki thinks I should open my own bookshop. She has big ideas, sometimes.' He turned towards Nicola with an affectionate smile. 'Darling, would you check the chicken? See it's not too high.'

We were in the middle of eating lunch when one of Mark's sisters and her friends arrived with their children. Instantly, space was found round the small table and the children sat on the floor. After a while I forgot that Nicola and I were the only white people there. Millie talked about the old days and complained how Brixton had changed from a black community – where everyone used to care for one another – to a horrible mix-up.

'Too many whites, you're saying,' said Nicola.

'No, Nikki. You're not getting my meaning. Too many boys looking like girls and girls looking like boys. It's mighty confusing. And they're all out for themselves. That makes them violent people.'

'When you're poor and you see some folks around here with big cars and Rolexes, you can get violent. There's too much struggling, struggling for the wrong things,' said Mark.

Millie leaned back in her chair, carefully wiped her fingers one by one and sighed contentedly.

'My boy's lucky. He's got good work and good housing. He's very lucky.'

'Don't forget Nikki,' Mark added.

'She's lucky, too.'

Nicola collected up the plates and handed round bowls of fruit. Then she went over to an expensive-looking stereo system and put on a CD, a Madonna song I half recognized.

'I didn't know you still had that.'

'Mark likes it.'

'Not so loud, Nikki,' he shouted, as she demonstrated the muscle power of the speakers. She turned it down only a fraction but nobody seemed to mind. Then she came to sit beside me.

'Will you come to see a film with us later?' she asked. She called out to Mark, who was encircled by the family group. 'We are going to the cinema tonight, aren't we?'

He swivelled round to face us.

'Sure. But we've got to make a decision. There's a good one on at the Ritzy I was telling you about.'

'Mum wouldn't want to see that! Just cos it won an award at some poxy film festival . . .'

'She accuses me of being a culture snob,' said Mark with a grin. 'But the way I see it, I put a lot of work into being educated, so why not? It harms no-one. Nikki, can you find *Time Out*? Then Sally can choose something.'

'I'm not sure . . .' I said.

'Please come,' Nicola begged.

'It's very tempting – but I'll have to get back. I've got lots of boring chores to do this evening. I never seem to find time during the week.'

'Shame,' said Nicola, giving me a penetrating look.

'Another time I'd love to,' I added, feeling guilty that I'd given such a feeble excuse.

I think our farewells were quite affectionate, if formal. Mark shook me warmly by the hand.

'You must come to Wengrave one weekend. There's a good train service from London,' I said.

'Sure. We will, Sally. But most likely we'd drive down. My old car should make it.'

I hoped Mark would accept my invitation, but I had no idea whether he would want to come or not.

'You'd be very welcome, Mark.'

'Thanks. It was good meeting you.'

Nicola and I walked along the concrete corridor, lit by harsh fluorescent strips, and waited by the lift.

'Do you like him? Tell me, Mum. What do you think?' I smiled at her.

'I think he's a really fine person.'

'Honestly, Mum? What would you have said if you hadn't liked him?'

This time I wasn't thrown by Nicola's directness. I was slowly beginning to treat her like an adult.

'I might have said, well, he seems quite nice but I've only met him once.'

'Yes, I can imagine you saying that,' Nicola said, with a laugh. She seemed oblivious to the growing crowd of people waiting for the lift. 'If Mark is promoted, we might rent a flat together.'

'Isn't it a little soon, darling?'

I couldn't help sounding a note of caution. She was only just becoming used to sharing a flat in London with her girlfriends and I didn't expect her to realize how different it would be, living with a man.

'Why? Do you think I shouldn't?'

'It's not that. But you've got a lot to cope with. College, living away from home . . . and you and Mark have only been together a little time.'

'I'll wait till I'm twenty then.'

She pressed the lift button again several times and sighed impatiently. The descending lift eventually came to a juddering halt, and we both travelled slowly down to the ground floor. As everyone streamed out, Nicola pulled me to one side.

'Promise you won't say anything to Dad. If I do end up living with Mark, he'd go absolutely wild, wouldn't he? My daughter with a black man? Sue him for abduction! I bet he would, too, if I was fifteen. Lucky I'm nineteen, isn't it?'

'There's no need to say anything to your father for the time being, is there?' I said.

We gave one another an affectionate kiss and I walked quickly towards where I had parked the car. Just before I left, I glanced back at the sprawling towers and the windswept sky. I was proud of Nicola. At nineteen, I would have been incapable of striking out as she had, of being so certain about her emotions. Would I be able to do the same?

I had finally given Paul his own key to the front door. It had taken some time for me to overcome my fear that one day Henry might come marching into the house unannounced and come face to face with my lover. I was convinced that he'd throw us both out onto the street until Paul reassured me that if such an unlikely thing were to happen, he would dream up a convincing explanation for his presence. I now trusted him enough to believe what he said. As I came up the drive, I could see a welcoming light shining through the window in the hall and a warm glow behind the drawing-room curtains. I was full of happiness, knowing that he was expecting me, that the house wouldn't be dark and silent.

There were some damp logs crackling and popping in the fireplace. I lay with my head on Paul's shoulder on the sofa where we had first made love, and told him about my trip to Brixton.

'So it went well then?'

'Much better than I thought. And I was impressed with Mark. You'd have liked him.'

'Who knows? Perhaps we'll get to meet one day. There's no reason why not.'

'You sound so sure,' I said, with a doubtful smile.

'Why shouldn't I be?'

I turned on my side to look at him. He was staring up at the ceiling, quite content. I envied his stillness.

'Who knows? I might run away.'

'I wouldn't lay bets on that one,' he said, with a laugh.

'Or you might decide to sail round the world.'

'Then you'd have to come with me, wouldn't you?'

We both lay stretched out in silence. I could feel Paul's steady heartbeat. He communicated such a sense of ease that I felt as though I was floating down a slow-moving river.

'Nicola and Joel will be coming for Easter. Perhaps . . . it might be a good time.'

'For what?' asked Paul.

'To tell them that . . .' I couldn't quite imagine what I would say. 'Well, to let them know that we're seeing one another a lot. Maybe if you came over for lunch to start with . . .?'

He suddenly sat up and took my hands.

'Sally. I'm not going to be here for Easter. But we'll go away together as soon as I get back.'

He must have seen desolation written all over my face. I had never considered that there might be a distance between us.

'How long will you be away for?' I murmured.

'A couple of weeks. I go camping in the New Forest with Mum and Dad every Easter. Sometimes my sister comes, sometimes one of my cousins. It's a family tradition and I couldn't let them down.'

'No. Of course you couldn't. I'll go and get something to eat.'

'I'll give you a hand.'

I had already worked out Easter in my mind. At first, I thought I might be on my own as Sheila had asked Joel and Nicola to her country cottage in Norfolk. I was relieved that Nicola refused to go but Joel was clearly looking forward to it. He sounded pleased, though, to spend the first week with me. Nicola would only be coming for a few days. Although I asked Mark to stay as well, she said he had family obligations and couldn't leave Millie. I suspected that she wanted to be alone with him, which I understood only too well. I dreaded the thought of facing two whole weeks when I couldn't hear Paul's voice, when I'd be sleeping in an empty bed, when the house would be deprived of his presence. I knew I'd miss him painfully and I couldn't bear the idea of being completely out of touch.

'I can call you on your mobile while I'm away,' Paul said.

'It would be risky. I might be with the children.'

'I thought you were going to . . . oh, never mind.'

*

183

We were now seeing one another every night. Usually Paul came round to me but occasionally, if he was working late, I went to his room. I found myself refusing all invitations, inventing excuses that became less and less convincing. It was childish and absurd but if I couldn't go out with Paul, then I wouldn't go out at all. Maggie couldn't understand why I showed no interest in meeting suitable 'possibles' that she'd cultivated for my benefit. I turned her down politely and also refused two of Patsy's theatre parties and Angela and Douggie's Japanese evening. I had stopped meeting them at the Café Rouge and I could tell that they were all becoming concerned about me. In the end, it seemed better to fabricate an all-embracing reason that would let me off the hook for several weeks at least. I allowed them to believe that I might have some debilitating, obscure illness that could be either psychological or physical in origin. All I needed was to rest as much as possible. They all guessed right. Yes, it could be what they called yuppie flu. ME, whatever that stood for. When I thought about it, I did feel ashamed that I had to resort to this kind of subterfuge but I couldn't find an alternative. I could only imagine them greeting my love affair with laughter and derision – or treating it as a passing diversion. And I wasn't prepared for that.

I used to wonder how Henry had managed it, finding plausible excuses for his absences for so long. Perhaps, in the end, he believed them himself. If you grew so accustomed to lying, would it become as natural as telling the truth? I had no intention of putting myself to the test. Somehow I hoped that a natural opportunity would arise, so that I could come out into the open. At least we would be together in public at the Hedgehog book-launch party. Every time I felt depressed about Easter, I would look at the bright red invitation card I'd put on the kitchen window sill, with Sally Linton and Paul Burridge written in large silver letters. I didn't dare admit to Paul how excited I was. And I was going through a minor agony, wondering how you behaved and what you should wear for a book launch. Was it a formal or an informal occasion? Henry could never understand it, why women worried about such trivia. I was beginning to wonder the same thing myself.

I consulted Ginnie, who was familiar with the nuances of social behaviour, or I thought she was.

'Book launch. Let me see,' she pondered. 'It's not my kind of thing, but I've been to a few. One in the Groucho Club, one in the Inn on the Park, another one in a private house in Chelsea . . .'

'Are they always so grand?' I asked.

'The ones I go to are,' she replied. Then she giggled. 'Then you're guaranteed some decent champagne. Why else would I go? Anyway, where's the venue?'

'In the house where the offices are, but they're going to tart them up. Knowing that lot, they won't do it by halves.'

'It must be difficult finding anywhere suitable out of London.'

'Not at all,' I said, indignantly. 'But we won't argue about that. What am I going to wear, for God's sake?'

'People in publishing are quite smart nowadays. Something simple, understated . . .'

'Your understated is different from mine,' I said, conjuring up my wardrobe. There were several dresses I'd worn that had been perfect for Mrs Farringford's appearance at Wengrave dinner parties, and a couple of silk suits. But it had been so long since I'd worn them, even though I hadn't managed to throw them out, that I couldn't summon up any enthusiasm.

'Trousers?' I suggested.

'Possibly. But you really need to come to London to find anything decent.'

'If I don't succeed in finding what I want, then I will,'
I said, to placate Ginnie.

'Then I'll expect you soon. Harvey Nicks Sushi for
lunch?'

'We'll see.'

I wasted a couple of lunch hours wandering round the
boutiques I used to frequent, feeling more and more
listless. I'd never been good at putting things together
and creating an effect and I couldn't ask Maggie or
Angela for help as I was meant to be laid low with the
lurgy. In the end – led on by an elegantly turned-out
French shop assistant – I settled for a pair of well-cut
black trousers, a black silk boned top that pushed up
my breasts and a short silvery grosgrain jacket. I was
convinced that clothes shouldn't be worn this tight, but
mademoiselle raised her eyebrows and assured me that
they were absolutely *comme il faut* and *très très chic*.
Finally, I made an appointment with a stylist who used
to work at Vidal Sassoon. Anyone would think I was
going to appear on television.

'I want your honest opinion, Paul.'

Freshly shaven, hair newly trimmed, washed and
gleaming, splendid in grey wool trousers and a dark
maroon shirt (he really did look stunning), Paul walked
back to take in my appearance. I was on tenterhooks for
his verdict.

'Yes. It's good, really good. Very . . . smart. Proper
clothes. All dressed up and ready to go. You'll be a
wow.'

'You don't like it?'

He walked round slowly, then stopped in front of
me.

'All lovely. But I don't know if I can live up to it.'

I instantly knew what he meant.

'I'll take it all off if you think it's wildly over the top.'

'Save that for later,' he said, with a grin. 'Like the hair, too.'

'Do you? I wasn't sure about the cut.'

He ran his fingers through my hair, ruffled it a bit and pulled a couple of strands from behind my ears on to my face. Then he removed the pearls from my neck.

'You don't need these. Now you're fantastic.'

He suddenly stopped in his tracks just before he reached the front door.

'Am I expected to wear a tie? If so, I might have to borrow one of Henry's. I'm sure he wouldn't mind.'

'No tie. Anyway, I bet you never wear one.'

'Not even for weddings,' he said, with a relieved smile.

The front door of the Hedgehog house buzzed open and large red arrows directed us to the top floor. As Paul followed me up the stairs I strained to catch the sound of music or the buzz of conversation, but it was unusually quiet.

'We could be too early,' I said, anxiously.

'Can't be. The invitation said seven,' Paul answered.

We were both a little nervous as we walked hesitantly into Matt's top-floor office. It had been minimally transformed, with all the furniture pushed back to the sides of the room, and in one corner there was a modest pile of Big Bear books leaning against a poster. Pickle, Jed and Matt were absorbed in talking to some of their friends who were standing with their backs to us, holding beer glasses. They must have come straight from work, without bothering to shave or change their clothes. What could they have thought when we came in? That we'd come to the wrong address, most likely.

'I wish I hadn't put all this on. Nobody else has bothered. I've completely misjudged it,' I whispered to Paul.

Pickle, standing in the far corner, suddenly caught sight of me and came rushing over, clutching an oversized bottle of wine.

'Great gear, Sal,' she remarked, before turning to Paul. 'Grab a couple of glasses from that table over there and I'll pour some of this in. It's not cold but it's OK. There's beer as well.'

Paul left my side and Pickle watched as he crossed the room.

'How's it going?' she asked, with a grin.

'I can't believe it,' I said.

'I can. He's a fantastic guy.'

'How can you tell?'

'Just can. Don't let him go.'

I smiled nervously, then turned away and gazed round the room. It was all very bare, with everything tidied to the sides.

'If I'd had more time, I'd have put some flowers around the place. And made you canapés or something.'

Pickle gave a wide grin that seemed to accentuate her higgledy-piggledy teeth and made her resemble an amiable troll. Onto her bottom lip she'd clipped three silver rings. I assumed they didn't hurt, otherwise she would have removed them by now.

'Don't worry, Sal. There's crisps and peanuts. No-one expects to get fed.'

'Won't publishers expect something when they come?'

'What, them? They've been here for ages.'

I could feel myself colouring. I realized I'd been fussing like an overanxious mum as Sally Farringford took charge. When I was nervous, I slipped into my former self almost without noticing. Perhaps it was the clothes. I wished I hadn't looked so expensive and out of place. I was relieved when I saw Paul returning with some glasses. Pickle tipped in the wine.

'Got something to ask you,' she said to Paul. 'I need some big rusty old chains for an installation I'm doing. Could you find me some?'

Paul was mystified. 'What's an installation?'

'Art thing,' replied Pickle. 'There's a theme and mine's called Apocalypse. I've made loads of different ones. If you drop round to my place, you can have a look.'

I glanced at Paul. Pickle spoke in a different way when he was near, tipping her head to one side, blinking a little faster than usual, making it clear that she found him attractive. This made me uncomfortable, a little jealous even. Although I'd tried to push it aside, there were moments when I was forced to recognize the impact of our difference in age. There was a natural intimacy between people in their twenties. I couldn't help comparing myself to her, wishing I could get away with the bright layers of clothing she'd flung on. Pickle must have caught my uneasy expression.

'Sal, you can come along as well. Though I don't think it's your thing.'

'You might be surprised,' said Paul, giving me a fond glance.

Pickle knocked back the wine in her glass and turned on her heel.

'I'd better go and do some chatting up.'

'Why? Are you on the hunt?' asked Paul, amiably.

'Not me. Miguel's coming later.' Pickle waved a hand in the direction of a small, tight group. 'Those are our new publishers, talking to Jed and Matt.'

I looked across the room at a striking black girl with tightly plaited and beaded hair who was wearing a long baggy shirt over leggings. Next to her stood a young man in jeans and trainers and a corduroy jacket.

'They look so young. I thought they'd be wearing suits.'

'Never! Not Jasmine and Ben. They're really cool. I'll introduce you.'

Jasmine and Ben were in the middle of an argument with Jed about the manager of West Ham. We all said 'Hi' and that was about it. (Joel's favourite club was Chelsea and I didn't have a clue about West Ham.) Pickle started enthusing about some footballer, but by now Jasmine seemed bored with the topic. She suddenly turned to Paul with interest and I heard her asking him if he worked with Hedgehog.

I wandered over to the jumbled display of Big Bear books and started arranging them more neatly. Matt came and stood by my side.

'Everything OK, Sal?'

'Fine. The publishers have done an excellent job, haven't they?' I said, with a bright smile. Matt stood back and surveyed the display.

'It stands out. Different. Yes, we're pleased. There'll be more people later. Our mates plus a few hangers-on. You need a fill-up.'

He took my glass and left for the drinks table.

Paul was still talking to Jasmine but I didn't want to interrupt them. It would take time, I thought, before I'd get used to being easy with everyone here. The buzz of conversation was getting louder. Pickle was throwing up her arms, probably demonstrating something she was making. Jed was sitting on the floor, leaning against the wall expounding some idea to Ben. Everyone looked animated, interested, involved. I couldn't help thinking of Henry. He'd have been amazed to see me with this crowd – but he'd never have known of their existence. In our social life, we'd met the same people for years. However uneasy I felt, I realized that I'd much rather be with the Hedgehog gang than having to endure yet another evening of stuffy conversation and predictable opinions. I wasn't used to having the freedom to say exactly what came into my head, to react honestly instead of considering what might be acceptable, to argue forcibly if I felt like it.

After another glass of wine, I began to feel less self-conscious. I might have been overdressed but nobody seemed to notice. I got into conversation with a couple of illustrators who had been with Matt, Jed and Pickle at art school and were getting into animation. I told them about my early days in the Themis Gallery. I was in the middle of a story about Theodore when Paul came over. He put his arm round my waist until I came to the end.

'We're about to have some music,' he said, gesturing towards Pickle. She was standing on a chair, getting down a CD player from the top of Matt's shelf. 'Matt's given in to gentle pressure. But if the neighbours object, she'll have to abandon the idea.'

Suddenly there was a loud burst of electronic sound. Matt shouted across the room and Pickle turned it down a fraction.

'Come on Sally. Let's dance while we can,' said Paul, propelling me into the centre of the room. He put his arms tightly round me but there was only space to rock to and fro. The numbers had grown and it was turning into a proper party. The music changed. It sounded like reggae but I wasn't sure. Well, what did it matter? We stayed locked in one another's arms. I didn't feel old and I didn't feel young but rather as though I'd landed up in a foreign country far from Wengrave.

Having put all our energy into a fast number, we decided to slow down and set off in search of Matt. Paul left my side to find something cool and refreshing and I was in the middle of kicking off my shoes when I heard a familiar voice.

'Hi Sally. I wondered if you'd be here.'

I whirled round and came face to face with Douggie. I scarcely recognized him as he was dressed all in black with a silver and black striped shirt open halfway down his chest. His grey-streaked hair was screwed back in a ponytail. Usually he wore it loose, his only eccentricity. I looked at him for a moment in horror. What was he doing here? When did he arrive? Had he seen me dancing with Paul? He misinterpreted my reaction.

'I've come straight from a creative meeting at the agency. So I had to look the part. I didn't have time to change,' he said, apologetically.

'Is Angela here?' I said, trying not to show my alarm.

'Somewhere. Oh yes. With Michael. He brought us here.'

He pointed to where she was standing with Jasmine and someone I didn't recognize.

'Do you know Michael French? He's a banker, thinking of investing in Hedgehog Graphics. Interesting man. Knows Henry. Mind you, everyone says they know Henry.'

'I . . . I don't think I've seen him before,' I stammered.

'I said you worked here. He'd be interested in finding out your views.'

'About what?'

'The company. Inside information is always useful. Michael is shrewd, brilliant at recognizing talent and has loads of ideas. He's sure Hedgehog has a future but they need to expand, get proper modern premises, maybe relocate to London, have a decent web site and so on. They'll need a business plan that stands up, of course. Anyway, as a first step we'll ask you and Michael round for supper.'

'That would be nice,' I said unconvincingly. 'But I'm sure that Matt, Jed and Pickle are happy working as they are. They like having a small outfit, it suits them.'

'They all think like that. Amazing the difference half a million makes.'

I didn't respond to Douggie's knowing smile. I'd never seen him in business mode.

'How long have you been here?' I asked.

'About twenty minutes. Angela said you hadn't been well. Sorry to hear that. But anyhow it looks as though you've recovered. Are you better now?'

'Yes, much better.' I noticed him staring at my bare feet. He must have seen my neck covered in sweat.

'Good.'

I never had much to say to Douggie, but least of all now. I couldn't decide whether I should bite the bullet and go up to Angela or stay rooted to the spot. I'd feel happier talking to Angela, I decided. I was about to wander off when Paul arrived holding a glass of mineral water. He handed it to me and looked questioningly at Douggie.

'This is Douggie. He's married to my friend Angela over there.'

'Oh yes. The one who has her paintings in Wengrave Gallery.'

Paul instantly shook hands.

'We haven't met before, have we? Are you from round here?'

'I live in Wengrave, yes.'

Douggie was looking up at Paul – he was smaller, which didn't help – with his eyes screwed up. He seemed to be weighing up whether he ought to have known him or not.

'But your accent isn't local,' Douggie insisted. Did he need to go into this?

'Cornish,' I said brusquely, before Paul could reply. 'He comes from Cornwall originally.'

'Interesting.' Douggie sounded bored. 'And what do you do?'

It was almost as though he was being deliberately insulting.

'I work,' replied Paul. Then he turned towards me. 'Finish that. Let's have another dance.'

I was glad to escape from Douggie. We had been dancing for a couple of minutes when out of the corner of my eye I saw Angela waving. I knew she would come over to us when the number came to an end. The moment I had disentangled myself from Paul, I found myself looking into her face.

'How lovely to see you – I didn't think I would,' she said, kissing me on both cheeks. 'You must be much better. I thought you looked so pale when you came to the gallery, but I didn't want to say anything.'

'I don't think you've met Paul.'

Angela smiled warmly and looked at him intently.

'Just a minute. Yes, I do remember. Didn't you go out with Nicola for a time? I believe I saw you once at one of Sally's lunch parties. Is that right?'

'It could be.'

'You're not the kind of person one forgets.' Paul glanced down in embarrassment.

'Poor Sally's had that awful illness that they can't do anything about. Yuppie flu they used to call it. Dreadful.'

'Oh? I didn't know about that,' he said, reacting with obvious alarm. I looked at Paul. Angela looked at me, then back at Paul. I could see her eyes flicking between us in fascination.

'Do you work here as well, Paul?' Angela asked.

'No. He came with me,' I said, before he could answer.

'Oh. I see.'

'I did exaggerate, about the illness. I'm sorry. I hope you weren't too worried.'

'Well, obviously . . .'

'Only, I suppose it was a cowardly way of saying I needed time to myself.'

We were awkward, all three of us. It was impossible to say anything more with the loud music and the raised voices. Angela looked quite shaken. She turned her head and gazed round the room, as though she was looking for someone. I didn't immediately realize the implication of what I'd said but I knew that Angela knew. I must have wanted her to. We had been friends for long enough to detect all the changing emotions that passed between us. I couldn't mask my feelings any longer.

'We're taking a friend out to dinner, so I'll have to go and find Douggie,' Angela said. She avoided looking at Paul. 'We'll all be away for Easter. But I do hope you come along to the Café Rouge – I'll call you when we're back. We've missed seeing you and it would be nice to catch up.'

'Of course I'll come,' I replied.

I tried to compose myself. I'd have a lot of explaining to do. Then I realized that there was nothing for it. I'd have to confess my affair and try and make light of it. Sally's little fling.

'Are the children with you for Easter?'

'Yes, they're coming . . .'

'That's something to look forward to, then. Well . . .' She seemed to be at a loss for words. Then she turned to Paul and gave a hesitant smile. 'I hope we meet again.'

We left soon after Angela and Douggie. Paul was rather subdued as we took the taxi home.

'Did you enjoy it?'

'I enjoyed being with you,' he said. 'But I don't think Angela approved of me one bit.'

'It's not that. But she doesn't understand. I can't expect her to.'

He settled into the back seat and closed his fingers round mine.

'I don't want you to lose your friends because of me.'

'Don't worry, I won't,' I said, with a confident smile.

# NINE

## • • •

With Paul gone, I felt quite empty and lacking in energy, only longing for the day when he would be back. Wengrave was sleepy and there were only a few boats hazarding the fast-flowing river. I forced myself to make a special effort for the children so I had Easter all planned out with visits and excursions. Even though I hadn't seen them for months and didn't particularly wish to renew contact, I'd managed to get us invited to friends of Henry's with children of a similar age who had a farm in Oxfordshire. They had a fine tennis court, so Nicola and Joel would be happy. There'd be a couple of parties. Supper with Martin. The Wengrave Easter Fair. A vintage car rally. I tried to fill up their diary.

It was as though I had to compete with Henry, to prove to my children that they'd have an equally good time with me. I often had a niggling feeling that Sheila would be much more fun than I would. A jolly good sort, as Martin might have put it. Joel had described her as loud and bouncing with energy and I'm sure he liked being in her company. He was going to help her and Dad construct a wooden fence. They'd go riding with Sheila's son. And best of all, he would get to drive her car. It didn't get any easier. My throat still constricted with anger the moment I heard her name and I struggled to show cheerful interest.

On Saturday Ginnie came down with Nicola and Joel. We all sat at the kitchen table decorating the Easter eggs, except for Joel who spent most of the time in Henry's study, glued to the Apple Mac writing emails to his friends. His contribution was to print out an Easter card, which originated from somewhere remote like Finland. I couldn't share his fascination with the Internet world. He said it was like suddenly being in touch with the universe and having it talk back at you. I still worried that he talked so little to me. But over Sunday lunch, Joel came into his own and carved the lamb to perfection. He said it was easy, as he'd watched Dad doing it thousands of times. He showed no sign of regretting Henry's absence and seemed to enjoy being the only man in the house.

I was waiting for an opportunity to slip away unnoticed. Luckily, Ginnie asked to borrow a bike so that she could go with Joel and Nicola on one of our favourite family trips to a bird sanctuary about ten miles away. I convinced her that I didn't feel up to it and would take a rest. When they had been gone for ten minutes, I pulled on my coat, tied on a scarf and jumped into the car. Taking the opposite direction to theirs, I headed for a public phone box at the end of a neighbouring hamlet and parked off the road in the entrance to a field. Standing in the traditional old booth with my face bent down so that I wouldn't be conspicuous, I looked cautiously through the misting glass.

Thankfully, there were no inhabitants to be seen. An occasional car roared past on the deserted road. My purse was full of coins and my heart was thumping. I dialled the number of the farmer Paul had given me – he would be camping in one of his fields. It took a long while to find him.

'I couldn't wait to hear your voice,' he said, sounding breathless. 'You just caught me in time. We were about to go on a hike but I knew you'd phone so I kept putting everyone off.'

'What did you say?'

'That my girlfriend was going to call me, of course. Mum and Dad said you should have come down with us. So I explained.'

'How?' I asked.

'I told them you had kids and they were coming home for Easter.'

His voice sounded close but I resented the miles between us.

'So they know, then?'

'About you? They've known for ages.'

He probably guessed what was going through my mind. How would his parents react to their son having an affair with someone only a little younger than they must be?

'How do they feel about it? Do they know . . . well . . . have they an idea of my age?'

'They've a rough idea. I said you were a bit older than me, that's all. Dad said he'd always liked being younger than Mum.'

The pips started to sound and I quickly inserted another coin.

'Where are you?' Paul asked.

I didn't want to admit that I couldn't bring myself to call him from the house.

'I went out to get some bread. There's an Indian supermarket that's open in Fawley Green. So I'm there, standing in a phone box. Ginnie's gone off with Nicola and Joel to the bird sanctuary.'

'How's it going?'

I laughed. 'All very well on the surface. But Nicola would rather be with Mark. I'd rather be with you. Sergei's in St Petersburg and Ginnie wants to be with him. After a couple of days enjoying being a family, they'd all prefer to be off. Silly, isn't it?'

'And Joel?'

'Joel spends hours with epic computer games or sending emails and surfing the Net. He said that's what holidays are for. Though he can't wait to go to Norfolk. Sheila's promised she'll let him drive her sports car.'

'That's very decent of her,' Paul said.

I think he was being ironical but even if he wasn't, Sheila had become a monster in my mind. And it was impossible to visualize a decent monster.

'Sheila's found an easy way of getting into his good books,' I said, then instantly regretted my acid comment. 'I'll be glad when girls are more exciting than cars, though.'

'Then the trouble starts. Give me a car any day,' said Paul.

It wasn't the ideal place to murmur intimate words to a lover but I tried to ignore the sour smell of the closed box and the crude graffiti in front of me.

'I spend a lot of the time thinking of you. I was awake most of last night, not feeling you beside me.'

'At least you weren't crammed like a chrysalis in a narrow sleeping bag. Mind you, there are compensations. Like cooking bangers over a fire, putting potatoes in the embers. And I'm getting in practice.'

'For what?'

'When we go off in a boat somewhere . . . Can you light a fire outside?'

'Only a bonfire in the garden. But I'd try.' I imagined his face, turning dark gold in the open air, his skin fresh with the smell of bracken and grass. 'I can't wait . . . I miss you horribly.'

'And so you should!' he said, with a laugh. 'But I might be back sooner than you think. Then you'll say, why the hell didn't he stay longer? I'm doing very nicely on my own and getting a decent night's sleep. By the way, when you're not with me do you go to bed naked?'

'Of course I don't,' I said, indignantly. 'Do you think I should?'

'I'd like it if you did.'

I was distracted by a ruddy-faced old man in a green padded jacket rubbing his hands together outside the telephone box. When he caught my eye, he jabbed a finger in the direction of the phone. I continued talking to Paul for a little while, until he came right up to the glass and grimaced at me.

'I'm being asked to leave.' I clung onto the receiver, reluctant to let it go.

'Ring me soon. It doesn't matter what time.'

After I'd finished the call and got into the car, I stared dreamily out of the window for several minutes without starting the engine. Eventually I remembered. We really did need some bread.

That evening, Nicola went off with Joel to a party and I was left alone with Ginnie. She was lying on the sofa in the drawing room, with one arm hanging down languorously over the edge. I was attempting to revive her with a glass of vodka but it appeared to do nothing for her aching limbs.

'I do take exercise, but it's extensive rather than intensive. And that's much better for you. My muscles are complaining.'

'You're making excuses,' I said. 'If you lived here, you'd be used to it.'

'I'd make sure I wasn't. Anyway, you're not going to stay here, whether you like it or not.'

'You're wrong there,' I said, a little smugly.

'I bet Joel ends up living in London. Or the States. Just imagine. In a few years' time, both the children will be happily settled in town and you'll be going to seed in this sleepy place. The higher you go up the Thames, the more soporific it is. Have you noticed?'

'Easter is always like this.'

Ginnie ignored me, sighed and stretched out her legs.

'I couldn't bear to think of you living on your own in this house. And how can you possibly meet anyone exciting? I bet even the window cleaners are pensioners around here.'

'Age isn't so important. I've stopped worrying about it.' Ginnie misunderstood my comment and immediately jumped in.

'Aha! Are you thinking about your young stud, by any chance? Is he still coming up to scratch?'

I think it was because she used that expression.

'You've got it quite wrong. I'm in love with him.'

Ginnie immediately sat up straight and stared at me for a moment. Her mouth dropped open.

'My God!' she exclaimed. 'Have you gone completely crazy?'

'He feels the same for me. And you don't need to tell me he's the most unsuitable man I could have chosen. Because he is.'

Rising to her feet, Ginnie made for the vodka bottle, poured herself half a glass and started pacing round the room. She ended up perched on the window seat, staring at me in amazement.

'I mean . . . you've been seeing a lot of him, obviously . . . and . . . it's fabulous that you're so happy . . .' I waited expectantly for a whole host of objections but none came. She looked pensive, as she walked slowly over to sit beside me.

'You really must tell me his name. Isn't it about time?'

'All right, then. It's Paul, Nicola's ex-boyfriend.'

'Oh. My. God. Oh my God,' she repeated, only this time in a voice of doom. But she quickly pulled herself together. 'So it is someone I've met. I never guessed it'd be him, not in a million years. Nicola's Paul. How did it start? When? How on earth did it happen?'

Taking a deep breath, I began at the beginning. At

first I was hesitant. It was strange, reviewing our history and trying to explain how, in just a few months, our attraction had grown into passion and the passion had expanded into love. It was the first time I had put the constant subject of my thoughts into words. It must have sounded so banal to Ginnie. I think she understood how it could have happened – she had declared herself in love after a matter of days – but she was mystified as to why I'd fixed my deepest affections on Paul.

'Of course, he's an incredibly good-looking man. I grant you that. But are you sure it's love? And not a bad attack of lust? Nothing wrong in that, of course.'

'I'm sure that I love him.'

'And you're sure that Paul feels the same?'

'Yes.'

'How do you know you're not having a delirious post-Henry reaction? Do you really think it's going to last? How old did you say he was?'

'Twenty-six. Coming up to twenty-seven.'

'You're not going to live with him, I hope?'

'It could work out. I think about it sometimes.'

Ginnie edged herself up on the sofa, and sat cross-legged in a yoga position, cupping her chin. We used to do this as children, holding our fists under our chins as we waited to be told a story.

'Ever since Henry left, I've been suggesting that you have a wild affair. It's the best thing that could have happened. But . . .'

'I know the buts. And I don't love him because I'm turned on by how difficult it's going to be. I haven't enjoyed keeping Paul to myself. I'm not used to keeping my life in separate compartments.'

I didn't admit to Ginnie how much I feared what would happen after Easter. I knew it wouldn't be long before I became the scandal of Wengrave. Angela would convey the news to Maggie, Maggie to Patsy and sooner or later I would have to provide an explanation. However unconventional Ginnie might have appeared, I knew that I had stepped across one of her boundaries. If Paul had come from a well-known family or been a brilliant painter or writer, it would have been different. Older women were admired for nurturing artistic talent but Paul had no claims to distinction. I didn't care but I knew it mattered to Ginnie.

'I know you don't approve, Ginnie. But I didn't expect you to.'

I knew she felt uncomfortable, as she began to twist the fine gold bracelet round her wrist, first one way and then the other.

'It's not about approval, not really,' she pronounced, rather weakly. 'Just . . . don't have Paul full-time. I'm saying that because of the odds, nothing more. I know it's hard to accept now but it's not going to be a lasting relationship. They never are. It might go on for a year or two at most and then he'll be off to find a girl near his own age who's dying to be a mum. So where would that leave you? You've been hurt enough already. I couldn't bear it to happen again.' Ginnie gave a nervous laugh and then added, 'That's my department.'

She looked at me expectantly, as though waiting for me to change my mind there and then.

'I've thought what might happen. And I'm going to take the risk. I'd rather be happy with Paul for a short time. I'd rather be with him than end up with someone else for a long time who didn't matter to me.'

'That's a brave thing to say,' said Ginnie, reflectively. 'Especially since you've never taken risks. You're not used to it, unlike me.'

'Then it's time I changed. I hope I am changing.'

The light was almost gone and we were sitting in the gloom. Ginnie leaped to her feet and began to pull the curtain cords around the room, releasing the folds of the heavy velvet. I went over to the fire and carefully put on a couple of logs. I thought of Paul's room and the mean gas fire. I wanted him to share everything I had. I wanted him to be warming his back against the frantic blaze of wood.

'Honestly, Sal. What have you got in common? He's obviously a nice young man and all that, but his background is very different from yours, let alone his age. Can you see him with your friends? Would you go with him to a dinner party? Or the theatre? He'd be utterly out of his depth. It's not fair on him.'

'He makes me happy and I love him,' I answered.

'It's madness. But I've said enough.' Ginnie took her glass and walked out to the kitchen.

I finished my drink and went after her. She announced that she would cook a light supper. Despising quick solutions, she turned down my offer of a bottled pasta sauce and began laboriously constructing a speciality of hers.

'I couldn't make you change your mind, whatever I said. Right?'

'Right,' I echoed, as Ginnie started meticulously peeling the skin from a head of garlic. Then she chopped each clove into minute slivers.

'You'll have to find a way of telling Nicola and Joel. I don't envy you. Nicola's going to be a real problem,' Ginnie muttered as she hunted for an onion in the vegetable basket.

'It'll be difficult, but at least she has Mark. I can only be honest. If she's so shocked that she refuses to see me, I'll have to trust her to come back eventually.'

'And how about Joel?'

'It might be easier for him than Nicola. He's so absorbed in his own world, he might just take it for granted. Mum with Paul. They used to get on well together. Paul took him fishing a few times.'

Ginnie gave me a doubtful glance, then suddenly broke into a smile.

'You do realize you'll have to move from Wengrave? You can't possibly stay here any more. It could be the best thing that's happened!' She sounded so gleeful that I giggled. She'd found yet another excuse for me to leave for London.

'Sorry to disappoint you, but neither of us is planning to move,' I said.

'Think, Sal. If you did end up staying with Paul, I'm willing to bet there'd be total outrage. It would be like putting an ad in the *Wengrave Gazette* saying you were opening a brothel. Shock! Horror! Everyone would have a fit.'

'It's not quite that bad. They'll get used to it,' I said, reassuring myself.

The next day Martin was expected and it was quite impossible to escape to a phone box. I paced around the house like a caged lion, wondering if the coast was clear enough to make a call. I knew I couldn't. Nicola or Joel could easily come looking for me, with a question or a demand for something they couldn't find. Where's this? Where's that? I felt like snapping 'Go and look for it yourself' but I made an effort to control my irritation, to be extra attentive. When you're a mother, I suppose you're always trying to show how much you care for your children. And when you don't have the day-to-day rhythm of living as a family, you try even harder to recreate things as they used to be, cramming everything into a few days. It started to irk me. Sometimes I found it a strain acting out my role as mother, slipping back into expressions and habits I had formed with Henry. Sometimes I was alarmed. I dreamed of running off with Paul to some distant, obscure place and leaving everything behind me. If he really wanted me to, I feared that I could. Ginnie had touched a nerve. Had I succumbed to madness? Had my reason deserted me? Isn't that what they said about the effect of love?

We heard Martin's arrival from all over the house. There was a screech of tyres, a loud clunk, then the repeated beep of a car alarm, then heavy footsteps crunching over the gravel, then silence. Joel walked out to greet him. I leaned out of a bedroom window and saw them trying to extract something from the back of the car. Joel heaved a large box onto his shoulder, Martin balanced several parcels in his arms and then they both walked inside.

'Come down and see!' Martin shouted up the stairs.

I knew he'd been to China on business and would be unable to resist bringing back a little something. This was a big something. By the time I arrived, Joel had unwrapped what appeared to be a cage for quite a sizeable animal. It was highly gilded and decorated with panels of enamel.

'I could just see this in your conservatory. Ideal place,' said Martin.

'It's wonderful. Fantastic.' I couldn't think where I could possibly hide the latest token of Martin's generosity. 'What on earth will I put inside it?' I asked him.

'Birds, of course,' said Joel. 'Though in China they put in small animals and eat them later.'

'How do you know?'

'I guessed,' said Joel, with a grin.

Martin opened his arms wide, waiting for me to receive a mighty hug.

'It's a wonderful present,' I said. 'And I don't know how you managed to get it back to England.'

'Oh, there's more!' exclaimed Martin.

We all gathered round as he unpacked his treasure trove. Somehow he'd found time to bring back something for all of us. Joel was given a leather sheath containing a fiendish knife with a carved handle, Ginnie a kimono and Nicola an enamelled jewel box. It was rather touching that although he travelled first-class in a plane, he still regarded himself as some intrepid explorer bringing back unique mementoes of his travels. I couldn't possibly mention that there was a shop in Wengrave where I'd seen identical kimonos and jewel boxes. They wouldn't have dared stock the knife. But the cage, I had to admit, was really unique.

'I won't be allowed this in school,' remarked Joel, sounding disappointed. He ran the blade lightly across the back of his hand.

'Never mind. It'll be useful in the country,' Martin replied cheerily.

'Right. When I go to Sheila's cottage, I'll take it with me.'

Martin looked at him quizzically. 'Sheila's cottage? Really?'

'Well, it's not all hers.' Joel glanced at me as though he'd said the wrong thing. It was difficult for him, repressing all references to Sheila.

'Joel told me that Henry pays some of the rent,' I explained to Martin, trying to sound neutral.

'But Dad says it's quite cheap considering,' Joel added. 'They go down there most weekends.'

Ginnie left the room, bearing the kimono over her arm. Nicola stayed seated at the table, trying to fit one of her rings into the box.

'I don't know why you're going to that cottage, Joel,' remarked Nicola. 'It sounds boring to me. Nothing but huge fields. Just because Sheila found it . . .'

'That's nothing to do with it.'

'Yes, it is.'

'It is not.'

It was obvious that a row was brewing. Martin gathered up the wrapping paper decisively.

'Before lunch,' he announced, 'we're all going on a little surprise outing. But you won't know where it is till we get there. How about it?'

'OK,' said Joel. 'Where's my green jacket, Mum?'

'Upstairs somewhere,' I replied.

I was left alone with Martin while Nicola went upstairs to collect Ginnie from her bedroom. Joel followed her a moment later.

'That was really generous, Martin.'

'I enjoy buying presents, you know I do,' said Martin. Then he squeezed my hand. 'We should meet more often. It's a real shame that I have to be away so much. I should call you more than I do, but you know how it is. What with business calls all day and often in the evening, you want to throw the damn phone away. Did you get my saucy cards?'

Martin made a point of sending me grotesque postcards whenever he went abroad.

'Oh yes. I had a giggle when I got those.'

'How have you been? I've thought of you a lot, Sal. Remember what I said when we last had dinner? You probably assumed I was drunk, but I wasn't. Well, a bit tiddly. What I said was . . .'

I answered with a smile.

'How could I possibly forget?'

'Could you manage a little trip this summer? I shouldn't be so busy then. Anywhere you like. Just say. As long as there's a palm tree and a comfortable sandy beach. No tourists, of course.'

'That's a tall order!' I exclaimed.

'I did mean it. I still want to take you away,' he said, sounding serious. 'Someone as gorgeous as you shouldn't be all alone.'

I was attempting to find a kind way of being vague about Martin's invitation, when I heard Joel and Nicola thundering down the stairs.

'I'd better drag out Ginnie. Knowing her, she'll be going through agony deciding what to wear – especially when she's no idea where she's going,' I said, finding a way to escape.

\*

After we'd piled into his car, Martin checked everyone's seat belts like a solicitous father. Then he took off
at his usual speed.

'This is a proper family outing,' he said, as he swung
into the road. I knew how much he loved being in our
company. I couldn't imagine him not being part of our
family, but I doubted whether he would ever come to
terms with my affair with Paul. He had been a friend for
so long. I could only hope, when it came to it, that the
years behind us would count. I tried to put these
thoughts out of my mind.

The moment Martin turned his car into a road
running along the edge of a field, I caught my breath.
Soon we would be in front of the great iron gate,
walking through the weed-choked yard. I should have
guessed where he was taking us.

'You're going to see my baby. I bet you never knew
this place existed,' he said, winding down the car
window.

'I've been here with Paul. He liked looking at the
boats,' said Joel, as he got out of the car to open the gate.

'But your launch isn't finished yet, is it?' I blurted
out. Then I hastily corrected myself. 'I mean, I thought
it took a long time to make one.'

'Getting along nicely. It won't be long now. They're
fast workers down here.'

I was relieved that the yard was deserted. Not even
Gabriel Edgeworth was working over Easter. The blue
plastic sheeting was flapping in the breeze and new
grass had sprouted all around it. Daisies, buttercups
and dandelions were pushing their way up through the
dry soil and the bushes were filled out with soft green
leaves. The sheds were silent. Martin strode towards
the plastic tent with Joel, and pushed open the flap. I
remembered how Paul had kissed me, the moment we
were hidden from view. Now I had to pretend I'd never
seen the gleaming hull before.

'It's truly amazing,' I said, tensely. Luckily, I wouldn't be called on to find more comments, as Martin was watching Joel's reaction. Obviously fascinated by the construction, he was stroking his hand slowly down the wooden planks. Martin pointed to the bow.

'Look at that workmanship and they'll be putting on fifteen layers of varnish!'

'The nails are brass,' Joel remarked, examining every detail. 'And I think the wood is yellow pine, though the frame is mahogany. What kind of engine are you putting in?' He bent down and examined the underneath.

'They're trying to persuade me to go for steam.'

'OK for old guys. But I'd want to go faster,' said Joel.

'Me, too. I'm not ready for sheltered housing quite yet.'

'I didn't mean . . .'

'No offence, Joel,' said Martin, patting him on the back.

'All very nice,' remarked Ginnie. 'But where does one sit?'

'The seats'll go in next. Then they'll be covered in blue velvet. All done by hand.'

'Very elegant. I approve.'

Ginnie grinned at Martin and then made a graceful exit backwards. I knew that she had little sympathy with the Wengrave passion for anything that floated.

'Your young Paul has done an amazing job,' Martin said to Nicola, who was standing by the opening, looking mildly interested. 'Though he's not your Paul any longer, I gather. Your ex-Paul, I should have said.'

'Did Mum tell you then?'

'Yes, I did. I hope you don't mind,' I interjected.

Nicola looked from me to Martin, with a distrustful expression.

'Sally doesn't need to hide anything from me,' Martin

said, putting a hand on her shoulder. 'And your secrets are always safe, if you want them to be secrets.'

'I don't care. Not about Paul, anyhow. What else has Mum said?'

'Nothing. Just that you're enjoying your course,' I said, firmly.

Nicola appeared satisfied with my reply and peered over the edge of the hull. I hoped nobody had seen the blush that I felt stealing over my face. It was becoming a strain, constantly fearing that I might give myself away.

'When are we going in it then?' Nicola asked, bobbing up again. 'Will you have a picnic basket and champagne? I won't come unless you do.'

'I'll consider it,' said Martin, with a laugh. 'But you'll have to wear a straw hat with flowers on it.'

'Oh all right. I'll borrow one of Mum's if you insist. But I'll take off the flowers, if you don't mind.'

I couldn't wait to leave but Martin insisted on taking us round the moorings to make comparisons with a couple of similar boats to his. Inevitably, they were neither as stylish nor as well made.

'Are you feeling all right?' Martin asked, as I leaned back wearily on the front seat of his car. 'I bet you've been doing too much as usual.'

'I suppose I have.'

As we drove back, everything weighed down on me. I imagined Paul in our company. How could it possibly work out? My secret was stretching me to bursting point and I feared that I might choose the wrong moment to reveal everything. I was afraid that I would betray myself, as I almost had with Martin. I even wondered if one of them might have guessed. I found a moment to be alone with Ginnie when she was in the guest bedroom, preparing to leave and packing a far too voluminous wardrobe into a tiny case.

211

'What shall I do? I feel such a fraud, concealing Paul from everybody. It's not fair on him, or on me. I know I shouldn't take it so seriously. I know you'd take it in your stride. But I can't. It gets worse and worse.'

Ginnie stopped folding up her clothes immediately, taken aback at my sudden outburst.

'I've never seen you at your wits' end like this. What are you afraid of? That you'll end up on your own, shunned by your family, an outcast amongst your friends? It's inconceivable. For heaven's sake, Sal. It's not the end of the world. It's not an imprisonable offence, to fall in love with a young man.'

'It feels like it. Almost like incest,' I murmured.

'You should come and live near me. You could be shacked up with a one-legged transsexual and nobody would mind.' She brought a smile to my face. 'If it's that important . . .'

'It is.'

'Why not start by saying something to Nicola? That worries you most of all. Clear the air. Even if she storms off, she'll storm back. She always does, doesn't she?' I nodded reluctantly. 'Come back with me to London. There won't be anything happening in your office. And then you can get on an even keel again.'

'You don't think I'm mad?'

'I don't know anyone saner than you.'

'Is that a compliment, I wonder?'

Ginnie grinned. 'Coming from me, it certainly is. I'm surrounded by people who need a mega dose of therapy. Including me. So don't talk about madness. Paul will come back and you'll feel normal again.'

'You think so? I miss him desperately.'

'Now throw some stuff in a case. You're coming back with Nicola and me. And Joel will come along too and sleep on my couch. He'd much rather be in London anyhow. Tell him I'll take him to our local Internet café.'

'But I'd arranged . . .'

'Cancel everything. Say you've had to go to London. Say your sister's in a state. Anything.'

Ginnie immediately rose to the occasion. She was always likely to change her mind and do the opposite of what she'd decided five minutes ago, so you never knew where you were with her. It used to drive me mad, but to Nicola and Joel it was absolutely normal. They loved a last-minute change of plans. As soon as we arrived in her Fulham flat, Ginnie rushed around clearing spaces where space was needed and handed Nicola and Joel a duvet each. I was given the spare bedroom, Nicola would sleep on the floor in Ginnie's bedroom, and Joel would curl up on the couch in the living room. Then she sent them both out to hunt down the nearest late-night shop as her fridge only contained yoghurt and mineral water.

'Here. While they're out,' Ginnie said, handing me a mobile phone. 'Get hold of that man of yours. I bet he's fretting just like you.'

I had to wait until the following morning. I knew he would be up early, so I dialled the number of the farm when everyone in the flat was asleep, holding the phone guiltily under the bedclothes.

'What happened?'

'Ginnie decided to take off back to London. And we all came with her,' I said softly.

'Are you all right?'

'Everyone's still asleep. Just a minute.' I heaved myself up the bed, gradually becoming more awake. Nobody would hear us. I didn't need to whisper. 'I was glad to get away from Wengrave. It seemed so empty. What are you doing?'

'I was making a fire to cook breakfast. Wish you were with me. You sound down.'

'Not really.'

'You can't talk?'

I thought I heard a noise in the living room. Even though Joel or Nicola was unlikely to be up at this hour, I tensed up immediately.

'It's difficult. But I'll ring you when I'm home again.'

'Don't forget I love you,' Paul said, lightly. 'It's cold. I put a sweater over my pyjamas and I'm still freezing.'

'So you don't sleep naked?'

He laughed. 'Neither would you out here. There's a thick dew and it's misty. How's Fulham?'

'Quiet.'

At that moment I heard a metallic object clatter onto the kitchen floor and Ginnie's voice crying, 'Bloody thing!'

'What was that?'

'Ginnie coming to her senses. She'll be making coffee. I must go.'

I was becoming calmer. Just hearing his voice steadied me, though I couldn't possibly express what was going through my mind. We had made contact. Just a couple of minutes and the world seemed different. Even the metallic grey sky looked more vibrant. I smiled as I flung on my clothes and prepared myself for the day.

The Easter holiday was over. I decided to take three days' leave from the office to spare myself the misery of coming home every evening to an empty house in Paul's absence. I remained in London, even though Ginnie and I were beginning to get on one another's nerves. It showed in small bursts of impatience but she assured me I could stay as long as I liked. Joel had gone over to Henry's flat, bound for Sheila's cottage in Norfolk. Nicola said she was returning to her flatmates but I guessed she'd be staying with Mark. Ginnie was tearing her hair trying to finish an article on domestic violence. I went to a couple of exhibitions and saw Theodore again in the gallery. He invited me to his next private view. I thought of going with Paul. I went shopping with Nicola but I didn't find the right moment to talk about him. Every now and then Ginnie reminded me, though I didn't need reminding. However awkward, I couldn't put it off any longer. I arranged to take Nicola to a smart place for lunch, which she would choose.

It turned out to be a wine bar, with nothing but sheets of glass enclosing a cavernous area of circular tables and minimal chairs, benches and banquettes, all in primary colours. I went in hesitantly, looking around at the clumps of young people packing out the space. The atmosphere seemed calculated to say 'No-one under thirty allowed in here' but it was probably because there was nowhere like this in Wengrave. I saw Nicola's eyes light up.

'Great, isn't it?' she said, squeezing herself into a corner banquette. She picked up a perspex-covered menu and read down the long list of dishes.

'Anything you like, darling.'

'Really?'

She picked out filo pastries stuffed with spiced aubergine and a Mexican coulis. I surprised her by deciding on a 'beeftek haché and frittes'.

'You know what that is, Mum? Hamburger and chips. And they've spelt it all wrong. Mark would have a fit!'

She delved into the carrier bags, gloating over the shoes and the Calvin Klein jeans I had bought for her.

'Dad never got me anything. He must have passed shops once in a while. He could have thought, "Oh, Nicola would like that." Why didn't he, Mum?'

'Men don't like shopping much. It wouldn't have entered his head, but he always gave you the things you needed.'

This time I had to come to Henry's defence. It was

215

going to be a hard battle, getting Nicola to allow him a place in her life.

'Mark comes shopping with me. He loves it.'

'Daddy liked going to auctions.'

Nicola sniffed contemptuously. 'That's not shopping, it's buying. Quite different. Anyway, you don't have to stand up for Dad any more.'

'I know. But wouldn't it be a good idea if . . . well, you could meet him for a drink occasionally?'

She looked quite affronted.

'What would I say to him? He doesn't understand what I'm about.'

'Why not give him the opportunity?'

'I might one day. As long as he doesn't say something stupid about black people.'

'Sheila might change some of his attitudes.'

'Fat chance,' Nicola said.

A young waiter dressed in jeans and a black polo-shirt delivered our order and stood looking at us.

'Everything all right?'

'Fine.' Nicola was smiling again.

'Enjoy,' he said with a dazzling smile, before walking away.

'Great place, isn't it?' she said again. I admired the way she could divert herself so effortlessly from what she found painful. It was the wrong moment to pursue the subject of Henry.

'My kind of food. That OK?' she asked, waving a fork in the direction of my plate.

'Small but perfectly formed,' I said, glancing down at the small hamburger sitting amongst a few leaves of lamb's lettuce.

We had almost finished our meal and I still couldn't think how I was going to mention Paul. Then Nicola gave me the opportunity.

'Will you and Dad get divorced?' she suddenly asked.

'Joel thought you would. He said you can't live with someone else and not be. He just sees it as a logical process.'

'Oh. I hadn't got that far. It's hard to be that final. At the moment, anyway. I suppose . . . if he really wants to marry Sheila . . .'

'Joel thinks he does. But I don't see why you need to get divorced, not until you find someone else. Why make things easy for Sheila? That's what I think anyhow.' She put down her knife and fork. 'Mum, do you see a lot of Martin?'

'We meet for a meal occasionally,' I said, with a smile.

'But you're not serious, are you?'

'No.'

'Good. I like him but he's not right for you now.'

'Oh?' I couldn't help laughing. 'So who is?'

'Someone younger, more laid-back. He's too old-fashioned for you.'

'I take that as a compliment.' I looked down at my hands. 'It's probably a big mistake, but I am seeing someone younger at the moment.'

'What?' Nicola's eyes were round with amazement. 'Why didn't I know?'

'I thought you'd object.'

'That's not fair. I never expected you to hang around on your own after Dad walked out. Why shouldn't you enjoy yourself? Is he nice?'

'Yes . . . yes. Definitely . . . yes, he is,' I said hesitantly.

'Good-looking?'

'I think so.' I had to stop Nicola's questions. She would worm it out of me anyway.'You know him. It's Paul.'

Nicola looked totally stunned, clasping her hands tightly together.

'What? Not my Paul?'

'It's very hard for me to tell you this. But it's not fair if I don't. I've been seeing him regularly for quite a while . . . after you split up obviously . . .'

'You having a scene with Paul?' she said in a loud voice. Then she quickly lowered it. 'Mum, you're not being serious. You must be kidding.' She stared at me in utter disbelief.

'I'm telling you the truth.'

I tried to explain to her how it had happened, that I'd never dreamed of being involved, that we'd seen one another more and more frequently, that we seemed to get on so well . . . Then she stopped me.

'Are you in love with him?'

'Yes,' I said, trying to keep my voice calm.

'It's disgusting. I'm sorry but that's how I see it. He's a kid compared with you. He's only a few years older than me.'

'I know.'

'Is it because you felt sorry for him because I'd ditched him? Jesus, I hope not.'

She looked as though she might burst into tears at any moment. I longed to comfort her but I knew there was nothing I could say. I took a deep breath.

'I never imagined that we'd fall for one another. It seemed the most unlikely thing in the world. But we did and I can't change that. Not everything happens according to neat little patterns. You can only do what you feel to be right. I felt right with Paul, from the beginning.'

There was a great explosion from Nicola.

'Mum, you're crazy, you're off your head. What's come over you?' She stared at me, not exactly hostile but completely uncomprehending. 'Why him? Why him? Apart from being so young, he's boring-looking, boring to talk to and his background is completely different from yours and Dad's.'

'I think you're wrong, but it doesn't matter.'

Nicola turned away from me, apparently watching the waiters moving to and fro. I knew she wasn't going to let me off lightly. Then she suddenly swung round to face me again.

'You could have chosen anybody. So why Paul? Because you knew him? Because he was around? And if you did fancy him, why make out it was love?'

'I don't expect you to understand. But I wanted you to know.'

'Does anyone else? Does Ginnie? Does Martin?'

'I only told Ginnie. She doesn't understand either. And she thinks I'm crazy, too.'

For a while Nicola was silent, once again ferreting in her bags, stroking the leather of her new shoes as though to reassure herself.

'I won't come home again if he's around.'

'He won't be. You don't have to worry.'

She relaxed a little and leaned on the table towards me.

'I've probably been mean about Paul. But I can't get my head round it, you and him. You can't ask me to, Mum.'

She kissed me goodbye, saying she had to get back to her studies. I wondered about all the confused emotions that must have been rushing through her head. In spite of our storms, we'd always managed to dredge out what we were feeling. If only Joel had been the same. Instead of going by bus, I took a taxi back to Fulham, to give myself an isolated space in which to reflect. I was still reeling from my conversation with Nicola. When I told Ginnie, she wasn't surprised. She thought it would be different in a few months' time, but I could see she didn't really believe we'd be together by then.

It still gave me a shock, all the pressing crowds of London. I missed the sounds of the country. I missed the clear brilliant song of early morning birds. I missed the fresh smell of river water and cut grass by the water's edge. I took the train home with pleasure, not only because I'd soon be seeing Paul again. I still felt that my life would always be in Wengrave.

I let myself into the house. Nicola and Joel's rooms were in a mess, but I would tidy them later. I missed their thundering feet, the calls from one room to another, the constantly ringing telephone. But even if I had come back with Henry, the house would still have seemed silent and empty. I began to wonder what it would be like if I were living somewhere else, somewhere smaller perhaps. Nearby there was a huge house with tennis courts and terraces and lawns going down to the river. I'd met the person who lived there. She occupied only one room of the twelve available, an elderly parent hanging onto the past, surrounded by framed family photographs heaping up dust on the tuneless grand piano. I didn't intend to end up like that.

I listened to various answerphone messages left for Nicola and Ginnie. Then I stopped the machine. I needed to hear this one again. It was from Henry, timed at nine p.m. the previous night. He usually called me from his chambers during the day if anything needed to be discussed. You didn't talk to wives in the evening, not with the other woman around. The other woman. I'd forgotten they used to call them that, but in any case Sheila was no longer an 'other woman'. I wouldn't have been surprised if she was already calling herself Mrs Farringford.

I pressed the play button.

'Hello Sally.'

There was something a little different about that. Oh yes, he rarely used my name. Just 'hello'. That was his usual greeting.

'I wondered if you could make lunch next week.'

I could hear sizzling in the background. He must

have been at home. Was she cooking up his steak?

'There are some things to sort out and it's better if we meet.'

That, too, was different. This wasn't an invitation to lunch. It was a business meeting. He sounded under pressure when he was meant to be relaxing at home. Perhaps they'd had a row. Or he could be dreading my reaction to his news. I made some wild suppositions. He was either about to tell me that Sheila had got sick of him (wasn't sure I'd welcome that) or that he wanted to marry her. If he wanted to marry her, then she'd aim to get as much of his money as she could. If this was a prelude to divorce, I'd better be prepared. There was still time. I immediately phoned Patsy, who had been through it all herself and knew every twist and turn of the matrimonial courts. And I said I'd see her on Saturday for coffee with the girls.

The day after that, I'd be meeting Paul from the station . . .

# TEN
• • •

I was furious with myself for agreeing to take a day off work to see Henry in London. If I'd only thought for a few seconds, I could easily have refused. But after he'd quietly insisted that he had a lot to discuss with me, that it couldn't be said in a letter or over the phone, that he was frantically busy but needed to see me, I instantly gave way. Why didn't I suggest that he could meet me in Wengrave? Why did I always let him have his own way? However much I had changed since I'd been with Paul, my first impulse was still to regard Henry's life as being far more important than my own. Until I could master that impulse, I thought, I would always be tied to him. I longed to be free. If the purpose of our lunch wasn't to discuss our eventual divorce, then I hoped I'd summon up enough courage to bring up the subject myself.

Paul seemed just as anxious as I was about my meeting with Henry. We had been living from one day to the next, so preoccupied with one another that we were reluctant to delve into the past too deeply. I'd never pressed him for all the reasons why it didn't work with Nicola or what other girlfriends he'd had before her, and he rarely questioned me about what it was like being married to Henry. But now it couldn't be avoided.

I was up early with Paul, even though I was in no

rush. We were in the bedroom and Paul was getting dressed. I caught him staring at a long-forgotten pale pink linen suit with a long tailored jacket, which I'd taken from the wardrobe and laid out on the bed.

'I've never seen you in that. You must be going somewhere grand for lunch,' Paul remarked.

'I'm meeting Henry in some Thai restaurant in Bayswater. God knows why he chose it – he probably has a meeting somewhere nearby. But I doubt if it's grand.'

'He should have taken you to the Ritz at least.'

Hopping up on a stool, I peered into the wardrobe and started hunting for a handbag on the top shelf. I scarcely remembered what it was like, having a ridiculously small container hanging by a chain from one shoulder. Handbag. I didn't even use the word any more.

'I expect Sheila suggested the Thai place,' I said, groping amongst several tissue-wrapped packages. '"Why not take Sally to that nice little place in Bayswater? Very reasonable, Henry."'

'Is she really that mean? I bet she'd like you if you ever met.'

'No question of that! And I don't care if she likes me or not,' I snapped.

At that moment, several handbags fell off the shelf into a heap on the floor. I glanced at Paul, who was suppressing a laugh, but I carried on regardless.

The suit no longer fitted me and the skirt hung down straight from my hips to well below the knee. Had I grown slimmer or was that how I used to wear things? I knew it was unflattering. The reflection in the mirror made me grimace.

'Why that?' asked Paul.

'My defence against Henry. I want to look as I was when he left.'

'You're a funny one,' he said, watching my performance with a half smile on his face.

I attached some pearl earrings and a matching necklace. Paul sat on the bed, while I applied an array of make-up. Some of the bottles had gone dry and I threw them angrily in the waste-paper basket. Catching sight of Paul grinning at me in the mirror, I smiled back.

'Crazy, isn't it? I really don't want to see him.'

'Are you sure?' Paul said, coming to stand behind me. 'He might come up with a nice surprise.'

'Like what?'

'He might want to come back to you. What would you do if he walked through the door with a suitcase? And said please Sally let me stay. Would you tell him to get lost?'

I was taken aback by his question. This time, Paul seemed serious. For a moment I wondered if I'd be strong enough to resist if Henry was determined to move back. 'Well, I don't know if I'd put it quite like that . . .'

If only I'd been able to deny wholeheartedly that I'd ever take Henry back, but I was still confused about my feelings and disturbed about the prospect of meeting him.

Paul didn't press me. He went over to the window and stared out into the distance.

'Sometimes I feel I've precious little to give you. I don't have a house, I don't have a car, I don't have much money to spend.'

'It doesn't matter! I just don't care about all that!' I exclaimed.

He suddenly turned round to face me.

'Can't you see? It's hard for me when I want to give you things and go to fancy places. I can't sweep you off to a West End show in a big Mercedes . . .'

'What difference would it make? I don't miss it, not even for a moment.'

Paul looked troubled and I didn't know how I could convince him.

'You must have wanted Henry back at the beginning,' he insisted.

I saw an uncertain, slightly sad expression steal over his face, like a child who's fretting when his parents leave for an evening out.

'For a while, yes, I did long for Henry to come back. There was a gaping hole in my life and I didn't see how I could fill it. But I don't feel that any more. You've changed everything for me.'

It wasn't often I told Paul what he meant to me – perhaps because I still couldn't quite believe what had happened.

'Will you be back tonight?' he asked, as he came over and covered my neck in kisses.

'Nothing will stop me,' I replied.

Just before I left for the station – I had decided I would arrive in a calmer frame of mind if I left the car behind – I decided to abandon the linen suit. Why did I find it so hard to shake off the habit of dressing as Henry would expect? Cross with myself for caring what he thought, I quickly pulled off the necklace and earrings, put on a clinging top that Maggie had given me and a pair of slim-fitting trousers.

I wished I'd arrived late at the Thai Garden but there I was, bang on time. The restaurant was almost empty and the waiters were craning anxiously towards the windows, trying to spot potential customers. Henry came in hurriedly a couple of minutes after I'd settled myself at the only table marked 'reserved'.

'Sorry I'm late. Dreadful traffic. You look different,' Henry commented as he pulled out a bentwood chair opposite me. He leaned over to kiss me on the cheek and sat back.

'Better or worse?' I asked.

'Perhaps it's the hairstyle.' I nodded. Clearly he wasn't overenthusiastic about my changed appearance, but he didn't elaborate. 'I'm so glad you could come.'

We were each handed a plastic menu by an expressionless Malaysian waitress.

'This is a surprise,' I remarked. 'I didn't think you went in for this kind of food.'

'I've had to change a few habits. Sheila's put me on an Eastern diet. It's healthier, apparently. My cholesterol count isn't what it should be.'

'You always seemed perfectly healthy to me,' I said. 'Is she rather neurotic about food? So many people are.'

Henry looked surprised at my comment.

'I wouldn't say that. Not really.'

While he was studying the short menu, I was thinking: why has he brought up her name so early in the conversation? I am Henry and Sheila, he seemed to be saying. It might have been easier to cope with if I'd been Sally and Paul. I tried to quell the hostility he aroused in me by attempting an imitation of Nanny Briggs, the north country woman who helped out when the children were small.

'You must be having too many health checks. It's not right, Mr Farringford. And if you've taken to doing that jogging nonsense round Dolphin Square, I don't want to hear.'

Henry gave a slight laugh, his eyes crinkled and his jaw jutted out a fraction. He did have a sense of humour and I felt a sharp pang of regret that I couldn't share it any more.

'That's one thing Sheila couldn't persuade me into. I leave that to her.'

I pretended to be examining the menu as my pang of regret instantly changed to resentment.

'We haven't met to talk about Sheila, have we? Or have we?'

'Er, no. But she's very anxious to . . . she believes it would help matters if we all met. Or rather, she'd love to meet you,' he said, looking slightly abashed. I couldn't help smiling. Sheila had obviously briefed him.

'Why does she want to see me? So I that could give my approval? Would it make her feel better? And what would we talk about? Which is your favourite position? How funny, I never liked that one.'

Henry looked at me as though I'd gone mad. In the past I would never have expressed myself so crudely. Now, I thought, it doesn't matter. I didn't care what he was about to say. In any case, he had given himself away. Did he really expect me to make up a cosy threesome? Were we meant to have an intimate dinner together? Was this Henry the New Man? What had come over him?

'Shall we order, Sally? Would you like me to recommend something? This place doesn't look anything special, but the food's meant to be very good.'

'It all looks pretty much the same to me. You choose, I really don't mind,' I said, with a smile.

After we'd been provided with a clean paper cloth and he'd given the order, Henry said, 'I do miss the wonderful boeuf en daube you used to make. Marvellous flavour.'

'Really? I've been experimenting since you left. When friends come round, they don't expect to have the same old recipes, do they?'

The moment I said 'friends' I could imagine his mind racing. Is she referring to men? Is she seeing somebody else? Who's coming into my house? But he was too tactful to put the question. I wondered if he might be relieved if someone had taken his place. There was an uncomfortable silence between us. I envied the two girls who had come to sit at a neighbouring table, giggling and chattering with obvious delight.

'Have you seen Martin lately?' Henry asked.

There were only a limited number of topics that you could discuss once intimacy had gone. It was hard to realize that we had been intimate. We'd led separate lives for little more than six months, yet he almost seemed a stranger.

'I meet Martin for a drink and a meal occasionally. He came over at Easter, when the children were at home.'

'Good. He was always so fond of you. Actually, Joel did mention it when he was at the cottage.'

Was Henry looking at me strangely or was I imagining it? I couldn't decipher his expression. Once I could tell almost everything going through his mind.

'What did Joel say exactly?'

'Just that you'd all gone with Martin to see his new boat. And he was going to take you out in it when it's finished.'

I guessed what Henry was implying and cut in quickly.

'We're not having an affair, if that's what you mean.'

'I wasn't going to suggest that for one moment.'

'Though I would if I fancied him.'

I could see that Henry was riled by this.

'I never thought that side of things was very important for you.'

By now we were both showing our irritation, which masked the guilt and resentment we were trying to suppress. I couldn't believe how pompous he sounded. I was becoming more and more reckless, rapidly discarding the habit of censorship that was once second nature.

'Fancy you assuming I didn't like sex!' Henry wasn't sure if I was teasing him or not, and gave a slight smile. I leaned forward as though about to confess all. 'Well, to be honest, I'm not bothered as long as I have it every couple of days or so.'

'You'll have to find yourself a young buck, then.'

'There are plenty around in Wengrave.'

Henry looked so uncomfortable I almost felt sorry for him.

'Indeed,' he said.

'Do all barristers say indeed instead of yes?' I said, softening my voice. There was little to be gained if we escalated into a row.

'That's a strange question. I've never given it any thought. It's a more positive affirmation than yes, I suppose.'

'Indeed.'

We both laughed, which broke the tension. The waitress silently reappeared and set down an array of small dishes that arrived so quickly they must have been hovering on a hotplate somewhere. Henry ignored her and scrutinized me carefully.

'You look remarkably well, Sally.'

I was taken by surprise. What did he mean exactly? Was he trying to say he still fancied me? I wondered what he might have said if he hadn't been my husband. That I looked attractive? Sexy? Younger?

'I'm glad you think so,' was all I said.

I took up the chopsticks and ate a couple of morsels. Henry did the same, but seemed in no hurry to eat. He suddenly rested both chopsticks on his plate.

'Are you getting decent money at that company of yours — what's its name?'

'Hedgehog Graphics.'

'Of course.'

This was Henry's way of having a mild ferret. What is Sally earning? Could I reduce her allowance? Was this the real object of the lunch?

'Some people wouldn't think thirteen thousand a year was decent, but I seem to manage,' I said.

'But that's appalling!' he burst out. 'How can you let yourself be exploited like that? It's barely above the minimum wage. You should ask for more.'

A piece of chicken escaped from between my chopsticks and I hastily took up a fork. I was feeling more and more exasperated, which wasn't helped by having to balance every mouthful of food between two pieces of slender bamboo. Suddenly I guessed what Henry really wanted to talk about.

'For Christ's sake! What do you want to tell me? Is our meeting about money? I'm quite capable of talking about it. Have things got out of control?'

I couldn't quite ask him if Sheila had been running him into debt, as I knew he would never have admitted it. But I wasn't prepared for what he said next. He ran his fingers through his hair and took a deep audible breath.

'It's rather bad news, I'm afraid. The partnership made a rather unwise decision a couple of years ago. We took on a client who turned out to be, well, unreliable. Mind you, at the time we could never have predicted . . .'

'Predicted what exactly?'

'There's no need to go into detail. But we've lost money. A lot of money. And then we had a huge tax bill. Pretty disastrous. It's been a tremendous blow. And I can't see an easy way out.'

'You know I'll keep it to myself. But I think you should tell me about it, Henry. I'm still your wife, after all,' I said, as he appeared to have lapsed into a ruminative silence. When he eventually spoke, he leaned towards me and lowered his voice almost to a whisper. I'd forgotten how secretive barristers have to be.

'Well, we'd been handling a huge fraud case for months . . .'

'The one you told me about? The man who took all that money from the research and development fund in his company?'

'Who is supposed to have. We got him off. And now he's disappeared, owing us near enough a million pounds. Unfortunately, this case took up too much time and we turned down smaller clients. A big mistake.'

'Easy to make, though,' I said, remembering his excitement when he first took on the case. It was a huge challenge for him, but he came alive with challenge.

'The financial situation is pretty disastrous. So we've had to take a huge cut in salary. It's going to affect both of us, I'm afraid.'

'Both of us? Aren't you forgetting Nicola and Joel? And I imagine Sheila comes into it as well.'

He frowned. 'I can't tell you what an idiot I feel. If you live by your judgement – and it lets you down – you wonder what's gone wrong. I should never have allowed it to happen.'

I sat back and tried to repress the mounting sympathy I felt. I knew how proud he was, what his reputation meant to him. But I couldn't help thinking that my replacement was unlikely to suffer.

'I hope Sheila is understanding about it,' I said.

'Luckily she accepted a good job in another company some weeks back. Anyway, I'm being forced by the bank to make severe adjustments . . .'

'Henry! Why can't you come out with it? You want to reduce my allowance. It isn't the end of the world. As long as Joel's school fees are paid and Nicola gets her allowance, I can make do. It's not as though I go on spending sprees every week.'

'I know,' Henry said, looking down at his plate. 'Joel and Nicola are my priority, naturally.'

'Naturally,' I echoed, wondering if he really meant it.

'I'm glad you're being so understanding. It does help.'

I felt sorry for him again. Then I had to remind myself not to feel sorry for him. He had Sheila to comfort him, perhaps even to shore him up financially. A whole list of things came flooding into my mind, all the practical details I'd pushed to one side.

'How much will I need to cut back? I'd rather know, so that I can budget. The house desperately needs some work on it, but I suppose that'll have to be put off for a while. The garage told me it was time to sell the Range Rover as it's getting rather long in the tooth. But I could hang onto it for the time being. And if things are really tight, I suppose I could do all the gardening myself. But I imagine you've worked out how I could manage. Or if you haven't, we could scribble down some rough figures now, if you like.'

I looked expectantly at Henry. He'd always disliked talking about money but he'd probably worked out every detail for how my finances were to be reduced.

'Unfortunately, it's not about small economies. If only it were. To put it bluntly, we're going to have to sell the house.'

They say people always bring up the most painful subjects in restaurants. Is that because they need an audience to share their agony? I sat rigidly still, resting my hands on the table, too shocked to speak. Henry put one pale soft hand over mine.

'I've done everything I could but it's the only solution. Otherwise I'd be on the way to bankruptcy. But it might work out better than you think. The market's strong, our capital will be released and we can both start proper new lives. There'll be enough for you to buy a pretty little cottage . . .' His voice trailed away. My eyes were blinking rapidly to hold back tears, my mind was a complete fog as though I'd been given a great blow to the head. 'I would never have made such a suggestion . . . if it wasn't the only way out,' he concluded.

Slowly I came to my senses and pulled my hand away from his.

'The way out of what? So you can carry on living a comfortable life with Sheila? So you can buy her cars and go on expensive holidays and eat out in the style to which you're accustomed? Is that right? Is that what I deserve?' Henry shifted nervously in his chair. He'd

rarely heard me raise my voice, let alone in public, and
he looked at me with alarm. 'I'm not selling Oakleigh
Grange. We don't even have to discuss it. It's my home
and my children's home. And I don't intend to leave.
You didn't honestly expect me to agree to that? Was it
Sheila's suggestion by any chance?'

Henry was trying to contain his anger.

'Of course not. But now the children are no longer at
home . . .'

'. . . it suits you to take it away from them. For God's
sake, Henry, you're still a father even if you're not
exactly a husband any more. And Joel hasn't even left
school. Where is he meant to come home to? Or has
Sheila got plans for that as well?'

His lips were pursed tightly together, his face tight
with frustration. He didn't need to say it. Sally, don't
get emotional. It only makes things worse. He always
tried to be reasonable and in the past I'd always
admired his calm temperament. But now I was enraged.
And so was he.

'Do you think I want to sell? Don't you think I've tried
everything I can? I'm trying to keep the partnership
together. You know what it means to me, surely?' His
voice was low but he sounded on the edge of hysteria.
I'd never seen him like this and Henry had always been
able to take pressure. 'Do you really want me to go
bankrupt? What would that solve?' He stopped in his
tracks and crushed a prawn cracker into papery
fragments. Then he went on more calmly. 'I beg of you,
Sally, this is just as painful for me. There's no other
solution.'

I looked him full in the face.

'I don't believe things are as bad as you say. How can
I be expected to trust you? You've never let me into
your financial affairs. For all I know, there's a nice pile
hidden away in Jersey or somewhere like that.'

'If you like, I'll get Sam Meerewitz to give you a

statement of my accounts. I've nothing to hide. Please be reasonable. You always have been in the past – it's one of the many things I admire about you.'

I stood up and removed my coat from the back of my chair.

'I don't care whether you admire me or not. I'm not selling the house and that's that. And isn't it time we started talking about divorce?'

'We'll talk about it another time.'

We had reached a stalemate. Henry took out a clutch of credit cards from his wallet to pay the bill and as I was walking out, I saw him beckoning to the waitress.

My anger began to subside into sadness as I sat on the train, staring through the rain spatters on the window at the sodden landscape. I couldn't even contemplate the idea of leaving Oakleigh Grange. I remembered so clearly the first moment I caught sight of the large solid timbered house, half obscured by mature trees. I thought that we would spend the rest of our lives there. It was practically the only decision I badgered Henry into making – he thought it too expensive at the time and said we could have had a Queen Anne house for that price. For me, it was comfortable, airy and well built. I didn't want anything architecturally significant, I wanted a home. Most of all, I fell in love with the garden sweeping down to the river. After we'd moved in, the house seemed to grow around us and we each cornered our own part of it. Henry's study, Joel and Nicola's room, my kitchen – they all contained our history and our identity and were filled with pictures and family photographs and objects collected at random that we liked. I couldn't imagine stripping them away and leaving an empty shell. And I couldn't believe that Henry really wanted it either.

When I told Paul what Henry had said about selling the house, I burst into floods of tears. It was as though my past was being ripped from me, to be given to somebody else. He tried to comfort me but I refused to listen. He tried in vain to suggest that Henry really might be in trouble, that it wasn't the end of the world, that he'd give any help he could but I just carried on sobbing. That night it did seem like the end of the world.

After work the next day, I went over to Patsy's place. She was the only person I knew who could help me face reality. Angela would have offered lots of sympathy and Maggie would have urged me to have a full frontal fight and get my own back on Henry. But I didn't want soothing words and I had no intention of being taken over by all-consuming hatred. I'd seen wives who never forgave their husbands and it poisoned their lives. As for Martin, I couldn't trust him to be objective, not where Henry was involved.

Patsy lived in a penthouse flat overlooking the river in one of Mustafa's developments. It had been a while since I'd sat in her living room. Not having children, she and Mustafa had opted for everything neutral or white. There were no pictures and the only touch of colour was provided by rich Persian rugs. I felt as though I was waiting in the foyer of some discreet intercontinental hotel as Patsy handed me a gin and tonic in a heavy modern glass. She listened carefully while I gave her a brief account of my meeting with Henry. I avoided mentioning that I'd spent the night before in tears, and hoped she wouldn't notice the dark circles under my eyes.

'Typical,' Patsy began, as though she'd heard it all before a thousand times. 'But he hasn't got a leg to stand on and he knows it. So Henry's got a cash-flow problem and wants to realize an asset. Namely, Oakleigh Grange. Worth a bob or two now of course but I bet he knows that.'

'I don't give a damn if it's an asset. It's my home.'

'Yes, yes,' said Patsy, impatiently. 'It is at the moment. What about his other assets?'

'I've no idea. He has a stockbroker, I believe, to manage his investments.'

Patsy turned her glass round thoughtfully.

'We've got to look at your future viability, though. And consider whether there's a positive or negative growth potential if you relocate.' She looked as though she could walk into any company and take it over, in her metal-grey work suit and crisp pink shirt.

'I'm not a business. I'm me,' I objected.

She gave a hearty laugh. 'Sorry. I was just thinking aloud. Want me to talk English?' She had an appealing way of sending herself up.

'I get the drift. Carry on,' I said, with a grin.

'Right. Let's look at the sale option. Number one. It's too big to have just for you and the children from time to time. And it needs a lot of dosh to get it up to scratch.'

'I know that. And so does Henry.'

'Number two. You don't want him to get his mitts on it. So let's work out the middle ground.'

'I'm not going to move.'

'Hang on, hang on. We'll do a "what if".'

'Oh?'

'The advantages of a seemingly negative situation. Get it? The business students love it when I give them that. Stock market crashes overnight. War breaks out in Wales. Hurricane sweeps away the Dome. Who benefits? That kind of thing.'

'Are you saying I should think about moving?'

Patsy gave another hearty laugh.

'I guess I am. But only as an exercise.'

'Get somewhere else?' I heard myself saying the words, which seemed to echo round the white walls.

'You could optimize your position.'

'Meaning?'

'Here's a rough projection. Have you got a sharp lawyer? Silly question, of course you haven't though I bet Henry has. I'll find you one. Get a settlement prior to agreeing to sell the house. You need, say, seventy-five per cent of the realizable value – after deduction of the agent's fees – to find a new family home and maintain your standard of living. Twenty-five per cent to Henry, give or take a per cent.'

'Twenty-five per cent? Why? I don't see . . .' I objected.

'Show generous. It's always a good ploy. Now, this is what I'd do. Sell in a peak market, rent for a while and then buy low for cash. You'd do really well out of it, Sal. And I could just see you in one of those highly desirable new riverside flats.'

'Mustafa's development, you mean?'

I smiled to myself. Patsy was an excellent promoter of her husband's property interests.

'Exactly. I'd twist his arm to give you a nice little discount.'

'Your analysis is brilliant,' I said, with a smile. 'You've given me a lot to think about.'

It was far too soon for me to have a clear plan of action, although I could see that for Patsy the solution was simple. Did I really have to go down that road? I was appalled at the idea of lawyers sparring at one another like pit bull dogs, with Henry and me staying safe on the sidelines trying to avoid one another.

Patsy made further attempts to persuade me that everyone was buying modern nowadays and who wanted the upkeep of an old pile like mine that wasn't even Grade 11 listed? She was rushing out to a banking dinner, but I promised that this time I really would meet her for coffee with Maggie and Angela. I hoped that my news about Henry's bombshell would divert them from speculation about Paul – Angela was bound to have mentioned bumping into us at the Hedgehog book launch. I was both glad and anxious about the prospect of seeing them all.

We all kissed and hugged, then took a good look at one another before we sat down at our usual table in the Café Rouge. Maggie's hair was even blonder, her lipstick redder, her jewellery heaped on more profusely than usual. Angela was wearing an Indonesian print dress – I recognized the design because we'd chosen the material and the pattern together. Patsy had on her version of Saturday casual, a sporty Ralph Lauren tracksuit. I was the odd one out, in a crumpled linen jacket and jeans. Really we didn't seem as though we belonged together at all.

I plunged in straight away and gave a more exaggerated version of the Henry story than I'd given Patsy.

'You poor thing. It's really frightful,' said Angela, sprinkling a pile of brown sugar onto her coffee.

'And he didn't even take you to a decent restaurant to break the news. Mean bastard,' commented Maggie.

'We mustn't let him do it. There must be a way of stopping someone from taking away your house. How about a sit-in?'

Maggie looked horrified at Angela's suggestion.

'You mean a squat? But nobody does that kind of thing here.'

'I hadn't thought of that. What fun!' exclaimed Patsy. 'But you'd need a gang of people. Still, there are plenty of students who need somewhere to live.'

'Sal shouldn't have to put up with that. I wouldn't. Get a smart lawyer and sue the pants off him. That's what I'd do.' Maggie looked to Patsy for the expected confirmation.

'Would you sue a barrister? Not advisable. Sally should go for an amicable legal settlement, helped along by some emotional stuff. Get the doc to say she's 'suicidal, that's a good one.' She grinned at me. 'You'd be good at that.'

'Can I get a word in?' I asked. 'I know he's behaving badly, but I don't want to go to war with Henry. For a start, think what it would do to the children?'

'It's your future,' said Patsy.

'When you have children . . .' Angela began.

'They get screwed up whatever you do. Who'd be a parent?' said Maggie. We all knew she had awful problems with her son, who'd been cautioned at least twice by his school for bullying. 'It just gets too much sometimes. No wonder we all want lovers. If only Jeff would understand that I still want to be a woman occasionally.' Taking a powder compact from her bag, Maggie examined her face, as though she needed confirmation of her female status. 'I need a touch-up,' she remarked. Then she rose from her seat and headed for the ladies' loo.

While she was absent from the table, Angela leaned over to me and whispered, 'She told Patsy she's having an affair. Someone from the tennis club who Jeff knows. Apparently he's very rich.'

'But married,' Patsy said, more loudly. 'She's bonkers about him.'

'And he plays the violin,' added Angela.

Patsy immediately qualified her remark.

'Not professionally. He's taking her to Nice for the weekend. Lucky her.'

'Don't say we told you,' said Angela, conspiratorially.

They were looking at me a little too intently, as though expecting me to exchange confidences. I was uneasy. Jeff was a decent, hardworking man who was good to Maggie in his way. I wondered if she would have been so carried away if her lover had no money. Then I wondered if we would be talking in the same way if we were all living on the edge. Was it merely our comfortable existence that brought us together? Was the bond we had based on genuine feeling for one another? Or would it melt away if our circumstances were different?

'Is that better?' asked Maggie, returning to the table. She turned her head from side to side and presented her face to us, waiting for our smiles of approval. 'Everyone for more coffee?'

Summoned by her wave, the handsome young French waiter immediately came over, twirled round on his feet and disappeared to the coffee machine. 'Couldn't you just go for him?' Maggie said to me.

'If I was twenty years younger I might,' I replied, with a grin. The instant I'd said it, I knew I'd given myself away.

'From what I hear, you wouldn't say no. Am I right?'

I could feel my cheeks burning. Now I was cornered. Angela's face, too, was bright pink but for a different reason.

'Actually . . . I know it was stupid but . . . well, I happened to mention your young man, the one at the book launch,' she said, haltingly. Then she gave me an apologetic smile. 'Still, it's not as though Henry's around, is it?'

'Angela thought you might be an item,' said Patsy.

'I couldn't help noticing the way he was looking at you. Quite adoring, I thought.'

'And we all desperately hoped that dream boy was your lover,' said Maggie, with a meaningful smile.

They were all looking at me expectantly, clearly showing their approval. But I was reluctant to be drawn.

'We're more than good friends, if that's what you mean.'

I attempted to adopt their light-hearted tone but it was taken the wrong way.

'There's no need to be so evasive,' said Maggie. 'Just because he once went out with your daughter.'

Angela gave a start and tried to interrupt her. 'Oh . . . I really didn't mean to . . .'

'You're with friends. We don't need to hide things,' Maggie went on. 'Anyway what does it matter? If I'd netted a young hunk, I wouldn't care where he came from. No wonder you went into hiding. What's his name?'

'I told you. Paul,' Angela said.

Now I was overcome with confusion. Could I continue being the person they expected? I was a spotlit actress alone on the stage, trapped in some terrible nightmare as I recited the words from the wrong play.

'Come on, Sal. You're bonking like crazy and we all envy you like mad.' Patsy's enthusiasm raised her voice several decibels. She quietened a little when Angela touched her arm. 'Let's face it, we're all getting to that age, aren't we? It's not our fault that we get sexier as we get older and our men get less interested. Nature's little joke! Why shouldn't we want a young stud?'

'Shame you can't get one from the doctor!' exclaimed Maggie, laughing raucously as she leant towards me. Angela and Patsy joined in and I waited for the laughter to die down.

'I know what you must have thought. But it really isn't like that,' I said quietly. The waiter set down four cappuccinos. Now all attention was focused on me. I tried to be as open as I could.

'I'm not in it for the sex or because he's young. Nor because I'm lonely. He's completely opened my eyes. He's the first man I've met who instinctively understands me. I'm in love with him.'

I looked at their puzzled faces. They remained silent but I didn't go on. Then Angela spoke.

'Oh dear. How wonderful, being in love.'

'No need to sound so sad. It's not an illness,' said Maggie brightly.

'It makes me sad because it can't last.'

241

'Not everyone wants things to last. Especially now-adays,' remarked Patsy.

Maggie stirred the froth carefully into her coffee.

'I hope he has some kind of work.'

'Oh yes. He does.'

Patsy and Maggie seemed completely nonplussed, as though I'd taken leave of my senses and they'd wait until I'd recovered them again.

'Are you happy?' asked Angela.

'Perfectly.'

'Then that's all that matters.'

Patsy and Maggie began gathering up their shopping bags.

'Does Martin know?' Maggie asked.

'Oh, goodness no,' I replied, feeling more uncom-fortable than ever.

I wished I hadn't told them, that Angela hadn't seen us, that I'd never been found out. I couldn't see how I could bring the two parts of my life together.

Maggie pushed away her half consumed cup of coffee.

'I hate to think of you moving from that lovely house. And make sure that Henry isn't having you on. If I were you, I'd do a little check on his financial situation. It won't do any harm. Do keep in touch, won't you?'

She kissed me goodbye and left with Patsy. Angela came and sat beside me.

'Are you upset, Sally?'

'A little.'

'I wish I hadn't said anything but I'm afraid the damage is done now.'

'I'm not upset with you. And I knew they'd find out eventually. I expect the whole of Wengrave knows by now.'

Angela glanced at her watch and then wrapped herself in a long patterned cardigan.

'I doubt if either Patsy or Maggie has ever been

romantically in love. We share some things but there's a lot we don't. I'm pleased for you. Really I am. Even if you get hurt, you'll look back and think how wonderful it was.' She had a faraway expression, as though she was recalling some private experience of her own. 'I admire you, Sally. You've found yourself a job and a handsome young man. And now, if you want, you can find a new place and start afresh. That must be so exciting. You should be proud of yourself.'

Walking back to the car park, I wondered why the others had been so disturbed when I tried to express my feelings. It was as though I'd broken some kind of unspoken code, like going into Wengrave Rowing Club wearing trainers and a blazer. It would have been far easier for them to accept, I thought, if I'd made light of my affair. Or did they feel awkward, believing that I'd made a complete fool of myself? If you've just confessed your love, what friend could possibly say, 'Don't be such an idiot!' I felt that only Angela had begun to understand, that she might eventually come round to accepting Paul. I didn't take in what she had said before we parted, but now her words began to sink in. I hadn't thought of what I'd achieved – it never entered my head. Perhaps she was right. But I still couldn't imagine how I'd cope with losing the house. It seemed like the final blow.

After a discreet call to Henry's partner, I had discovered that the finances of the partnership were as dire as he'd intimated. When I talked to Sam, our lawyer, he said the only way out was to put the house on the market. I also discovered that it was in Henry's name. I had no idea. It had never crossed my mind to ask. It was then I brought up the subject of divorce and Sam gave me a long lecture about making an effort to save my marriage. What marriage? I said.

*

243

The late blossoms were falling softly to the ground, the tulips furling outwards in the warmth of the sun. Usually I welcomed early June when the garden burst into colourful life, but it was one of those days when a grey pall seemed to have settled over everything. I found myself reflecting on Henry's sudden departure, wondering what I'd have done if I hadn't met Paul. Would I have made a greater effort to ask him to return? Should I have insisted on seeing a counsellor to sort out our marital difficulties? Had I tried hard enough to pull Henry through his mid-life crisis? I even wondered if I had a part to play in his disastrous case. Hadn't I encouraged him to take on the client, when Henry had his doubts? I remembered saying that after the case was over he could take a sabbatical, that we could go away for a couple of months . . .

When Paul came over, I was sitting gloomily on a garden bench, next to a wheelbarrow half filled with weeds I'd pulled up from the vegetable beds. Our gardener was getting too old to do a thorough job. Still, he wouldn't be coming for much longer.

'How were the girls?' Paul said cheerily. 'What's really going on? What should I know? Did you have a good time?'

'All right,' I replied. 'Nothing special. Except Maggie's having an affair with somebody.'

'I thought she was married with kids.'

'People have affairs, even here.'

Paul looked puzzled.

'Are you cross with me?'

'Of course I'm not.'

He took me by the hand and dragged me off the bench.

'You seem down. Leave this. I fancy sitting on the terrace with a beer. Go out there and I'll bring you one. Isn't it a fantastic day?'

Usually being in Paul's presence made me forget

everything that was troubling me. But today I couldn't respond.

'I don't know why I bother with the garden.'

'You love it. What are you talking about?'

'Why slog away for someone else's benefit? The house has got to be sold. It's in Henry's name, anyhow. I can't stop him. I talked to his lawyer.'

I felt that Paul could have shown more sympathy. Yet why did I expect him to understand? There were times – though rare – when the gap between my experience and his seemed difficult to ignore.

'People move around. Why stay in the same place all your life? You might find somewhere you like better, anyhow.'

We were sitting on the terrace, looking down the sloping lawn towards the dancing river. I couldn't imagine being anywhere more beautiful.

'Better than this? I couldn't bear not being within sight of the water, watching the swans drifting past . . .'

Paul looked at me and smiled.

'There's this old nomad on his camel, gazing out at the endless desert. His son's riding along on another camel beside him. Bits of sand are stinging his face. He's hungry and fed up and wants to move to a town. Dad's thinking, I couldn't bear not seeing all this golden sand going on for ever and ever. It's so beautiful. And his son's thinking, when's Dad going to get real? Why can't we sell our mangy camels and get a nice little pad in the souk?'

I laughed.

'So I'm the old dad, am I?'

'I'll take back the old bit. But only on one condition.'

'What's that?' I asked, anxiously. I saw his eyes dancing, but I still found it hard to judge when he was being serious. What did I have to promise?

'Come away with me. It'll have to be your car, but I'm working on that one.'

'But, I can't . . .'

'Yes, you can. Pack a bag right now. And take a map. First we'll go by my place and then we'll set off somewhere.'

I looked at him in astonishment.

'You mean now? But I thought we'd decided . . .'

'Change of plan. Don't you like change of plans?'

'Where are we going?'

'Where we feel like.'

I'd never moved so fast. I found an old sports bag of Henry's, threw in a change of underwear and shoes. In no time I'd jumped into the car beside Paul. We roared out towards the M4.

'Are we going to Cornwall by any chance?' I asked, after we'd been driving for a while.

'Not quite. We'll stop around six, wherever we are, and find somewhere to stay.'

'But we might be in the middle of the country,' I objected.

'Then we'll kip down in the back. There's loads of room.'

This was our first time away. I rested my hand on Paul's knee while he drove, watching the urban sprawl of Reading, the glassy office blocks of Basingstoke and Swindon give way to bright fields, splashes of yellow and rolling hills as we went deeper into the countryside.

The sweet smell of early summer wafted through the open window. I couldn't ever remember having felt such elation.

# ELEVEN

• • •

'How about here?'

We had ended up on a winding country road and found ourselves in the High Street of a market town. I drove slowly past a large timbered building with trails of wisteria over the façade. The hotel seemed neither too off-putting and expensive, nor too depressing.

'Looks pretty good,' said Paul.

We parked in the hotel car park and Paul went over to the reception desk. Even if the room was only adequate, I knew it didn't matter. But I was anxious for Paul, even though he'd seemed quite easy as he strolled up to a boy in a maroon uniform who was on duty. Would they ask both our names? What would he say? Should we have talked about it earlier? The days when unmarried couples booked under Mr and Mrs Smith were long over, but I still felt a twinge of guilt, as though I was an adulterous wife slipping away for a weekend of sin. I hung around a little way away, pretending to examine a row of old sepia photographs.

'Have you got any rooms available?' I heard Paul ask.

'I'll just have a look, sir.'

The boy with savagely short-cut hair behind the counter couldn't have been more than twenty or so. He must have been training there, I thought. Pulling out a shabby leather book, he leafed through the pages.

'You don't have computers yet, then?' Paul asked.

'No, sir. Not here.'

The boy repressed a smile, as though he'd been given instructions to look serious at all times. He looked up at Paul.

'I don't seem to have two single rooms. In any case all the en suite rooms are taken, I'm afraid sir. And I'm sure your mother would like a bathroom. But I can recommend somewhere else.'

'Thanks but we'll move on,' Paul said.

I could hardly believe what I'd heard. Out of the mouth of babes. Baby-snatching. What made him come out with that? Your mother would like a bathroom. Could I really have been taken for Paul's mother? What had he seen? Middle-aged woman, young man. He'd only expressed what everyone must have been thinking every time they saw us together. Don't say anything but . . . if you didn't know you'd assume she was his . . . yes, old enough to be his mother. How on earth must Paul have felt? How humiliating! And how silly of me not to have foreseen that this might happen. We had to leave. Horrified, I rushed out and shut myself in the car. Paul walked out of the hotel and sat down calmly beside me.

'Don't worry. We'll find somewhere better.'

'I want to go back, I can't take this. And you shouldn't have to,' I said, tensely. Then I turned the ignition key. Paul gently took my hand away.

'He was very young. And he didn't have a clue. Don't be upset.'

I leaned back against the car window, my eyes half closed.

'It's always going to be like this. Every time I go out with you, we're going to get strange stares and pointed comments. I know I should just laugh it off. But I can't. It's hurtful. And it's terrible for you as well. It's not fair on either of us. I should have said something before. If I'd thought for a moment . . .'

'Don't be so silly, Sal. Who cares? What does it matter?'

He looked so unconcerned that I flared up.

'It does to me. And it must be even worse for you. I know you're making light of it, but it's only because . . .' My voice was catching. I felt outraged for Paul more than myself. 'You were in an impossible situation. What were you meant to have said? That's not my mother, she's my girlfriend? Why should I expect you to put up with that? What if it happens again? It's better if we don't go away.'

'If that's how you feel.'

'It is.'

'At least let me drive now.'

'All right,' I said.

I wanted to shut out the beautiful evening sun. I hated the boxes of flowers lining the pavement. I hated this smug little town. Everything seemed to be conspiring to tell us that we weren't wanted. I moved grudgingly over into the passenger seat.

'We'll find our way out of here, if I can crack the one-way system,' Paul remarked.

I put on my dark glasses, so that I only had a dim view as we wound our way out of the town. Paul was observing everything around him, pointing out odd things that he found interesting. But I didn't respond. How could he sound so unaffected, when I felt I was growing older by the minute? I removed my sunglasses and pulled down the mirror on the shade in front of me to examine my face. I needed some make-up but I'd left it in the bag stowed in the boot.

'Where are we going?' I asked, petulantly. The sun appeared to be coming from the same direction as before.

'Wait and see.'

Paul half turned and smiled indulgently at me as though I was his kid sister in a bad mood. I suddenly felt ashamed.

'I'm sorry. I shouldn't have taken it out on you. I was overreacting and I've been a pain.'

'I can take it, ma'am,' said Paul, gritting his teeth John Wayne fashion. He suddenly swerved off the main road and we were bumping down a narrow track.

'Where on earth . . .!' I cried.

'Ah. You didn't notice. Back there, I saw a small board. It said farmhouse B and B with en suite and TV. Evening meals by arrangement. Might be OK.'

'And if not?'

'We'll find a barn somewhere. And there's always a field.'

Another sign directed us to a low grey-stone farmhouse, where a cockerel and several chickens were scratching in the grass. To one side there were rows of lettuces, feathery carrot tops and spinach.

'Promise you won't get all worked up? I know what I'm going to say,' Paul said, as we came to a halt next to a mud-spattered van.

'What?' I asked, doubtfully.

'Something like – have you got a room for my wife and me?'

'Wife? Just as bad. That makes me sound old and married,' I said.

'You can stay in the car if you like.'

'No, I'll come inside with you.'

The farmer's wife, a freckle-faced woman in a short floral dress, greeted us with a delighted smile, as though she'd been waiting for our arrival. After we'd briefly glimpsed the room, we decided to stay. Supper would be waiting until eight if we wanted it. Paul ran down to collect our bags while I washed my face in the spotless pink basin, surrounded by sachets of cleansers and shampoo and bubble bath. A large shiny pine double bed with a pink duvet took up most of the space on the polished wooden floor and on a table next to it

250

was a glass vase filled with dark, heavy-petalled roses. There was the sound of wood pigeons fluttering and cooing near the window. I opened it and breathed in the comforting smell of freshly watered soil. Below me I could see a collie, which was barking and scratching away at the back door. I had never been anywhere like this, and Henry certainly hadn't. I doubt if he'd have even known what B and B stood for.

'Just made for us,' Paul said, as he deposited the bags and rolled onto the bed.

'Did she say anything?' I asked anxiously, coming to lie beside him.

'What the lady said is this: there's cucumber soup to start. Then you can have lamb chops or liver and bacon. I said make it lamb chops. OK? We've got half an hour.'

'Wonderful.'

'And she said something else, too. But it's best not to tell you. Otherwise you might freak out again.'

'Oh? What? Tell me!'

'Are you ready? You won't jump down my throat?'

'No, I promise.'

'No smoking in the bedrooms but you're allowed to in the conservatory at the back. Oh yes. And no sex after ten o'clock. So we'd better get a move on.'

'What?' I said, quite taken in. 'She can't have said that!'

Paul laughed and began to slide his hands down my thighs.

We soaked together in the large pink bath and then I decided to dress for dinner, changing my cotton trousers for a skirt. Paul produced a bottle of wine from his bag and then we took our place in a small room where four pine tables were laid out for supper. A wide-eyed child stared at us in amazement until the farmer's wife dragged him away. Then the collie dog took his place, sitting with its mouth open, dribbling with anticipation by Paul's side. The meal was fresh and wholesome, the kind I would have cooked at home. After we'd consumed an apple tart, the farmer's wife – whom we knew as Jean by the end of the meal – presented us with a bowl of chocolates.

'Happier now?' asked Paul, stretching out his arms.

'Couldn't be more,' I said, smiling.

The following morning we breakfasted on crisp bacon and deep yellow eggs, sitting in the small garden at the back with the sun pouring onto our faces. I couldn't bear the thought of leaving. I was languid and slow from lovemaking, while Paul was bursting with energy. He walked round the garden, examining the fruit trees and throwing sticks for the dog. Then we both lay on the freshly cut grass, cups of coffee at our side.

'I can't believe we're here,' I said. 'It's all so unreal, as though my alarm clock's about to go off, I'll wake up in a panic and be late for work.'

'I dreamed about running away with you right from the start. After we'd made love the first time, I kept imagining you in all different places. Sally in the jungle. Sally in the desert. Sally basking like a seal on the rocks. And I thought of you swimming naked underwater. I bet you're a good swimmer.'

I grinned. 'Not bad. But I can't dive.'

'Neither can I. But I can stay on a surfboard. Most kids can who grow up in Cornwall.'

He began to talk about his childhood in Falmouth and I tried not to think what a short time ago it seemed. What had I been doing when he was ten and cadging trips on fishing boats, playing truant from school? I'd already been married to Henry for a few years. When he was ten, I'd have been . . . twenty-six.

'What were you up to when you were a kid? I bet you had a pony.'

'I did, I'm afraid. So did Ginnie. Hers was a terror, of course. Always bolting.'

'And a school uniform.'

'Oh yes. With a little grey pleated skirt and a blue Viyella shirt that itched like mad. And a gingham dress for summer.'

'Have you got any photos? I'd love to have seen you then.'

'Somewhere,' I said, vaguely.

Paul rolled over onto his back, staring up at the fluffy summer clouds slowly drifting above us.

'Tell me some more.'

'It was a long time ago,' I said.

I sat up cross-legged and finished my coffee. I found it impossible to elaborate on my childhood. If I gave any more details, I would be setting myself firmly in what for Paul would be a far distant past. The Sixties clothes, the music, the cars – they would all be history to him. He wasn't even born when I was ten. It would be like turning the pages of an old yellowing magazine you'd found in an attic. But I couldn't keep my past hidden for ever. I couldn't be sure that one day I wouldn't give myself away with a slip of the tongue.

'You've never asked me how old I am,' I began. Paul didn't stir. 'But you must have wondered.'

'Not really.'

'The lads at the yard must have asked.'

'Never. Only your name.'

'Well . . .' Paul lazily turned to look at me. I took a deep breath. 'I'm forty-two.'

I was expecting disbelief, astonishment, and even outrage. Forty-two! Really! How could you be! Why wasn't he in a state of shock? His expression hadn't changed. Had he known all along? Had someone told him perhaps? How long had he known? What could he be thinking now? She's even older than I thought. How can I stay with a woman over forty?

'Girls always worry about age, don't they? Even Sam. I'm getting old, she says. I'm nearly twenty-one.' I winced, wishing he hadn't brought up her name. 'I've never thought age was important. It doesn't matter to me, anyhow. You remember some things I don't. But I remember some things you can't. What's it about? Your memories going farther back than mine? So what if you can remember the Second World War?'

'But I can't! I'm not that ancient,' I said, indignantly.

'All right. The Festival of Britain.'

This time I did realize he was pulling my leg. 'There are other things besides memories . . .'

'Like?'

'You must look at my body sometimes and think, I wish she was twenty years younger.'

'Never. Do you really believe that I'm sizing you up and down, comparing you to a page three pin-up in the *Sun*? Your body is fantastic. It's you. I can't separate the two.'

'I thought that's what men did.'

'I wouldn't know about other men.'

We lay in the garden until the sun began to grow hot.

'How about staying another night and leaving early tomorrow?' Paul suggested. 'We could walk to a pub across the fields . . .'

'I can't,' I said. 'Joel's calling at six. I've got to be home.'

'Couldn't you phone from here?'

'I can never get hold of him during the day.'

'Oh.' Paul looked disappointed and a little impatient. Then he smiled. 'You still have to remind me sometimes that you're a mum.'

Reluctantly we had to pack up our bags and begin the drive back. I stayed at the wheel while Paul navigated, finding a network of obscure back roads to delay our return. If only we had had longer.

'I can't imagine ever going away without you. There'd be no point,' Paul remarked, as we meandered eastwards in the rough direction of Wengrave. It was then that I must have realized we would be together for a long time. During the summer holidays, I decided, I would tell Joel. I couldn't exclude Paul from my family for much longer and I was growing impatient for my future to be settled. Henry's shadow was still lurking behind me.

A few days later I had a meeting with my new lawyer, Jane Bradley. Having taken Patsy's advice, I was preparing myself for a major battle. However determined I'd been to hang on to Oakleigh Grange, I now had to face up to the fact that it would have to be sold. Jane kept assuring me that she'd insist on a decent percentage from the sale. I couldn't work out what was fair or what wasn't. Hadn't Henry paid for the house? Worked hard to pay off the mortgage? What had I done? Part of me still wanted to leave everything in Henry's hands and take whatever was offered me. But Jane quickly scotched that idea. A marriage is a working partnership, she told me. For two weeks she had been battling with Sam Meerewitz, attempting to secure an agreement.

We'd had a particularly harassing day at Hedgehog Graphics and were in the middle of the June strategy meeting. Jed lost his temper with Pickle and I was trying to mediate between them. Just when I thought I had suggested a workable solution to their differences – which usually centred on whether to spend more time on commercial ventures and less on poorly rewarded ones – the temporary secretary rang through to Matt's office on the red phone reserved for urgent calls.

'For you, Sal,' said Matt.

'Are you sure? Who is it?'

'Someone called Jane. She's holding for you. It's urgent. I'll put her through to your office.'

I ran downstairs to my desk. Jane sounded jubilant.

'Meerewitz has given way to my last demand. At last! We've got a workable agreement and you'll be safeguarded. There are one or two clauses I'm still not happy about, but we might give in to Henry on those. See what you think. But we've got the percentage I discussed with you. And a cash settlement later if and when the partnership turnover improves.'

'You've done well,' I said, without enthusiasm.

'Aren't you pleased, Sally?'

Jane sounded rather indignant and I couldn't blame her. But my heart sank. Soon the house would no longer be mine. Everything would be packed away. All that would be left would be marks where the pictures were, damp patches and worn carpet. Removal men would trample over the flower beds I'd planted year after year, and rip up the carefully tended lawn. I could only see devastation.

'It may be inevitable, but it's still a trauma for me. I'm not used to selling houses. Especially mine. And where is my son meant to stay in the holidays? It couldn't have come at a worse time,' I answered, my voice rising with emotion. 'Are you sure there wasn't a way round it? Have you really done everything you can?'

I could hear an impatient sigh.

'We got beyond that point days ago. Do I need to go over it again?'

'I suppose not.' I was silent for a few moments. 'When exactly will the house be on the market?'

'As soon as possible. Henry did point out that this is the best time for an above-market price. Obviously one will aim for that.'

'Obviously.'

Above-market price? That would be Sam's phrase. Or

was it Sheila's? I'd never known Henry to be pre-occupied with market prices. Unlike the husbands of most of my friends, he'd never fussed over figures. He hated talking about money. It was either there or it wasn't. I used to admire the lofty contempt with which he dismissed predictions about property or high-tech investments. No longer. He was probably poring over account sheets at this very moment. Poor Henry.

A few days later, I was in Jane's office signing away the house. Or that was how it felt. Even though she did her best to convince me, it was hard to believe that it had nothing to do with Sheila. In low moments, I suspected that Henry's financial crisis was a manipulative lie dreamed up by her. What was her ultimate goal? To take away everything I had? To turn the children against me? To make it seem as though it was my fault that Henry had left?

I wrote a letter to Joel giving him the news, explaining the situation and trying to sound enthusiastic about finding somewhere a little smaller. When I spoke to him, he said it was all lousy for me. But he seemed more interested in whether we'd make more than a million. No doubt Sheila had given him a lesson in housing markets. Nicola hit the roof, cursed and swore, and then offered to come and help me pack up when the house was sold. Ginnie commiserated briefly, then congratulated me (or rather Jane) on getting a good deal and said I'd get a presentable three-bedroom flat in Fulham for that kind of money.

I had seen Jane in the morning. By late afternoon I had received a call from Jeremy at Maxton's saying how delighted he would be to handle the sale of the house. (Henry had been unusually quick off the mark, I thought.) They'd get a brochure out in no time and Jeremy had already drafted the description, which he read out. 'One of the most desirable family residences

257

in Wengrave with superb gardens and river frontage'. With the buoyant market, he could assure me of a quick and extremely profitable sale. I could hardly believe that my life could be turned upside down so quickly. One phone call was all it took. A large board in gothic lettering was put up, despite my objections, by the front gate. Two photographers roamed round the house and garden choosing the most flattering angles. They had barely packed up their aluminium cases when the first 'clients' (Jeremy's words) rolled down the drive in a Porsche. I hadn't even tidied up.

After they'd left, having shown 'very keen interest' according to Jeremy, I had a welcome call from Martin. He was in Buenos Aires visiting some factory or other and telling the boss what to do. Or that's what he said. I almost wept as I told him the fate of our house. I thought he'd be as devastated as I was.

'Of course it's terrible,' he said. Then he corrected himself. 'A bit of a shock, I mean. Not necessarily terrible.'

'A terrible shock, Martin.'

'It should never have happened. Henry's been a damn fool. I said to him at the time, don't take on that case. It didn't smell right. Know what I mean?'

'Oh? I never knew you'd discussed it.'

'He wouldn't listen. Typical Henry.' (Thank God I brought it up. So it wasn't entirely my fault that Henry had taken the wrong decision.) 'You'll need some help with the house. When it gets to a serious buyer, I'll see that Maxton's are doing their job properly.'

'The house is likely to be sold before you even get back,' I said, after Martin had given me the dates of his comings and goings. 'I did want you to come over one last time.'

'Seeing you is the most important. And guess what? I'm taking delivery of the new boat. They tell me young Paul has done a splendid job. Know what I'm calling her? *Water Gypsy*. So book in yourself and the children for a river cruise. Champers, naturally. I'll call the moment I'm back.'

Since my visit to the boatyard, Paul had scarcely mentioned the progress of Martin's boat. All he said was that he didn't approve of his choice of engine – unnecessarily powerful for a craft like that. The summer season was getting into full swing and he was constantly busy keeping boats in riverworthy order, harried by their anxious owners. *Water Gypsy* had been finished over a month ago, but he'd forgotten to tell me.

'You can report back on what Martin really thinks. People always find something they don't like. Watch out, though. I could be spying on you from the riverbank,' said Paul, when I told him that Joel, Nicola and I were booked for the maiden voyage.

'Don't you dare!'

'We'll see,' said Paul, with a laugh.

'I'm afraid Martin isn't great with anything mechanical. Anything he buys has a habit of breaking down.'

'Don't worry. I'll take him through it. I'll make sure he's clued up on the engine and controls before he takes you out. It's an easy boat to manage. But I'd take your lifebelt just in case.'

'Oh dear. You think I should?'

'You can all swim, can't you?' he said, with a grin.

Martin arrived back a week later. He delayed the date he had fixed for his outing until after Joel had taken his exams. I immediately phoned Nicola but she made several weak excuses not to come so I pressed her a little further.

'Is it because you don't want to come on your own? I'm sure Martin would like to meet Mark. Why don't you both drive down here, stay the weekend . . .'

259

'No. I . . . I don't think so, Mum.'

She sounded hesitant.

'Paul won't be staying, so you won't have to see him.'

'Well then, maybe I will. I'll call Mark, see if he's free.'

I knew this was not the time to tell her how I felt. For one weekend, Paul and I would have to be apart and I wouldn't be able to mention his name. Nicola was still adamant that she couldn't accept we were together. It pained me but for the moment I could do nothing. Nicola rang back after a few minutes.

'Mark's got to talk at a library conference that weekend. But I'd really rather not come, nothing to do with him, though.'

'Yes?'

'It's about the house.'

'I haven't hidden anything from you. You know all the reasons,' I said, gently.

'I still don't see why you agreed to sell it. I really don't. I think you're giving into Dad. You're letting him walk all over you.'

'That's just not true.'

'Mark says you can get a lawyer to stop people selling things. It's our home, Mum! Just because Dad's spun you a yarn about being broke . . .'

'It isn't like that and he hasn't. I didn't believe it at first, but I'm afraid it's true. Anyway, why don't you just come for Sunday? Martin would love to see you. And Joel's going to be here.'

'I'll see.'

That was the nearest Nicola came to committing herself. The day before, she left a message to say she'd promised to have supper with a friend, which she'd forgotten about completely.

On Saturday morning I collected Joel from the station. I wondered if he would comment as it was hard to

one with long dark hair.' I nodded. She used to love climbing the largest trees in the garden. 'Only I promised her one of my CDs.'

'You don't have to ask,' I said.

I suddenly remembered what it was like, the first time when you tentatively approached someone you fancied, apprehensive and a little ashamed of your boldness. Then Joel's expression changed, and he became a worried little boy.

'When the house is sold, will all my things be safe?'

'Of course they will. I'll pack them up myself, don't worry.'

Martin's house used to be a second home for Joel and Nicola. It was a ten-minute car ride away from us, a typical riverside wooden ranch house set amongst trees. As soon as the weather grew warm, we all used to gather on his terrace. I knew the barbecue would be lit so that Martin could begin the lunch ritual half an hour after we arrived. He always went into a frenzy of activity when the children came round. Looking back, I suspected that he would have been a better father than Henry.

I was keeping an eye on Joel from under a sun umbrella, sipping champagne and freshly squeezed orange juice. He was driving Martin's tractor at a vertiginous speed around the rough grass at the side of the house.

'Can he control that thing? I hope he doesn't do any damage,' I said to Martin, who was bent over the outdoor barbecue, controlling the heat of the charcoal with a pair of bellows.

'He won't. It's an all-terrain vehicle,' Martin commented proudly, without looking up. 'And it brings a whole new perspective to gardening.' He rose to his feet and turned over a selection of ribs, chops and sausages blackening on the grill. 'Jo-el!' he yelled over the sound of the tractor. 'Grub's up.'

Martin threw himself into everything with such energy, as though proving to the world that he wasn't a day older than forty, though he must have been a couple of years over sixty by now. If I dwelt on the past and the happy times we had spent with him, I'm sure the children would have welcomed it if we'd ended up together. But now it was impossible. I couldn't go back on what had happened with Paul, even if we didn't stay together. Nor could I 'keep Martin in reserve' as Maggie had once suggested. It wasn't just cowardice that prevented me from saying I had fallen for someone who was nearly forty years younger than he was. I couldn't bear to hurt him, to see the humiliation on his face. Would there come a time when I would lose him as a friend? In moments of doubt I felt as though I had made a terrible bargain, that by staying with Paul I would have to give up everything. I tried not to think that the days of sitting on Martin's terrace would soon come to an end.

By the time we'd eaten the gargantuan lunch, I'd drunk far too much champagne and followed Joel and Martin rather unsteadily down the twisting path that led to the river. Martin stopped by what appeared to be a newly put-up garden shed. Then he handed a black electronic device to Joel.

'Stand here and press that.'

The doors slid apart and there, bobbing gently in the water of the boathouse, was *Water Gypsy*. The hull had been varnished to a mirror-like surface and the boat was decked out with a blue-striped fringed canopy and velvet-cushioned wicker seats.

'Proper wood, not that fibreglass rubbish,' Martin said to Joel, glowing with pride and pointing at the large curling gold letters painted on the side. 'And wonderful workmanship. All proper brass screws. You'll never guess who made it. Remember Paul Burridge?'

'Of course. He used to play football with me. And we went fishing, too.'

'He's working at Edgeworth Marine. Doing very well, they tell me.'

Joel grinned. 'He was ace at making things. It's brilliant.'

My skin prickled as though I'd been given a mild electric shock.

'Can we get in it now?' I asked.

'I'll take down the canopy first. Then you can get the Riviera suntan.'

Martin eased down the canopy, grasped hold of my hand and guided me into the boat.

'It's all right, Sal,' he said, mistaking my slightly drunken hesitancy for fear. 'You'll be quite safe. Sit next to me. Joel can go on the back seat, check the exhaust.' He lowered himself down onto the captain's seat and put a small key into the ignition and turned it. There was a muted roar. 'Old Edgeworth wanted to put in some piddling little engine. I soon changed that! Joel, you can have a go later. Now watch this.'

We lurched out into the river with a wake large enough for a paddle steamer, and in no time we were rushing upstream, with ducks, geese and moorhens scooting out of our way. Martin was showing as little concern for speed on the river as speed on the road, and I was feeling queasier by the minute. When we came to a wider stretch of river, he suddenly accelerated even more.

'Feel the power in that!' Martin said, glancing back at Joel. He allowed himself a few seconds to demonstrate while I clung to the side of the boat. Then, to my relief, he slackened off the engine. 'Now I'll keep to cruising speed.'

There was still a huge wake behind us and I turned round to see how Joel was taking it all.

'Fantastic, isn't it?' he said, with a huge grin.

Joel took over from Martin, handling the boat with far more expertise. We'd travelled another couple of kilometres when the wind suddenly rose and a big raindrop splattered against my face. Martin noticed the large dark cloud coming in our direction.

'Better head back. Swing her round,' he barked.

On the few occasions I'd been on a friend's boat, the mildest man turned into a dragon when at the wheel. Martin was no exception.

'No need,' shouted Joel. 'If you pull into the bank, I can put the canopy up.'

'The canopy's to keep the sun off, not the rain. It won't last long and we'll soon dry off at my place. I'll take over now,' he said, coming forward to take Joel's place. Obediently, Joel made way for the captain and crawled over to the back seat.

'She's going well, isn't she?' Martin said, settling back on the damp velvet, clearly unperturbed. The rain slackened off and turned into a light drizzle. Another twenty minutes or so, and we should be back. Glancing back at Joel, I saw that he had twisted round on his seat to face the stern.

'Martin,' he called out. 'There's a lot of black smoke back here.'

'Nothing to worry about,' Martin replied. 'New engines always smoke.'

I glanced back at Joel, who shrugged and made a face, unconvinced by Martin's diagnosis.

'Might it be sensible to slow down?' I suggested.

'Not at all. If I go faster, then I'll burn off the oil.'

Joel edged his way forward and knelt by our seat.

'I'd take it easy, if I were you.'

'Everything's fine. Sit back and enjoy yourself.'

There was nothing we could say and I could sense Joel's frustration. I imagined us drifting helplessly in the strong current. I kept glancing back as the smoke developed into a pall of black that hovered over the water. After another five minutes the engine began to wheeze and splutter. By now even Martin had begun to admit defeat.

'We'll be at Edgeworth Marine in a few minutes. There should be someone there to sort us out.'

'Can't we stagger on?' I said, trying to dissuade him. But Martin refused to listen. He just made it to a pontoon and jumped onto dry land while Joel tied up the boat.

'Why don't you come in with me? This might take a while,' Martin called out.

'I might as well stay here,' I said.

'There's no point, Mum. We won't be going back on the boat,' Joel remarked. 'I bet they have to take out the engine. Rotten luck.'

By now I had completely sobered up. I didn't know whether Paul would be at the yard, but he had said he might drop in for a couple of hours. With any luck he would have left by now. A bell rang as we came through the door of the Marine Stores, and Sam appeared from the back and walked quickly towards us. She gave me a curious look and then smiled winningly at Martin.

'How's the boat? Everything OK, Mr Hunt?'

'Just a spot of engine trouble, that's all,' he said. 'I wondered if Paul was around. I'm sure he could sort it out.'

'You bet,' she said, sitting on the counter and crossing her legs. Today she was wearing a short skirt instead of her usual jeans. Her legs were long and tanned, and Martin couldn't take his eyes off her. Then she leaned backwards so that her T-shirt pulled tightly over her breasts.

'Paul!' she yelled. 'Can you come?'

At the far end a door opened and Paul appeared. Even now, after I'd got to know him so well, I still had the thrill of recognition. It wasn't often I saw him at a distance. I was sure I'd given myself away and could only trust him to handle the situation. I kept a smile on my face to conceal my frayed nerves. Sam slithered off the counter and ran up to him.

'*Water Gypsy*'s got some trouble. And your girl-friend's here,' I heard her say.

My heart missed several beats. I glanced at Joel, then at Martin, but they didn't seem to have taken in what she said. I was so unnerved that I was on the point of inventing an excuse to leave. Paul didn't appear to have noticed either, greeting us all in the same friendly manner. Martin had lost his captain's persona and seemed rather flustered.

'Well, I suppose one expects these things. I invited Sally and Joel for the maiden trip. First she went like a dream, then we had a bit of a let-down. Not your fault, I'm sure,' said Martin.

'Let's take a look,' said Paul.

He went off to the mooring with Joel and Martin, while I hung back. Sam came up to me.

'Paul should've gone with you. He'd have sorted it.'

'Yes,' I said, beginning to walk into the yard.

As there were no customers in the stores, Sam strolled out and caught me up.

'Fancy you knowing Mr Hunt. Paul never said anything. Is he a relative or something?'

I assumed she was insinuating something more, though later I realized she was merely being curious.

'No, we aren't related,' I replied, rather brusquely.

'Just friends, then,' she said, settling herself on a log. Then she looked up at me and smiled brightly. 'I wonder if you and Paul will get engaged. He's very keen, you know.' Her remark was so unexpected that my mouth dropped open. 'Sorry. I can't help being nosy. They're always telling me off about it. I don't mean to be rude but it just comes out that way.'

'That's quite all right,' I mumbled. Then I turned

towards the river. 'I'd better see what they're up to down there.'

'See you later, Sally,' she called out as I began to walk away.

Martin came striding towards me along the wooden pontoon, with Joel on one side, Paul on the other.

'A few days' hospital treatment for *Water Gypsy*. That'll do the trick.' He put an arm round my shoulder. 'We'll take a taxi back to my place. Could you get us one, Paul?'

'Sure,' he said, setting off for the stores.

'He's a good lad,' commented Martin, slipping his arm through mine.

For the rest of the evening, I'm sure I was dreary company. I sat outside, staring at the oversized urns of spilling geraniums and the lawn dotted with statues of nymphs and fauns that Martin had collected. Joel and Martin had set up a ping-pong table on a corner of the terrace, and were engaged in a furious game. I ought to have joined them but I was overcome with gloom. I couldn't see a way out. If I stayed with Paul and openly admitted his existence, I didn't see how I could face the pain and dismay it would cause. My feelings were becoming too intense and I began to wonder if I should see him less often, to try and distance myself.

Sometimes it felt as though we were worlds apart, anyway. Was I deluding myself that it didn't matter? I couldn't imagine creating a life together. I couldn't fit our dream into any kind of reality but once the house was sold, I hoped my life would be easier. I would throw myself into finding somewhere that I would like, where the children would feel comfortable. I would make an effort to relish my independence.

Everyone seemed concerned about where my next home should be, as though it was the most important decision I would ever make, and that my identity would be forever fixed by which street I chose, what kind of house I ended up in. All my friends rustled up property experts to advise me, while Maggie and Patsy spent a serious amount of time working out the relative benefits of old build and new build. Even in the Hedgehog office, my move was a constant topic of conversation. During the lengthy breaks for coffee and doughnuts (the summer was usually a quiet period for them) finding 'Sally's new gaff' was a major pre-occupation for Pickle, Jed and Matt.

'You know what I'd do, Sal?' said Pickle, on one of these occasions. 'Buy a barn and live in a great big open space. Wouldn't that be brilliant? Then you could give parties every week and we could all come.'

'I'd go for a horse-drawn caravan myself,' said Jed. 'Then if you got bored, you could move around.'

Matt ambled over to give his contribution.

'You could try living on a houseboat. I've got a mate who's got one near Sonning. It's great. Why not take a look?'

Pickle instantly changed her mind.

'Better than a barn. Really cool, cos you can play music all night and there's no crappy neighbours. How about it, Sal?'

'It's an idea,' I said with a smile. Did Pickle really think I'd be staying awake playing my favourite CDs at top volume? She probably did. 'I've been wondering about this one. Here, have a look.'

I passed her a crumpled leaflet from a pile on my desk. I hadn't mentioned it to Paul. Whenever he asked me if I'd seen anything I liked, I gave a vague answer. Jed came and peered over Pickle's shoulder.

'My mum would love that! And you've got the river at the end. Nice view.'

For some reason I couldn't explain at the time, I kept coming back to this unlikely, rather genteel residence.

There was a three-bedroom top flat for sale in a timbered Thirties block. I never expected such a place to meet with the Hedgehog gang's approval – and it certainly wouldn't have impressed Ginnie or any of my friends. It was unmodernized, with a Seventies kitchen and bathroom that reminded me of the flat I had been living in when I met Henry. The rooms were spacious and I had already begun to imagine how I might change them. There was a balcony that ran the length of the flat. I couldn't explain exactly what appealed to me, except that I felt a welcoming atmosphere the moment I walked through the door, as though the previous occupants had been happy living there.

'Has Paul seen it yet?' asked Jed.

'No. He's been too busy,' I said, hastily.

'Let's see.' Matt took the leaflet from Pickle. 'Ah yes. I know that place. It's an old block they did over way back in the Seventies. It used to be an old folks' home.'

'That'll do me, then,' I said with a grin.

'You'll have to wait at least forty years!' retorted Pickle.

She sat herself on the corner of my desk, munching a doughnut and ignoring the crumbs straying over the surface.

'Are you going to live in your new place with Paul?' she asked.

'I'm not sure . . . Well . . . It's not really on the cards at the moment. I mean, it's a big step to take,' I answered, haltingly.

'Good thinking. You got to be your own person, Sal. Why should he land himself on you? I had a bloke once, wanted to move in after our first weekend. No way, I said. You can come when I ask you.'

Whenever I felt myself weakening, I would take courage from Pickle. She had grown up taking for granted the freedom I had only briefly experienced. But I wondered if she had ever fallen in love? If so, would she have been so skilful at defending her own interests? So sure of her own ground? I began to fear that against my will I was starting to become too dependent on Paul, that very soon I'd slip back into a wifely role and give in to him in the same way as I'd given in to Henry. On one occasion I remember Paul saying he wished we could live together, that it was ridiculous going back to separate places. Then, I rejected the idea because of Joel and Nicola and never questioned whether it was what I really wanted.

Now I was beginning to wonder . . .

# TWELVE

● ● ●

Oakleigh Grange was sold, signed over to a stranger and the final procession was beginning to rumble down the drive. A vast pantechnicon, which would carry away most of the contents of the house to a storage centre, was followed by a smaller truck containing a few of my personal belongings and the minimum of furniture. I kept my eyes firmly fixed in front of me as I went through the gate for the last time. I refused to look back at the luxuriant blooms, the roses and peonies in the beds, the fuchsias and lobelias hanging down in profusion from the stone urns by the front door, the whispering willow by the river. It was hard to imagine that Fernwood Court would become my home, but it was now mine in name and the first place I had ever owned.

It was like burying someone, leaving a house. I wanted to put up a blue plaque outside to remind everyone that Oakleigh Grange used to belong to us. Here lived the Farringford family – Henry and Sally, Joel and Nicola. A year ago it would have been inconceivable that I would be leaving everything behind me. I didn't ask Paul to come with me, nor any of my friends. I didn't want anyone to witness my final separation.

How small it seemed! Every room of my new home was piled up with boxes and furniture, even though I had done my best to rid myself of anything I didn't like or never used. I couldn't think where I would start, though my first instinct was to unpack Joel and Nicola's boxes, to arrange their rooms in case they came unexpectedly.

I had managed it! Found a place and moved into it without consulting anybody. On my first night alone, I was jubilant. I tore open the box marked Day One, pulled out a plate and a mug, heated up some soup on the old cooker and sat on a kitchen chair. Then came my first phone call.

'How are you? Are you settled in?' asked Paul.

I perched against a box, balancing the phone on my lap.

'I'm like a refugee who's suddenly been given a place to live. I'm here! I can't believe it.'

'You sound over the moon.'

I thought I heard a slight tone of regret in his voice and was on the edge of saying, 'Come over now' but I checked myself. However tempting, I wouldn't allow him through the door until I had created some order and unpacked a few things that would stamp my identity on the bare rooms. He had only seen the flat from the street, and I'd tried to make him understand why I wanted to wait before I invited him in. But I doubted if I'd succeeded. I knew I placed far more importance on where I lived than he did. He'd never wanted to own his own home and had always said he would take off happily to anywhere in the world if the opportunity came his way.

'Are you sure you don't need anything? I'll come over if you like,' he went on.

'I'm fine, really. I've something to sit on and something to sleep in and lights that work and a cooker that just about works.' The buzzer suddenly sounded. 'Hang on. There's someone here.'

I opened the front door and there was a courier,

holding out a bottle-shaped package with a huge red bow and a card.

'Who was that?' asked Paul.

'The Hedgehog gang have sent me some champagne. Isn't that wonderful of them? And they've insisted I take the week off.'

'When can I see you, Sally?'

I knew Paul had had a long day and I'm sure he thought I was being difficult and unfair and selfish. But I was afraid of giving in.

'Tell me, is it going to be months, weeks or days?'

'More like hours,' I said, with a laugh. 'I'll call you after Angela's been. She's coming tomorrow to help me get straight.'

'Don't phone too late. But you know where I'll be – down at the Raven with the lads, as usual. Come along if you're fed up.'

'Perhaps I will,' I answered.

Ginnie rang next, wanting to know every detail of my move and offering me the services of Sergei as decorator. I said he was far too grand for me but I'd think about it. Then Nicola called. I suspected that Ginnie had reminded her, as she seemed surprised that I'd already installed myself in the flat. The first question she asked was whether I'd put a double bed in her room because she might want to come down with Mark – as long as Paul wasn't there, she added. Both she and Ginnie sounded as excited as I was.

When I got up the next morning, my euphoria had subsided. All the walls and paintwork were so grubby, the kitchen was smaller than I thought it was and I hadn't noticed that some of the flimsy fitted cupboards in the bedrooms were coming off their hinges. I don't know why that bothered me, with so much to sort out, but it did. And the dripping tap in the bathroom. And the awful curtains in the living room. Was that a damp patch in the hall? Something the survey had over-looked? And was that a small crack in the balcony or merely the marks of a leaking gutter? What had I taken on? Had I made a terrible mistake? If Paul had been with me, he would have laughed at my fears. I missed him. And I guessed he was growing more and more impatient with me, though he rarely showed it.

Angela buzzed the intercom. My first visitor. I opened the unimpressive front door and heard the laboured groan of the narrow lift as it struggled to my floor.

'How lovely, to be so high up. You're so lucky!' said Angela, coming in with a huge basket. 'I've brought some food along because I'm sure you haven't had time to bother.'

'You're a darling.'

I felt a rush of affection. Sometimes Angela seemed to be in a world of her own, but I could always rely on her to be positive and generous. She put down her basket and immediately began to wander round the flat.

'It's all in a terrible state, I'm afraid.'

'Oh, that doesn't matter,' she said, opening a window and gazing out. 'It's a wonderful view. I always prefer to see the river glimpsed through trees, don't you?' She left the window and followed me into the kitchen, which led off the L-shaped living area.

'I'll have to get used to a small kitchen,' I commented.

'Well, you won't be having huge dinner parties every day, will you? It's perfect for one, I'd have thought. And who needs a large kitchen nowadays?'

She unpacked her basket and began to decipher the workings of the cooker. Within minutes she'd prepared – or rather heated up – a delicate meal. And she had thoughtfully brought along some cutlery, plates and glasses, knowing that everything would still be packed up. I opened a bottle of wine and we sat on two kitchen chairs with a box for a table. The dining table we used in the house, which seated ten in comfort, was far too cumbersome for this room, so I'd left it for Henry.

'You could do so much with this flat,' she remarked. 'How exciting it all is. We'll have to find you a decent builder.'

'There's no hurry,' I said, imagining huge bills that I'd be unable to pay and remembering the thousands I'd spent on the house without a thought. 'I'll have to be quite careful from now on.'

'You don't have to spend a fortune. And I know Douggie will help you with ideas. He's brilliant with interiors.'

'I'll probably paint everything white,' I said.

'Just think of the possibilities! Now you can experiment, do whatever you like and there's no need to consult anyone. I envy you, I really do. Douggie and I always have enormous arguments when it's decorating time.'

'Yes,' I said, feeling encouraged. 'Though I'm not artistic with interiors like you two.'

'Everyone can be artistic if they want to be. They just don't bother to use their eyes.'

'What about Patsy then?' I asked.

Patsy prided herself on being completely philistine and not giving a toss about appearances. White and clean was all she demanded.

'Patsy's different. She's clever and intellectual,' Angela commented, as though that was sufficient explanation.

After lunch we began to rip off the plastic sheeting covering the living-room furniture. Soon we had a smallish table, six chairs, two armchairs and a sofa to position. Angela and I heaved and pushed, trying first one place then another. Finally we agreed on an arrangement and collapsed into the armchairs.

'It'll be a tight squeeze, when the children come,' I remarked. 'But I'm sure they'll get used to it.'

'They'll have a nice large bedroom each, won't they? And if you have lots of people in the living room, they can sit on the floor. Kids usually prefer it – mine do, anyway.' She sipped her tea thoughtfully, then looked up. 'Has Paul seen your flat yet?'

'Not yet. I wanted to get straight first, even though he offered to give me a hand. He's been very reassuring. There's not nearly as much to do as I thought. And he doesn't see the point in getting a builder. There's nothing complicated, he says, nothing he can't tackle. And he's going to teach me a thing or two about decorating. Do you know, I've never painted a wall before? Not even as a student. Paul was amazed. Isn't it ridiculous?'

Angela gave a slightly embarrassed laugh.

'Not at all.' Then she leaned forward, with her hands clasped. 'So you've been seeing a lot of him?'

'Yes, I suppose I have.'

'I did wonder whether . . . well, you know how these things happen. You might find that before you knew it, he'd suddenly moved in with you.'

'I . . . well, I don't think that's likely. Not for the moment, anyway.'

She looked at me a little sternly, as though she knew I was being evasive.

'I'd be worried if it did happen, though.'

I finished my mug of tea, wondering whether I should talk frankly or not. Although we were good friends, I still wasn't sure of her attitude to Paul.

'I've often wondered what would happen if he came to live with me, if it could work out,' I began.

'Of course you have,' she said, encouragingly.

'At the moment, I can't make up my mind. Sometimes the idea horrifies me. I'm afraid that if he comes, I'll end up being the same as I was with Henry. Since he left I've become more independent, used to making my own decisions . . .'

'. . . yes, and we all admire you for it,' Angela interjected.

'At other times, I think – why should I be so afraid? It's so difficult knowing for sure whether you've really changed for good, isn't it? I might suddenly slip back to being the old boring Sally. You would tell me if I did, wouldn't you?'

Angela seemed surprised.

'I never thought you were boring for a moment. I've always thought of myself as the boring one. I spend most of the day saying nothing, painting away. And my pictures aren't going to change the world. Douggie says I'm slightly better than Prince Charles but not much.'

'That's cruel. And not true.'

'As long as I sell a few watercolours to friends, I'm not ambitious,' she said, laughing it away. 'But we're not talking about me.' I was aware of Angela's hazel eyes looking intently into mine. 'I hope you don't mind me saying . . . but . . . I'd think hard about whether it's a good idea for Paul to share the flat with you. But not for the reason you gave.'

I immediately jumped in, defensively.

'You think he'd take advantage of me? I assure you, he's not like that. He's the most considerate person imaginable. We never get on top of one another and he always shares everything he has. I don't have any worries about him. It's just Nicola and Joel. That's the problem.'

Angela sighed, as though unwilling to continue.

'I wasn't being critical, Sally. We all want everything to work out wonderfully for you. It's just that . . .' Her voice trailed away.

'That?' I echoed softly.

'. . . you've known one another for such a short time. It's just possible that you might be building up your hopes, dreaming of a future . . . that's not going to be.'

'You mean, he might walk out like Henry?' I said.

'Not exactly.'

I began to be a little exasperated by Angela's reluctance to say what was on her mind.

'Please don't try and spare my feelings. I'd rather know what you really think.'

'Let's have some more tea first,' she said, rising to her feet.

When she'd put on the kettle, she came and sat on the floor beside me. I think she always felt more comfortable sitting cross-legged, her skirt flowing around her.

'I hate telling you this.' She paused, shifting her position. 'A couple of days ago, I'd just delivered a painting to the gallery and I was walking past the Raven. A group of people came out, and then one couple stayed behind. They leaned against the front wall of the pub and I could see Paul's face, lit by the window. Then this girl flung her arms round him and kissed him on the lips. Was I wrong to tell you? I just didn't know what to do.'

I could feel myself crumpling like a waterless plant.

'What did she look like?' I said, my voice quavering.

'Blonde hair, long legs, tight black jeans, skimpy white top. I only had a general impression. She looked quite young.'

I rushed off to the kitchen, groped for a couple of tea bags and a carton of milk, and made two mugs of tea. I'd even forgotten that Angela didn't like milk, but she didn't comment.

'I know who it was, outside the pub,' I said, my hand trembling as I handed her a mug. 'It was Sam. I've met her a few times. She's part of the Edgeworth team, the first girl they've employed.' Angela put down the mug and began to twist round a strand of her long hair. We were nervous and it was equally difficult for both of us. 'Sam's very uninhibited, flirts with everyone. I expect she'd had a drink or two. I . . . I don't think it would have meant anything to Paul. He's always making fun of her.'

Angela relaxed into a smile as though she wanted to be convinced by my explanation. But I was feeling completely hollow inside. I tried to steel myself, barely hearing Angela's remarks.

'I'm sure you're right. Young people behave quite differently now, don't they? They don't take things nearly as seriously as we do. I do hope I wasn't wrong to tell you, though.'

'I'm glad you did,' I said. 'But I'm sure Paul would let me know if he'd fallen for someone else. He couldn't be dishonest if he tried.'

I was trying my utmost to sound unconcerned. If only I could believe what I was saying . . .

'That's marvellous,' said Angela, taking up her mug.

We began to tackle the dreary business of taking china, glass and cutlery from packs of newspaper, placing everything haphazardly on the toffee-pine shelves. Then we moved to the room I'd chosen for my bedroom. Half-heartedly, I unpacked a box of linen and began to make the bed with Angela. The great wooden bed was far too large for the room, far too large for one. I wondered where Sam lived and what kind of bed she slept in. Would she still have teddy bears and dolls piled up round her pillows?

When Angela left, she said I shouldn't do everything at once and invited me to come over for dinner. Paul wasn't included in the invitation. I excused myself by saying I was exhausted and would go to bed early. That night I hardly slept. Again and again I asked myself if Paul was as straightforward and honest with me as I'd assumed. I tried to remember the conversation we'd had about Sam when I first met her. 'Some of the lads can't keep their eyes off her, but she doesn't do anything for me. She likes winding me up because she wants me to fancy her. As I don't, that makes me a challenge.' Did he mean it? Did he react a little too quickly, suspecting that I'd guessed the truth?

Next morning I called Paul at the yard and told him that there was still chaos and I'd need a few more days before I'd allow him to come round. He didn't sound too disappointed, saying he'd work late and get ahead on a couple of projects. A suspicion started to worm its way into my mind and I couldn't root it out. No wonder he hadn't complained, for I'd given him an opportunity to meet Sam again. They would probably go off somewhere. What if Angela was right? Had she witnessed more than she was prepared to say? I couldn't bring myself to talk to Paul, even though he phoned me several times, leaving messages. At the weekend I could bear it no longer and escaped to London. Ginnie and I drank a lot and laughed a lot, and I said little about Paul. Then, on Monday, I returned to work.

Pickle couldn't understand why I refused to come to the phone when Paul rang. Things were a little difficult at the moment, I told her. Sally Linton wasn't available for the time being.

'Quite right, Sal. Don't let him walk over you. Give him a hard time,' she said, having summed up the situation to her satisfaction. She decided that he was taking me for granted, though I'd implied nothing of the kind. I think I mentioned needing 'space for myself' and she'd drawn her own conclusions. It took all my self-control not to answer him, but every time I was about to call, I stopped my impulse with the thought that he had probably fixed his next date with Sam.

Sam was in my mind for most of the time, persistent as an old stain that couldn't be removed. It wasn't quite jealousy because I knew I wouldn't stand a chance if Paul was really involved, but rather anger. I felt irrational anger that she was still at the yard, that she could insinuate herself so easily into Paul's affections – but most of all, that she was the right age. They were within reach of one another all day, every day. And Sam was exactly the kind of girl that Paul would get on with so well, the knowing, confident new generation like Pickle or Nicola. They had so much in common: the same interests, the same kind of background, the appropriate age. How could I possibly compete? Faced with such a temptation, how could Paul have remained faithful to me? We'd never talked about fidelity. There was no need to. Even the word sounded as though it had been taken from an out-of-date dictionary. I didn't want to put it to the test.

By Monday evening, my resolve had weakened. When I arrived home I listened to Paul's recorded message, even though I had been about to delete it.

'Sally, I do hope you're all right. Or are you angry with me? Whatever it is, I love you. Please call.'

Half an hour later we were standing outside the lift, locked in one another's arms. I quickly drew away when he started to kiss me, and strode through the open door of the flat.

'What's happened, Sally? Do you want me to go away?'

'Of course I don't,' I answered, torn between saying yes and no. He came inside, barely glanced at his surroundings and stood by the window in the living room.

'I'll get something to drink,' I said.

The bottle of champagne from the Hedgehog gang was in the fridge, unopened. I didn't feel like celebrating and pulled out a half-consumed bottle of wine standing next to it. When I came in, Paul was still by the window. He was silent while I sat down at the dining table and poured out the wine. Then he came to sit opposite me. He looked tense, biting his lip, and I'd rarely seen him like this. I wanted to get it all over as quickly as possible. However distressing, he'd have to make a choice and bring everything out into the open. We might never see one another again. I'd have to be prepared. We were both on edge and I feared that if I burst out in anger he might suddenly leave. I didn't want him to leave.

'What's worrying you?' Paul asked quietly, picking up his glass.

All my prepared words dissolved into a haze. I couldn't see how I could confront him. It would all sound so banal, like a wife checking up on her husband's movements.

'Oh, nothing really. I'm fine. Everything got on top of me, that's all. Moving was harder than I expected.'

I knew my words were coming out in a tired monotone. Paul gazed straight at me, unsmiling.

'There's something else, isn't there? Has Henry called? Has he upset you?'

'No. It's not Henry.'

I could barely keep the tears from escaping. Paul got up and came behind me, putting his hands on my shoulders.

'I'd hate it if I did anything to make you unhappy. You must tell me. Will you promise? Silence is the worst.'

He slowly took his hands from my shoulders, pulled up a chair and swung round to face me. I took a deep breath.

'It's about Sam.'

'What about Sam?'

'I know you're really attracted to her. I suppose I've been feeling low and a little jealous. It happens sometimes.'

'You're not still bothered by Sam?' he said. I couldn't trust myself to respond. 'I thought we had that out ages ago. Nothing's changed.'

Paul seemed genuinely mystified. I searched his face, as though I'd see the marks of deception hidden beneath the surface. His clear blue-grey eyes looked straight into mine without flinching. I took another deep breath.

'When Angela came round, she happened to remark that . . . oh well, never mind. It was only gossip. But even gossip hurts.'

'I can take it. I've lived here long enough,' said Paul, with a slight smile.

'She was taking a picture to the gallery and saw you and a blonde girl who sounded like Sam. You were outside the pub.' I thought there might be a flicker passing over Paul's face, as though I'd touched a nerve, but there was none.

'Is that all?' he asked.

'She was kissing you, Angela said.'

'This is crazy. So you jumped to conclusions and assumed we were having an affair. Is that right?'

I'd never seen Paul look so angry. His eyes suddenly went dead, his mouth set. Was he angry because I'd found him out? Or because I even bothered to pass on what Angela had told me? I shuddered. Were we about to have a huge row?

'Listen, Sal. Have you ever drunk rather too much?'

'You know I have,' I answered, nervously.

'Has a man ever lunged at you and kissed you almost before you realized it?'

'Mm. Maybe,' I said, thinking of Martin.

'Sam turned up at the pub – she'd been drinking lager all evening. So Pete bought her a couple of whiskies, which wasn't a good idea. Outside the pub she threw herself at me. She was in such a state, I'm sure she didn't even know who I was. It could have been any man. Then Pete grabbed her arm and took her back home. I don't know what happened after that, but I can guess. Is that really what upset you? Why you refused to speak to me?'

For a moment I was quite taken aback. He made it all sound so trivial but I still had lingering doubts.

'I didn't mean it to sound like an interrogation,' I said. 'And I've no right to stop you seeing whoever you want. But I'm not good at sharing someone.'

'Crazy girl. Do you think I want anyone else? I don't. And that's that. You can't honestly see me ending up in bed with Sam, can you?'

'You must be tempted sometimes.'

'Then you don't know me very well. I'll have to do something about it, won't I?'

I emptied my glass. I could have left it at that but my thoughts were still racing feverishly. Even if he was about to leave, I felt compelled to go on.

'When . . . if you do meet another girl that you want to be with, I'd rather know. I couldn't bear it if we had to hide things from one another.'

Paul came and put his arms round me. We were both silent and I was swallowing rapidly, trying to keep my tears at bay.

'Stop dreading the future, Sal. I love you. And if either of us is stupid enough to fall for someone else, there'd be no need to lie about it. Would there?'

'No,' I said, gradually regaining my confidence.

Paul smiled at me and reached into his satchel.

'You need a refill. They told me this was special. I said it'd better be.' He popped open the cork and poured out two glasses of champagne. 'Here's to Sally's place. Can I look round now?'

'It's all a mess still.'

'You mean you haven't got everything organized? I shouldn't have come, then,' Paul said, with a laugh.

The tour ended in my bedroom, which was where we stayed. We made love hungrily, as though we'd been apart for a year. The evening breeze came into the room, scented with overblown roses, dried grass and the smell of the river. The boxes were still heaped around us, the orange patterned curtains I longed to tear down were pulled right back. But now that Paul was here, I no longer minded and I felt the flat truly belonged to me.

Paul lay on his back, his hands under his head.

'I was thinking about why you were so upset,' he began. 'I'd probably have felt the same way. But there's something I don't understand. Do you think all men have to go to bed with any girl who's attractive? That we have to prove ourselves the moment we get an opportunity, like tomcats on the rampage?'

'Mostly, yes,' I murmured.

'Not true. Not for me it isn't. I don't believe I'm so different from the others.'

'Just better-looking.'

'And brainier, of course, and smarter.'

'Of course.'

We both laughed and Paul rolled over onto his side, resting his elbow on the pillow.

'I love you and I don't dream about having other girls. You're the sexiest woman I've ever met and I like being with you more than anything else. If I was good at romantic compliments, I'd say something more original.'

'And then I wouldn't believe you.'

For the rest of July, Paul and I rushed back from work and immersed ourselves in renovating the flat. Won over by his enthusiasm, I was surprised to find that with a little tuition I could wield a roller, hammer in nails, remove paint and sand down window frames. Maggie thought I was quite insane and offered to lend me some money to have a proper job done, but I said I was doing a proper job. I liked getting my hands dirty and watching the result of our labour each day. When it came to painting, everything was white except for Joel's room – he'd asked for grey – and Nicola's room, which had to be a vibrant yellow. She wanted to inspect her room first, before settling on the exact shade she had in mind.

Once I'd assured Nicola that she wouldn't bump into Paul, she arranged to come down for the day. Although she complained about my plans to paint everything boring white, I think the flat met with her approval. I made sure that Paul wouldn't be there, but I couldn't hide the evidence. His things were around – a few tools, some clothes, books and CDs – and it seemed dishonest to pack them away. She pointedly ignored everything. It was only when I was driving her to the station that she mentioned him.

'Is Paul around most of the time?' she asked, suddenly.

'Well, more or less,' I answered.

'I thought you'd have got fed up with him by now,' she remarked.

Then she dropped the subject. It was too much to expect that she might have changed her attitude, but at least she hadn't sounded resentful.

The flat had to be ready and finished by the middle of August, when Joel would be coming for a couple of weeks. He'd been staying with Henry and Sheila in a villa they'd rented in Tuscany. (I longed to ask Joel who was paying but I knew I couldn't.) Together Paul and I ripped out cupboards, removed the worst of the carpet and sanded the floor in the living room. We chose a new dining table together, as well as a fridge and a cooker. I'd never imagined that I'd such reserves of energy, working in the office all day, sharing a quick takeaway and then throwing myself into physical work. By the time we'd finished each evening, it seemed natural that Paul would stay. I occasionally reminded myself that this was only a temporary arrangement. Once the flat was in order he was bound to spend the occasional night in his own place, which would suit us both. And then, having spent several mornings and evenings in his company, I saw no particular reason to bring up the subject, not just yet anyway. If the moment came when I began to be oppressed by seeing him every day, I could mention it then. It would be another matter when the children came to stay.

One evening, we'd taken our usual bath. Paul was wrapped in a towel and I was sitting on the floor in my robe, leaning against the sofa, feeling exhausted but comfortable. My hair was growing long again. I hadn't bothered to have a session at the salon for some time. Strange to think I used to go every week. Strands of hair hung damply all round my neck and face. Paul pushed them back and handed me a cool glass of orange juice.

'I seem to be living here. Are you getting sick of me yet?'

'Not yet,' I said, with a grin.

'Don't forget to tell me if you are. And I'll need five minutes to pack up my stuff.'

I couldn't quite make out if he meant it or not.

'Do you think it would work out?' I began tentatively, looking down at my glass.

'If I lived here permanently, you mean?' I nodded. He glanced at me shyly. 'What's your view on this one?'

'It's too soon . . . I can't talk about the future. But I love every minute that you're here. I thought you might start telling me what to do and you haven't.'

'Why would I do that? It's your place. I wouldn't dream of it, anyhow.'

'It hasn't quite sunk in, that . . . that my life could be so different from . . .'

'From what?' he insisted.

'. . . from how it was with Henry. I keep waiting for the cracks to appear. Then nothing dreadful happens and I wonder why not. Everyone seems to expect it, anyhow.'

'The Wengrave Ladies Circle, you mean.'

I laughed.

289

'All right, yes. But most people would probably agree with them.'

'Most people? Surely what you mean is, the ones around you. What is "most people"? Forty million? Fifty million? Or just four or five? You know what old Edgeworth says when someone wants a new boat built? "Most people choose this design." Which means – he chooses it. He wants to save himself the trouble of drawing up new plans. He'd rather do the same old things in the same old way, with small changes.'

'I don't quite understand,' I said.

'I may be wrong, but it seems to me that your friends want to impose their views on you. They don't mind you being a little bit different, but now you're going too far. You're the new design and they don't like it.'

'You may be right,' I said, reluctantly.

'Can I have the last word this time?' Paul asked, smiling at me.

'Go ahead.'

'I'd like to live with you. I've no doubts about that.'

A couple of days later I received a letter from Nicola. When I saw the scrawled address in her handwriting, I was apprehensive. She made a point of never writing letters if she could possibly help it. 'What's wrong with the phone?' she always said, when I urged her to write a card or a thank-you letter. I tore open the envelope, my hands trembling.

*Dear Mum,*

*I've been thinking a lot about you and Paul. I hope you don't mind, but I told Mark you were seeing him a lot of the time. (All I said was he was my boyfriend ages ago.) When you first told me, I was horrified. It was all so sudden. I think I'm beginning to feel a bit differently now. Mark said that everyone has to make their own life. You're making yours and I'm making mine. I'm sure you can't really understand why I'm crazy about Mark and I can't figure out what you see in Paul. If he hadn't been my boyfriend, I wonder if it might have been easier for me to take? But I know it's silly thinking like that.*

*Mark suggested we both drove down to Wengrave and had a day out with you and Paul. He's never been before but he's read* Three Men in a Boat *and wants to see the river and maybe visit a pub or two. Sound OK? If you agree, don't worry, I'll behave myself! I won't let the side down!*

*Lots of love. Nicola.*

Paul carried in some tea and toast and set it down on the dining table. Without saying anything, I handed him the letter. As soon as he'd read it, I hugged him. And then I read the letter again.

'Would you come out with us?' I said.

'I might,' he replied, with a grin. Then he said, 'You're going to start making plans, aren't you?'

'I'll just see how it goes,' I said.

The day before Nicola and Mark arrived, I couldn't quite manage to throw off all my old habits. Part of me was still stuck in the past – especially where the children were concerned – and I found myself feeling guilty about not having made a greater effort for Mark's first trip to Wengrave. I took extra time off for lunch, and kept adding to my shopping list all morning.

My Waitrose trolley was filling up at an alarming rate. I was contemplating the red-hot sauces, tins of exotic chillies and blocks of coconut, wondering if I should change my mind and try cooking something more exciting than the roast I had planned.

Suddenly I caught sight of a woman in a bright emerald jacket wheeling an overloaded trolley and swaying her ample hips. Unmistakable.

'Maggie!' I called out. 'I haven't seen you for ages. I was wondering how everything was working out.'

I couldn't ask about her lover in the middle of a supermarket, but I assumed she'd guess what I meant.

'Everything's fine,' she answered, in the kind of bright voice that said, I wouldn't tell you if it wasn't. 'And you? How's the new flat?'

'Wonderful. Quite transformed. You must come round,' I said.

'It's dreadful. I just don't have a moment these days. I've taken on far too much charity work. Quite honestly, I never stop.'

I glanced down at her trolley, almost spilling over and topped with several packets of vol-au-vents and frozen prawns.

'This looks like serious entertaining.'

'Some business friends of Jeff's are coming round.'

'I thought you always refused to do that kind of thing,' I said, smiling.

Maggie observed few rules, but this was one of them.

'I'm making an effort now.'

She was screwing her eyes up as she smiled, as though she'd either become very short-sighted or was in pain.

'Have you seen Angela or Patsy?' I asked, even though she was obviously reluctant to stay parked at my side.

'Oh yes. We meet quite often as a matter of fact. We're all going to that lovely new health club. It's such fun. Wildly expensive, but there's a fabulous pool.' Then she abruptly changed direction. 'Sorry, Sal. Must rush. My parking ticket's running out.'

Maggie couldn't have made it clearer that I was out of favour. She hadn't phoned for weeks and neither had Patsy. Angela had rung a couple of times after she visited me at the flat, saying I really must come for dinner but failing to arrange a date. She must have told the others that Paul might be moving in and I thought their silence was a cowardly way of showing disapproval. Would they have felt so compromised by asking us both over for a drink? I made excuses for them but I couldn't help feeling hurt. Ought I to have made a greater effort to win them over? If all went well with Nicola and Mark, it might make it easier. And then there was Joel. If my family came to accept my involvement with Paul – and I hoped in time they would – surely my friends would come to accept us too?

Nicola and Mark arrived the next day, a couple of hours late as they'd had some trouble with his ancient Volkswagen. I was afraid that lunch would be spoiled and was already planning a stand-by meal. Paul was working in Nicola's bedroom, rushing to finish off some paintwork he'd overlooked. Then the doorbell rang.

'Sorry we're late. But you have to be tolerant with old bangers,' said Mark, shaking my hand. Nicola gave me a hug and ran inside the flat.

'We had to keep stopping.' She opened the kitchen door and gave a hearty sniff.

'Oh good. Roast. I hoped we'd have one.'

Once they'd settled themselves in the living room, I called out to Paul.

'They've arrived.'

'I'll clear up and put on something decent,' he shouted from the bedroom.

Nicola turned her head slightly but made no comment. She was rocking back on her chair, which she always did when she was nervous. Still, I'm sure I was equally nervous. I brought in some beer and wine, which Mark opened.

'I hope you've finished my room,' said Nicola.

'Paul wanted to get it done before you came. It should be ready now.'

'I thought you were doing it.'

'We both are.'

Nicola glanced towards Mark, who smiled.

'Can we go have a look?' he said.

When Nicola came face to face with Paul he was still in his paint-spattered shirt, tidying away the paint cans and brushes.

'Hi,' was all she said.

We all smiled at one another until Paul broke the silence, addressing Mark.

'This is Nicola's choice. What do you reckon?'

'It's a hell of a colour,' Mark said. 'You'd have to wake up in the morning, looking at that.'

'Is it OK?' Paul asked Nicola.

'Great,' she answered, looking at me. Then she turned to examine the faded green curtains. 'You're not keeping those, are you? I want blue blinds, please.'

'Steady on. Maybe Sally's got other ideas. This is her place,' said Mark, giving Nicola a reproving smile.

During lunch, Nicola was more reserved than usual and avoided looking at Paul. But he and Mark seemed to be getting on well, and the conversation was easy.

'This is the first time I've entertained here,' I said, as Paul and I began removing the plates from the table. Paul quickly corrected me.

'How about when Ginnie came?'

'That doesn't count. She's my sister.'

'I don't feel like a guest,' said Mark. 'Entertaining is for guests.'

'And we're family, aren't we?' added Nicola.

'Yes,' I said with a smile. 'I believe we are.'

After coffee, Paul suggested that we showed Mark around the town. The day, which had started off cloudy, had suddenly brightened and a warm breeze had cleared the sky. We wandered down the High Street and took detours round the narrow streets running off it. Mark seemed to know far more about the history and architecture of Wengrave than I did.

'I thought you'd never been here before,' I commented, as he pointed out a pub that had once been visited by Boswell.

'I haven't,' he said with a grin. 'But I read it up before I came. Nicky couldn't understand it, but when I showed her some old photos in a book she started getting curious.'

We walked on, slowly catching up with Nicola and Paul who were ahead of us. I was pleased to see that they were having an animated conversation.

'I like your Paul,' Mark continued. 'Nikki finds it difficult but my bet is, she'll come round to you and him being together. He's very natural. That's good. I know she went out with him once, but that's in the past. I'm not jealous of the past. I've been married, too, you remember.'

'It takes a while to get used to it, not being married,' I remarked.

Mark turned to me and grinned.

'Seems you're doing pretty well.'

After a drink in the Raven, we took a walk by the river and ended up at Shiplake. By the time we returned to the flat we were all feeling drowsy with the sun and river air. It was as though all our anxieties had been washed away. Nicola seemed to be her old self with Paul – she had even started bickering again. Then she quickly realized and stopped abruptly, grinning sheepishly at me. The most difficult moment for me came after we'd finished supper.

Paul and I had agreed that, for Nicola's sake, he would go back to his place. I was only too aware that it would have upset her, knowing that we were in the bedroom next to hers.

'I'll have to be getting back,' said Paul.

Mark answered immediately.

'Oh. Can't you stay?'

Nicola glanced at me, with an uncertain expression. Paul turned to Mark.

'My mum and dad are coming to stay with me tomorrow. I'll have to tidy up my place. It's in a state at the moment.'

I hoped it didn't sound as though it was a pre-arranged excuse. He grabbed hold of his jacket and said his goodbyes.

Nicola and I weren't able to have some time alone until after breakfast the next morning, when Mark decided to take a walk and collect the papers. We took a couple of chairs out onto the balcony and sat drinking coffee together.

'Mark said he likes Paul,' she remarked.

'Were you worried he wouldn't?' I asked.

'A bit. Well, more worried that Paul wouldn't get along with him. I mean, he wouldn't have met someone like Mark in Wengrave, would he?'

'I suppose it's unlikely,' I admitted.

Nicola stood up and leaned against the balcony.

'Last night you didn't have to ask Paul to leave, you know.'

'I didn't.'

'He could have left early in the morning.'

'Perhaps.'

She reached down for her mug and returned to sit beside me. I suddenly felt inadequate, and thought how well Ginnie would have handled it.

'I thought it was better if he didn't stay,' I added.

'Even though he usually does?'

I knew that expression on Nicola's face so well. I want to know.

'Yes. He usually does.'

She suddenly broke into a smile.

'I don't think I mind, Mum. Not any more. Anyway,

Paul's changed. He's not nearly so moody. He used to worry about being inferior to everyone, that he hadn't been abroad and got a degree and a classy job. But he doesn't seem bothered now. Know something? He never looked at me like he looks at you. Mark said you can always tell.'

'I'm so glad that . . .'

I couldn't finish my sentence but I think Nicola guessed what I was feeling.

They stayed a few hours longer until it was time for Mark to start coaxing his old car back into wheezy action for their journey home. We were standing outside in the entrance of Fernwood Court when Nicola suddenly threw her arms round me.

'Thanks for everything,' she said. 'We love it here. Mark says I'm very lucky to have you for my mum.'

There was a jubilant cry from Mark as the engine fired, and Nicola ran off to jump into the car. Then she shouted through the open window, 'Don't forget the blue blinds, will you.'

Left to myself for a few hours, I thought how I had underestimated Nicola. She had worked through her initial revulsion and anger at my behaviour and come to her own conclusion. How many daughters, I wondered, would have been so generous? Now we could both go our own ways, without recrimination. Even if nobody else sympathized or understood, I knew that Nicola did. She had given me the freedom to love Paul as I wanted to. I could never have asked for more.

# THIRTEEN

• • •

One afternoon Paul called me at the office to say that he would be coming home early. Coming home. It was then that I suddenly realized that we were living together, even though neither of us had made a momentous decision to do so. He no longer said 'I'll come round to your place' but I couldn't remember exactly when it had happened. Paul still kept his room, which he used to store things in, but he hardly ever went there. The occasional letter arrived for Mr Paul Burridge and his friends began to call my telephone number. I wasn't ready to tell my friends, who in any case were all away for the summer.

At home with Paul, I was surprised how easy it all was. The flat had come together sooner than I'd imagined and it gave me pleasure to see a few of his things around the place, side by side with mine. If I asked his opinion about details, he'd say what he thought but otherwise he didn't interfere. The only time I felt under pressure was when we went into town together. I couldn't help noticing the occasional curious glances when we visited shops I regularly frequented. On one occasion, while we were choosing something for supper in our nearest delicatessen, the Spanish girl at the counter asked me whether Paul was my son. When I said he wasn't, she gave me a meaningful woman-to-woman lucky-you smirk. It would take a while before it made little impression on me, but if I looked back to our weekend away – when I was so mortified by the young trainee in the hotel – I was starting to accept that from now on, this would be every stranger's reaction to seeing us together.

More than anything, I was concerned about what would happen when Joel arrived, but at least I could now consult with Nicola. In the end we decided that it would be easier for all of us if I was able to be open, without hiding that we were living together. Then she took the initiative herself. Without telling me, she met Joel while he was in London and she and Mark took him out for a meal. Afterwards, she mentioned that Paul was sharing the new flat with me.

'What did he say? How did he react?' I asked, wanting to know every detail.

'Well, he wasn't amazingly surprised but you know Joel. He did ask whether Dad knew, though.'

'So how did you answer that one?'

'I said I didn't think he did. And I also said it was best to keep quiet for the moment, that you'd let him know when the time was right. You know what he told me then? If Dad had Sheila, he was glad that you'd found someone, too.'

'Do you think he meant it?' I asked, anxiously.

'There's no need to worry, Mum. Really, there isn't.'

I smiled to myself when I heard Nicola reassuring me as though I was her daughter. Then I wondered how much Joel was hiding. He always appeared to be calm on the surface but I never quite knew what lay below.

'Thank you for being so understanding,' I said. 'I will tell Daddy, though, before someone else does.'

'I wouldn't. What difference would it make? I don't see the point in telling him anything.'

'I don't see it that way.'

Nicola refused to listen. I felt powerless to alter the situation between her and Henry. She was convinced that if he met Mark he would never talk to her again, and I couldn't persuade her otherwise. I hoped she would change her mind when everything had been finally resolved between Henry and me. I almost felt as though I was already divorced, although it would take some time for our affairs to be settled.

Not long after Nicola's phone call, Henry rang to say he would drive Joel down to Wengrave and was looking forward to seeing me in my new flat. This was so unexpected that I assumed he'd had an attack of guilt and wanted to make up for it in some way. I could only stammer that it wasn't convenient for him to come, that I preferred to meet Joel from the station. He sounded genuinely sorry and I guessed what he must have been thinking. Sally is still angry. She has every right to be. Then he asked if he could see me in London. That would be my opportunity, I thought, to tell him about Paul.

Once Joel had arrived, he quickly made himself at home. I stood by his bedroom door while he made a brief tour to check there was nothing missing from his shelves, drawers and cupboards. Then he plugged in his laptop and placed it on his desk.

'Thanks Mum. This is perfect. Much better than my room at Dad's.'

He looked up with a smile and swung round on his old stool to get a panoramic view. Then he began to unpack his bag, taking out a pile of carefully ironed T-shirts, some jeans and immaculately folded underwear.

'Sheila did all this. God knows why. She says she enjoys ironing.'

'Some women do,' I said.

He grinned at me, as though we were sharing a secret.

'My guess is, Dad won't marry her, though,' Joel remarked, as if it had something to do with Sheila's ironing.

'Why do you say that?' I asked.

'Don't know really,' he answered.

'Are they getting on all right?' I said, then instantly regretted it. The last thing I meant to do was to pump Joel about Henry.

'Seem to,' he said.

He carried on unpacking, and wanted to know exactly where each item should go. I would have expected him to throw everything into a heap and leave it to me. Was that Sheila's influence? Or had they drummed it into him at school?

The phone rang in the living room. Joel reacted immediately.

'It might be for me.' He was about to leave the room but I hurriedly stopped him.

'I'll take it,' I said, expecting a call from Paul.

When I came back into his room, Joel had already started up his favourite computer game. He was instantly in another world and I tried to bring him back into mine.

'Did you know Paul's living here?'

'Oh yes,' he said, his eyes fixed on the screen. He sounded as though he'd just remembered.

'He'll be back from work around half past six. And he's looking forward to seeing you again,' I said.

I moved closer, trying to see from his expression if he was worried by what I'd told him but he was frowning with concentration, clicking frantically with his mouse. After a loud explosion on the screen, with limbs scattered in all directions, he appeared satisfied and swivelled round on his stool.

'Nicola took me out to dinner with her boyfriend. She told me then,' he said. 'We went to a great place in Brixton somewhere. Mark's OK. He gave me an interesting CD. I'll play it for you.'

I didn't know whether he'd refer to Paul again or pretend to ignore what I'd said.

'I thought we could take a trip together while you're here,' I began.

'Nicola and Mark?'

'No. Me and Paul.'

'Fine,' he said, swivelling back to face the screen. 'Is Paul building anything else in that yard?' he added.

I had to get used to sharing my conversation with a computer screen, as he continued playing his game.

'Not at the moment. He's doing repairs as someone's always breaking down on the river.'

'Like Martin. Has his boat gone phut again?'

We both laughed, recalling the awkward scene on the river with *Water Gypsy*.

'I haven't been invited since that time,' I said. 'Anyhow, Martin's away holidaying in South Africa. He's always off somewhere. So I'm afraid you won't be able to beat him at tennis.'

'Never mind. I can always play with Paul,' said Joel.

The phone rang for the second time and he leaped up from his stool, following me into the living room.

'It's Sarah,' I said, and a great smile spread over his face.

I was pleased to see Joel throwing himself effortlessly into our way of life. I sometimes caught him staring at Paul, as though he was trying to fathom his relationship with me. But he didn't change with him and seemed to accept Paul's presence, as far as I could tell. He didn't mind when meals weren't on time, or when we had takeaways delivered. I sometimes thought how different it must have been when he stayed with Henry and Sheila.

'Things are rather casual around here,' I commented one morning, when the dirty dishes from the night before were still piled up in the sink. Even though I'd taken time off from Hedgehog to be with Joel and could easily have cleared up, I had lost the habit of being meticulous. I suddenly felt rather ashamed, as though I was slipping into sluttish ways and letting down my son.

'That's OK, Mum. It doesn't worry me.' He went over to the sink and began to stack up the dishwasher. 'I'm on holiday. So you can be too.' He glanced at me and grinned.

I did my best not to be an organizing mum, but to let Joel suggest what he wanted to do. We went out rowing on the river, he played tennis with his friends, went to a couple of parties and towards the end of the week he asked me hesitantly if he could have a little cash to take Sarah out for a meal. He spent hours getting himself ready. Finally he stood in front of Paul and me.

'Do I look OK?' he asked, shyly.

'A million dollars,' said Paul reassuringly.

A second later he shot out through the front door. I was looking forward to having an evening alone with Paul.

'You've been so good with Joel,' I said, as we sat out on the balcony to catch the last of the sun. 'I know it must be hard sometimes.'

'We get on fine, he's a nice lad. It's only been a week, after all. And I don't have to pretend to be Dad.'

'I hope it goes on that way.'

'No reason why it shouldn't. If Joel sees you happy, he's not going to have sleepless nights, is he?'

There was no answer to that, but I was still battling with the belief I'd always had, that if you have children, you have a duty to maintain the status quo to give them a stable background. I regretted that Joel and Nicola would join the armies of children of divorced parents and feared they would have a jaundiced view of marriage. I couldn't rid myself of the idea that it was my fault.

'Do you think it'll work out all right for him?' I asked.

'Why ever not? He's done brilliantly in his exams and he's keen on a girl. What more do you want?'

'You don't think one day he'll blame me for mucking up his life? Or decide never to get married?'

'Joel doesn't think like that. On the whole, kids don't. Only parents.'

Soon after Joel had gone back to London, I agreed to meet Henry at his club.

It was only just before I left that I remembered. Ladies were not allowed in wearing trousers. I'd quite forgotten all the formalities I used to adopt without a thought.

In the club reading room Henry pulled up an enormous armchair, protected either for privacy or draughts by concealing wings. He pointed to a smaller version apparently intended for visiting ladies. As I would have been sitting well below his level, I placed myself opposite him on a hard, shiny leather chesterfield.

'It's better if I sit next to you,' Henry decided.

So there we were, side by side, both of us feeling uncomfortable. Henry drew one leg up onto the other, while I half reclined in a corner. All I could see around me were pink and white newspapers screening the occupants' faces.

While he was making a vain attempt to summon a drink, I had a good look at Henry. His hair was longer than usual, straggling towards his collar, and his face seemed a little gaunt. I'd expected him to be exactly the same as he'd been when we lived together, as though time would never touch him. We addressed one another quite formally to start with.

'I trust you're happy in your new flat.'

'It suits me very well – for the moment, that is.'

Henry cleared his throat slightly.

'Yes, of course. One can only hope things will improve.'

'I wasn't talking about money or getting somewhere larger,' I said.

He looked puzzled.

'Oh? Does that mean you're thinking of moving from Wengrave?'

'I might,' I said with a smile. 'I might do anything. I know it's silly at my age, but I feel that anything's possible now.'

'You're not exactly old.' Henry smiled back, then reached down and picked up the briefcase at his feet, extracting a box of small cigars. 'Mind if I have one of these?'

'Of course not,' I said.

'They're not allowed in the flat. Sheila has a long list of forbidden pollutants that I find impossible to remember. She can see danger in a carrot. Incomprehensible, as far as I'm concerned.' Having unwrapped his cigar, Henry lit it with relish. 'Joel had a happy stay with you. He told me you've a very nice flat.'

'Good. I'm glad,' I said quickly, trying to guess whether Henry knew. It would have been so easy for it to slip out. I went with Mum and Paul . . . I needed something to drink before I could break it to Henry.

'Would it be possible . . .?' I said, gesturing to a distant figure dressed in black who might have been a waiter.

'Ah. Bob's arrived. A glass of wine perhaps?'

'A large vodka and tonic.'

Henry laughed and waved in the direction of the elderly man in black.

'So you're drinking vodka now. That must be your sister's influence? Isn't that her favourite?'

'She likes it now and again,' I remarked, already on the defensive.

'How is Virginia?'

I could tell that he was only asking for old times' sake. He just about tolerated Ginnie.

'She's still seeing Sergei.'

He looked a little blank.

'Sergei? I don't remember that one. Still, I always lose track with her amours.'

Whenever we mentioned Ginnie, Henry always managed to make a disparaging reference to her boyfriends. Luckily the waiter came to take his order before I could make some irritable comment.

'Nicola hasn't been in touch for a long time,' Henry continued, as though going through a list of what had to be discussed between us. 'I've tried getting hold of her at her flat, but they say she's never there. I know I haven't exactly been a satisfactory father, but it doesn't seem right . . .' His voice trailed away, as though he'd thought better of what he was about to say.

'I have asked her several times to contact you. But in the end it's up to her,' I said.

Henry was holding his cigar in one hand, contemplating the smouldering end.

'You start off at the beginning with all these ideas of having a lively, devoted family, life running reasonably smoothly . . . then . . . ah well.' He abruptly halted his train of thought and looked up at me. 'Sign of age, isn't it? Running down the balance sheets, wondering if things might have been different.'

'If you hadn't met Sheila, I suppose you mean,' I said. 'Who can answer that? She gave you something I couldn't, though God knows what that was.' When Henry didn't answer, I continued. 'Still, I'm sure it will all be easier once everything's settled. It's hard for both of us at the moment, I realize that.'

'Indeed.'

The waiter had stopped at a discreet distance with a small tray. As soon as he received his signal to advance, he placed our drinks and a bowl of nuts on a table and drew it up next to us.

'I'm only allowed one small whisky a day,' Henry

remarked, picking up his glass.

After he'd taken a sip, he continued. 'It was good of you to come to London. But I wouldn't have asked you unless . . . well, it's important to say certain things face to face. And besides, I wanted to see you.'

I started to fiddle with the strap of my handbag. Henry pretended not to notice but I knew he had. He was irritated by women who fiddle and was always telling Nicola off for not being able to keep her hands still.

'I do find all this very difficult,' I said, looking directly at Henry. 'Actually, I found it difficult last time. We're not a husband and wife, we're not exactly friends and we're not lovers. All we can do is to talk about the children and make polite conversation. We could do that over the phone.'

'I see what you mean.'

'Do you?'

Henry crossed and uncrossed his legs, then leaned back and loosened his tie.

'Sally, things have altered a little.'

'What do you mean – a little?' I said, dreading what he was about to say. Sheila was pregnant. A marriage was about to be announced. The second Mrs Farringford was going to confirm the new family line. The father of my children was about to become the father of her child. I could feel my anger rising to the surface, as though she'd become pregnant deliberately, to spite me.

'I was referring to Sheila,' he said quietly.

'Let me guess. She's having your baby.'

I was waiting for him to say 'How on earth did you know?' Instead he shook his head.

'A couple of days ago she had the offer of an extremely good job, to run a large legal practice in New York. And she took up the offer, without consulting me.'

'Oh. Why did she have to consult you? Or wasn't it her decision?'

'Of course it was. But she must have known I couldn't possibly relocate to New York. I mean, I couldn't understand why she hadn't discussed it. When I objected, she said she had to give an instant reply when the job was offered, that I was being high-handed and lots of people commuted to New York nowadays. And then she accused me of wanting to stand in her way. When all I intended was for us to talk it through.' He gave a deep sigh, which he then tried to disguise with a cough. 'I've done my best to adapt, not to be set in my ways, to help domestically, that kind of thing . . . but it seems that I've failed. It does count, the difference in age . . . I was stupid to pretend it doesn't. I'm sorry. I shouldn't be going on like this.'

'Henry, please. We know each other well enough.'

He gave a grateful smile, as though I'd given him permission to be the old Henry. Then his expression changed and became more determined. He seemed to be gearing up for the final stage of some important case. Barristers have a way of sifting through evidence and presenting it piece by disjointed piece until it can be organized into one final telling statement. I had an instinctive fear of what the final statement would reveal.

'Quite honestly, I don't believe Sheila and I have a future together. She's a very ambitious young woman . . .'

'What's wrong with that?'

'Nothing. Nothing at all,' he said, rather unconvincingly. 'But she wanted me to change, to be more . . . modern. That was how she put it. I was fooling myself when I thought I could be someone else, though. Even though I made the effort, I often felt inadequate.'

'Don't we all?' I murmured.

'You? I never thought I'd hear you say that!' he exclaimed.

'Then you don't know me,' I answered.

I agreed to have dinner at the club, even though it meant I'd be home late. There was still so much to have out in the open. And yet, in spite of everything, I wanted Henry to feel that I would always be a friend, that I hadn't wiped him completely out of my life. Over the fish soup, which I barely touched, Henry continued his confession. The dining room was almost empty and all you could hear was the clattering of the meat trolley being manoeuvred into position near our table. Then he began to review our marriage, as though it would throw light on what had happened since November.

'You always gave the impression of being so independent, so in control. I used to watch you packing up Joel's things when he went back to boarding school, everything in neat piles, beautifully folded. There was always calm in the house – furniture polished, flowers in all the right places. When a man is making his career, he has to take all these things for granted. I should have been more considerate . . .'

'Ah, but I was bred to it. I was taught that being a wife was an honourable profession. I took my duties seriously. I wish I'd had the guts to be a rebel but I never quite managed it. I envied people who believed in something so strongly that it swept them along, who didn't have all the petty doubts I seemed to have.'

A huge platter of sliced beef surrounded by a glutinous wine sauce was placed on our table, accompanied by a silver platter containing mounds of overcooked vegetables. We both ate for a few minutes in silence, until I laid down my knife and fork, unable to take any more.

'Shall we have coffee in the library?' Henry suggested.

I walked up the great marble stairs behind Henry and

wondered how many times Sheila had followed in my
footsteps. They didn't make a distinction here between
wives and mistresses. Womenfolk. That's what we
were. I wondered what Paul would have made of it all.
I could imagine him gazing in admiration at the
elaborate metal balustrade, the great crystal chandelier
above us. We were directed towards four leather chairs
placed round a low table laid with coffee cups and
liqueur glasses.

As I was sitting with my hands on my lap, I caught
Henry staring at them. I quickly realized that he was
looking at the ring finger of my left hand. A few weeks
ago I'd taken off my wedding ring and had never put it
back. It felt like a supreme act of rebellion. Henry
suddenly raised his head and looked straight at me.

'Sally. Would you live with me again?'

I was so taken aback that I jolted the table with my leg
and sent a cup flying over the carpet. A man sitting
nearby struggled to his feet, picked it up and hobbled
over to replace it on the table. Henry thanked him and
then drew closer to me so that the ancient club member
was obscured from view.

'Well, darling?' Henry murmured.

'I . . . never even thought . . . I . . .'

Henry must have taken my hesitation for a positive
reply. I didn't mean to encourage him.

'You don't have to answer straight away. You can
think about it. It would be quite different from the old
days. We could start afresh. I'd do everything to make
you happy.'

What if Henry had made that suggestion before I'd
met Paul? Would I have gone back to him? I couldn't
begin to imagine. Too much water under the bridge.
Too much pain. How can you push yourself back in
time and pretend that the marks made by events can be
cleaned away?

'I'm really sorry but I can't see that it would work . . .'

Henry leaned towards me and clasped his hands together tightly, as though he was praying for me to relent. For a moment I put my hands on his. I understood what it must have cost him to admit that his affair with Sheila had been a failure.

'I know you've changed, but so have I. We've both moved on, but in different directions.'

'I'm not so sure, Sally. We have years behind us. We had a good marriage and could make it good again. I admit I made mistakes. Surely we can begin where we left off?'

I knew I would have to dash all his hopes, however I expressed it. If only he'd come out years ago with what he'd just said. If only he could have admitted that he wasn't always right. I waited until Henry had lit up another cigar.

'Henry, I'm living with another man. I'm sharing the flat with Paul.'

'Paul? Paul who? Do I know him?'

'Paul Burridge.'

'Not the boy who knocked around with Nicola for a while?'

'Yes. Her old boyfriend.'

He slowly put down his cigar onto the ashtray and stared at me for a moment as though I'd gone completely out of my mind. Then he gave me a pitying smile.

'Darling, I'm not condemning you. I can understand why it's happened. You had the right to try a new experience. It must have been terribly lonely for you. I've often thought about it.'

All my self-control suddenly deserted me. How dared he be so patronizing? I couldn't bear the complacent smile on his face. I had an irresistible urge to sweep everything off the table and storm out. Instead, I glared at Henry, my eyes hot and blazing.

'I'm in love with Paul. And he's in love with me. I'm not living with him because my bed gets cold at night.

I was used to that, after all. Wasn't I?' Henry flinched but I continued. 'I'm happier than I've ever been. And I don't care if you won't or can't believe it.'

Henry slowly poured out some more coffee from the jug, then looked up calmly.

'It's so easy to confuse sexual gratification with something more serious. I see it all the time.'

'Henry! How can you?' I burst out. 'I could have said the same about you and Sheila.'

'Then you might have been right. I doubt if I was ever really in love with her. But how does one know? Friends and colleagues never tell you what they really think.'

'You'd never have listened anyway,' I retorted.

Henry folded his arms and hugged them to him.

'We're both adults, you and I,' he said quietly. 'One makes mistakes at our age, everyone does.'

I shook my head vehemently.

'Paul isn't a mistake. We're building our lives together. It might seem crazy to you, but there it is.'

He picked up his cigar again and began puffing away to bring it into life.

'My dear Sally,' he said, in the patronizing tone he'd used before. 'You're deluding yourself. What can you possibly have in common with a boy from a dubious background, little education . . .'

'For God's sake, Henry. It isn't true and what if it was? Why should that matter?'

'Because you're being used,' he said, starting to become angry.

'How exactly?'

'I've seen it all before and it happens again and again. Older women falling head over heels for totally unsuitable men, young men on the make – or older men on the make. Flattery and competence in bed are all that's needed, it seems, to persuade women to give up all they possess.'

'So what you're saying is that once women reach a certain maturity, they all become weak and hopeless. Good God, Henry! I never knew you had such a low opinion of the female sex.'

'There's no need to be so strident. It doesn't suit you.'

'I don't give a damn.'

Henry put out his cigar, hammering the end into the ashtray. We stared one another out like two dogs spoiling for a fight. I couldn't remember ever having been consumed with such rage. Then Henry sat up straight and took a few deep breaths. We both sipped some coffee and tried to calm down. The waiter came up and quietly refilled the pot, as though he was officiating at a funeral.

'Do the children know?' Henry asked, when the waiter had retreated to a safe distance.

'Yes. It took some time to adjust but they seem quite relaxed about it now.'

Henry frowned and pursed his lips.

'They won't be quite so relaxed when your young man starts looking around elsewhere.'

'I don't believe he will but I'm going to take the chance.'

'I'm afraid it's inevitable, Sally. Don't fool yourself. I couldn't bear to see you being hurt.'

'For a second time, you mean?' I said. Henry looked away. 'I can't explain logically why I'm living with Paul. I just know he's right for me. I can't weigh everything up and start worrying where I'll be in ten years' time. Or five.'

Henry put down his cup carefully on the tray.

'What on earth do your friends think?'

'I've no idea. I haven't asked them,' I snapped.

The waiter came to remove our cups and I asked him for my coat.

'My offer's still open. Do think about it,' Henry said quietly, as I got up to leave.

'I'm sorry, Henry. I'm not interested. As soon as it's legally possible, I want a divorce.'

We walked quickly down the marble stairs without saying a word. Henry hailed a taxi and I just caught the last train to Wengrave. I sat back in the half empty carriage, feeling leaden, empty and sad. Now our marriage had really come to an end and I knew I could never go back.

Paul was already in bed, hidden beneath the blankets, but the light was on. I slipped off my shoes, crept to the bathroom and looked in the mirror. I hoped he was asleep so that he wouldn't see my grey, colourless face, my eyes tinged with red.

'Sal? You back?' he called out, when I opened the bathroom door. I came slowly into the bedroom. 'Tell me. Was it dreadful?'

I sat on the bed, my shoulders hunched, with my face turned away.

'Yes. I said I wanted a divorce as soon as possible.'

'And was he angry?'

'I lost my temper. And then afterwards I felt sorry for him. He asked me to . . .'

'There's no need to talk if you don't want to.'

I slipped in beside Paul and clasped my hands round his neck. The warmth of his body lulled me into sleep.

It took a few days for me to recover. In the office, Pickle made various attempts to lighten my mood but I found it hard to join in the banter.

'Something up with you and Paul?' she asked, one morning.

'I must finish this. Everything's wonderful,' I replied, continuing to type.

'Honest?'

'Leave it out, Pickle,' Jed said, from the other side of the room.

She went back to her drawing board, but I could see she wasn't concentrating, ripping off sheets of paper and throwing them on the floor. Then she abandoned her attempts and swivelled round to face me.

'Sal?' I looked up for a moment. 'You're working too hard. You need to do a fun thing.'

'Like?'

'I dunno.'

'A knees-up?' volunteered Jed. 'We'd all go for that.'

'A party! A proper one. How about it? You've been moved in ages.'

'I'm not nearly ready for that.' Pickle looked so crestfallen that I couldn't help laughing. 'D'you think I should have one, then?'

'Course you must. So your friends can come along and be jealous. And bring you silly things for the flat. Who cares if nothing's ready? I'll do the invite, if you like.'

'And I'll organize the sounds,' added Jed.

'We'll see about that! OK. Now let's fix a date,' said Pickle, already putting herself in charge.

Before I'd had time to consider whether it would be a good idea or not, I found myself going along with it. It would give me a chance to show how much I appreciated being with Hedgehog, a small way of thanking them for their friendship. Since any kind of party was their idea of heaven, I was soon swept away by their enthusiasm. We circled a date towards the end of September, when all my friends would be back from holiday. Then it dawned on me that it would give me the ideal opportunity to let everybody know that I was no longer on my own. I had become part of Paul's circle of friends and now he would become part of mine.

It was a Sunday morning towards the end of September. I was downing cups of black coffee, feeling more anxious by the minute. Paul and I had decided that

315

we'd have open house from lunchtime until early evening, so there'd be less pressure and everyone could come at different times. Ginnie had swept down from Fulham and instantly thrown herself into party mode. She was making minute but essential adjustments to the great vases of lilies and white roses placed around the living room. Paul was bent over the work surface in the kitchen, concocting Mediterranean dips from her recipes. I was running backwards and forwards, unable to remember what I should be doing and in what order.

'What's got into you, Sal?' asked Paul, as I checked yet again to see if he had everything he needed. 'We're only having a few people round.'

'But I must have asked eighty at least.'

'If half of them drop in, that's only forty. And they're not likely to come all at once.'

I left the kitchen, ran into the bedroom and changed what I was wearing for the third time. Why was it such an effort? Ginnie always looked right and ready for anything.

'Will this do? Not too over the top?' I asked, appearing in front of Paul in flowing white silk trousers with a bright peacock blue camisole top. These were nothing like the clothes I used to have, which I'd bundled up and taken to the charity shop just before I moved.

'Perfect. Now for God's sake sit down,' Paul said.

He seemed so unconcerned, so relaxed. Why couldn't I be the same? His fine blond hair was just touching his shoulders and he was in cream linen trousers with a short-sleeved shirt. I couldn't see how I could live up to this handsome man.

'Sal, I think you need a drink,' he said.

'Did someone say a drink?' came Ginnie's ebullient voice from the living room. 'Count me in.'

The buzzer sounded for the first time. Trish, a friend of Maggie's who always invited me to her barbecues, came sailing in wearing a large-brimmed silk hat and a flowered cocktail suit. She was followed by her husband Jeremy, who was in a blazer and pink in the face.

'Sally! What a darling little flat!' Trish enthused. 'But why did you leave that lovely house by the river?'

Paul came forward and handed them both a glass of sparkling wine. Jeremy immediately took a great gulp.

'Champers. Jolly good.'

I hoped he'd drunk enough before he came so that he wouldn't be able to distinguish the cheap bottles of méthode champenoise from the real thing.

'This is Paul,' I said.

He was standing beside me, but at first neither Trish nor Jeremy appeared to have registered him. Now Trish turned to face him.

'I've seen you somewhere, I know I have,' she gushed. 'Aren't you from Edgeworth Marine?'

'Course he is,' Jeremy chimed in. 'You chaps look after our launch. *Trish's Treat*. You must know her.'

Now was the moment. I had to make a start. Ginnie would have done it so much better.

'Paul lives here with me,' I said.

Jeremy gave a puzzled glance at Trish, but she ignored him and beamed a smile.

'It's such a good idea to have a lodger. Lots of people we know do.'

I was dying to say, 'You've got it wrong — actually we're lovers' but I didn't have quite enough bravado. Paul immediately set off for the kitchen. I couldn't have imagined a worse start to our party. I rushed after him and whispered in his ear.

'I'm so sorry. Don't take it to heart, will you? Trish means well but she always manages to put her foot in it.'

'Still, she knows how to wear a hat,' said Paul, with a grin.

The buzzer sounded a few more times. Some acquaintances arrived from the Henry days whom I hadn't expected to come. Three of Paul's friends came and sat in a corner, talking amongst themselves. Nicola, Mark and Joel were coming later in the afternoon. What if Mark's car broke down again? What if Matt, Pickle and Jed had overdone it the night before and failed to turn up? I smiled with relief when I opened the door to Maggie and Jeff, closely followed by Patsy and Mustafa. They were always good at parties, taking pains to meet new people and to make them feel at home. They embraced me warmly and immediately demanded a tour of the flat. Mustafa approved, saying it was an excellent investment, and Jeff made some comment about 'decent-sized rooms, not like the poky places they put up overnight and call executive dwellings'.

'You must meet Paul. He'll get you something to drink,' I said, waving towards the kitchen.

Paul came over and I introduced him. Maggie and Patsy both stared for a moment, gave a brief polite smile and continued a conversation with Jeff and Mustafa about yet another person they knew who'd been quite unfairly breathalysed and was over the limit after only one drink. I'd heard it so many times before. I couldn't understand their behaviour. It was so unlike them. Didn't they have anything to say to Paul? Even if it was only something trivial. We were about to move away when Mustafa suddenly withdrew from the conversation and turned to address Paul.

'Sorry about that,' he said, gesturing towards Maggie's group who were now discussing speed traps in loud voices. 'Once they start, I can't stop them. My wife's always terrified of losing her licence or getting a huge fine. Luckily I have someone to drive for me. Where do you live? Are you from Wengrave?' he asked.

'From Cornwall originally but I live here, with Sally.'

'Patsy wanted me to buy into this block but I had

other things on. I should have taken her advice. Still, you've done all right, haven't you?'

'Sally has.'

'Ah. I see,' he said with a smile. Then he turned to me. 'You must come round for supper. We met some interesting people on holiday – I'm sure you'd get on. They've just moved round here and one of them is a cosmetic surgeon.'

Patsy immediately pricked up her ears and joined in our conversation.

'Oh yes. He's quite marvellous, so they say. Maggie and I are going for a consultation. He'd give us a discount. Fancy coming?'

'You can't be serious!' exclaimed Paul.

'They say it changes your life,' remarked Patsy.

'Mine's already changed,' I said with a grin, taking Paul's hand. 'Did you know that we were living together?'

My clumsy announcement failed to make the dramatic impact I'd hoped for.

'Angela said it was on the cards.'

Patsy raised her eyebrows and briefly glanced at Paul. Then her eyes followed Maggie and Jeff as they made their way towards the drinks table. Finally, she beckoned me to an empty corner of the room. I was expecting some comment about Paul.

'Listen Sal,' she said, standing close to me. 'Just so you'll know. Jeff's found out. They had a big row on holiday and Maggie's dropped you know who. They're both seeing someone from Relate. Shh. I'll tell you later.'

I looked at her blankly.

It didn't take long for the living room to become crowded and the buzz of conversation grew louder. There seemed to be a good atmosphere, though I couldn't be sure. I'd never given a party in such a small space and there wasn't nearly enough seating. But Paul and his friends seemed happy enough sitting on the floor, and soon they were joined by Matt, Pickle and Jed. By now I had stopped explaining that Paul and I were living together. Some guests betrayed a slight curiosity when I introduced him, but most of my friends and acquaintances looked mildly surprised and then quickly turned to other matters. Sooner or later, I thought, they would have to accept us. I wished I hadn't invited so many people who – I was now beginning to realize – really didn't mean much to me.

Most of the married couples left after an hour or so, pleading other engagements. I felt much easier in the company of Paul's friends, who appeared not to notice their absence. Yet the differences that divided them didn't seem to depend on age. It was as though all the couples around my age had been coached to act in a certain, rather rigid manner. I found it hard to identify myself with them. Even if I couldn't identify myself completely with Pickle and her gang, I felt at home with them, as though the years between us were irrelevant.

As I half expected, Nicola rang to say that they'd all be late. For a while I gave up being the perfect hostess and came to sit on the floor beside Ginnie. She and Pickle were comparing notes on the sexual habits of fourteen-year-olds, with Ginnie providing the statistics. Pickle was clearly a great hit with Ginnie and I heard her saying she'd love to interview her for the mag.

Jed's music was starting to pulse round the room when there was a hammering on the front door. I leaped to my feet and ran to answer it. A florid Martin hurtled towards me.

'At last! I kept asking for Sally Farringford. No-one knew you. Knocked on the wrong door. Not too late am I? Haven't cocked things up again?'

'I didn't think you were coming,' I said, leading him into the flat.

'Got back late last night. Saw your invitation. Couldn't miss Sally's party.'

Staggering into the living room, Martin gave me a hasty kiss and then homed in on Ginnie. It was obvious that he'd already had something to drink. I was praying that he wouldn't ask searching questions about Paul. It would be best, I decided, to break the news to him gently when we were alone.

'Is there some Scotch hidden away? Or gin at a pinch?' Martin asked, grabbing hold of my arm.

'Try some of my Russian vodka,' suggested Ginnie. 'I've kept some hidden for special guests.'

'Later on would be better,' I said, giving a warning glance at Ginnie.

Martin released my arm.

'To tell you the truth, I've had a bit. Can't drink as much as I used to. I could do with a nice lady to stop me being naughty.'

He fixed his gaze on the faint outline of Ginnie's breasts, showing temptingly through her lacy top.

'What you need is a nurse,' she said, icily.

Martin quickly backed away from her, clasped my hand and pulled me through the crowded room towards the window.

'Sally, my dear. You can't live in a place like this. You'll go completely bonkers. Not enough room to swing a cat.'

I smiled awkwardly.

'It's all I need. And it's very spacious for a flat.'

Martin put his arm round my shoulder. With any luck we'd be screened from view, as Paul and Jed had pushed back the furniture and people were starting to dance in front of us.

'This flat'll do for a while,' Martin continued, slightly slurring his words. 'But I'll be able to whisk you away sometimes. Palm trees and a golden beach. I know just the place.'

321

'Martin, please don't.'

I tried not to sound too severe, but he had already extracted a small silver flask from his pocket and was unscrewing the top. Without pausing, he gulped down a good helping of its contents. At a certain stage, nobody could stop him. I prayed he wouldn't get out of control – which, on rare occasions, he did. He slipped his hand down my behind and I unobtrusively pushed it away. This didn't deter him and I knew it wouldn't.

'Sally, darling. I think of you every day. Always will. Can't get you out of my mind. Always. Love. Loved you. Do anything you say.'

'You know it's not possible. I only love you as a friend,' I said.

I felt enormous tenderness towards him and I didn't care if he was drunk. I was familiar enough with his pattern. Soon he'd drop off into a doze and then he'd suddenly wake up and demand a cup of coffee.

'I'll . . . live . . . in Timbuktu . . . or a desertisland. See you in my dreams.'

He gave a little hiccup and then without warning lowered his head and kissed my neck, clinging there limpetlike and leaning heavily against me. I didn't want him to make a fool of himself by falling asleep on my breasts, so I tried unsuccessfully to lift him off. Suddenly Paul was by my side.

'What's happening? What on earth are you doing?'

The response was a grunting sound as Paul prised Martin away from me.

'He's a little drunk. Let's sit him down somewhere.'

'Not drunk. Little tip . . . tip . . . tipsy.'

With difficulty, we edged Martin through the whirling feet towards a chair backed up against the wall. His head slumped onto his chest.

'Will he be all right?' I asked Paul.

'He'd better lie down in the bedroom for a while.'

Martin attempted to raise his head.

'Be fine in a tick. No need. Gone to the head.' He made another effort to sit upright, pushing himself up from the seat of the chair. 'People here I don't know.' His swimming eyes fixed on Paul. 'Know you, though. Name escapes me. Had a bit to drink at the golf club . . . and blow me . . .'

'You know perfectly well who I am,' Paul cut in.

'Paul,' I added quickly.

Reaching out, Martin took hold of one end of my belt, trying to pull me closer to him.

'Lovely girl, Sally. Never taken her to bed. More's the pity.'

'Don't take any notice,' I said to Paul, but he wasn't listening.

'Just keep your hands off. Right?' he said, his voice sounding rough and menacing. I looked warily at Paul. I'd never heard him come out with anything like this. I felt as though we'd been plunged into a pub brawl and I had no idea what to do. It was my fault for having been such a coward. I should have written to Martin a long time ago, but I'd kept putting it off. It was the wrong time, but I had to say something now.

'Paul and I are living together,' I said to Martin.

He leaned his head backward to focus on Paul, who was standing over him, his face set and unsmiling.

'Made my boat. That the one?'

I had to repeat it, slowly and clearly.

'Paul and I are living together. In this flat.'

Having given a brief nod of acknowledgement, Martin turned to watch the dancers. He looked like a blind man who is pretending to see.

'I'll get him a jug of water. With any luck, he might sober up.'

I was about to go but Paul pulled me back.

'Wait here. I'll get him some.'

Once Paul had left us, I crouched down beside Martin. The music had temporarily stopped and I began to speak quietly, hoping he could hear me against the buzz of conversation.

'I was going to tell you, Martin, but I didn't know how to. I didn't want to hurt you.'

Martin was still staring ahead, as though in a trance. Then he suddenly swung round to face me.

'You thought I didn't realize? When you kept putting me off? Well, I did. There must be . . .' His voice was rising and he checked himself. 'There must be a chap somewhere,' he continued, more quietly. 'Hadn't heard, no more chats. Good-looking girl like you. Didn't imagine it would be whatsisname, though. All you girls want youngsters in bed.'

'That's not why,' I said.

'No, I get the picture. I don't blame you. Not that I like it, but I don't blame you. You're a modern girl now. They do things differently, so they tell me.'

I stood up and opened the window wide to let in some cooler air. The room had become uncomfortably hot, but nobody appeared to notice. Pickle and friends were about to leave, waving frantically to me across the room. I waved back. I saw Paul escorting them out, and then he returned with a jug of water and a glass.

'Be right as rain in a mo,' said Martin, swilling down the water. 'Got to see the children. Are they coming?'

'Soon, I hope,' I replied.

'He ought to get back home. I'll get him a taxi right now,' Paul insisted.

'No, no. Wait a while. He hasn't seen Nicola and Joel for ages and I know he'd hate to miss them,' I said.

Paul immediately walked off without saying a word. There was little I could do. If only he hadn't witnessed Martin at his worst. I wanted Paul to appreciate Martin for what he was, a good-hearted man – who occasionally drank too much. I needed my friends to be Paul's friends, at least the ones who'd shared my life and been close to me for so long. In a flash, I realized I

324

wanted my old life and my new life. I wished to hop happily from one to the other, but it wasn't possible. Gradually it was dawning on me that I would have to make a choice, but it seemed that Paul was forcing me to do so, as though he'd given me my voting paper with a list of names and I was only allowed to make one cross.

Ginnie was coming towards me, bearing a tray of drinks. I left Martin's side to join her.

'Nicola's just rung on her mobile. They'll be here in ten minutes.' She peered into my face. 'What's up, Sal? You look miserable.'

'Martin. Drunk. He's disgraced himself. Paul wanted him to leave.'

By now I was close to tears. Ginnie put her arm round me.

'Tomorrow it'll all be forgotten. Come on, Sal. Cheer up. You don't want the kids to see you like this. And if Paul can't cope with Martin, he's not the man I thought he was.'


Martin stayed long enough to spend some time with Nicola and Joel, and it wasn't until nine o'clock that the last guest was persuaded to leave. Then we were left together – Nicola, Mark, Joel, Ginnie, Paul and myself. Paul was extracting some splinters of broken glass from the carpet. My feet were swollen and my mouth was aching with having to smile all day.

'Do you think it went all right?' I asked.

'Fantastic, wasn't it?' said Nicola, glancing at Mark.

'Sure was,' said Mark.

'I'm sorry about Martin,' I said to Paul.

'Forget it. It was a great party. Now I could really go for an Indian. How about it, everyone?'

As we set off, all my weariness suddenly disappeared. It hadn't been a total disaster. The disappointment I'd felt at the half-hearted reaction of my friends was beginning to fade away. Paul and I would find new friends together and I would see less of old ones. I felt the rush of pleasure that comes from doing something with people one loves. They didn't care about making the right impression or obeying conventional rules of behaviour. I hadn't been such a dreadful mother, I thought, as I joined in the unrestrained laughter coming from our table in the Posh Spice Indian restaurant.

# FOURTEEN

• • •

Just over a year after Henry announced he was leaving me for Sheila, she moved out. There was no question of my going back to him, and when he saw how determined I was, Henry promised that he'd go along with a divorce by mutual consent. In another year, I could officially change my name back to Sally Linton.

Whenever I passed Oakleigh Grange I no longer slowed down to see what the new owners had done to the house. Angela told me they'd put in a wavy-shaped swimming pool where the vegetable garden used to be and planted leylandii all along the front wall. She was the only one of my friends I used to meet regularly who passed on the Wengrave gossip. After my party, I received the usual polite messages thanking me for my hospitality but the invitations I received in the next few weeks failed to include Paul, so I sent my apologies. Whenever I bumped into Maggie or Patsy, they enquired if everything was all right and then left it at that. They weren't unkind but puzzled, as though they were unable to relate to the Sally they knew so well.

I was discovering that Paul had quite an eccentric and varied collection of friends – but they were all easy with me, as though we'd known one another for years. None of them referred even indirectly to my being so much older than him. The question didn't seem to arise any more and I rarely thought about it. I was forty something. I'd stopped reminding myself of months and years. And I rarely peered into the mirror searching my face for puckering skin or the early signs of wrinkles. Then one evening, a friend of Paul's and his pregnant wife came to supper.

After they'd gone, I stretched out on the carpet, warming myself in front of the imitation log fire – not the same as a real one but near enough.

'Jean's quite young to be having kids, isn't she?' Paul remarked, coming to lie beside me.

'I was about her age when I had Nicola. In one way, you cope better then. You just get on with it.'

Paul patted my stomach.

'Have you ever thought about us having kids?'

'It's rather soon for that,' I replied, praying that he wouldn't elaborate.

'I don't mind waiting. But I'd love to see you with a big belly. Did you like being pregnant?'

'I think so. I can't really remember.'

'Maybe you'll get the urge, in a year or so. There's no hurry.'

'I . . . I'm not sure it's a good idea for me to have babies again.'

'When you're divorced from Henry, we could get married. Would that make it easier to decide?'

'No, it's not that. But is that a serious proposal?' I said with a smile.

'Everything I say is serious.' Paul's eyes were dancing.

I sat up and stared into the fire. How could I possibly explain? How could I tell him that even if I wanted to, it was almost out of the question to start a family at my age? Even though I knew women were having children much later, I couldn't face it myself. In a very few years I'd be menopausal. The idea of babies hadn't even entered my head.

'What's the matter?' Paul asked. 'Have I said the wrong thing?'

'No, you haven't. Not at all.'

'If you don't see yourself with kids just at the moment, that's all right by me. I'd like to be a dad but only if you wanted it too. It's not something we have to think about right now, is it? We can decide later. You might change your mind – who knows?'

Even though I'd confessed my age when we went away together, I'd always refused to give Paul the exact date of my birthday, with the excuse that after twenty-one, I couldn't see the point of marking the passing years. Now I'd have to spell it out.

'My birthday was last week and I'm forty-three now,' I said hurriedly, before Paul could interrupt me. 'I'm getting on a bit for babies.'

'Why didn't we celebrate?' asked Paul, in amazement.

'Because . . . oh . . . it just reminds me of the time between us.'

'I thought you didn't care about that any more.'

'Only for you.'

'Do I seem to care? Do you think I wake every morning saying to myself, "Forty-two. She's forty-two!" '

'Forty-three.'

'OK, have it your way. Forty-three. Plenty of women have babies after forty. My Auntie May had her youngest when she was forty-five. Popped out like a pea from a pod, she said. And you're a good strong girl, just like her.'

The idea of wheeling Paul's baby down Wengrave High Street was so unthinkable that I began to giggle, either through nerves or relief that we were able to discuss it.

'What's funny?' asked Paul.

'You calling me a good strong girl. But that's not everything, is it? Time's running out for me but it's different for you. One day you'll want to be a father and have children, and do all the normal things I'll be too old for.'

'Too old? That's crazy. My gran's got more energy than me and she's ancient. Twice a week she walks down to Newlyn harbour to buy her fish – and that's three miles away. We can have kids. In a couple of years I should be earning good money.'

Now that Paul had mentioned it, I did wonder what it would be like to have his child. Physically, it would be possible. And I could visualize a baby who looked like Paul, who would grow up into a wonderfully gifted beautiful child. But I knew it had to remain a dream. Imagine my telling Nicola and Joel that they were to have a baby in the family! Going out to buy maternity clothes, all the paraphernalia of motherhood . . .

'I can't see myself getting pregnant,' I said, with regret. 'I don't think I want to do all that again.'

'Never mind. It was only a thought, Sal.' Paul rolled over onto his side and propped himself on his elbow. 'You look so lovely, lying there.'

He had an expression of tender happiness, as though nothing would ever go wrong between us.

'One day you'll meet a girl and you'll think of starting a family. It's perfectly normal. And I know I'll some-how have to accept it. You're so good with kids – you always have been.'

'I love you,' said Paul, kissing me gently on the lips. 'I'm staying with you. I'm not looking for anyone else. I belong here.'

I was slowly growing confident that Paul would be part of my future, but I did miss the close relationship I used to have with my friends. He urged me to keep in touch, even though he had little in common with them, as he didn't believe in shutting off people you were fond of. When he spent the odd evening alone with his friends,

I no longer feared he was having a rendezvous with Sam. Occasionally I'd drop into the Café Rouge and Maggie, Patsy and Angela would be chatting about subjects I now cared little about. 'Still with Paul?' they'd ask, with a surprised smile. But they never asked us round. I enjoyed their company for a short while, but I think Martin was the only person I truly missed. There had been a long silence. After the party I called him several times but he had gone away again and didn't phone me back. Then, one day, he rang me in the office as though nothing had happened, inviting me – as always well in advance – to have lunch at his favourite pub by the river.

I could see no sign of Martin's old Jaguar outside the pub. I went in and was just about to order a beer, when he appeared by my side.

To my surprise, he looked younger and healthier, with a rosy bloom on his skin. He was dressed in an expensive, well-cut navy suit with a bright striped tie. His thinning, usually unkempt hair was trimmed very short and square. I must have looked scruffy beside him – my hair had grown, and the old cashmere sweater I'd put over my trousers had seen better days. I'd given up wearing jewellery and used the minimum of make-up. I felt more comfortable now that way, more relaxed, more like myself.

'Allow me, Sally. Champers as usual?'

'Just a glass.' I smiled. 'Lovely.'

'I've already ordered,' he said, with a beam. 'The best one they've got. Not marvellous but it'll do for us, won't it?'

'Isn't that a touch extravagant?'

'I can't stop making money. I'm earning more and doing less work than I ever was,' he whispered. 'Silly, isn't it? It's all legal, though. I'm a corporate consultant now.'

'Sounds very grand,' I remarked. 'But what do you actually do?'

'Corporate planning, strategies, mission statements, bit of Euro-babble plus a wild prediction of export markets. And that gets me a brand new TVR sports job. I'll give you a lift home in it, goes like the bloody wind.'

'My God, Martin!' I exclaimed. 'Why get one of those?'

'You're only old once! Come on, let's find somewhere quiet.'

He led me to a couple of panelled oak settles either side of a narrow table. We had barely sat down when the barman came bustling up to us with a bottle of champagne in a bucket. After he'd popped it open and poured it out, Martin sampled it and then squeezed my hand.

'Just like old times. And you're looking years younger. You know, I wondered if you'd ever forgive me after I'd disgraced myself. I thought I'd better lie low for a bit. Drunk as a skunk at your party, I was. That Paul of yours must have been horrified. I bet he told you to get that seedy old bastard out of the place.'

'Of course he didn't, Martin. Everyone expects a bit of bad behaviour at parties. Otherwise they wouldn't be fun, would they?'

'So I'm forgiven?'

'Naturally you are.'

He reached across to examine the state of the bottle.

'I'll get another. Why not?'

'Martin. One's enough. No more.'

'Quite right. I'm driving you home. Aren't I impossible?'

'Absolutely impossible. I don't know how I put up with you.'

Martin had ordered some oysters, which arrived on an enormous platter surrounded by seaweed and chunks of lemon.

'I had to see you eat these. I know you love them.'

He waited until I'd downed the first one before taking one himself, giving me a mischievous look as though we were eating a forbidden food. Then he suddenly became serious.

'You know, Sally, I've just turned sixty-two. It makes you think.'

I naturally assumed that he wanted reassurance.

'Nobody would ever guess. You're in great shape.'

'Thanks, Sally. But that's not quite what I meant. I've been thinking a lot about us.'

'Oh?'

I couldn't hide my alarm. Surely it was plain enough by now?

'Don't worry, I'm not going to propose,' he said, with a laugh. 'I know perfectly well you'd have been mad to get married to me. I wouldn't advise it myself as a matter of fact. I've given up my hopes, or maybe they were illusions. And that's better for both of us.'

'You're very wise.'

I really did admire him for having the guts to say what he had to say with such good humour and a complete lack of self-pity.

'To celebrate my non-proposal, I've bought you a present. It was meant to be for your birthday but I was gadding around in foreign parts.'

'You sent me a wonderful card. Very saucy.'

'Thought you'd appreciate it,' he said with a smile. 'Anyway, the moment I saw these I knew you'd have to have them.'

He handed me a small pink gift-wrapped box and I slipped off the sparkling string. Inside was a pair of chunky gold earrings in the shape of horseshoes, with coloured stones where the nails would be.

'What fun! You really shouldn't have. They look awfully expensive,' I said.

'Real stones. Emeralds and rubies. Designed by a

333

chap with a fancy Italian name. I asked for a young style because I know you don't like pearls and things any more. Put them on. I must see them on.'

When I'd threaded them through my ears, Martin leaned back to admire them.

'I knew they'd suit you, Sal. Young and bold. Equally suitable for day or evening wear, that's what the pretty girl said in the shop.'

He kissed me to celebrate his purchase. Dear Martin.

Our meal wasn't prolonged because Martin was dying to show off his new car. When I stepped in, he promised not to exceed fifty miles an hour and I was given permission to keep an eye on the speedometer. However, he couldn't resist an initial acceleration, which knocked me back into my seat.

'Easy!' I cried.

'Just a taster,' he said, dropping down his speed. 'Now, where's it to be? We could go out to Cliveden and have a whopping great tea.'

'I'm really sorry, but I have to be back in the office.'

'Of course you do. Shame about that. I'd forgotten about your little job. What's it called, the company?'

'Hedgehog Graphics.'

'Well,' he said with a laugh. 'Prickly Hedgehog it is.'

I managed to persuade Martin to park round the corner from the office. I couldn't quite face the barrage of questions if one of the gang happened to notice our arrival.

'How's life with Paul?' he suddenly said, as he gazed affectionately at the dials in front of him.

'Pretty good,' I said.

'I'm wildly jealous but I know he's a good lad. I've made sure you're in safe hands. We couldn't have some no-good taking advantage of you, could we?'

'I can judge for myself,' I answered, smiling at him.

'I know. But these days, you can't trust anyone.

More's the pity. Anyway, I didn't think it would do any harm to have a quiet chat with old Edgeworth.'

'You what!'

'Don't worry. It was just a casual enquiry. We happened to be talking about *Water Gypsy* and I said I was interested in Paul's progress. Well, I had started him on his way.'

'And what did he say to you?'

I had dreadful visions of Martin making credit checks on Paul's past history.

'They all think he's tremendous. A nice lad – man I should say – and a serious worker. If he stays with him, Edgeworth told me, he might eventually take him on as his junior partner.'

'Fantastic! Am I allowed to tell Paul?' I asked, excitedly.

'Don't see why not. But why don't I tell him myself? We could all meet at the pub one weekend when I'm home. Or I can take you both out to dinner, if you'd prefer.'

I looked at him doubtfully.

'Are you sure?'

'I mean it,' he insisted.

I swung myself out of the car and watched as Martin started up the throaty engine, then attempted a Grand Prix start, sending birds scattering from the trees in the quiet street. Seconds later he veered round the corner out of sight, tyres squealing.

'Wow!' said Pickle, staring at me open-mouthed as I walked through the office door. I instantly put my fingers to my ears. I'd forgotten to remove the earrings as I ran up the stairs.

'Where on earth d'you get those?'

'They've just been given to me by a wonderful friend. The best in the world. But he isn't exactly a style guru.'

We both giggled as I slipped them off.

*

Towards the middle of the afternoon, Matt appeared
with a long woollen scarf wrapped several times round
his neck. The whole house was invaded by icy
draughts as the central heating was being renewed.
The old paraffin heater provided by Jed did little to
increase the temperature and we'd opened the windows to lessen the stifling smell. Pickle and I were
trying to get on with things, sitting with chilled fingers
at our desks.

'Bloody freezing! Typical, isn't it? Trust Hedgehog to
put in new radiators in November. Let's go off to the
pub. We need a warm-up.'

We were able to thaw out in front of the gas-fired
flames lighting up the saloon bar of the Raven. Matt
brought over some steaming soup and we sat warming
our hands round the thick pottery bowls.

'I should have given you some time off till the
heating's in,' Matt said, apologizing to me. 'But
knowing you, I thought you'd want to carry on.'

'You guessed right!'

'You must have got used to us by now.'

'Just about,' I said, with a laugh. 'I've been here for
nine months, after all.'

'Christ! That long! I never thought we'd last more
than six.'

'Why ever not? You've worked hard, haven't paid
yourselves much . . .'

'You can say that again,' said Jed, making a face at
Matt.

'Not for much longer, though.' Matt looked serious
for a moment. 'What do you think, Sal? We've had an
offer from a film animation company. They want to
take over Hedgehog and are offering loads of dosh.'

'Sounds great,' I said. 'But you wouldn't want to lose
your independence, surely? What would you get out of
it, Matt?'

'New premises. Posh front. Marketing budget. And for starters, a contract to script and design six animation films. It would mean hiring new people.'

'Expansion,' added Jed, with an ironic grin.

'What do you think, Sal?' Matt repeated.

'Well, I'd like to have a good look at their proposals. And how about getting in a business consultant before you commit yourselves? Actually I know someone who'd be ideal,' I said, thinking of Martin.

'I talked it over with Pickle and Jed last night. Me and Pickle are in favour. Jed's not sure. But we've got to decide by next week.'

'Fast-track decision, that's what,' Pickle remarked, glancing at Jed.

While we finished our soup, I began to go through in my mind what my position might be. If Hedgehog were taken over, they'd want to replace me with some smart incredibly qualified high-powered management secretary. But I knew they deserved to be successful, even if I had to leave.

'In principle, I think you should go ahead.' I tried to hide my regret with a bright smile. 'And I'm sure you'd do really well.'

Matt looked up at me.

'We couldn't do this without you, Sal. When we discussed things last night we agreed. If this deal goes through, we'd like you to be our projects manager. We're pretty hopeless at the paperwork stuff, as you know. You're as much part of the company as we are.'

'And what's more, you'd get a raise!' exclaimed Pickle.

'How about it?' asked Matt.

'Say yes,' ordered Jed. 'Then I might.'

'And you'd get a few shares as well,' added Matt.

'Goodness! I don't know what to say. I mean, I don't know if I'd be up to it.'

'Course you will. Otherwise we wouldn't have asked.'

'It has to be yes,' I said, beaming. 'Of course I'd love to be part of Hedgehog.'

'Deal, then.'

Matt, Pickle, Jed and I stood up, formally shook hands and sat down again.

My mind was racing. Hedgehog would need new offices – I couldn't see them staying in the little terrace house for long. I could count on Mustafa to find the ideal place.

'You'd need flashy new premises, I imagine,' I said.

'You bet.'

'Hold on. If I agree . . .' Jed began.

'You have agreed. I said so.'

'OK, Pickle. Then I want a huge big desk with space to put my cactus on and pics of my dog.'

She groaned, shrugging her shoulders.

'They want us to move to Covent Garden,' Matt continued. 'There's a converted warehouse just off Long Acre. Do you know that area?'

'A wonderful location.' My face fell. 'So you'd all be going to London.'

'Thassit. If I agree,' said Jed.

As we walked back to the Hedgehog house, I was in turmoil. It was an impossible decision for me and a brilliant opportunity for them. I'd have to grit my teeth and start looking for another job. I would see Matt in private to explain my reasons.

'You're asking me to leave Wengrave. How could I, Matt? It's a huge step. I haven't lived in London since my early twenties. I don't think I could take it.'

'Look. We've talked about it. We'd all help one another find somewhere to live. Pickle thinks we should all rent a house together to start with. See how it pans out.'

'What about my children?'

338

'They'd love it. We'd find a corner somewhere, don't worry.'

'It's rather late for me to make such a radical change.'

'You've made quite a few since we've known you. One more won't make any difference, surely?'

'I can't see it, Matt.'

He brought me a cup of tea and after clearing a space, I sat on the edge of his desk.

'You're thinking about Paul, I know,' Matt said.

'A good guess,' I said, with a smile. 'You know how much I'd like to stay working for you. I'm sure Pickle wouldn't approve, but I couldn't give up Paul. He'd never leave. We're both settled and happy. What would he do if he left the boatyard? He'd be completely lost in London.'

'There's plenty of boat places down the Thames. I bet he'd find something,' Matt said, sounding impatient. 'Listen, Sal. What I'm offering is a great opportunity for you as well. We need you and think you'd do a fantastic job. What's the alternative? If you stay in Wengrave what will you do? Find something really exciting with a local estate agent? Type out contracts for some deadbeat lawyer? Sell trainers and golf clubs? I can't see you doing anything like that. You'd hate it and you're too good.'

'Am I?' I said, doubtfully.

'And I bet Paul wouldn't want it either. For Christ's sake, do you realize what you'd be doing with us? Helping to build up an exciting young company, one you understand. Think about it. We want you to come. Talk it over with Paul and let me know by Sunday night. And don't forget. First you said yes.'

I could barely concentrate for the rest of the afternoon. If I told Paul I'd accepted the job, it would be the same as telling him that it was all over. Or that was how I saw it. Yet I couldn't bring myself to totally reject Matt's proposal. Since Henry left, I'd been testing my reactions to challenges. Could I manage to hold down a job? Could I live with Paul and keep my independence? Could I face upsetting all my friends? Could I manage to keep my friendship with Martin? It struck me that I'd been plotting my own course, however haphazardly. Would I be able to continue?

For once, I concluded that I had to make this decision on my own. There was no point in being swayed this way and that by listening to the views of others. Ginnie would have told me to come to London and so would Nicola. Martin would have said the opposite, as would Angela. I knew what their reactions would be. But what about Paul? Would he see it as an affront if I accepted? Would he jump to the conclusion that my love was waning or – as he teasingly suggested – I was getting bored with a cosy domestic life? I veered alternately between negative and positive. I wouldn't talk to Paul until I had the arguments clear in my mind.

Reasons Against (I always seemed to put the negative first):

I'd never considered myself ambitious. I imagined that you'd need a certain kind of ruthlessness that I had no desire to cultivate. Hedgehog would be competing in a tough environment – it couldn't remain the relaxed little business I was used to. And my new home? How could I possibly give up the place that Paul and I had created? And lastly, the most overpowering of all the reasons for deciding against: how could we possibly live apart?

Reasons For:

Taking another risk. Pushing myself. Feeling proud that I'd grasped another opportunity however fearful I was. Even if I failed, I wouldn't be able to reproach myself for not having tried. Learning something new. Making new friends. Living in a city I used to love. If my affair with Paul did come to an end, I wouldn't be

340

left empty and hopeless as I was when Henry left. I'd see Ginnie and Nicola more often. It would make things easier with Joel and he'd be happier with me in London.

Conclusion (for the moment):

Now was the time to be ruthlessly honest. I began to incline towards Reasons For.

Why?

I might have protested too much that I could never live in London. Suppose it was just a way of opting out of pressures everyone took for granted? Wasn't I too young to be satisfied with a gentle haven, more suited to motherhood or retirement? Could I only thrive in the undemanding slow pace of a Thameside town? Could I see myself drifting into old age seeing the same people – who were already becoming distant from me? In twenty years' time, would I still be content to meet up with Maggie, Angela and Patsy in the Café Rouge?

I tried not to anticipate what Paul's reaction would be and I was steeling myself to tell him. We had just finished dinner, which he had cooked, and I was making the coffee.

'It's time we went away on a proper trip,' Paul began.

'I'd love it,' I said, pressing my hand down on the coffee grinder. When the rasping noise had stopped, Paul said, 'I've been thinking, Sal. If we got a boat of our own next year, we could go on a long journey, through the canals to Wales. Could you get three weeks off?'

'I don't see why not. But actually . . .'

'Don't worry about the money. I'm sure I could find something reasonable, a wooden cruiser that needs repairing. If they're in a bad state, nobody wants the trouble of putting them right. But I'd love to.' He sounded so enthusiastic that I couldn't interrupt him.

'I've worked it all out. Edgeworth said he'd give me a loan if he approved of the boat and I've saved a bit to put down. Imagine – going wherever we wanted, waking up on the water, breakfast on the bank . . .'

'I can't think of anything better.' I meant it.

Paul gave a sheepish smile.

'There's a boat I've got my eye on. It's moored in Reading and I've talked to the owner. He's an old guy. Used to be in the Navy. He couldn't manage to keep his boat up to scratch and it's too big for him now. I know I'd persuade him to sell cheaply. It would be ideal for us. And there'd be room for Joel and Nicola as well if they fancied a trip . . . Will you come and see it with me this weekend?'

'Well, yes. I suppose I could.'

I laid out the cups and began to pour out the coffee.

'You don't sound too keen. But I wouldn't expect you to do anything. I'd work on it in my spare time and I could get it ready for late spring, when the bluebells are out.'

'It sounds like a huge project,' I remarked.

'Not for me. Never mind, I can always do it up anyway. Then I could sell it and we'd have enough money to go somewhere hot and sunny abroad. You'd probably prefer that, wouldn't you?'

I shook my head.

'I can't make any plans at the moment. Matt's offered me a new job.'

Paul leaped up and gave me a hug.

'Why didn't you tell me earlier? That's great news. About time, too.'

'He wants me to become projects manager. That means I'll be in charge of all aspects of the work they do – budgeting, marketing, future proposals, that kind of thing.'

'Why aren't we celebrating?' A broad grin spread over his face. 'I'm so pleased for you.'

'I'm giving Matt an answer tomorrow. But it's a huge decision to take.'

'Then you must go for it, Sal. Jump in feet first.'

'It's not that easy.'

'You always say that.'

I paused, biting my lip. Then I took a deep breath.

'Hedgehog will be moving to London. They're about to accept an offer from a big company so they're expanding.'

The smile faded from Paul's face, and he turned away as though bracing himself for my answer.

'Will you go with them?'

'What do you think I should do?'

It took a few moments before he answered.

'It's not up to me. You know I'd be devastated if you left. But I can't stop you, if you really want to go.'

'That isn't fair,' I burst out.

'It's selfish of me, but I'd do anything to make you stay. That might be wrong but it's how I feel. Couldn't you get another job round here? I'm sure you'd find something.'

He didn't sound convinced. I couldn't look him in the face. I knew this moment would be the worst.

'It'll never happen again. I'll never get another offer like this. I've decided to accept.'

I glanced up at him. Paul was staring fixedly at me, as though willing me to change my mind.

'I see. Yes . . . well . . . I'm sure you're doing the right thing. You must have thought about it a lot.'

'I have. It's been agony.'

Paul got up and went over to the window. I could only see the side of his face as he gazed out into the darkness.

'Sally, I can't come to London with you. It's impossible. Do you really want to live there?' He turned swiftly round to face me. 'I thought you loved being in Wengrave. I thought we were happy together.'

'We are. We are.' I was fighting back tears. 'This doesn't mean . . . I'm not saying . . .'

'I can't take half measures. I just can't. Don't ask me to. Could you see me phoning you up in London each evening, saying how much I wanted you here? Remember with Nicola, when I used to visit her at weekends? I couldn't wait to get back home. It just wouldn't work out. There's no point in pretending it would.'

I felt as though I'd just crashed into a brick wall.

'Sorry, I shouldn't have said that,' he said.

I intended to make some more coffee, but all I did was to stand by the cupboards, staring vacantly into space.

'I know I'm being mean,' Paul went on, 'but I can't bear the thought of giving you up. I could have said I'd go to London with you, but if it came to it, I wouldn't have. There's no way out, is there?'

I turned round slowly to face him.

'What would you do, in my position?' I asked, desperately searching for a compromise.

'If I'd got a bigger and better job away from here? I'd have taken it.'

'And then?'

'I'd have persuaded you to come with me.'

'And if I'd refused?' I said.

'I don't know. I really don't know. But I'd have tried to find a solution somehow. What's the point of talking about it? When would you go?'

'After Christmas.'

'I'm still getting that boat.'

There was one last thing I had to say.

'Paul. When I go to London, would you rather . . .' I couldn't bring myself to finish the sentence.

'Rather what?' he said, sharply.

'That we stopped seeing one another.'

'Yes.'

His reply was so immediate, I knew he meant it. And

I also knew that I would have to turn down Matt's offer. I couldn't go through with it. I was about to tell Paul that I'd changed my mind and nothing was worth destroying our happiness together. Before I could marshal my thoughts, he began to speak.

'I wouldn't want us to end in resentment and tears. I know some couples live in different places – different countries even – and manage to keep everything going. But I couldn't. It's an old-fashioned thing to say, but it wouldn't work out. Not for me.'

I watched helplessly as he walked out into the hall and took down his jacket.

'I'm going to the pub, Sal. I need to,' he called.

When I heard the door slam, I dissolved into tears. I didn't know if or when he was coming back and it felt as though I'd just made the worst mistake of my life.

I was half-asleep when I heard Paul moving softly round the room. I was aware of him throwing off his clothes, then getting in beside me. He lay over the far side of the bed, almost dropping off the edge, as though he was getting into practice for being apart from me. By the time the dawn came we were both still awake, both refusing to speak. I finally broke the silence.

'I'll make some tea,' I said.

A little while later Paul appeared, looking pale and desolate. We had never seen one another in the depths of despair.

'I won't take the job.'

I expected to see Paul's face come back to life, but his eyes remained lowered, his mouth set.

'That's not the answer. You've already decided. Anyway, I think you should.'

'Then somehow we'll have to find a way of managing.'

Paul waited a few moments before replying. I searched his face, hoping for a glimmer of encouragement.

'There's no point in pretending,' he said. 'I know I'm

not going to change my mind. You probably think I'm being stubborn but I have been through it all before. And I can't go through it again.'

Soon after Paul had left for the yard, I called Matt to say I needed a little more time. I'd give him my decision at the end of the day. Although I came in to the office and sat at my desk, I was unable to think of anything except my conversation with Paul. I took an early lunch break and walked through Wengrave towards the river, hardly aware of where I was going or how long I'd be gone.

I sat down on the bench where I had told Nicola about Henry's departure. Would I soon be telling her that Paul and I had split up? I tried to stop tears flooding my eyes. Was I witnessing the natural end of my affair? Had the truth finally emerged, that Paul preferred me to stay as I was and didn't care about any ambitions I might have? Was it time to face up to the fact that Paul and I were desperately unsuited to one another? Supposing I had misjudged him all along? So far, life had been easy for us. But now there was a challenge, he had failed to respond. He had honestly admitted his limitations but would I be able to accept them? What of the future? Every one of my friends had warned me that it would end. Perhaps I had built him up too much and seen in him far more than there was. I had always doubted that I was the right person for him. But was he the right person for me?

The house was dark and quiet when I came to see Matt at the end of the afternoon and I was relieved that Pickle and Jed had already left. He was crouched down on an old rug in front of a TV screen, holding the remote control and running backwards and forwards through a video. After a couple of minutes he stopped, poured us out some wine and sat me down in his only armchair. I told him how difficult it had been but my answer was yes.

'What about Paul? Will he be moving with you?' Matt asked.

I glanced away.

'I don't think so. No. He won't consider the idea and I can't persuade him to come with me. I've been wondering if . . . if it's his way of telling me that everything is over.'

Matt looked startled.

'You don't honestly believe that, do you?'

'If . . . when I mean . . . I go to London, he wants us to . . .' I hesitated, then forced myself to continue. 'To stop seeing one another. I was shocked. It almost seemed like blackmail. I never thought I'd be pressured into making this kind of decision. But I promised myself after Henry had left that I wouldn't let any man dictate what I should do. I shouldn't be talking to you like this. I'm sorry.'

'I'm glad you are,' said Matt. 'But I'm sure the last thing Paul wants is to split up. Perhaps he's frightened of losing you in the bright lights of London. Or feels he can't compete with all those cool guys you'll be mixing with. I bet that hadn't even crossed your mind.'

I managed a slight smile. By now, I thought, Matt would be itching to leave for the pub but he sat quite still, contemplating his glass. We sat talking for at least an hour.

Paul came home late, greeted me briefly and began to run a bath. A little while later he emerged, looking weary and drawn.

'How was your meeting with Matt?' he asked, as though unwilling to hear my reply.

I looked at him anxiously.

'Would you try something . . . as an experiment?' I asked.

'Depends.'

'I had a long talk with Matt. He suggested that I could

spend four days in London with them and then come back here on a Thursday evening. And then if things were quiet, I could even work from home on the odd Wednesday.'

'It wouldn't work in practice,' Paul said, as though his mind was already closed to the idea.

'Please listen. If we both want things to work out, they will. Give me three months. Then if you agree that it's a hopeless arrangement, I'll think again.'

He sighed. 'We'll give it a go, then. If that's what you want.'

Next day, when he'd adjusted to the idea, Paul seemed more positive. We'd each make a wholehearted effort to make it work. It wasn't going to be easy but at least we would both know how strongly we felt for one another. My doubts about Paul began to fade. The moment I was in his company, even when he was tired and depressed, I knew that I could never consider anybody else and that I wouldn't stop loving him.

For three months I took the train early on Monday morning, travelled to the high-tech offices in Covent Garden and stayed with Ginnie until Thursday. On Thursday evening I was home again, which meant we were only apart for three nights. Although at first Paul refused to spend any of the three nights at Fernwood Court – my guess was that he didn't want to wait for my phone call – he slowly adapted to being there without me. After a few weeks, we began to grow used to our way of life. The time we had together seemed more precious and we never fell into the stale acceptance of a routine, nor did we take one another for granted. But every time I left for London, it was as though I'd put on a new persona, which didn't really fit.

I longed more and more for the soft air and gentle ways of Wengrave. Everyone I met seemed to be wound up like a coiled spring, eagerly pursuing a goal or frantically maintaining their position. Now Hedgehog was part of a large company they all worked in a huge open-plan office with low dividers shielding them from the others. Pickle and Jed no longer wandered round when the mood took them. Matt had a small office to himself, in a glass box at one end of the room, and when I passed I hardly ever caught his eye. We rarely went out to lunch together – a trolley brought round sandwiches in the office so that the employees wouldn't waste time lingering in a pub somewhere.

One morning Matt asked me to have coffee with him in his office. I slid back the glass door and sat down in front of his desk, which was completely bare except for two telephones and a small, leather bound notepad.

'I hardly ever see you except from a distance,' he said, stretching behind him to take down a thermos of coffee and two white beakers from a shelf. 'There's good news. That American deal looks a cert. So we'll be ferreting around for a second team. Will you sit in on the interviews? We'd like your input.'

'Of course.'

'And I was wondering if . . . well, you know our workload. Could you do a couple of Fridays? Just till we get in the swing?'

I hesitated. 'I'm not sure, Matt. I mean, I'm afraid I can't.'

'Something special on?' he said, pouring out the ready-made coffee.

Our relationship had changed. Now I was in danger of becoming a cog in a machine that Matt didn't control.

I shook my head. 'It's just not possible.'

'Oh. I'll have to work around it, then.'

I was waiting for him to object, to try and persuade me but he didn't. I looked hard at him. He was the picture of well-paid urban man. Black Paul Smith suit, hair shaped perfectly round his ears and neck, a silk tie and glossy shoes. His hands were snow white – no

349

longer stained with ink and paint as all the work was generated from a computer programme.

'You really need someone to do a five-day week,' I remarked. 'Though if I had an assistant . . .'

'Sorry Sal, but they won't allow that.' Matt pulled a face. 'They've got a strict personnel-limitation policy. So we have to stick by it. I had to fight to get an extra team in – and it's only for a short-term contract.'

'I hope it's all worth it for you,' I said.

'You bet, Sal. We've gone from mud huts to sky-scrapers in one move. It's all been so sudden, I sometimes think "Christ! Tomorrow I'll wake up."' He grinned at me. 'Are you sure you couldn't stretch to a Friday? I'll make it worth your while.'

'Thanks but no. It's one of my few rules.'

'I thought you didn't believe in rules.'

'One or two I keep. Just for old times' sake.'

'Then we'll stick to the usual arrangement. We'll manage somehow. It's amazing but we always have done, haven't we?'

Matt smiled, glanced at his minimal black-faced watch, finished his coffee and half stood up as though to indicate the end of our meeting. Then he appeared to have second thoughts and abruptly sat down again, leaning forward towards me and looking intently into my face.

'You're not thinking of leaving us, are you?'

I looked away, wondering whether I should express my doubts or reassure him that I had no such intention.

'I would like to talk some things through . . .' I began but Matt instantly cut me short.

'Don't tell me. Someone's made you a really good offer. I know we should be paying you more. In a few months, I should be in a position to . . .'

'You've got it quite wrong, Matt,' I said quickly, astonished that he could make such an assumption. 'I'm actually wondering whether to move back to

Wengrave full time. I'm not convinced that I'm cut out for London life. I mean, of course I appreciate it but . . .'

He looked so genuinely upset that I wished I hadn't brought it up. 'It's because of Paul, isn't it?'

'He's part of the reason but only part.'

Matt relaxed into a smile and tipped back on his chair. Now he seemed more like his old self.

'Right, Sal. Miz Linton is resigning in order to spend more time with her family.' He paused for a moment. 'You're not really going are you?'

I could have stalled, given a vague reply, but we had been through too much together. I felt I owed it to Matt to be honest.

'I've been so happy working with you all. It'll be very hard for me to go. But I can't see any other way,' I began.

'We like having you around,' he said, then immediately fell silent. I tried to gather my thoughts. I hadn't intended to have this conversation so soon.

'I knew things would be different when Hedgehog was in London. But I had no idea how different. I tried to persuade myself that all companies grow up, that they have to grasp opportunities but . . .'

'You think we've made a wrong move?' said Matt, with a look of alarm.

'Not at all. I'm only saying how it seems to me, though of course it's early days. I knew it might take me a while to adapt to your new set-up but . . . well, I suppose I found myself wishing that I was back in the Hedgehog house in Wengrave. I know I'm not supposed to say this, but I preferred it how things used to be.'

'Small is beautiful?'

'Small is more fun,' I answered, with a smile.

I suddenly realized that I had been coming to this conclusion for some time but refused to acknowledge it. It had been hard to disentangle whether I was unable to face the continued challenge of working in London or whether I genuinely wanted to spend all my time in Wengrave.

'I know what you're saying, Sal,' said Matt, as he got up and came round to my side of the desk.

I looked up at him. 'I think you should start looking around to find a really good person to replace me. I'd help them into the job, of course.'

Matt let out an impatient sigh. 'Are you sure that's what you really want?'

'Yes. Only I didn't realize that until now.'

'I'm glad you told me. But if you are leaving, it doesn't mean there isn't an open offer for you to come back. Who knows? Things are bound to change. Our aim is to pump up the whole group so in a few years' time someone will come along and make a huge offer for the lot. Then we can do anything we like.'

'Whatever you decide, we'll keep in touch. I know you'll surprise me,' I said, rising to my feet.

'No'. Matt shook his head. 'It's more likely you'll surprise us.'

Shortly after our conversation, I wrote a letter to Matt confirming that I had decided to leave. After I'd sent it, I realized it was the second time I'd resigned my job. Major Carter would have died by now. What a long time ago that seemed!

Now I'd made up my mind, I was dreading the moment when I'd have to break the news to Ginnie. I had become part of her life for four days in every week. We often met up after work and went back to being girls together – eating popcorn in the Odeon or meeting a gang of her friends and giggling over a late drink in her favourite wine-bar. She was always inviting Paul to stay and dropping suggestions in my ear about how we could induce him to move. She was convinced he'd give way given enough time and assumed that my working arrangement was only a temporary solution.

There was no doubt in her mind – Paul would join me in a year or two. But once I'd had confirmation of my letter of resignation, I couldn't put it off any longer. I would have to tell Ginnie that my life was about to change yet again. Now there was no going back.

I found my opportunity one evening when Ginnie came home in extra ebullient mood. She handed me an extravagant array of shopping bags from Harrods food hall so I knew she'd had a good day.

'And how about you?' she asked, having told me of the rapturous reception given to her latest piece for the mag. 'How are the Hedgehogs? Gone dot-com yet?' She lovingly unwrapped her carefully selected treasures and arranged them on the kitchen table.

'I really don't know. I'm not involved with those kind of plans, even if they are.'

Ginnie gave me a pitying look.

'Has it been one of those days?' she asked. 'If so, have a glass of this and it'll feel better.'

She unscrewed the top of a narrow bottle and filled up my glass with some sour cherry vodka, her latest passion. After a few slugs, I felt I could say anything.

'I'm not sure about the direction the Hedgehogs are taking,' I began. 'When they were in Wengrave, they used to be much more individual. They cared passionately about everything they did and spent hours getting things right. Now it seems more a question of seeing how many deadlines they can meet in a given time.'

'What did you expect?' said Ginnie, going over to the sink to wash some scallops.

'Things happen faster here, that's all. Just because they're powered up, making quick decisions and working the speed of light doesn't mean they've dropped their standards. That's the buzz of working in London. That's why we all like it so much.'

'Well, I've come to the conclusion I don't. Or rather,

it doesn't suit me even though I admit I find it stimulating a lot of the time. So I've handed in my notice.'

Ginnie covered my words in a rush of tap water so she must have only heard half of what I'd said. I waited until she'd rinsed the scallops, taken down her favourite cookery book from a kitchen shelf and leafed through the food-stained pages to find a suitable recipe for the meal we'd probably end up having around midnight. Having alighted on one that satisfied her, she marked the page with a rosemary sprig.

'This is it, Sal. The ultimate scallop recipe with a retro feel. Cream and a splash of Armagnac, OK?'

'Perfect.' I watched in silence while she collected the ingredients she needed and arranged them in order of preparation. Then, at last, she sat down.

'I've handed in my notice,' I said again. 'I've decided not to work for Hedgehog any more.'

I was expecting Ginnie to let off her usual stream of expletives but she didn't.

'You must be feeling depressed,' she remarked, thoughtfully. 'Is something happening between you and Paul?'

'No, everything's fine. I am in my right mind and I've sent off the letter.'

Now she let out a despairing groan.

'Oh God, Sal. I give up. You land yourself this fantastic job, great company, great location and then . . .'

'Please don't go on,' I said firmly. 'Listen for a bit and then you can jump down my throat.'

I told her about my conversation with Matt, how he wanted me to devote more time to Hedgehog and why I felt I couldn't. And how — whenever I saw them together — Jed and Pickle seemed to be having a row. Apparently Pickle had threatened to set up on her own on several occasions. And they both felt that Matt often did things without consulting them. The atmosphere had completely changed.

'That just sounds like teething problems,' said Ginnie. 'Not exactly grounds for walking out of the door.'

She set me to work peeling a heap of radishes in narrow stripes, which allowed me plenty of time to reflect.

'Sometimes you feel something to be true but then your mind tells you the opposite.' I paused, wondering if she would understand.

'Go on, Sal.'

'Well, recently it dawned on me that I'd stopped looking forward to going to the office. I kept longing to be in Wengrave again. In the middle of writing a report I'd break off and start wondering which flowers and shrubs would be flowering, what the river would be up to. I began to wish that I could be with Paul every evening. I didn't like having to cram everything into the weekend. Then I'd hear this horrified voice inside me. Sally, what are you doing? You're chickening out! Are you really going to slip back into being the homey wife again? Only now, instead of devoting yourself to Henry, you'll be devoting yourself to Paul. What you want will always take second place. Isn't that precisely what you reacted against? Aren't you worth more than that? Can't you face the challenge any more? Do you really want to go back to the life you had before?'

'Putting words into my mouth,' said Ginnie.

'But that isn't what I want. The Henry days are gone for ever. Being with Paul has changed everything, but perhaps I would have changed anyway. I know I could never go back to being Mrs Farringford. Can't you see? I've created a completely different life for myself in Wengrave – different home, different friends and quite a different way of life.'

'Well, yes, of course you have. I'm not disputing that,' Ginnie said grudgingly. 'But it's just so easy to

355

slip back into it, after all those years. That's what worries me, to be honest. I just couldn't bear it if you got stuck in Wengrave again and Paul turned out to be another Henry. He is quite a traditional man in many ways, after all.'

'I don't think he could be another Henry if he tried. In any case, I wouldn't allow him to,' I answered, with a smile.

'That's something, coming from you,' said Ginnie.

'There's only one thing I regret. If only I'd discovered what I really wanted years ago. I wish it hadn't taken so long.'

A couple of hours and several phone calls later, we sat down to Ginnie's lavish supper. All through the meal, my mind was racing, as though a burden had suddenly been lifted from me. After we'd finished, we sat up talking even though it was way past the time when we usually collapsed into bed.

'There's something else I'm going to do. I'm going to look around for some work to do in Wengrave. Something completely different. Just you wait.'

Ginnie looked astonished.

'Sal . . . what can I say? Give me a clue. I bet you've thought about it.'

'Not telling.'

'I wonder how Joel and Nicola will react to all this? Mum's gone nuts again, probably. Gets a fabulous job, then chucks it.'

'They must be getting used to me by now,' I answered.

Suddenly Ginnie got up and hugged me.

'The best of luck, Sal. I hope things work out, I really do. But I'll miss you. It's been great having you here. Still, you can always change your mind again.'

She must have thought I was taking the wrong path. This time, though, I wasn't going to take it to heart if she or Nicola or Joel – or anyone for that matter – expressed their disapproval. What I was doing felt right for me.

It's now five years on and Paul and I are still living together. In fact, he's looking over my shoulder at the computer screen right now, trying to distract me.

'Is that the end?'

'I think so. It seems the right place for it.'

'I wonder if Henry's going to sue.'

'Why should he? It's all true, I haven't made anything up.'

Now he's opening my chapter summaries. (He read parts of the book before I'd finished but he didn't make any comments. He said I had to come to the end.)

'What about our first boat and the holiday we had with Mark and Nicola? The time when Joel came down with Sarah and she nearly drowned? Our trip to Norway? How you started writing for the Wengrave Gazette? You've missed bits out.'

'You have to.'

Paul brings up the last chapter again and scrolls down to the last page.

Now I can type it in. *The End*.

'Why stop there?' he asks.

'Because you can't write a long book about a happy couple.'

He lets my remark sink in.

'The next one will have to be fiction, then.'